Ambition

Ambition

A. O'Connor

POOLBEG

This novel is entirely a work of fiction. The names, characters and incidents portrayed in it are the work of the author's imagination. Any resemblance to actual persons, living or dead, events or localities is entirely coincidental.

Published 2009
by Poolbeg Press Ltd
123 Grange Hill, Baldoyle
Dublin 13, Ireland
E-mail: poolbeg@poolbeg.com

1 3 5 7 9 10 8 6 4 2

A catalogue record for this book is available from the British Library.

ISBN 978-1-84223-396-2

Typeset by Type Design in Palatino 9.5/13
Printed by
Litografia Rosés, S.A., Spain

www.poolbeg.com

About the Author

A.O'Connor has written three previous bestselling novels published by Poolbeg, *This Model Life, Exclusive* and *Property,* and is a graduate of NUI Maynooth and Trinity College Dublin.

Acknowledgements

As ever a big thank-you to Paula Campbell and Kieran Devlin and all at Poolbeg. It's always a complete pleasure to work with the dedicated team at Poolbeg Press.

Thank you to my agent, Caroline Sheldon. And, of course, to Gaye Shortland, a great editor. Thanks to Louise Harvey and Gina for the background information. And the booksellers for their continued support.

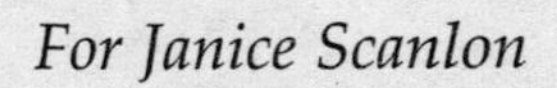
For Janice Scanlon

Chapter 1

Nicola Newman was attacked on her way to work that morning. It happened just after she had fallen in love. Both events were a first time for Nicola and she didn't know which one shocked her most. That morning she had left her home, a beautiful sprawling farmhouse just outside a picture-postcard village, and was on the train doing her usual forty-minute commute to Liverpool Street Station. From there she would get two tubes to Knightsbridge where she was the Human Resources Director of the landmark retail store, Franklyns.

She sat on the train as the countryside whizzed past her, a copy of the newspaper opened in front of her on the table. It was early summer and the sunshine was promising a lovely day. She always made sure to leave late in the mornings, so as to avoid the rush-hour crowd and ensure she travelled in comfort. Again, she often left the office late in the evenings in order to miss the crowds.

She sat back in her seat and glanced around the carriage and that was when she saw him. The man was seated across the aisle from her, one seat down and facing in her direction. He was dressed in an immaculate suit, his fair hair cut fashionably short and she was immediately drawn to him. He exuded an air of confidence and the charm of somebody for whom life had gone without a hitch. He was talking to another man, similarly dressed and seated opposite him. Because of the sound of the train and the distance between them, Nicola couldn't hear his voice. She was surprised by the fact that she was becoming agitated because she couldn't hear him talk. Shaking her head, she tried to read her paper but, finding it impossible to concentrate on the article, she slowly lifted her eyes to look at him again. She guessed him to be thirty-five, making him slightly younger than her. She looked down at the black business suit she was wearing and was annoyed with herself for not dressing differently that morning, for not wearing something younger. He didn't seem to notice her. Trying not to stare, she found it impossible not to as she became disturbed by the feeling he was evoking in her. Realising how silly she was being, she tried to focus on looking out the window. But her gaze continued to be drawn back to him.

As the train pulled into Liverpool Street, the man and his colleague got up and, taking their briefcases, left the train quickly. Nicola found herself irritated with the old woman in front of her who was obstructing her progress. Finally she managed to get past her and onto the platform where she walked quickly, trying to catch up with the man. As he entered the main part of the station, she saw that instead of going to the Underground, he and his friend began to head towards the steps that would lead them out onto the main street. She stopped in the middle of the station for a while, thinking hard. Not understanding herself, she abandoned the next leg of her commute and was suddenly heading across the station as well, almost running to catch up with the man. She normally never ran and soon found herself getting out of breath. Hurrying up the stairs, she continued out of the station and spotted the two men walking along the pavement. As she followed them down the main street outside the station, she wondered how far she was prepared to go to find out more about him. The men paused for a second, chatting. Then they turned into a quiet sidestreet, which was known as a route taxis took for a short cut and where you could flag one down easily thereby avoiding the queue at the station's rank. She hurried down the side street after them. She watched anxiously as they stopped suddenly, wondering what their next move would be. Then her man looked up and down the street and, seeing an approaching taxi, put out his hand. She felt panicked that he would disappear into the taxi and she would never see him again.

Suddenly there was a bang to her right arm that sent her flying. Knocked to the ground, she was filled with confusion, then realised it must have been an accident when she saw the young man standing over her. He reached his hand down to her and she offered hers so he could help her up. She was surprised when he ignored her hand and continued to reach down, then suddenly he grabbed her pearl earring and ripped it off her earlobe. A second later the other earring was ripped off. She later remembered thinking how glad she was that she had opted for clip-ons that morning rather than pierced earrings because, judging from the ferocity with which he had grabbed them, he wouldn't have cared if he had injured her. Next he grabbed her diamond necklace. Then his hands were on her handbag and she made a half-hearted attempt at keeping it but his strength quickly won out. She felt him grab her hand and then he was pulling her two rings off her fingers, her engagement and wedding ring. She put up more of a fight for them and clenched her knuckles shut, obstructing their easy removal. He shouted at her and caused her pain as he forced her fingers to stretch out. She quickly realised a fight wasn't worth it and she felt the two rings that had been sitting on the same finger for fourteen years being pulled off. Her attacker turned and disappeared off down the street, running towards the main street. She looked after him, saying goodbye to her rings silently. Then she quickly looked around to see the man she had fallen in love with, but he had gone.

* * *

"Did you notice anyone following you from the station?" asked one of the two police officers.

She was still outside Liverpool Street, leaning against a wall, trying to regain her composure.

"No, I didn't see anyone," she said, running a hand through her fair hair.

"What did he look like?" asked the other officer.

"I didn't get a good look at him – he was wearing a hood."

"So you can't give us a detailed description of him?" repeated the first officer.

"I told you I can't!" snapped Nicola.

The officers gave each other a quick glance.

"Could you come down to the station? And can we get a friend or a relative to collect you?"

Nicola sighed. "Maybe you could bring me to my husband, Commissioner Oliver Newman – he's based at Scotland Yard."

The two officers again looked at each other and then stared at Nicola. "Of course, ma'am. Our car is around the corner."

The two officers drove her to Scotland Yard, sitting in silence. Their amicable manner on the street had been quickly replaced by ultra-professionalism when she had revealed her husband's identity.

She was shown into Oliver's office. There was a look of shock on Oliver's face. One of the officers made a brief report, then hovered at the door, only leaving when Oliver nodded to him.

It was only after the officer had gone that Oliver came from behind his desk and went to her, gently putting his arm around her and leading her to the chair in front of his desk.

"What the hell exactly happened?" he asked.

"I was mugged," she explained, in an almost nonchalant voice.

"But where?"

"At Liverpool Street Station."

"In the station? But how could that be? The place is packed with police with the terrorist threat and –"

"Not *in* the station – outside."

"Outside? But you always get the Tube."

"I was late for an appointment, so I was getting a taxi."

"A taxi?" He looked confused. "But the traffic would still be desperate – it would have made more sense to get the Tube."

"Oh, Oliver!" she snapped loudly. "Will you stop going on. I don't need to hear this." She began to massage her temples.

"Of course." He looked sheepish and put his arm around her shoulder again.

They sat in silence for a minute.

"What did he take?"

"My earrings, my necklace, handbag . . . rings."

"Your wedding ring?" His face went red with a mixture of fury and disbelief.

She nodded.

He got up quickly, walked to the window and looked down at the street.

"The bastard!"

As she looked at him, she almost felt his anger was directed at her. Crime didn't happen to them. They were the establishment. They made decisions that affected other people's lives. He was a Commissioner and she an HR boss at a world-renowned store. Her father was a respected and long-standing Conservative MP.

Observing his stress, she felt the need to quickly reassert his confidence and his position – their position. To show they were not victims.

"Could you call me a taxi?" she asked.

"A taxi?" He spun around, looking incredulous. "Where are you going to?"

"To work, of course," she said. She began to smooth her hair with her hands.

"You can't go to work!"

"And why?"

"Because of what happened, of course. I'll take you home."

"Nonsense. I've a very busy day at work and I'm not going to allow a silly incident like this to upset my schedule."

She saw something else in his face now. An admiration and regaining of confidence.

"Nicola, no! You can't go into work –"

"I don't want to hear another word about it. I'm going." She stood up and smiled.

"I'll drive you then."

* * *

Franklyns stood proudly amongst the other emporiums in Knightsbridge, confident of its place amongst them, confident of its place in history, two hundred years old. As the crowds of shoppers swarmed through the main glass entrance, they had no idea that Franklyns' grand history was about to take a new turn. It was about to become repossessed by the bank.

Rachel Healy had taken her time as she entered the store, soaking up the rich atmosphere that exuded from the shiny black floors, the mirrors and glass walls.

She made her way up to the personnel offices on the fifth floor for her eleven o'clock interview. An hour and a half later, there was still no sign of the HR Director Nicola Newman. Rachel was just about to go and ask Mrs Newman's PA if there was a problem when a blonde woman stepped out of the elevator, quickly cut across the floor and entered the director's office, closing the door after her. A second later the phone on the secretary's desk rang and she answered it, then quickly disappeared into the office.

* * *

Nicola took off her blazer and sat down at her desk.

"Everything all right?" asked Yvette, Nicola's personal assistant.

"Yes, why wouldn't it be?"

Yvette knew from Nicola's cold tone not to pursue her nosiness.

"Who's out there waiting?" asked Nicola, taking up the CV left on her desk.

"An Irish girl, Rachel Healy." Yvette thought it better not to mention that Nicola's lateness had meant the girl had been sitting there for an hour and a half. "She's here about a position in the press office."

Nicola scanned through the CV. "Twenty-five . . . marketing degree . . . send her in." Nicola cast the CV to one side and massaged her temples, trying to forget the morning's events. There was a knock on the door and in walked the Irish girl.

As her smiling figure approached, Nicola decided her dreadful morning really didn't need to be finished off with this pretty young girl with her glossy chestnut hair and expressive dark-blue eyes.

* * *

Rachel detected that Nicola Newman's faint smile did not carry to her eyes as she took a seat on the other side of her desk. She was immediately struck by Nicola's presence. There was a steely coldness behind her English rose appearance. Rachel thought she was actually very pretty but her hair, make-up and style had the look of an older businesswoman.

"Have you been in London long?" Nicola opened the interview.

"Just a month or so. I've been staying with an aunt in Hampstead. Just getting to know the city."

"I see." Nicola returned to the CV and scanned through it.

"But I think it's time to stand on my own two feet now and I'm looking at a flat this evening," Rachel continued with a friendly smile, her blue eyes sparkling.

"I see." Nicola sounded uninterested. "You spent some time working in Brown Thomas in Dublin and your reference is obviously excellent. You worked in the press office there?"

"Uh huh. I was involved in everything from the fashion shows to running promotions to general press-secretary duties like answering queries and media-monitoring. I dealt with a lot of designers personally about their PR." She smiled, hoping all this would impress Nicola.

"I don't think we'll be letting you loose on any of our designers at this stage." Nicola pushed the CV to one side and fixed Rachel with a steely look. "Because working in the press office is a very responsible position, we actually never recruit from outside the store. You have to have served in a department within the store for a time and then apply internally."

Rachel continued to smile and nodded, but her eyes glassed over slightly.

"You see yourself as having a career at Franklyns as opposed to just a job?"

"If opportunities arose I would certainly not shy away from them."

"More a case of whether they shy away from you. Why did you come to London instead of staying in Dublin?"

"I've always been fascinated with London and really wanted to give myself a chance to live here. And the experience of working at Franklyns, well . . . " Rachel left the unspoken to speak volumes.

Nicola decided the girl was in a travelling phase and would only stay in London for a few months before returning home.

"If you are agreeable to serving some time in a department other than the press office initially, I would like to offer you a position here at Franklyns."

"Yes, I would be delighted with that."

"I will have your contract and terms of employment drawn up. I have an induction course beginning on Monday. Can you start then?"

"Sure." Rachel beamed a smile.

"Good. Report here at ten on Monday morning and we'll go through the necessary paperwork and you'll meet your manager."

"What office will I be working in?" pushed Rachel.

"I haven't decided yet. You'll be informed on Monday."

"Thank you. I'm really going to enjoy working here." Rachel stood up and put out her hand for Nicola to shake.

Nicola looked at it hesitantly for a moment before shaking it quickly.

She waited for Rachel to leave her office before picking up the phone.

"Yvette, I don't want to be disturbed for the rest of the day."

She hung up, sat back in her chair and closed her eyes, reliving the morning's events.

What had she been doing following that stranger? She felt she was to blame for allowing her normal routine to be disrupted. For being so consumed by that man that she hadn't been alert to the danger.

She stood up and unbuttoned her blouse, getting a shock at seeing the purple bruises on her arms from where she had been shoved and from the fall. She did up her blouse, sat down again and began to massage her temples, still unable to comprehend the feelings she had felt for that man on the train.

* * *

Karl Furstin sat at his desk in his office which was situated on the top floor of Franklyns, reading an article about himself in *The Mail*. There was a huge photo of him and his wife Elka underneath the heading *'The Baron Of Knightsbridge'*. The article was taken up with the Furstins' lavish lifestyle and spending habits. Karl read a small part of the article: *'Money seems to be no object to the owners of Franklyns. For Elka's birthday last year a private jet rushed the guests to a party at a French chateau. The theme of the event was 'The Last Days Of Versailles'. And from rumours that spilled out about the night, the party did give the last king and queen of France a run for their money with out-of-season orchids everywhere and the female guests being presented with gifts of diamonds and emeralds at dinner.'*

The phone ringing on his desk interrupted his reading.

"What?" he snapped down the phone.

"Paul is waiting for you," said one of his personal assistants.

He slammed the phone down and walked over to the bathroom which was off his office. The bathroom was huge and designed to his specifications with marble and mirrors throughout and a chandelier in the centre of the ceiling. He quickly inspected his appearance and smoothed down his grey-blond hair. Tall and thin, with cold grey-blue eyes set in aristocratic features, Karl was in good shape for a man in his sixties.

Leaving the bathroom he walked briskly back through his office and out into the reception area.

Paul Stewart braced himself as he saw Karl swing out of his office. He did not enjoy being in his company. He didn't know anybody who did. But he could handle him . . . just. He tried to decipher what mood Karl was in today and judged it to be bad.

Paul was tall and broad-shouldered, with a light tan and brown hair that had become flecked with grey recently. He was given a very generous clothing allowance by Franklyns which ensured he was always dressed in expensive Italian suits. Appearance was important in his job. He often had to give a television interview at a moment's notice about something to do with the store and he was always conscious he represented Franklyns.

Two security men were also waiting for Karl. Although these men were on the Franklyns' payroll as security, Paul knew they were different from the normal security in the store. They were from a group of six personal security staff hand-picked by Karl and sent on special training courses. They doubled as his drivers.

The men made their way past the warren of offices on the sixth floor. Paul often thought that this floor, dripping in opulence and luxury, resembled a Saudi prince's palace. All the offices here were occupied by Karl's personal staff.

"I was expecting you at two," said Karl.

Paul hid his irritation. The appointment was definitely for three.

"We have to schedule our tours at more convenient times. This late in the day does not suit me." Karl had a faint accent which was from his German origins.

"Why don't you just let me know whenever you want to meet and I'll rearrange my schedule to suit you," said Paul. He always adopted a patient tone when speaking to Karl.

Karl hit the button and, as they waited for the elevator to arrive, turned and fixed his grey-blue eyes on Paul.

"You're obviously not that busy if you're free at all times," he said.

The elevator door opened and they stepped in.

"What have you done to increase the sales in the cosmetics department?" Karl asked loudly and abruptly.

"Ah, we've got quite a lot of promotional material coming in with L'Oréal – and free gifts for purchases over £100. Discounts on repeat purchases from Clarins." The elevator door opened on the fifth floor and they began what Paul called Karl's 'tour of duty'. At least once a day, Karl would walk from one end of the store to the other. It was his way of keeping in contact with the grass-roots of Franklyns. Without them, he felt he would lose touch in his ivory tower.

"Fucking discounts to be cut out of magazines?" snapped Karl. "This is Franklyns of Knightsbridge, not Superdrug! What the fuck are you coming up with something as tacky as that for?"

Paul swallowed the retort he wanted to make. Karl took great pleasure in humiliating people. He took pleasure in talking to Paul in that manner in front of the security men. He enjoyed undermining his authority.

"Maybe you want to go work in Boots or something? Maybe that would suit your talents better?"

"When it comes to marketing this store, I think nothing is out of the equation," Paul insisted. "Maybe we could learn a few things from Boots."

They walked down an escalator to the next floor.

"I don't need ideas, I need good ideas," said Karl. "And if you can't supply them to me, then I'll replace you with someone who can."

Paul raised his eyes to heaven. "If you feel I'm not doing my job, replace me any time you want," he said calmly.

Karl stopped abruptly and fixed him with his cool eyes but was at that moment distracted by a young male employee leaning over a counter while he talked on the phone.

"What is this twit doing slouching like that?" Karl snapped.

Paul walked over to the man.

"Will you straighten up?" he said quietly. "Furstin will have you out on your arse otherwise."

The young man immediately stood bolt upright and hung up the phone.

They continued on their tour.

"We're having Louise Stirling coming in tomorrow to launch her new book," said Paul. "We're expecting a very big crowd."

"Let's hope her book sells better than her perfume."

"The publishers are expecting huge sales and we are the first point of call for her."

Karl suddenly stopped as he spotted a blonde girl standing behind an information desk.

"Who is she?" he demanded.

"I haven't seen her before. She's probably just started."

"Go find out who she is."

Paul went over to the girl. From her blonde hair, vivid blue eyes and sculptured face, he guessed her to be Scandinavian.

"What's your name?" Paul asked.

"Ingrid," she said.

"How long have you been working here?"

"Just a week."

"Where are you from?"

"Stockholm," she smiled, feeling unnerved by Karl's stare in the background.

Paul went to speak to Karl, and Ingrid watched nervously as they chatted. Then Paul nodded and came back over to her.

"Right, you're to start working up in the offices on the sixth floor tomorrow morning."

"What?" Ingrid shook her head in confusion.

"You've just been given a promotion – you'll be working in the Chairman's offices."

"But doing what exactly?"

"It'll be explained in the morning when you go to the sixth floor. You should be delighted – it'll be extra money for you. Just let Personnel know you're transferring there."

Ingrid nodded and watched as Paul rejoined the others and they continued their tour.

Chapter 2

As the taxi manoeuvred through the London traffic, Stephanie Holden sat in the back, legs crossed, dressed in a business suit and groomed to within an inch of her life. Gazing out of the cab window at the beautiful sun, the day reminded her so much of another day over twenty years ago. A day when for ten minutes the whole world was watching her. It was the day of Live Aid and she was one of three backing singers for the The Yell. She was only eighteen at the time and had been with The Yell for two years as they emerged as an eighties phenomenon. Not bad for a young girl who had only been in the music industry for a short time. But then Stephanie had always stood out from the crowd.

She remembered the excitement of going out on stage that day, dressed in a tight black dress and high heels. Danny McKay, lead singer of The Yell and eighties pin-up, had winked over at her and they had exploded into music. She remembered thinking that this was their moment and they had to give it everything. As Danny's voice had boomed around the world, she had poured her heart and soul into her singing and danced in the stylish energetic way The Yell's backing singers were known for. It was the last performance she ever did with The Yell or anyone else. Her mind drifted to that night after the concert, the night she had got pregnant.

She forced her mind to stop dwelling on the past. She wasn't a teenage backing singer any more, she was a forty-one-year-old businesswoman. She was en route for one of the most important meetings of her life and didn't need to dwell on the past. She quickly took her mobile from her handbag and dialled her son Leo's number, hoping he would answer.

"Yeah?" Leo's tone was uninterested.

"Hi, just checking how you are? I haven't seen you in ages."

"Been busy."

"Too busy for your old mum?"

"What do you want, Mum?" Leo said impatiently.

"I was just hoping you could come home this evening. I could cook us something to eat and we could catch up –"

He cut her short. "I can't, I've got something on."

"I see." She tried to keep the disappointment out of her voice.

"Listen, I've gotta go." He paused and added as an afterthought, "Maybe I'll see you at the weekend."

"Oh, will you try?" Her voice lifted.

"Right, gotta go. Bye."

"Leo, I love –" Stephanie paused as she realised he had hung up and quietly added the word "you."

She switched off the mobile.

"Kids, eh?" said the taxi driver, not in any way trying to disguise the fact he had been listening in. "You wonder what's the point in having them. It's all take take take, no give. I've got two teenage daughters and do you think they ever care about how much worry they cause us?"

"I'm getting off just here," she said, grateful she didn't have to listen to his saga.

She quickly paid the driver, got out of the cab and looked up at the building of Barons Bank headquarters situated in the heart of the city. As she walked down the busy pavement filled with suited executives, she stood out. Her figure was as good as it had ever been, thanks to regular work-outs in the gym. Her sleek black hair fell gleaming straight past her shoulders. Her face was still strikingly beautiful. She walked through the revolving doors, announced herself to Reception and was told to go straight up to the Boardroom on the tenth floor. She steadied herself as the elevator transported her to the meeting. She suddenly felt nervous. No matter what she had achieved in life and how far she had come, she always carried that feeling that she was an outsider, especially when she was going into a heavy meeting with these super-educated professionals. She banished the feelings of inadequacy. She was there because they needed her.

* * *

Conrad Richardson rose from the head of the Boardroom table as his secretary showed Stephanie in. He hadn't seen her in quite a while but she hadn't changed. But then she never did. He supposed she could be described as beautiful.

"Stephanie!" He approached her, smiling, and when he shook her hand he clasped it in both of his and stared warmly into her eyes as if they were old friends. They weren't.

"Good to see you again, Conrad," she smiled back.

Conrad was about fifty years old and was dressed

immaculately in a pin-striped suit, his brown hair combed back. She observed that his eyes were as lively and smug as ever.

"Stephanie, I'm not sure if you've met David Stafford before?" Conrad indicated the other man in the room who now rose from the head of the Board table and came towards her..

She smiled as they shook hands, noting that he was very handsome.

"Thank you for meeting us at such short notice. Please take a seat," said Conrad.

The three of them sat down.

"It sounded urgent on the phone," she said, resting back in her chair and crossing her legs.

"Well, I suppose it is."

Stephanie imagined if Conrad Richardson was informed a nuclear bomb was heading towards him in twenty minutes, he still would not lose his relaxed and in-control manner. He sat back and smiled.

"Well? Let's get down to business," Stephanie prompted.

"Franklyns of Knightsbridge." He paused to examine her reaction. He could see she was intrigued.

"Yes?" she pushed.

"It's not been looking too healthy recently."

"I was in there last week. It looked very good to me. In fact, better than ever."

"On the surface it looks good, with all the renovations done over the past couple of years. But financially it's a very different matter."

"And what have Barons Bank got to do with that? That's more Karl Furstin's problem, isn't it?"

"I'm not sure if it is necessary for you to know exactly

the details of our interest but we need somebody with your track record to – well, to turn the place around."

Stephanie studied Conrad and then glanced at David Stafford. She leaned forward.

"Conrad, I do need to know all the details. So cut the bullshit and tell it to me straight."

Conrad remaining cool, scrutinising the woman at the other side of the table. Stephanie Holden would never be his first choice of business partner. But he needed her. He needed her ability. In the past ten years she had grown into something of a legend in the retail world. Working up from the shop floor at the John Hewitt department store, she had risen to the position of Brand Manager and under her expertise brought the store firmly into the first division. She had quickly been poached by an ailing rival store and within a year had transformed their fortunes. She had then moved on to the nationwide chain, Blackthorns, which she had quite literally snatched from the hand of the receiver and transformed it into a powerhouse of fashion and profit. She was the best in the retail business. And he needed the best at Franklyns.

He glanced at David, who was coolly playing with his fountain pen.

"So, what's going on?" said Stephanie.

David looked over at Conrad and nodded.

"Very simple really," said Conrad. "Years of declining sales have meant Franklyns has been making losses. They attempted a major revamp by modernising the store a couple of years back. We financed the loans for the revamp and we have been financing their deficit. They can't repay the loans any more."

"What you're telling me is you're sending Franklyns into receivership?"

"Yes," Conrad nodded but continued smiling.

"But it's an institution!"

"A badly in-debt institution."

"And you want me to go in and sort it out?"

Conrad got up, walked over to the window and stood looking down at the street below.

"Yes, your appointment would be as Brand Director. Despite the modern appearance the revamp has given it, the place is stuck in two hundred years of history. It won't be an easy environment for you to operate in. You'll have to work with some existing department heads there, before you decide who stays and goes. But you need to change the place completely, so there will be a lot of resentment."

"I'm used to resentment."

"And then there's Furstin. He obviously won't be happy losing his pride and joy. Do you know him?" Conrad swung around and looked at Stephanie.

"I know his reputation – who doesn't?"

They looked at each other and didn't need to say anything else. Stories had been circulating about Karl Furstin since he took over Franklyns sometime in the eighties. He could be dynamic, brilliant, strange, threatening and sinister. His and his wife's glamorous lifestyle were tabloid fodder. He was originally German and the son of a retail dynasty who had owned a chain of department stores there. He had been sent to England for education, and proved himself a brilliant businessman as he sold the family business in Germany and then bought and sold a number of retail groups in the UK. Back in the eighties he had bought Franklyns from under the nose of stiff competition. At the time Franklyns had been in the Franklyn family for nearly two hundred years. A dynamic family that effectively built up the business through the decades, each new generation after the war had become increasingly lazy and more interested in country pursuits. The world-famous store had become neglected and ripe for a takeover by the eighties. Karl had used the same dynamics with Franklyns as he had with his previous retail groups and the store had enjoyed a period of modernisation and growth.

Conrad turned and looked at her. "We want to get our money back from Franklyns and we want to do it quickly. Our plan is to put it on the stock market in a year and sell it off so we can recoup our losses. It was Furstin who took out the loans and as he is the major shareholder by far we are foreclosing on him. There are a number of other very small shareholders but they really don't have any say in running the store so won't really interfere with us. I think collectively they own five per cent of the business. With our planned launch on the stock market, Franklyns has to be transformed in that period so that it is seen as an excellent investment and we get our money back."

David sat back in his chair and said, "I'm going to be the new Financial Controller at Franklyns, so although our areas are obviously very different, it will be down to us to turn this store around."

"I don't come cheap," Stephanie warned.

"I never thought you did," said Conrad.

* * *

"What's your opinion of her?" David asked after Stephanie had left.

Conrad sat back and put his hands behind his head.

"Creative, I suppose is the best word for her. Knows

her retail. Has a keen eye for knowing exactly where a retail organisation is going wrong and where it needs to move to become successful. She tries to give the impression that she's a complete bitch. But she's not so bad really under it all. She's not frightened to make tough decisions and carry them through, but I'd say she goes home at night and cries about it."

David nodded. He liked to know as much as possible about the people he would be working with. Especially for such a huge project as Franklyns. If he was to have Franklyns financially ready to be launched on the stock market in a year, then Stephanie Holden would be the key to that.

"Is she married?" pursued David.

"I don't think so," said Conrad. "She's notoriously private about her private life. There were a lot of rumours that she was going out with one of the Blackthorns when she worked for them. I believe she has a son but that's all I know. She can be slightly tricky to work with. She wants her own way all the time. You won't find her hard to deal with?"

David stood up and closed over his briefcase before smiling and saying, "I can deal with anybody very easily as long as they are bringing in the money. I'll be watching her very closely to make sure she doesn't lose the run of herself."

Chapter 3

Oliver Newman stared down at the photo of himself and Nicola, taken when he received his OBE. Certainly one of the proudest moments of his life. And well deserved. He had been an excellent law enforcer and instrument for good for his country. He quickly put the framed photo back in a drawer. He admired the way Nicola had handled the morning's events but there was a rage inside him over it – that somebody would have the audacity to attack his wife. How many criminals and gangs had he defeated and put away over his years of cleaning up the city? And yet some hoodlum had done this. He thought of the wedding ring and engagement ring they had spent hours picking out years ago ending up on some chav's hand. He would get them back and he didn't care what it took to get them back. They were a symbol of his marriage and he would not allow them to be dishonoured. And he would get the bastard who attacked his wife and he would wish he had never been born. The little fucker didn't know what he had come up against when he had picked his random punter that morning. There was a knock on the door and the two policemen who had brought his wife in that morning entered. "I want you to return to Liverpool Street Station and get every bit of CCTV footage you can lay your hands on in the area. Inside the station, outside the station, in the McDonald's, in the Tube station, everything. You understand me?"

"Yes, sir."

"I want to piece together my wife's journey as she made her way through the station up to where she was attacked. We're going to get his face on footage and get the bastard."

* * *

Rachel crossed over Waterloo Bridge and walked down the Embankment, inhaling the sights and sounds of the capital. She stopped at a coffee shop, ordered a cappuccino and sat down at an outside table. It was nearly six and crowds of people were walking quickly by, making their way to the nearby Tube station to get home.

She felt excited at the start of her new life in London. She had anticipated moving here for so long that it still didn't feel real. She took out a copy of *The Evening Standard* and leafed through to the accommodation section. Money wasn't too much of a problem, thanks to her father. She marked an X beside the accommodation that interested her. And after she had gone through all the columns she took out her mobile and started to phone to make appointments.

Four hours later she wandered back to her aunt's house in Hampstead where she was staying. The accommodation had either not been to her standard or else too out-of-the-way for her to get to work easily. She remembered one house she viewed. It was a tiny cramped house that was really just four bed-sits with a shared kitchen. A potful of spaghetti lay poured out into the sink while wallpaper was peeling off the walls. Maybe finding a place was going to be more difficult than she had expected.

Her aunt and uncle had three teenage children. They were all very welcoming and delighted to have her but, as she heard the commotion that could be made only by three teenagers under the one roof, she realised that she really didn't want to stay there very long.

* * *

Glancing down at her watch, Nicola saw it was almost seven in the evening. Everyone in the offices had long since gone. She got up and, walking to the window behind her desk, glanced down at the traffic below. Her mobile rang and she reached over her desk for it.

"Hi, I'm downstairs," came Oliver's voice, a forced cheeriness in his tone.

"I'll be down in a minute," she said and grabbed her blazer from behind her chair.

They drove back to Hertfordshire in Oliver's Range Rover in relative silence. Oliver punctured the quietness occasionally with some tale of his day's work. Now and again he reached over and patted her hand, both of them painfully aware of the missing rings. He turned into their gravel driveway and brought the car to a halt.

She sat in the car for a minute, watching him open their front door and turn on the lights inside the house. She looked up at their beautiful period home, set in the beautiful countryside. The old farmhouse was her dream home. She and Oliver had spent a huge amount of time and money restoring it and now the interior was luxuriously refurbished. Yet she felt so empty as she made her way to the front door. And yet, as she closed it, she felt so safe there.

Oliver had put on some classical music and had gone into their extensive kitchen where he was beginning to prepare them dinner. She crossed over into the living-room and fixed herself a large port. Downing the drink quickly, she refilled her glass and went and sat down. As she sipped her drink, she gazed up at the array of photos on the walls. They were all of significant moments in their marriage. There was also one from many years ago, not long after they had first met. He looked handsome and smiling but as ever had a slightly uncomfortable look about him. Oliver was now forty-three but had always been older than his years. She wore a big floppy summer hat. She seemed very carefree. She had been back then.

She remembered meeting Oliver for the first time. It had been at her sister's wedding. She had been twenty-one at the time and he not much older than her. She had been working as an assistant in Harrods after graduating from college and was discovering the delights of being an independent young woman. It was a just a fluke she had ended up in Personnel. She had studied History of Art at college and upon graduation discovered it didn't really qualify her for anything. A family friend was working in Harrods at the time and suggested he sort her out with something. She ended up in the personnel department there. She had a natural flair for the job and it suited her. She had gone to the wedding with her then boyfriend Jack. She had known him since college and he was the most unreliable man she had ever encountered. But she found him exciting and dramatic.

The wedding was a glamorous affair. Her father being a respected MP meant there were plenty of politicians and dignitaries in attendance and a telegram of congratulations from Downing Street. She had noticed Oliver looking at her in the church. And afterwards at the county golf club where the reception was, she spotted him nervously glancing over at her. Out of curiosity, she made some enquiries and discovered he was a friend of her sister's new husband. He didn't have a partner at the wedding and as a single man he was getting a lot of attention. But he didn't venture far from his group of male friends.

Jack was impossible for the day – spoilt and petulant and, as he got steadily more drunk, chasing every available female, oblivious to her embarrassment or her family's fury. As she looked at her sister dancing with her accountant husband, she thought they seemed very grown-up and as she looked at Jack falling off a chair and sprawling on the ground beside her, she felt very un-grown-up. When the newly married couple were doing their first dance, she happened to be standing beside Oliver. Jack at this stage had his arm around some barmaid's waist and was leering into her face, intent on groping her. She felt mortified. When the other couples started dancing on the floor, she and Oliver stood awkwardly beside each other.

"Eh . . . do you want to . . . ?" He made a gesture to the dance floor.

She turned around and managed to smile and nod.

"You're Kate's sister," Oliver said, almost as if it was an accusation.

"Yes," she nodded, one eye on him and the other on Jack who now seemed to be having an argument with a barman who happened to be the molested barmaid's boyfriend.

"What do you do?" she asked.

"I'm a police detective," he answered.

She thought that it was incredibly dull but responsible.

The song ended.

"Thank you," Nicola had said, smiling, and before Oliver had time to engage her in further conversation, she rushed off to rescue Jack from the brawl he was now in.

Much later, Nicola and Jack were out in the carpark. A lot of the guests had left to go off to their respective hotels and now she was trying to convince Jack that the wedding was over and to get into the awaiting taxi to take them back to their hotel. But Jack was insisting he wanted to go on to a nightclub in the nearby town. As Oliver came out of the golf club he saw them arguing.

"You can go on your own, Jack! There's no way I'm going to a bloody nightclub after this long and horrible day!"

"Suit yourself then!"

Before she knew it he had jumped into the taxi, instructing the driver to take him to the nearest nightclub. She stood in disbelief as the taxi took off and left her standing on her own. She felt like crying but it wasn't her style.

"Are you all right?" asked Oliver as he came and stood beside her.

"Eh . . . yes." She was taken aback at seeing him. "I'm just . . . er . . . you know weddings, they're such long bloody days. I need to order another taxi."

"Where are you staying?"

"The George Hotel."

"So am I. Look, if we order another taxi it might take an hour to arrive. It's only a ten-minute walk if you want to walk with me."

She thought for a second. The thought of going back

into the golf club and waiting for an hour was too much. She nodded.

They walked in silence along the country road back to the hotel. She didn't know if she was shivering from the cold or from her humiliating day. And it was stupid, because she never cried, but suddenly silent tears were falling down her face. She had been brought up in a very safe and privileged background. There was hardly an argument between her parents in all their married years, and she as their daughter had been indulged and given a great sense of confidence and belief in herself. As they walked along, her anger shifted from Jack to herself. She was angry with herself for becoming so attracted to somebody as irresponsible as Jack.

Oliver had noticed her shivering. He took off his jacket and draped it over her shoulders and, as they walked along, he put his arm around her and she found herself leaning into him, silent tears falling down her face.

They had now been married for fourteen years. And time had gone slowly. She was thirty-eight and Oliver five years older than her. She was looking forty in the face and it was looking back at her and not smiling.

The phone ringing cut into Nicola's memories. She shook her head to dispel her wandering thoughts and, getting up, crossed the room and answered it.

"Nicola! Are you all right?" asked a dramatic voice. Nicola recognised it as that of Liz Williams. Liz and her husband Edward were two of her and Oliver's closest friends and lived nearby.

"Of course. Why wouldn't I be?"

"Well, Oliver told Edward about you being mugged and I've just been worried about you all day. You haven't been answering your mobile . . ."

Nicola let Liz drone on and cursed Oliver for telling Edward. It would be all around their circle of friends now and she just wanted to forget about the damned incident.

"Dinner's ready!" Oliver shouted from the kitchen.

"Liz," she interrupted her friend's flow, "I'm afraid I have to go. Oliver is calling me for dinner."

"Well, if you're sure you're all right?" Liz sounded unconvinced.

"I am and thank you for your concern. Bye, Liz." Nicola hung up.

She finished off her drink and went into the kitchen where Oliver had prepared a feast of steak, roast potatoes and peppered sauce. She smiled at him and sat down at the large country table.

"This looks beautiful," she said as she began to eat.

"Nonsense, it's nothing!" he said as he joined her but he was delighted by her remark.

"That was Liz . . . I wish you hadn't mentioned to Edward about the mugging."

"Oh, I just wanted his help really." He went red in the face.

"His help for what?" she queried, noticing him blush.

"Just about a new criminal bill I think should be brought in. We need to get tough on these hoodlums on the streets." Edward was a solicitor who was on some government committees.

"Oh, Oliver, don't make my mugging into a crusade!" She looked at him angrily. "I want to just forget about the whole bloody experience. I contacted the insurance company today and we should be reimbursed for everything. I just wish I hadn't worn that diamond necklace – it cost over twenty thousand after all."

"I know the necklace was expensive but I was thinking

more about the rings . . . an insurance company will never be able to replace your engagement and wedding rings." He looked very upset.

"There's nothing we can do." She shrugged and continued to eat.

"I'll get them back for you. I'm going to head the investigation myself and get the guy who attacked you and get your wedding and engagement ring back."

"Oh, Oliver, it's hardly worth it! Just let it go. This kind of thing happens to people every day and they just have to get on with it and forget about it."

"It doesn't happen to you – to us. I'll track him down. I'm going to scour the CCTV footage from Liverpool Street Station tomorrow."

Horrified, Nicola had visions of Oliver, with that dogged determination he had once he got going, sifting through hours of CCTV and seeing her run across the station and out onto the street after some stranger.

"Oliver!" She slammed her fork and knife on the table. "Will you just drop it? What's happened has happened and that's an end to it! I don't want to hear another word on the subject. And I *don't* want you making a vendetta of it!"

Seeing she was upset, he reached over and rubbed her hand. "Of course, whatever you want."

* * *

The beautiful sunny day had given way to a wet and windy night. Stephanie emerged from the headquarters of the Panther Fashion Group. She had been their Brand Director for the past two years. They had been shocked when she'd handed in her notice. They had asked her to reconsider, then they had pleaded and when that failed threatened her with legal action. Finally they had accepted the inevitable and parted company amicably.

She was happy enough to be leaving. She felt she had come to the end of the road with the chain and would have been looking for another position soon anyway, even if Conrad Richardson's offer hadn't landed into her lap. She sat in the back of the black cab as it made its way down the Kings Road towards her home at Chelsea Harbour as the rain splattered against the windowpanes. Conrad said he would have the terms of her contract forwarded to her home the following day. She would have the contract meticulously picked over by her solicitor before she signed.

"Where to, love?" asked the cabbie.

"You can leave me off just here outside this chip shop," she instructed.

She hurried inside the chip shop through the rain.

"Oh, how are you?" asked the owner, Antonio. "You not off out tonight to some posh do?"

"No, darling – this is the weather to stay in with fish and chips and a bottle of wine!"

"You're right there," chuckled Antonio as he shook the basket of chips he was frying. The music on the radio was an old track from The Yell and Stephanie leaned against the white-tiled wall as the music began to take her back again.

There was a respite in the rain, so once her order was ready Stephanie decided to walk rather than hail another taxi. She made her way down the street and then turned into Chelsea Harbour. Smiling at the concierge as he opened the glass doors for her, she walked through the lobby to the elevator which took her to the upper floors and her apartment. She let herself in and closed the door firmly behind her and locked it, feeling that relief of locking the world out and being on her own.

Her apartment was enormous, with direct views onto the Thames. It had cost her a fortune, but hey, what else did she have to spend her money on? She turned on the spotlights and went into the kitchen. Grabbing a plate, she unwrapped the takeaway onto it. And, as she had promised Antonio, opened a bottle of wine.

She went into the sitting-room and turned the TV on but kept the volume off. Listening to The Yell's song in the chipper had made her want to put on one of their albums and so she put on a CD and ate her fish and chips while she looked out at Battersea across the river. Funny, twenty years or so ago when she was a single mother living on social welfare, she had lived in one of the council tower blocks there. She smiled to herself. It was amazing what the difference a few streets, a river view and luxury interiors made. About a million bucks, she thought wryly.

Sipping her wine, she thought of her son, Leo. With his sallow skin and black hair, he had always been a great-looking kid. He looked very like his father. She had a lot of great memories from his childhood, despite the fact it had not often been in the easiest of circumstances. She would give anything to get that closeness she'd had with her son back but it had been taken away. She hardly knew anything about his life any more. All she knew was that he had fallen in and out of bad crowds since hitting teenage life. She knew she wasn't a perfect mother but always tried to do her best for him.

Chapter 4

The following day Leo Holden was standing at the top of the hired function room in The Selfridges Hotel while a video on a giant screen behind him showed a series of developments and landscapes in Spain. Beside him stood a beautiful girl called Daniella.

The video clip came to an end.

"Ladies and gentlemen, as you can see, this latest development we are offering is a wonderful opportunity for you to have your own holiday home in the sun and also a wise investment that will offer you serious capital appreciation over the coming years. A £5,000 deposit today will secure you your apartment in our new luxury development, Villa Las Palmas. Then we will be in contact over the next two weeks to organise for you to travel to Villa Las Palmas at a time that suits you so that you can see this wonderful investment opportunity for yourselves. If you then want to continue with your investment, contracts must be signed within two weeks. If you don't want to proceed, we refund your £5,000. Any questions?"

Daniella looked on admiringly as he then expertly answered the questions fired at him.

By the end of the session, five people came forward and wrote cheques out to Las Palmas Property.

"Not a bad afternoon's work," smiled Leo happily as they came out of the hotel and sat into his awaiting open-topped sports car.

"Not bad at all," said Daniella. She glanced down at her watch. "We'd better hurry back to Franklyns. I'm late for work." Daniella worked as a salesgirl in the cosmetics department there.

"I'll have you back in a jiffy."

Leo tore off down the street and quickly negotiated the London traffic to Knightsbridge.

"What time will I pick you up tonight?" he asked as he pulled over to let her out. It was Friday and he was in the mood to party.

"Usual time, six thirty," she said, leaning over and kissing his lips.

She stepped out of the car and hurried towards Franklyns.

Leo put on his sunglasses and drove off. He was delighted with the afternoon's work. He would go to the bank and lodge the deposit cheques into the newly opened Villa Las Palmas business account. Then, once the cheques had cleared, he would withdraw the money and close down the account. Then he would close down the swish offices he had temporarily leased and do a disappearing act. He would be long gone before the would-be purchasers realised their would-be dream investment didn't exist nor did their deposits any more. Certainly one of the best scams he had ever pulled.

Just then his phone started to ring. He picked it up and, seeing it was his mother, Stephanie, he turned it on to silent and threw it back down on the seat beside him.

* * *

Two police officers came into Oliver's office, carrying boxes loaded with disks.

"This is all we got from all the CCTV footage, sir," said one.

"Start going through it and call me as soon as you pick up my wife on the tapes," Oliver ordered. He handed over a photo of Nicola. "Also ask all the shopkeepers and British Rail staff if they saw her . . . I want to get this bastard and I don't care what we have to do to achieve that."

"The problem is she wasn't attacked in the station, sir, but we're in the process of collecting all the CCTV from businesses on the street outside the station."

"Good. I want to be kept informed of everything." Oliver turned around on his swivel-chair and stared out the window as the two policemen left the office. He wouldn't tell Nicola he was pursuing this. She just wanted to forget about it. But he couldn't forget about it. And he wanted her jewellery back. Especially her rings. Nicola had pretended the whole attack hadn't fazed her. But he could see she wasn't herself.

He decided he would leave work early, go and collect his wife, and try to make sure that she relaxed and rested over the weekend.

Chapter 5

In Human Resources you become an excellent judge of character very quickly. Nicola prided herself on being able to read a person's disposition and background within a few seconds of meeting. As Rachel sat in her office on Monday morning, her first day of work at Franklyns, Nicola knew that she was from a moneyed background. It wasn't just the expensive diamond necklace or the discreet Cartier she was wearing – it was her whole demeanour and confidence. The way she wore her clothes. Not that it impressed Nicola. Her career in Human Resources in Knightsbridge had been littered with children of the very wealthy. A store like Franklyns offered these children, some who might not be the brightest or most confident, a role in life. Saying they worked at Franklyns or Harrods or Harvey Nichols was a perfectly acceptable form of occupation until they decided what they wanted to do in life. Her personal assistant, Yvette, was a classic example of this – a girl from a Chelsea background who took great pride at working in Franklyns. Then there were the Europeans and Americans who came to work at the store. These were often just travelling through for a year or so . . .

if Karl didn't take a shine to them and whisk them up to his offices. The cosmetics department was slightly different. The girls who worked there weren't from moneyed backgrounds. Their glamour got them their jobs. And often they didn't mix with the rest of the store. Oh, the politics of it all, thought Nicola, as she sat back observing Rachel.

"I'll give your bank details to our payroll office," said Nicola. "Your wages will be paid into your account on the last day of every month."

Rachel nodded, slightly intimidated.

There was a knock on the door and a glamorous blonde entered who Rachel judged to be in her early thirties.

"This is Christine Mountcharles who is our overall sales manager for first and second floor. Christine, Rachel is starting work today. Show her to her position, please."

"What department am I starting in?" asked Rachel as she rose to her feet.

"Cosmetics on the ground floor," informed Nicola coolly.

"Cosmetics?" Rachel was startled.

"Yes – have you a problem with that?"

"It's just that I was expecting something in an office environment." Rachel began to look very concerned.

"I've no cosy office job available for you, I'm afraid. You'll have to take it or leave it."

Rachel thought for a few seconds. "It's fine." She forced herself to smile. "I'm sure I'll really get to know the store there. It will be great experience for when I work in the press office."

Nicola looked down and started doing paperwork, indicating that the interview with Rachel was concluded.

"Right, follow me," said Christine.

Rachel looked down at Nicola who was busily writing. "Thank you, Nicola," she said. When Nicola didn't raise her head, she turned slowly and followed Christine out of the office.

Nicola looked up and speculatively watched her go.

* * *

"Where are you from?" Christine asked as they entered the elevator.

"Dublin."

Christine looked at Rachel. "Word of advice – you never question Nicola."

"Right," said Rachel meekly.

The elevator door opened and they walked over the black porcelain tiles through the busy store.

"We're incredibly busy," Christine said. "Louise Stirling is coming into the store today so there will be oceans of people coming in for a look at her."

"The model? She's doing a fashion show here?"

"No," Christine said dismissively. "Her modelling career was finished in that drugs scandal a couple of years back. She's written a novel and has a book-signing session here today. This is about the fifth career she's tried since her modelling career was destroyed. She was in last year promoting her new perfume called Survive. It survived on the shelves about a week before it was sent back to the factory due to disastrous sales." She glanced down at Rachel's Cartier. "Is that real?"

"Eh, yes . . . it's a gift from my parents."

"No boyfriend then?"

Christine's blunt manner was unappealing to Rachel.

"Nobody at the moment," she answered briefly.

They moved through the huge ground floor, making their way through the crowd of shoppers. Rachel took in all the glamour. Huge encased eight-foot-tall glass boxes had fountains inside splattering water continuously against their glass confines. As they walked through the cosmetics department, the glass square tiles on the floor continuously changed colours electronically from black to white to gold to indigo. A central staircase had also been equipped with a colour-changing mechanism with each step automatically lighting up in a different colour as customers walked up and down. All this with classical music wafting down from the very high marble dome ceilings.

"Nicola said you worked in Brown Thomas – so how much experience have you got?"

Rachel decided to be honest. "I'm afraid I was mainly in the press office. I've no real shop-floor experience."

"I see." Christine raised her eyes to heaven.

As they reached the Chanel counter Christine beckoned a dark-haired beauty over to her.

"Daniella, this is Rachel – she's starting here today. I'm going to leave her here with you for now. She has an induction course at two. Send her up to Personnel for that, will you? Right, I'll check on you in half an hour." Christine turned and marched off.

"I'd like to say she's not as bad as she seems, but she is," said Daniella as Rachel went behind the counter to join her.

"She seems a bit to the point all right," Rachel smiled.

She felt a wave of excitement as she looked out at the store from behind the counter, observing the passing crowds.

Daniella looked Rachel up and down. "Are you seeing anyone?"

Rachel felt perplexed that this seemed to be the first question everyone asked her.

"No, not at the moment."

"There's some rich pickings around here. The security guards try it on with all the new girls starting here so just avoid them like the plague. You can have a bit of fun with them, I suppose, but I mean what can they offer? Do you see that girl over there?" She nodded at a glamorous redhead at a nearby counter. "A guy from Florida came in about a month ago and asked her out. And he turns out to be a multimillionaire! She's going over to his place in Miami next week to check out his set-up."

Rachel frowned. "I haven't really come here to find a boyfriend. I was hoping more for a career."

"In Franklyns?" Daniella looked confused.

"Yeah, it's a big company – there must be opportunities to get on?"

"I guess. I mean you can get to a supervisory position on the shop floor."

"I was hoping for something up in the offices."

"They like to keep the power to themselves up there." Daniella went to serve a customer.

A large American woman tugged on Rachel's sleeve from the other side of the counter.

"Hey, honey, what you got that looks expensive but don't cost too much?" she asked.

Rachel smiled at the woman but she screamed on the inside. The last thing she wanted was to be stuck doing this job and if, as Daniella said, the opportunities of getting up to the management offices were very limited then she would go quickly mad.

* * *

"At first I thought it was a joke but Paul seemed very serious," explained Ingrid as she sat opposite Nicola explaining her change of occupation.

Nicola viewed the girl. She had interviewed Ingrid herself for her sales post and thought she was pleasant and unassuming.

"No, Paul was being very serious," she said. "Mr Furstin often employs his personal staff internally."

"I wonder why he picked me?" Ingrid said excitedly.

I wonder indeed, thought Nicola knowingly. The sixth floor was outside Nicola's domain and it always had been. She might have power over the staff through the rest of the building but once they went up to the sixth floor they had nothing to do with her any more. That suited her. She and Furstin got on just fine. He always treated her with the greatest respect. She wouldn't have stayed if he dealt with her any other way. They kept out of each other's way and jurisdictions. He often asked for her judgement on matters he wasn't sure of. And she had been called upon in the past to advise on legal matters concerning members of staff on the sixth floor. Furstin was a well-known man and even with staff as well vetted as Franklyns' the occasional bad apple – in Furstin's terms – could get through the net.

"Your net salary will be increased by 20% from tomorrow," Nicola informed the delighted girl.

* * *

Paul strode into the book department. Security was tight and there was a huge throng of people waiting for the arrival of Louise Stirling. There were life-size cardboard cut-outs of her, and the book was displayed all around the department. All over the store were banners with the book's title, *Secrets,* followed by its advertising logo: '*She wanted it all – but got more than she wanted!*' Crikey, Paul thought as he read the corny slogan. He glanced at his watch and saw they seemed to be behind schedule.

He saw Christine approach him with her usual determined stride.

"Where's Louise Stirling?" he asked.

"She's in the stockroom and she won't come out!"

"Why?"

"I don't know what the fuck is wrong with her. She seems to be having a panic attack or something."

He quickly made for the stockroom.

"You didn't answer my text last night," Christine accused as she walked alongside him.

He looked straight ahead and lied: "I didn't get it until this morning."

"We need to talk, Paul."

"Not now!" he snapped as he slammed through the double doors of the stockroom.

He found an assortment of people gathered at the end of the room, including the book department manager, three of Franklyn's security guards and two PR girls called Emma and Sarah from Louise's publishers. They all surrounded Louise, who was sitting on a box containing her books. Her long model figure was clad in tight jeans and a tight top and over this she wore a long leopardskin coat. She sat, her legs crossed, smoking a cigarette theatrically.

"Louise, come on – *please!*" begged Emma.

"This was a mistake," announced Louise. "I should never have agreed to these book-signing sessions."

"But you did agree to it as part of your contract," Sarah reminded her gently.

"Is that a threat?" Louise turned and looked at Sarah menacingly.

"Of course not," Sarah spluttered.

Paul came up to Louise and, taking her hand, smiled down at her. "Louise, it's so good to see you again." Realising she hadn't a clue who he was, he continued, "I'm Paul Stewart, the general manager here at Franklyns – we met when you launched your perfume here last year."

Still not remembering she gave him a courteous smile, the one reserved for fans.

He squeezed her hand tightly. "It really is good to see you again. You know you pulled the biggest crowd of any celebrity we had here last year with that appearance."

"Did I?" She looked sceptical.

"Sure did. Even more than Madonna."

"Well, for all the good that did me. They didn't buy the damned perfume – it had disastrous sales."

"And who could blame them?" Paul smiled.

"Do you mean who could blame them for wanting to gawp at me or for not buying the damned perfume?"

"Both," Paul said decisively.

There was a sharp intake of breath from everyone.

"Are you telling me you're not surprised that my perfume failed?"

"That's exactly what I'm saying. Unfortunately, it smelt like . . . detergent."

Sarah and Emma looked at each other in horror.

Louise uncrossed her legs and, dragging on her cigarette, said icily, "Detergent?"

"My wife agreed with me. We wondered how you could ever have put your name to it."

"Well, it wasn't my decision! It was my manager who arranged it all!"

"Well, I hope you've got rid of him."

"As a matter of fact I have."

"Anyway, I've a bone to pick with you about your new book as well."

Louise suddenly looked very fragile and insecure.

"What?" She seemed almost afraid to ask.

"You're causing a rift in my marriage. My wife won't put the book down. She was up all night reading it."

Louise's face visibly relaxed and she looked joyful.

"She's enjoying it?"

"She can't wait for your next book to come out. The difference is, the perfume was a management decision, whereas the book is yours, written by you and coming from your heart."

Emma and Sarah gave each other a cynical look. The book had been ghost-written.

"I wonder, if I got a copy, would you sign it for my wife?" ventured Paul. "She'd never forgive me otherwise!".

Lousie stood up briskly, threw the cigarette on the floor and stamped it out. She turned quickly to her PRs. "Come on, Sarah and Emma, we haven't got all day. Let's get this session started!" She walked quickly out towards the shop floor, followed by her entourage. As she opened the double doors there was a cheer from the waiting crowd.

Christine sidled up to Paul. "I have to say – very impressive."

Paul fixed his tie. "I thought so."

"And did your wife really enjoy the book?"

"She glanced through it and said it was a load of crap."

Outside, Lousie was surrounded by fans.

"I'm a big fan of yours!" A young girl handed her copy of *Secrets* to Louise.

"Ah, thank you, darling!" Louise signed her name with a flourish.

"Is the main character based on yourself?" asked the girl. "It is, isn't it?"

Louise looked up and smiled. "Let's just say I can identify with her . . . I too wanted it all . . ." she sighed before adding, "but got more than I wanted."

Paul looked on, his arms folded, smiling. The book-signing was turning into a huge success, as was evident from the beaming Emma and Sarah who stood protectively either side of Louise.

Paul's mobile rang and he answered it

"Hi, Paul, it's Gordon here."

"Hey – how's Joanne and the baby?" Gordon Holban was Franklyns' marketing manager and an old friend of Paul's. His wife, Joan, had just had their first baby.

"Brilliant. Just brilliant. Just left the hospital now. They are doing great and I could do with a drink. You around after work to wet the baby's head?"

"Sure I am. I'll see you after work in The Blue Posts."

* * *

Christine stood behind the counter with Rachel, showing her how to work the till.

"The Arabs are fantastic. They never check the prices for anything and just keep buying. Americans are always good. The Russians are the new Arabs. Lots of money.. The Home Counties set will spend but will check the price of everything and look for value for money – and the British aristocracy will spend but charge it to their account and never pay. There are some lords and ladies who own half a county and owe the store over a hundred grand – and the credit-control department can't put any pressure on them except ring them up and politely ask them for a payment whenever they get a chance. The Japanese don't really spend like they used to. And look out for days like Valentine's and, of course, Christmas. If you get a hassled businessman looking for presents at the last minute because he hasn't had time, he will literally hand over his credit card to you and you can go to town. If you get a businessman on Christmas Eve who's had a few drinks, he'll let you put anything on his credit card."

"Hello," said a friendly voice.

Christine and Rachel looked up to see Paul Stewart standing there smiling, his arms folded.

"Paul, this is Rachel. She's started working here today."

Paul smiled at Rachel.

"This is our general manager, Paul."

"Oh, I'll be nice to you then," Rachel smiled at him.

"No, don't be nice to me because of my position, but because you want to be," said Paul.

He walked off down the aisle and Christine quickly came from behind the counter and marched quickly after him.

Daniella appeared at Rachel's side. "What do you think of Paul?"

"Seems friendly," said Rachel.

"I think he's very attractive."

"He's not my type." Rachel had observed that anyone who appeared to have money or power was Daniella's type.

"By the way he was looking at you, I think you're *his* type."

"Don't be stupid."

"Paul's the store's ladies' man."

"Wasn't that a wedding ring on his finger?"

"You spotted that quick enough, didn't you?" Daniella looked at Rachel knowingly, causing her to blush. "Listen, are you up to anything tonight?"

"I'm due to see a couple of apartments to rent."

"There's a pub across the road, The Blue Posts – we all hang out there and there's a crowd going over for a drink after work if you want to join us?"

Rachel smiled and nodded. "That would be nice."

Chapter 6

That evening The Blue Posts was packed, mainly with Franklyns staff, as Paul pushed open the door and made his way through the crowd, looking out for Gordon. Different staff members quickly stepped out of his way as he walked through, occasionally greeting him with a respectful "Paul".

Music from the Kaiser Chiefs was blaring loudly.

"Hey, congratulations!" Paul shook Gordon's hand firmly, sat up on the spare stool Gordon was keeping for him, and ordered two more Heinekens.

"So everything went fine?" he asked then.

"Just great. And she's absolutely beautiful. We're calling her Beth. I'm telling you, it's like when I first saw her my whole perception of the world changed in a moment. It's hard to describe but everything changed."

Paul forced a smile.

"I'm telling you, nothing and I mean *nothing*, prepares you for that moment." Gordon's emotions were racing from hyper-excitement to contentment.

The barman placed the pints in front of them and Paul handed him a ten-pound note.

"Well, then – to Beth!" said Paul.

They raised their pints and chinked glasses.

As two members of staff came up and congratulated Gordon, Paul spotted the new girl he had been introduced to walk into the pub with Daniella and watched them as they headed across the bar to a group from their department.

"You know, you and Anna should really give it a try, Paul."

Paul felt very uncomfortable. "We're a bit too busy at the moment to be having babies."

"You two have been married years! There's never a perfect time. You just have to go for it. You'd never regret it."

Paul felt himself become even more uncomfortable. Why did people always think they could speak with authority when they had managed something that someone else hadn't? He wanted to end this line of conversation.

Gordon continued, "We plan to go again soon. No point in hanging around. Having one child is a mistake."

"And having two is a worse one. Anna is a very successful journalist. She doesn't really have time to have children."

"She doesn't have time?" Gordon looked incredulous.

Paul spotted Christine enter the pub.

"Oh oh – here's trouble!" said Gordon. "That's not still going on, is it?"

"No!" Paul looked angry. "It's long over. And I hope you never mentioned it to Joanne – because if we're all out to dinner sometime and Joanne lets it slip . . ."

"Relax, of course I said nothing. What goes on tour stays on tour. Has she dyed her hair?"

"Yeah."

"You went to bed with a brunette and woke up with a blonde! Having said that . . . you're lucky you didn't wake up with the clap, mate!"

Paul decided to change the conversation quickly. "Furstin wants to know when you'll be back at work?"

"You joking me? This is the first time off I've had all fucking year and he's moaning already?"

* * *

As Nicola got into her awaiting taxi at the back entrance of Franklyns, she saw the new girl Rachel head into The Blue Posts.

It hasn't taken her long to start socialising, she thought. But, she's young and she's pretty, so why shouldn't she?

As she heard the laughter and music pour out of the pub, she was consumed with a jealousy of their enjoyment. She guessed Paul would probably be over there. He was a man and could get away with drinking over in the pub with the boys. If she dared to go over, her image would be tarnished and she felt her position would be undermined. She was still feeling envious as the taxi whisked past the pub to bring her to Liverpool Street Station.

* * *

"Oh, no, I don't want another one!" objected Rachel as another gin and tonic was put in front of her.

"Too late," said Daniella, sitting down at the table.

Daniella's mobile bleeped as she got a text. She checked it and smiled.

"It's from Leo. This guy I'm kind of seeing at the moment. I did a job for him and he's just thanking me."

"Is it serious?"

"I'm not sure. He's very exciting. Loaded, of course. He worked in the city and made his fortune. Now he runs different businesses."

"Where did you meet?"

"In a bar up in the city one night!. He's not the most reliable . . . but he's much more reliable than the last guy I was seeing. He was a case of wham bam and not even so much as a thank-you ma'am!"

Rachel laughed. She liked the girl. There was something endearing about her.

"You've been at Franklyns a while, haven't you?"

"Too long, love!"

"What were you saying earlier about it being hard to get ahead in Franklyns?"

"Oh, nothing. It's just that Franklyns is two hundred years old and I often think it belongs in another century. All the senior management are a certain type. I mean, I'm just from a normal background myself. I applied to do a couple of things in the store but got nowhere. Not that I give a shit. The store is just a means to an end. I'll get my break one day."

"Break?"

"I do a bit of modelling. You might remember I did the Tia Maria advert a couple of years back?"

"Oh, yes, I think I do," said Rachel, trying to sound convincing. She couldn't remember her in the least.

"Paul Stewart and Nicola Newman, they think they are so important. I went up and asked Nicola Newman about moving up in Franklyns one day. I had an idea I wanted to be a buyer. She let me babble on for thirty minutes about how much it would mean to me to train as a buyer and then she calmly said – 'Not a chance!' I was humiliated!"

"That's terrible!" said Rachel.

"And who the fuck are they really?" continued Daniella "One day they'll be running around after me. That's what I kind of love about Leo. He just knows what he wants and goes for it and doesn't give a fuck about what anyone thinks. He says life is there to take what you want from it. Nicola Newman can piss off. I won't be asking her for any more promotions."

* * *

Christine sidled up to Paul, catching him on his own. Gordon had gone to the loo and been waylaid by a couple of friends as he returned.

"You can't continue ignoring my calls and my texts," she said.

"You shouldn't text me when I'm home," he retorted. "I don't want Anna getting suspicious."

"What the hell has she got to be suspicious of? We haven't been together for ages."

"Christine. It was last Christmas, we were both drunk the first time and we should have left it at that. It was a fling. Let it go!"

"You can't just dismiss me like that, Paul." She felt herself getting angry. "You're just bored with me and want someone new."

"Actually, no, Christine. I want some space to try and make my marriage work."

"Your marriage! Don't make me laugh. You never thought about your wife when you were fucking me!"

"Well, now I am thinking about her."

Paul felt the pub was crowding in on him, what with Gordon going on about children all night and Christine hassling him.

He stood up abruptly. "I'm going home."

"Paul, I'm not finished talking to you!" Christine almost shouted as he pushed his way through the crowd.

He walked down the streets towards the Tube station. He didn't want to go home yet and so passed the station and continued walking.

It was something Paul did often on his way home to Wimbledon. Get off a Tube stop early and walk the rest of the way. It helped him clear his head.. He liked walking. It was a habit he had got into when he was growing up. His own parents' marriage had gone through a bad patch when he was a kid and there had been many arguments. Sometimes he would just walk around in the evenings or at night after visiting his friends' houses, delaying getting home.

He looked at his watch and seeing it was approaching eleven thirty he picked up his pace.

His thoughts drifted to meeting Anna the first time. After a brief and not particularly successful spell in college, he wasn't sure what he wanted to do, so got a job in Selfridges and managed to get on a graduate management scheme. Anna had been working at Selfridges in the press office at the time. He remembered meeting her and being bowled over by her. She was so intelligent and sophisticated and just plain nice.

He turned down the leafy street that their home was on.

Anna had found him interesting. She thought he was witty and clever or at least made him feel like he was those things. Paul hadn't been used to people finding him interesting then and was very flattered when she asked him out. And suddenly they were seeing each other.

Seeing the lights were off in the house, he gently let himself in. She was still the nicest person he had ever met. He quietly went up the stairs and into the bedroom. Her still figure lay in the bed. He slipped off his suit and got in beside her. They had gone out together for a long time and had married ten years previously. When they had got married, he felt his life was beginning. They both worked hard and got lucky breaks and rose up the ladder. One day they expected to have children that would make their home complete. But the children never came. He looked down at her sleeping face. Her compassion for the world, for people, her love for him still overwhelmed him. And yet he had betrayed her. With the promotions came the confidence and the attention from females which had given him even more confidence. And he was seduced by the glamour of Franklyns and the power he had there. When Christine had come on to him at the Christmas party, he was flattered. Drink and his ego got the better of him and they had ended up together that night. It had developed into a brief affair. It certainly hadn't been the first time he had been unfaithful. And now as he looked down at Anna, he was filled with regret. He would never let it happen again. He was going to turn over a new leaf. There was no excuse for his behaviour in the past. He had thought that what Anna never knew never harmed her. Now he realised that wasn't good enough.

She stirred in her sleep. She opened her eyes and looked up at him, his face half lit from the light from the hall.

"Hi," she smiled.

"Hi," he smiled back.

"What's wrong?" she asked gently.

"Nothing," he whispered.

* * *

Karl Furstin tossed around in his sleep. He was dreaming and he was a child again. He was only four and he was so happy and safe in a beautiful manor in the country.

There were a lot of other children there and they all lived together. This was their home. There was one particular nurse and she was called Gerty and he was her favourite and she made no secret of it. She spoiled him and looked after him. She would sing him to sleep every night. He and the other children wanted for nothing in that big house. And then suddenly everything changed as bombs started raining down on the manor. There were screams and bloodshed. And he was racing through the manor trying to find Gerty but she was gone. And then there were soldiers and he and the other children were being rounded up and placed in a horrible place, a grey place.

He woke up with a start and was covered in sweat. He was panting and reached over to the switch and filled his opulent bedroom with light. He wiped the sweat off his brow and got out of bed. He opened the curtains and looked out at the lights of Knightsbridge. He was safe. He was in his penthouse. He tied a silk bathrobe around him and walked into the sunken lounge off the bedroom. His wife Elka stared dreamily down from four portraits that hung around the room. Each artist had succeeded in capturing Elka's beauty spectacularly.

He was still shaking from the dream and went and poured himself a cognac and sat down on the sofa drinking it. If only he could wipe out the bad memories.

He was a child of the Lebensborn project. Hitler wanted to create a perfect super race and during the war years he had encouraged what he considered to be good specimens of the Aryan race to come together in special resorts and procreate. The fathers were mostly SS officers, the mothers were often government staff. The women would be looked after in considerable style in special spas until after they had given birth and then they would give their children over to be brought up in luxurious institutions. The women were pleased that they had done their duty for the Reich. Some women from outside Germany were also recruited, largely Poles and Norwegians considered racially pure enough to be added to the programme. These children were to be Hitler's future ruling class, born and bred to rule his empire. And that was what Karl owed his existence to. After the war, as was common for most Lebensborn children in Germany, Karl was adopted. He was taken in by a wealthy family who owned a chain of stores throughout the country. He spent many years living in shame because of his origins but then decided he shouldn't be ashamed of who he was any more. In fact, he should be proud.

Was he not always destined for greatness?

He let his mind turn to work and an issue that needed resolving. He reached over to the phone beside him and dialled Paul Stewart's number. He regularly rang his management at all hours in the night. With the amount of money he paid them, he expected them to be available whenever he needed them.

Chapter 7

Oliver was in his office early on the Tuesday morning.

The two police officers who had been assigned to investigate Nicola's mugging had been working overtime, sifting through CCTV footage. They had managed to piece together the footage of Nicola making her way through the station. They were now playing it back for Oliver on a DVD player in his office.

Oliver watched his wife get off the train and walk down the platform. He was watching not only her but also the people around her for signs of the mugger. As he followed her progress from the platform into the main station, he was struck that she wasn't moving in her normal elegant and steady fashion. She was walking in a very strange and uncharacteristic way. He squinted closer to the screen to make sure it was Nicola, her demeanour was so strange. What was she doing? Now she was almost running across the station. She stopped abruptly, looking around frantically. And then suddenly she was racing across the station and nearly running up the steps. And then he noticed her gaze was fixed on two men in front of her and realised that it had been all along.

He paused the tape, frowning.

"What about footage from outside the station? What have you got?" he asked the officers.

"Very little as yet, I'm afraid," one of them answered. "We're still trying to collect it from different businesess and shops who have CCTV trained on the street outside the station."

"Okay, well, it doesn't look like there was anyone stalking her inside the station, so we need to concentrate on the footage from outside. Get those tapes in immediately, will you?" There was an impatience in Oliver's voice.

"Yes, sir."

The two officers turned and left.

Oliver rewound the tape and watched the sequence of events again from the beginning, this time concentrating on the two men in front of her.. And yes, Nicola was trying to catch up with the men. He watched the tape over and over again. Studying the men, they looked like wealthy businessmen and certainly not suspects for the mugging. They also seemed to be completely unaware of Nicola. It was his wife who looked to be stalking the men.

* * *

Like Furstin, Nicola liked to take a daily walk through the store, usually in the morning. She would choose a senior manager and they would start at the basement and walk through the entire building.

There was a tier management structure at Franklyns with floor managers, then managers over two floors like Christine, then department managers and then they all answered to Paul. But Nicola's strong personality meant that her power and influence went way beyond the HR department. If Nicola decided something related to any department, few people would overrule her.

That morning, Nicola arranged to meet Christine at the front entrance before the store had opened. Christine dreaded the exercise. Nicola's tour of duty could on occasion take up to two hours and Christine would have to be deferential for the whole time. Still, it was good to have Nicola's ear for that amount of time, and as long as you were on Nicola's regular list of walking companions it meant you were in favour. Nicola seemed to like the last security manager a lot and he used to be regularly chosen to accompany her on her walkabout. However, he had suddenly fallen out of favour and was replaced at lightning speed. Nobody knew what he had done to displease her.

Nicola was already waiting at the door, dressed in a beige suit and sensible shoes. Christine felt slightly nervous, as ever, about talking to her. She tried to analyse what it was that was so intimidating about this woman. It wasn't just her position in the store. It was her ultra-respectability, her level-headedness. This woman didn't need to lose her temper to frighten people – all she had to do was fix them with a cool look.

"How are sales figures this week?" Nicola asked as they made their way through the ground floor.

Staff were preparing for the day ahead at their different work stations. Tills were busy being loaded with their float from the cash office. Shelves were being rearranged.

"Good," Christine said. "Lots of tourists flocking in."

Nicola stopped as she saw the new Irish girl at a counter. She was passing boxes of stock to the girl Daniella who in turn was stacking them on shelves.

They were talking as they worked and Rachel tossed her hair and back and laughed.

"Christine, look at this," said Nicola, gesturing at the girls. "This isn't a social club. It's a workplace."

"I'll be back in a second," said Christine and marched over to the girls. "Will you stop talking and concentrate on your work," she snapped at them.

Daniella and Rachel looked around in surprise.

"We've been watching you over there. Nicola has marked your cards, Rachel. If you don't pull up your socks you'll be out. "

Rachel could see Nicola standing in the background, looking on with an icy half-smile.

Christine returned to Nicola and they continued on their walk.

"What's their fucking problem?" snapped Rachel when the two bosses were at a safe distance. "We're working away, aren't we? Retail is supposed to be a fun and lively environment so the customers get a sense of that too." Rachel felt herself consumed with anger by the pettiness of it.

"I'd better go to the other end of the counter," said Daniella.

Rachel looked at her, surprised to see her cockiness vanish.

* * *

Nicola made her way up to the sixth floor, past Karl's reception and knocked on his door. She was the only person at Franklyns who had free access to Karl without needing an appointment.

"Yes!" he called.

She opened the door and slipped into the room.

"Hello, Nicola," he smiled.

"Karl, I've got these documents I need you to sign," she smiled back and placed the paperwork on his desk in front of him.

She sat down as he glanced through them.

"They are just some dismissal notices that I need a second signature from you on," she explained.

He nodded and scribbled his signature on each document. He had nothing but the utmost respect for Nicola Newman. She was a lady in his eyes, devoid of any whiff of scandal – but was also extremely tough, a trait he admired even more.

"I have a problem with one of my staff," he said, sitting back in his chair.

"Really?" She crossed her legs and sat back.

"She's a young Italian girl by the name of Silvia? Do you remember her?"

Nicola cast her mind back and remembered a glamorous young Italian being whisked up to the sixth floor from the haute couture section.

"Yes, I think I do," she nodded.

"Bad attitude. I don't want her around any more."

Nicola nodded. "Will I find alternative employment for her in another department?"

"No." He shook his head violently. "I want her out of the store. Just get rid of her, if you can."

"Leave her to me," Nicola smiled.

Karl smiled back, confident of her ability.

* * *

As Stephanie made her way into the Barons Bank for a

meeting, she couldn't stop thinking about Leo and worrying about him.

"Mr Richardson is just in a meeting, Ms Holden, if you'd like to take a seat?" said Conrad's secretary.

Stephanie smiled at her and sat down.

Leo never returned her calls any more. And when he took a call from her, he barely carried on a conversation for longer than a minute before rushing off on some pretence. If she knew what she had done, she could rectify it. But this mystery was the worst. Maybe this was the result of bringing him up on her own. Maybe, despite putting him first and working hard to give him everything, she had failed him as she hadn't given him a normal family life with a father.

She picked up a magazine and glanced through it. In the social pages she was confronted with a photo of Danny McKay of The Yell with his wife Hetty. In spite of the time lapse since seeing him in person, seeing a photo of him gave her the same old pang. And she saw him often, between his guest appearances on television and these silly society pages. It seemed she would never be able to leave that part of her life behind her.

* * *

Stephanie had always loved music. All she had wanted to do when growing up was to be a singer. Much to her parents' dismay. She came from the East End where there was never much money. But it was such a hive of activity! Everyone was wheeling and dealing back then. On the street where she lived there were loads of small businesses: tiny greengrocers, bakers, timber yards, pubs, coal shops, hardware shops, clothes shops. Her own parents had a small general store that crammed in everything from shovels to sugar. If they didn't stock something they could get their hands on it within twenty-four hours. She and her brother were expected to help out in the shop whenever they were free. Stephanie didn't mind. In fact she enjoyed it. She was always rearranging the stock, and spending time doing the window display. She loved Christmas when she could go to town on making a dramatic window display. She'd watch her father in awe as he wheeled and dealed. There was a lot of bartering going on with the other shopkeepers. A bag of coal from the coal merchant for a week's groceries from their shop. But it was a survival game. No matter how much they worked, money was always very short.

School bored her and she couldn't wait to get out into the world. She knew she wanted to work singing with a band. She had become obsessed by all the singing stars and their glamorous lifestyles and wanted to be a part of that. She left school at seventeen and her mother brought her up the West End for a job interview in the Oxford Street store. She started working there in the fashion department as a salesgirl. She loved the excitement of working in the West End, earning a wage and having fun with the other girls working there. But what really grabbed her attention was the loud pop music constantly playing in the store. After much pestering, a friend of her brother allowed her to try out as a backing singer to his band which were well known locally around the East End. She looked great, had a knockout figure and a powerful voice and soon came to be in demand. She was introduced to different managers in the music industry and got gigs with some well-known bands singing backing vocals. Then one manager told her he had just a signed a new band called The Yell and they were looking for a couple of permanent backing singers. He sent her into the music studio to listen to them play. She immediately loved their sound, their look and if she was honest with herself, their lead singer Danny McKay. She met with them and they got on famously and offered her the position of backing singer with two other girls.

It was great money, she got to travel a lot, stayed in glamorous hotels and went to fabulous parties, as The Yell enjoyed considerable chart success. She tried to fight her feelings for Danny but she became more and more attracted to him. A lot of other men asked her out but she said no to them all, hoping that one day something might happen between herself and Danny. But he seemed to like a certain type. Danny was from an ordinary family and grew up in a town just outside London but his new-found fame brought him into contact with a lot of different celebrities and those from moneyed circles. And Danny had a penchant for girls from aristocratic backgrounds. Stephanie was introduced to a string of girlfriends who seemed to all look the same – pale skin, soft hair, clipped accents – and whose families lived in stately manors. Despite realising that she was the very opposite of the type he went for, she still couldn't get him out of her head

They were at a party to celebrate the end of a tour at Annabel's one night. She couldn't keep her eyes off Danny who was downing drinks with the rest of the band. The tour manager was a guy called Gary Cosgrove and he had asked Stephanie out lots of times in the past. She had constantly turned him down. He was in his thirties, with a failed marriage behind him and a pushy personality. She didn't find him remotely attractive. At the party he hit on her again.

"Look, no, Gary. It's not going to happen," she said, smiling at him. "So, get over it and move on."

He walked away angrily.

"I'm getting worried about you, Holden," Danny said, laughing, as he sidled up beside her.

"Yeah? How so?" She looked at him quizzically.

"Well, the fact is every man in this room has asked you out at some stage and you've turned every one of them down."

She looked at his laughing face. "I just have high standards."

"Whoa! Excuse me!" he laughed.

"Anyway, not every man in the room *has* asked me out." She looked at him brazenly, emboldened by the champagne she had been consuming.

He looked at her, confused for a moment before realisation dawned.

"You're the only one not to have asked me out."

"Yeah, but –" He looked at her, confused. "We're mates."

She suddenly felt stupid as he was obviously not interested and turned to walk away.

"Hold on!" He grabbed her arm and swung her around.

They stared into each other's eyes for while.

"Eh – do you want to go out with me?" he asked awkwardly.

"*Yes!*" She nearly shouted it.

* * *

Stephanie quickly put the magazine down as the double doors of Conrad's office opened and Conrad came out.

"Ah, Stephanie! Do you want to come in?"

She stood up and went into the room. David Stafford was seated at the Board table.

"Good to see you again, Stephanie," nodded David.

"Likewise," she nodded back at him.

"So how are we going to do this?" she asked.

"An element of surprise is always the best," said Conrad.

"All the legal work will be completed by Wednesday so we can send the company into receivership any time after that," David explained.

"I vote we storm the place next Friday morning in that case," said Conrad.

"What will be our strategy?" asked Stephanie.

"You all congregate at the store on Friday morning," said Conrad. "David will have his financial team with him and my legal team will be present. You enter the building, make your way to the fifth-floor offices."

Stephanie wasn't surprised that Conrad wasn't offering to be present himself. Conrad would always get somebody else to do his dirty work for him.

"The entire accounts department is to be fired immediately apart from a couple of juniors," said David, "so they can't have a chance to remove paperwork from the building or cover anything up."

"Furstin is to be immediately escorted from the building," said Conrad.

"He mightn't go easy," warned David.

"Leave him to me," said Stephanie confidently. "I've taken care of much worse than him in the past."

Conrad gave her an admiring glance. "I'm sure you have. Then, Stephanie, you hold meetings with the department heads saying they now report to us and that we are in charge. Then you can take it from there – who stays, who goes, where we can make cuts. Who's worth keeping. What do we know of the senior management?"

"Nicola Newman is the HR over there," said Stephanie. "She's kind of notorious for being a cold bitch, to be honest with you. However, she is highly respected and so I advise we approach her with an open mind."

"A good HR on our side can be a real bonus when we take over," said David. "I know the last business we sent into receivership was a nightmare because a) the HR was ineffective and b) not willing to help us. It made getting rid of people very difficult."

"Then there's Paul Stewart. He's been the general manager for years there. I believe he's very loyal to Furstin."

"Well, Furstin made him who he is," said Stephanie. "He made a pact with the devil to get ahead."

David coughed and creased his forehead slightly. "I actually know Paul Stewart from years ago – we were at school together."

Stephanie and Conrad both looked at David, surprised.

"And what's he like?" Conrad asked.

"He's a good bloke from what I remember. He kind of came late to our school and, you know, he was always there but never really at the centre of things. As I said, I haven't seen him for years.. I was really surprised when he used to crop up on television giving interviews, singing Franklyns' praises or defending Furstin. You know how they always wheeled him out for comments when they suffered bad press."

"Why were you surprised?" asked Conrad.

"Well, who'd have ever thought he'd have the gumption to be running such a big business?"

"He obviously didn't or the place wouldn't be going into receivership," said Stephanie. "He sounds too loyal to Furstin to have a future with us and, as I am effectively replacing him as the new boss, we'll have to see what his future is."

Conrad looked at her pointedly. "So what plans have you come up with for Franklyns?"

"None as of yet," she answered honestly. When she noticed the surprise on their faces, she continued. "I never make plans until I'm working in the store. See how it's working from the inside and what I feel would be the right moves."

"We were rather hoping you would start implementing strategies straightaway," explained David.

Stephanie sat back. "It doesn't work like that. I have to have a feel for the soul of the place and I can only do that from the inside. You're paying me a lot of money to put this thing right and that's what I aim to do. Retail has become a national – a world – obsession. We've all gone shopping mad. There are reasons why Franklyns isn't working right in today's environment and I look forward to putting it on the right track."

"How can you be so confident you can do it?" asked David.

"Because I understand shoppers. I understand what makes them shop and where. I know how to get into their minds and convince them to spend money. It's just all psychology. Think about it – we convince half the planet that their skin is too dark and so get them to buy lightening kits to make their skin lighter. We convince the other half of the world that their skin is too pale and convince them to spend billions on fake tans or tanning lotions to make them darker. The answer to everyone's problems is shopping." She paused and, seeing she had their complete attention, continued. "If you're overweight we can sell you the right make-up, clothes, slimming aids to make you feel better. If you're underweight we can get you to buy products to make you look bigger. If you have straight hair we convince you your hair is lifeless and lank and you need to buy products to give you curls and bounce. If you have naturally curly hair, we tell you your hair is frizzy and unkempt, but hey, we've got products to straighten your hair. The key to retail is to realise we aren't selling products. We are selling happiness. The products represent an illusion of happiness that they can acquire. We are giving power to the shoppers and letting their money change their lives by buying our products, whatever products they may be. And we need to keep those products changing and inventing new ones before people can realise that what they've bought hasn't made them happy." Stephanie paused. "Franklyns just didn't keep up in the race."

* * *

Nicola viewed the glamorous Italian Silvia whom she had called to her office.

"I have unfortunate news for you," she informed her in a professional manner. "Your position is being made redundant."

Silvia paled in shock. "But I've been working very hard," she objected. "And beyond work –"

"I'm sure, but your position is no longer needed." A streak of mascara fell down Silvia's face as a tear overflowed from her eyes.

Nicola leaned forward and put her hands together.

"Now, Franlyns is prepared to offer you a free gratis payment of £5,000, combined with your last month's salary which will be tax free."

Silvia wiped away a tear. "I'll take it."

"It would be the sensible option."

"Can I just say that working here at Franklyns has been the worst experience of my life?"

Chapter 8

"I don't think I like that Nicola Newman," commented Rachel as she and Daniella left Franklyns, thinking about being reprimanded earlier.

"Who does?" laughed Daniella.

"Looks like she's just on a a power trip to me."

"The whole world is on a power trip, love. We're just the minions at the bottom who have to put up with it." Daniella took out her phone and checked for messages. "The bastard hasn't phoned me back."

"Who?"

"My supposed boyfriend, Leo. I bet he's in the Oxo Tower Bar with his mates – he lives in that place." She thought for a second and then suddenly flagged down a passing taxi. "Come on, we're going to go for a drink!"

"No, I can't, Daniella, I've got an appointment to see a flat," objected Rachel but she found herself being dragged into the back of the taxi by Daniella.

"To the Oxo Tower Bar," she directed the taxi driver.

* * *

Leo walked into the reception area of the Oxo Bar.

"Good evening, Leo, and how are you this evening?" asked the doorman, smiling broadly.

"I'm good, Danny. I'm good," Leo smiled back and discreetly put a fifty-pound note into Danny's hand.

He walked into the bar and found that Tom and the others had taken up a corner of the bar. Smiling broadly, he approached them and there was much slapping on backs and greetings. He had been genuinely popular with all his former workmates. Now they believed he was doing fantastically in property development.

"So how're the markets today?" Leo asked Tom.

"Offloaded some shares I bought in a Danish bank and made quite a good profit on it."

"Yeah?"

"And I got the rest of the bonus I'm owed, which is bloody fantastic."

"What are you going to do with it?" Leo felt himself becoming envious as he imagined the size of the bonus.

"I might invest in some foreign property – if you've any good deals going let me know."

"Of course I will, mate," Leo nodded.

"You know, I've been taking helicopter flying lessons as well, so I was thinking of buying my own chopper. You were talking about doing that a couple of years ago, weren't you? Did you ever buy one?"

"No," Leo shook his head earnestly. "My motto is: if it flies, fucks or floats – then rent it!"

"True," laughed Tom. "True."

As the traders began to discuss the deals they had made that day, Leo pondered his present situation. How he missed being a trader and those bonuses, the respectability and the camaraderie! It was his natural environment. And he knew that scams could never pull in the money he could earn as a trader.

"Thought I might find you here," said a voice in his ear.

He turned around to see Daniella.

"Ah, hiya, love! Was just about to phone you!" He leaned forward and kissed her.

"Hmmm!" She gave him an unconvinced look. "Hi, everybody!" She nodded to his friends. "This is my friend, Rachel."

Rachel nodded to them, smiling.

Tom was straight over to Rachel. "Can I get you a drink?"

"No, thanks. I'm just off to the bar myself. What do you want, Daniella?"

"A margarita for me."

"Who's your friend?" asked Tom as he watched Rachel go up to the bar.

"She's just started working with me at Franklyns."

"Bit standoffish for a shop girl," remarked Tom.

"You watch your manners!" Daniella gave him a pretend hit, while she put her arm around Leo's waist.

Rachel waited for the cocktails at the bar and wished she hadn't bothered coming.

She didn't like the look of this lot. Full of their own importance. Lots of ready money and no class.

"I think Tom could fancy you, if you play your cards right!" whispered Daniella into Rachel's ear when she came back.

"I'd say Tom would have a thing for any available female who came through the door," Rachel said cynically.

"Don't be like that. He's worth a fortune! You could do a lot worse than him."

Rachel looked at Daniella, half-draped across Leo and

felt a pang of irritation. She was like a lot of the girls who worked at Franklyns whose sole ambition in life, it seemed, was to marry a rich husband and live off him. That's when they weren't preoccupied with their other obsession – permanent diets. Size zero? Some of those girls were aiming for a minus 1 in Rachel's opinion. She examined Leo. He was very good-looking, with sallow skin and thick straight black hair swept back. He seemed very cocky and she imagined Daniella was just a plaything for him.

"So how are you finding Franklyns?" Leo asked her.

"Ah, so far so good. Nice crowd, you know," she smiled.

Leo checked out her jewellery and did some quick mental arithmetic.

"Rachel's just moved here from Dublin," said Daniella. "She's finding it impossible to find a flat. Maybe you could help her, Leo." She turned to Rachel. "One of Leo's companies is a letting agency."

"Oh, there's really no need!" said Rachel quickly. "There are tons of adverts in *The Standard*!"

"But all you do is complain you can't find a nice place! Leo, sort her out!" insisted Daniella.

Leo took out his phone. "Give me your number and I'll set up some viewings." Rachel felt uneasy as she called out her number.

As Leo tapped her number into his phone, he thought that one of the clients he had on his property-letting database might actually get a client for once.

* * *

Leo put his arm around Daniella as they walked down the Embankment after putting Rachel into a taxi.

"She seems like a nice girl," he commented.

"Rachel? Yeah, she's a laugh. Bit uptight though."

"Didn't seem to have much interest in Tom or the others," he commented.

"As I said – a bit uptight. Now, you will sort her out with a flat, Leo, won't you? No bullshit here, a nice one."

"I said I would, didn't I?"

* * *

That evening, Stephanie was alone in her apartment looking out at the Thames, having a glass of wine.

She looked down at a photo in a tabloid of Louise Stirling signing her books at Franklyns. Part of her was looking forward to starting work there and another part was dreading it. When a company was forced to change as Franklyns was about to, there was always a lot of resentment and resistance to change and she would be the main focus of the resentment. The likes of David Stafford wouldn't be getting down to the nitty-gritty of dealing with the people who worked there. He would be just directing the finances from his lofty office.

She sighed and shook her head in exasperation. She was feeling a little sorry for herself this evening and she knew why. She allowed herself to slide back into the past again.

* * *

When she and Danny had started seeing each other, she was over the moon. She was where she wanted to be with the man she loved. They got on brilliantly. Everyone in the band and their record company knew they were seeing each other but they kept it a secret beyond that. She would find herself getting insanely jealous when fans tried to get to him. They never talked about the future or made plans. They just had a laugh all the time.

A month before the Live Aid concert, which was due to be their biggest exposure ever, the band were in the middle of writing a new album. Things weren't going so great with the recording and the band went and hid themselves away for six weeks in a country estate to try and concentrate.

"I'm really missing you," Stephanie said down the phone to him. She, along with the rest of the entourage, had been banned from going near them.

"I know – me too. But it won't be for that much longer."

And on stage in the warm July sunshine at the Live Aid Concert Stephanie put everything she had into the performance and watched Danny give it his all. Afterwards, they embraced each other backstage, engulfed in euphoria, and kissed each other.

"I love you," she said out of excitement.

"Yeah, me too," he smiled and they went off for their showers and to prepare for the big party that night.

But at the party that night, Stephanie waited anxiously at the bar but there was no sign of Danny. When he finally did arrive in, she was shocked to see he was accompanied by Hetty Barrington, who was one of the troop of aristocrats he had previously dated. Hetty had always stood out from the other girls he had been with, for sheer determination if nothing else. Even after he had finished with her, she would still show up at all the parties and events and try to capture his attention and keep him to herself. Hetty was outraged when Danny began seeing Stephanie and behaved ignorantly to Stephanie at every opportunity.

"What's she doing here?" Stephanie demanded, taking him to one side.

"Look, Stephanie, me and Hetty kept in contact all along and, you know, I kind of missed her. Anyway, we're back together."

"What?" She was horrified.

"Don't be like that, Stephanie. We've had a great time and a good laugh. But both of us knew we weren't on for the long haul, didn't we? We're too alike. I want somebody different from me."

"You're so fucking sad!" she spat. "You just want her because you're impressed by her background and her connections!" She turned quickly and walked out of the party.

As she swung out of the front doors, Hetty smiled triumphantly at her and flashed the engagement ring Danny had just given her.

Tears stinging her eyes, Stephanie bumped straight into Gary Cosgrave.

She was filled with anger and hate and humiliation.

"Gary, do you want to go with me now?"

"What do you mean?"

"Just go with me wherever I'm going! You've asked me long enough and now I'm offering myself to you." He looked at her curiously and then nodded.

They spent the night together in the hotel they were all staying in. It was the strangest night she ever had. She didn't enjoy being with Gary. She was heartbroken about Danny and couldn't believe how stupid she was. She was just a nobody backing singer who Danny never had any intention of being with long-term.

The next day she walked away from the hotel she was staying in with the group and never came back to them.

She stayed alone nursing her hurt to herself as she saw Danny announce his engagement to the world in a sea of tabloids. Soon after that she realised she was pregnant.

* * *

A boat floating down the Thames below her brought Stephanie back to the present moment. She was thinking too much of the past – she needed to force herself to stop.

She thought instead about Leo and the distance between them. She had always felt guilty that she couldn't give her son more when he was growing up. And then when he was a teenager and she was concentrating on building her career, she wasn't there for him. She was so busy that she missed the signs when he started making wrong turns. But that was the past and she wasn't going to live in the past any more. Okay, so her son might be an adult now but for the first time in her life she was in a position to give him both help and attention. If he would let her.

Chapter 9

Ingrid sat in her new office on the sixth floor, the computer in front of her switched off. It was now Thursday and she had been working on the sixth floor all week with nobody coming near her. She ventured out into the hall outside and stopped as she came face to face with a girl who looked the same age as herself.

"Excuse me," Ingrid smiled, embarrassed. "I was just wondering what I'm supposed to be doing. Nobody has given me any work to do."

The girl looked at her blankly. "Just stay in your office until someone gives you something. I'm sure they'll let you know what's expected of you soon enough."

* * *

Paul was walking through the store when a security man came over to him, looking hassled. He was followed by an Arab woman dressed in her traditional black garment, half her face veiled, accompanied by a man in a suit.

"Paul, this lady has been in looking for Rolex watches but she says her boss is parked outside the store and wants the merchandise brought out to the car for her to inspect."

Paul took a quick look at the woman who seemed, from the expression in her eyes, to be bored and uninterested and the man beside her who looked stern and forbidding. It was completely against Franklyns' policy to allow merchandise to leave the store without payment but he knew the spending power of the people who had made the request. The woman in front was probably a high-ranking assistant and the man a bodyguard.

"Yes, certainly that can be arranged," smiled Paul before turning to the security man and saying, "Stay close to us."

Paul quickly led them through the store towards the jewellery department which was approached through archways and designed like a beautiful white marble palace.

As opposed to the rest of the store this area, though large, had a more hushed feel to it. There were far fewer customers which meant they could be given leisurely one-to-one service by the sales assistants.

Rachel happened to be taking a short cut through the jewellery department and came face to face with Paul.

"Follow me, would you?" he said.

"Er – I was just off to my break," she objected.

"Come with me," he ordered.

Confused, she joined the small group following him.

Paul approached a large counter filled with different watches and said to the assistant working there, "Give me that one, that one, that one and that one." He pointed quickly to watches laid out in the counter. "And several more Rolexes."

He turned to Rachel. "Hold out your arm."

"I'm sorry?" She shook her head in confusion.

"Your arm!" He grabbed her wrist and held it out and then pushed the sleeve of her blazer up and started putting the watches on her arm all the way up.

She felt uncomfortable and his touch made her feel vulnerable.

"Eh, Paul, I would prefer not to be doing this," she said.

One look from him silenced her.

After he was finished with that arm, he grabbed the other and added several more watches to it. Rachel noticed from the little price tags sitting in front of the stands from which Paul was removing the watches that none of them was cheaper than £10,000.

Paul turned to the Arab man. "Where are you parked?"

"To the front."

He nodded and then pulled down the sleeves of Rachel's jacket over her arms, covering the watches.

Rachel walked alongside Paul numbly, aware of the other salesgirls' looks as she passed by.

"Who are these people?" she whispered to Paul.

"I don't know. Oil rich or could be royalty. This one is probably the lady-in-waiting." He nodded to the woman in front of them. "Sometimes you're better off not knowing."

Paul swung through the front door and, sure enough, parked on a double yellow line was a stretch limousine with tinted glass. Another bodyguard was standing at the car.

The back window opened and the lady-in-waiting stepped forward, leaned in through the window and spoke a few sentences before turning around to Paul and Rachel and beckoning them to approach.

Rachel stepped forward and looked through the open

window. Inside was a very big woman, also dressed in voluminous black garments with a traditional gold mask covering half her face. Rachel could make out that she was extremely old. A shiver ran down her spine and she wanted to run away. The whole scene was unfamiliar to her and she disliked it – this stranger having people run around after her.

Paul leaned forward and smiled through the open window.

"Welcome to Franklyns. We've selected an array of watches for you to see."

He nodded to Rachel and she pulled up the sleeve of her jacket and carefully stretched her arm in. The old woman grabbed her hand, yanked it further in and started examining the watches. Rachel felt her take off some watches to examine them.

The contact made her skin crawl. She didn't want to be touched by this stranger.

The woman chose some watches quickly and then beckoned her lady-in-waiting forward and spoke to her.

"She would like to see some more," said the woman.

As Paul led them back into the store Rachel said, "I'm not comfortable with this. If I wanted to be a model I'd have joined a model agency."

"But you became a sales assistant in a store instead. And that's what you're doing – assisting in a sale." He looked at her pointedly.

They spent an hour going back and forth to the woman in the car. And eventually she chose to buy eight watches. Rachel stood by Paul as the salesgirl put the watches through the till point in the jewellery department. The bill came to £100,000 and the lady-in-waiting opened her handbag and paid in brand-new £50 notes.

As she did, Paul drew Rachel aside.

"In future, when I ask you do something," he said, "I don't want to hear moans that you're going on tea breaks, that you're not a model or any other objections. You just get on and do it, do you understand me?"

Rachel glared at him before uttering, "Perfectly."

Paul nodded at her and turned back to the woman.

"Now, allow me to walk you back to your car." He smiled at the woman and led her away.

Feeling angry, Rachel headed off and waded through the crowd to her break, only to encounter Christine.

"Rachel, get back to your position – your break was over half an hour ago!" snapped Christine.

"Christine, I haven't had a chance to take any break – I –"

"*Now,* Rachel!" she snapped before walking away.

Rachel looked after her in disbelief before turning and heading back to her counter.

Chapter 10

Rachel walked down Brompton Street to get a packed lunch from Boots. It was Friday and she was dreading another weekend at her aunt's. She really needed to get her own place. As she walked along in the sunshine a porter of an apartment block opened the door and out stepped a man of about sixty, tall with grey-blond hair, with a man in a dark suit behind him. She nearly bumped into the tall man.

"Oh, I'm sorry!" she said.

The man turned and smiled at her. There was something about him that made her very uneasy. His eyes from his smiling face bored into her and she felt she had to get away from him as quickly as possible, as even his aroma reached out and seemed to pull her to him. She quickly walked past him. Glancing around she saw him get into a chauffeur-driven car.

She continued to a Starbucks opposite Franklyns and sat down to have a coffee while leafing through a magazine. Her mobile rang. Not recognising the number, she answered it.

"Hello, Rachel speaking."

"Hi, Rachel, how's it going? It's Leo here, Daniella's boyfriend."

"Oh, yes, hi." She had almost forgotten she had given him her number.

"How's tricks?" He sounded chirpy.

"Fine. Just on my break from that madhouse."

"Good, good. Listen, I've found a flat that I think might be just what you're looking for."

"Oh! Look, really you shouldn't have bothered. I'm seeing another couple of places this evening."

"Cancel them. You'll take one look at this place and you'll be moving in by tomorrow."

She thought for a while. She really would prefer not to meet him. She hadn't particularly taken to him and didn't want to be beholden to him. On the other hand, she was finding it difficult to find somewhere suitable and it might upset Daniella if she declined their offer of help.

"Okay. What's the address and what time will I meet you there?" she asked, taking a pen out of her handbag.

* * *

Paul chose to have his office not in its appointed place on the fifth floor but on the third floor, just off the shop floor through double doors leading to the loading bay. He preferred it that way. There, he felt he was closer to the vibrancy of the store as opposed to the stifled hush of the fifth floor. It also made him more accessible to sales managers and staff who did not always feel comfortable going into Nicola's territory on the fifth floor. His office was large. Cream carpet ran through it and his desk was glass-topped, situated in front of a row of windows that looked down on Knightsbridge. There were fifteen television monitors on the wall, offering him different views of the store.

"Paul," said Nicola as she walked in, "I've just had that new security guard, Matt Short, in to me and he's very interested in moving into sales management."

Paul searched his memory and put a face to the guy. He was young and cocky and thought he was God's gift to women. Paul didn't like him. Looking at Nicola's expression, she obviously did like him.

"We're not recruiting anybody onto the management training schemes at the moment," said Paul.

"I'm obviously aware of that. But I do think that he would be an amazing asset to the company and is wasted in his present position, and so I'm arranging for him to start work as a trainee manager from tomorrow."

Paul looked at Nicola and felt his temperature rise. Nicola consistently did what she wanted with the personnel without ever discussing it with him or anybody else. If somebody was in favour, their career would experience a meteoric rise. Falling out of favour began an equally fast career descent. Her superior attitude infuriated him and yet what could he do? As he looked at her faint smile and cool attitude, he knew she was above reproach. For the most part they kept out of each other's way and he wouldn't risk their *entente cordiale* by challenging her now. This sudden promotion of security man to management was bizarre, and yet he had seen Nicola make the most improbable business and personnel decisions in the past. Some of them worked out and if they didn't she simply disposed of the situation.

* * *

As Karl heard a knock, he stopped admiring the portrait of his wife Elka hanging on the wall and, swivelling around on his chair, quickly turned to the door.

"Come in!" he called.

Ingrid came in and stood there nervously. He inspected her from across the office.

"Sit down there. Take up that notebook and pen. I want to dictate a letter."

Ingrid nodded and took up the pen and notebook. She wondered should she mention that she couldn't do shorthand or really type that well. But she thought better of it. She had been sitting in her office for a week doing nothing and she didn't want to start complaining about the first thing she had been given to do. Besides, she was intimidated by him.

"Dear Louise, I would just like to take this opportunity to personally thank you for your recent appearance at Franklyns. Although regrettably I was not present on the day to meet you personally, I trust you found my staff attentive to your every need. I have long admired –" "I'm sorry – y-y-you'll have to slow down a little," said Ingrid, looking stressed..

Karl sat back in his chair and viewed her. "Why did you apply for the job if you couldn't do it?" he questioned harshly.

"I-I didn't apply. I was approached."

There was a silence during which Ingrid wondered if she dared to say that it was he himself who had promoted her to the sixth floor.

"Well, what *can* you do?" he asked then, peering at her.

"I want to work hard but if I could maybe have some training –"

"I can't waste money training you. Why should I bother?"

He looked at her, then reached into a drawer, pulled out a duster and threw it at her.

She looked at him, puzzled.

"Clean my office," he commanded.

"What?" she asked.

"You have to earn your wage some way. Clean my office."

His grey-blue eyes bored into her. She put down the notebook and pen and took up the duster. Slowly, she stood up.

"Start with the coffee table," he demanded.

She went over to the coffee table and started to wipe it. She stopped and looked up at him.

"Clean!" he all but shouted.

She jumped, bent over and began to polish it.

She cleaned it thoroughly and then stood up and turned around to him.

"Do it again. It's not clean enough," he said.

She looked down at the sparkling top but bent over and started to clean it again.

* * *

Leo gave the flat a once-over and glanced at his watch. It was seven and he expected Rachel any minute. He had quickly come up with a nice one-bed flat in a mansion block down by the river in Chelsea. The rent wasn't cheap but wasn't stupid money either. He guessed Rachel would be able to afford it and it wouldn't be just her wages at Franklyns that would be paying for it but Mummy and Daddy back home.

The doorbell rang.

"Come on up, second floor," he said into the intercom and then opened the flat's front door.

Rachel got out of the elevator and saw him waiting there, smiling, his hand resting against the door frame.

"You found it easily then?"

"Yes, you gave good directions."

He moved into the flat and she followed him. She immediately liked the place. It was by no means huge but there was a good-sized sitting-room and it was tastefully furnished. The floorboards were painted white which matched the two white sofas that faced each other across a coffee table. She liked that new fashion of painting old floorboards – it brightened up small spaces amazingly. The large bay window gave the living-room a light and airy appeal. The room was finished off with a black iron fireplace. There was a nice kitchen off it, a bathroom that had been recently refurbished and a bedroom that was bigger than the usual cupboards she had been viewing, with a double black wrought-iron bed, again on white floorboards. Most importantly the area felt right. It was safe and convenient to work. And the place wasn't overly expensive. In fact, she was delighted with it.

"It's just what I'm looking for," she said, returning to the sitting-room.

"You want to take it?" he asked.

"Yes! I can write you a cheque now for the deposit and first month's rent." She reached into her handbag for her cheque book.

Too bad, he thought, that he couldn't pocket the cheque and not bother giving it to the landlord. But he couldn't shit on his own doorstep. Daniella would go mad. Besides, there was something about this girl that he liked. He certainly hadn't bothered to show her the apartment for the commission he would be getting from the landlord. He had wanted an excuse to see her again.

"That's fine. I've got the contract here for you to sign." Unzipping a folder, he produced a thick document.

"Oh, could I take some time to read that?" she asked.

He looked at her and said, "Sure. But I've someone else very interested in this place so it would have to be quick. Tell you what – there's a pub at the end of the road. Why don't we go for a drink and you can look through the contract and I can explain anything you're unsure about?"

She smiled. "Sounds good."

* * *

Leo took a joint from a silver cigarette case in a toilet-cubicle in the pub, placed it between his lips and lit up. He leaned against the wall and inhaled three leisurely drags before firing it into the toilet and flushing. He then walked out into the bar and collected the two beers waiting for him on the counter and went outside to the tables on the pavement. Rachel was seated there, flicking through the contract, her sunglasses perched on her head. The pub was near the river and a soft breeze was radiating from there. A James Blunt song spilled out onto the street from inside the pub

"Thanks," said Rachel as he placed her beer in front of her.

"You're welcome."

"This all looks straightforward," she said, glancing through the last page.

"It is," he confirmed. "Just no all-night sex parties as there's a lot of old dears living in that block and we don't want to upset them." He smiled and winked at her.

"I'll try to remember that." She looked at him wryly.

"And definitely no all-night sex parties if I'm not invited," he added.

She raised an eyebrow.

"Joke!" he insisted, and raised his glass. "Cheers!"

She clinked her glass against his and sat back in her chair.

"So how long have you been seeing Daniella?" she quizzed.

"About six months."

"It seems to be quite serious."

"Is it?" He looked at her.

"Well, she seems to be quite serious, whatever about you." She sipped from her drink.

He looked across the river to the distant council towers in Battersea, behind the swish glass apartments on the river front.

"I grew up in a tower block like that," he said.

She followed his stare across the river.

"My old mum still lives somewhere near here," he added.

"Will you pop in to see her after this?"

"Nah. I don't really go home much."

"You're not close?"

He looked at her. She seemed so clean and fresh and as if nothing bad had ever happened to her. He envied her.

"Not really. As soon as I could I got out of there and kept going. I was the only one of all my mates growing up who got out of there of my own accord. Started off doing a computer course and I was the best in the class. Then got a job in IT support up in the city. I tell you, it didn't take long before I was working as a trader."

She studied him as he talked, full of confidence and swagger. She imagined how a girl like Daniella would quickly fall for his talk. However, his charms had no effect on her. In fact he was the type of guy who had her putting up her guard.

"You know Tom, my mate you met in the oxo bar?"

Rachel nodded.

"He has said to me on so many occasions that he would never have got through his first year working as a money boy if it wasn't for me showing him how to do it and covering his ass."

"You must have been a good friend to him," she said as she put on her large sunglasses.

"So he keeps insisting! I tell you we made so much money that first couple of years. The bonuses were amazing."

"Why did you leave then?"

Her question took him off guard. He had a flashback to his tribunal at work after his insider-dealing scam was uncovered – his boss looking at him angrily and saying: 'You have brought disgrace on this company.'

"I guess I'm a bit of a free spirit. That's me for you. On top of the world with something and then I need to move on and conquer something else. So I left and started up my own businesses. I like being my own boss."

He didn't like the huge sunglasses she was wearing – they were putting up a barrier between them and obstructing him from reading her expression.

"So you're in the letting business now?"

"That's just one of my companies."

She nodded and glanced at her watch, wondering how long she would have to stay without it looking rude to leave.

They sat in silence for a while. Her indifference annoyed him. He tried another approach.

"It's kind of strange that me and Daniella are

together. I usually go for blondes. You know, Scandinavian-looking." He glanced at Rachel's chestnut-brown hair. If one thing worked with women, it was to make them feel insecure about their looks. They started wondering what was wrong with them and down came their defences.

"Maybe you should suggest she dye her hair," Rachel smiled. "Listen, I'd better be going." She took out her cheque book, wrote him a cheque and handed it over to him. "Thanks so much for sorting me out with the apartment. I'll be singing your praises to Daniella." She got up and put out her hand.

Surprised, he looked at her hand for a few seconds before taking it and shaking it.

She took the keys for the apartment, dropped them into her handbag and then walked off down the street in the sunshine. Daniella is wasting her time with him, she thought. He lives for the moment and if someone else came along he wouldn't hesitate in dumping her.

It wouldn't have taken much encouragement that afternoon.

* * *

Kanye West's "Stronger" was blaring in the East London club called The Chambers as Leo made his way in the door. He greeted the doormen like old friends, and slipped them some cash.

"Hey, Leo, haven't seen you for a while," said the pretty girl on reception.

"Been busy. How you keeping?"

"Just fine."

He opened his wallet to pay the entrance fee but she shook her head as if he was insulting her.

"You can buy me a drink later," she said and waved him in.

He walked through the reception into the club. It was large and packed. He had been coming to this place since he was sixteen.

It wasn't the kind of club that was featured in gig guides. The same clientele came every week and no outsiders were admitted. It was more than just a club or a social venue. It was a business centre. In between all the loud music, the drinking, the dancing, subtle business transactions were being conducted. He sat up at the bar, ordered a beer and looked around. He spotted a regular drug dealer talking to a supplier over a drink in one of the many seating cubicles. He noticed two other men having a heated discussion. He knew one of them quite well – he produced counterfeit money. They were all doing deals. Dealing drugs, dealing stolen goods and, he thought, as he spotted a pretty blonde girl he knew was a prostitute go by with a much older man, dealing themselves.

As he looked at them all, he couldn't help but think of Rachel and how she was a million miles from all these people. She had unnerved him. He could usually take people in very quickly. But she seemed immune to his usual charm techniques. He was tempted to just pocket the deposit and first month's rent and do a runner. That would teach her when she went to move into the apartment and found the landlord screaming at her door when money had failed to materialise in his account. But he couldn't with Daniella involved.

"Leo, my man, where have you been hiding?" asked a voice beside him.

He turned to see a young guy called Joseph Maguire. He had bought some stuff off him in the past. But he didn't like doing business with him. Joseph had no redeeming qualities whatsoever. Leo knew that he had a violent reputation and didn't like handling his stolen goods.

"I've been busy. You know how it is."

"Got something to show you I think you might be interested in." Joseph smiled and beckoned him to follow him over to a booth.

Reluctantly Leo got up and went over. He sat into a discreet booth, out of sight of the main club.

"You okay for coke?" Joseph asked.

"I don't want any, thanks." Leo stood to get up but Joseph reached forward and grabbed his wrist, pushing him back into his seat.

"I'm not offering you coke, man. Got something a little more substantial for you." Joseph reached into his pocket and held out his hand in a fist. Then he turned it over and opened it, revealing a diamond necklace in the palm of his hand.

Leo reached forward, took up the necklace and studied it discreetly. He was immediately impressed by the quality of the diamonds.

"Interested?" asked Joseph.

"I might be if the price was right."

"You can have it for fifteen grand."

Leo knew the necklace would be worth a lot more than that. It was a deal too good to refuse.

"I'll give you ten," he offered.

Joseph's face turned sour and he reached forward and grabbed the necklace.

"Forget it. You know there's a hundred guys I can sell this to in here tonight. I just thought I'd offer it to you because we're old friends."

"Very thoughtful. Okay, fifteen grand. I'll have to

arrange to meet you tomorrow to give you the money."

"Cool," Joseph slipped the necklace into his inside pocket. "I'll keep this safe for you until then."

* * *

Nicola sat in her drawing-room with the television on. The sound was low and a glass of wine was balanced in her hand. It was late on Friday night and no sign of Oliver home yet. She hoped he wouldn't be too late as they needed to make an early start in the morning to go to an art auction in Oxford. She reached for the remote and turned off the television.

She got up and walked through the beautiful house and upstairs to their en suite where she looked at herself in the huge mirror. Analysing her face, not any part of her had aged badly. Her skin was smooth and line-free. Her body fit and slim. Why then did she feel old? Why did she feel she looked old? Was it the way she dressed? The way she carried herself in that non-compromising fashion? Her demeanour? She had worked to be the ultra-respectable figure and that was what she was. And so why was she now so unsatisfied, even though on the face of it she had everything she wanted?

Oliver went on and on about the blasted rings every night and all she wanted to do was scream that she was delighted they were gone, that she felt younger not having to wear them any more. But she couldn't say it to Oliver. She didn't want to hurt him. He had been too good to her to hurt him.

But the marriage left her unsatisfied. It was the main thing in her life that did. Her thoughts drifted to the man on the train and she wondered who he was and tried to understand what he had stirred in her. She sighed and shook her head. She needed to be more appreciating of Oliver and her life. She went to the phone in the bedroom, picked up the receiver and dialled Oliver's mobile.

"Oliver, where are you?"

"I'm still at work. Sorry, I've been held up here. Don't wait up for me."

"Oliver, we have an early start in the morning. I don't want to miss that auction. And we're over to Elaine and James's tomorrow night for that dinner party. Remember, it's going to be a late one. "

"I'll be leaving here shortly."

"All right. I'll see you soon." She hung up the phone.

* * *

Oliver hung up the phone and turned his attention to the CCTV footage playing on the screen in front of him. His officers had managed to get their hands on CCTV from the different businesses outside the station and piece together Nicola's movements after she left the station. The quality of the footgage was grainy and bad. But he could still see Nicola as she headed down the steps outside the station and quickly made her way down the main street. He could clearly see the two businessmen up ahead and, just as inside the station, she seemed to be trying to keep up with them. And then the men went down a sidestreet and she paused again before heading off down the same street.

And that was where the footage ended. His men couldn't get any CCTV from that sidestreet and so there was no film of her being attacked. And as much as he looked at the film outside the station there were no suspects. Nobody who seemed to be paying any attention to Nicola. Nobody suspicious.

He had kept trying to bring up the mugging at home with Nicola but she didn't want to discuss it. He would have liked to ask her what was she doing going into the sidestreet. Why she was half running in such an irregular fashion? Why she was following those men? But she just shut down whenever he approached the subject. She would be furious if she knew he was looking at CCTV footage of her. He imagined how she would lose her temper. He knew he had to tread carefully. She'd had a terrible shock and he didn't want to upset her further.

* * *

Rachel was delighted to be moving into her new flat over the weekend. She really did owe Daniella and Leo one for sorting her out.

On her first evening she unpacked her clothes. She hadn't brought that much over from Ireland with her. She ordered a Chinese and after eating it sat back, enjoying her new surroundings.

Things certainly hadn't gone according to plan since arriving in London. She had expected to be at the very heart of Franklyns, working in the press office, not stuck behind a counter listening to whining customers. But maybe this was better. She was actually hearing much more gossip on the floor than she ever would in the offices. And really seeing how the store was working. After she had been reprimanded by both Nicola and Paul, she quickly realised Franklyns didn't give a damn about employees. You were there to do a job. So she had decided if that was the way to play, she could play it better than anyone else. She had worked very hard at selling and was hitting fantastic sales targets. She hoped it would get her noticed and with that a promotion to where she wanted to be.

Her mobile bleeped and she opened it, seeing that it was from her ex-boyfriend, Simon, in Dublin. He said he hoped she was settling in London and that everything was going fine for her. It was almost like a text from a stranger, with no hint of the relationship of eighteen months they had had. Simon had just graduated as a doctor and he hadn't wanted her to go to London. He wanted them to move in together and settle down. He couldn't understand all the things she wanted to achieve first and he felt that she had put her career before him. She wanted to get somewhere in life, see a bit of life and enjoy a bit of life before she settled down.

Chapter 11

On Monday morning, as Paul studied the sales figures, he was struck by the increase in profits at the Chanel counter in the past week. They were up fifty per cent. He ventured down to the cosmetics department and observed. The Irish girl, Rachel, was being very enthusiastic. Instead of doing what the other girls did, namely standing around looking glamorous and waiting for custom, Rachel was actively seeking custom. Going out of her way to attract customers over to her, not caring that she was being loud.

Christine spotted Paul and came over to him.

"She seems very good," Paul commented.

"I guess. I've asked her to tone it down a bit. She's a little too loud for an exclusive store like Franklyns."

"No, don't. Her sales figures say she's doing it right." He walked over to Rachel.

She had just finished a sale and was thanking a customer profusely

"Glad to see you have more enthusiasm selling perfume than you had with Rolexes,"he said smiling.

"I'm very enthusiastic about selling anything as long as

it's not during my coffee break."

He gave her a dubious look..

"You don't want to separate me from my coffee!" she quickly added, smiling,

"I'll try to remember that in future. We're due some new products in tomorrow. They are a new exclusive brand. I'm going to assign them to you and you can let me know the level of interest."

"Good. It's about time we got something decent to flog in this store." Her eyes twinkled.

Looking at her, he laughed and said, "You're a cheeky one!" and then, still smiling, he walked off.

* * *

Paul pulled his BMW into the driveway of his house in Wimbledon and spotted his wife's Mini already parked there. He was delighted as she had been working late all week trying to get an important feature finished for the newspaper where she worked. He got out of his car and looked up at the fine detached five-bedroomed house. When they bought it they had firmly in mind a family home to raise children in. He put his key into the front door and let himself in.

"Hello?" he called.

"In the kitchen!" Anna shouted.

He walked through the porcelain-tiled hall to the sitting-room. His shoes sank into the plush pile of the cream carpet as he flung his briefcase onto the exquisite couch. He walked through the double doors into the extensive kitchen.

Anna stood examining the contents of a pot on the cooker on the island in the middle of the kitchen floor.

"I thought you'd be still stuck in your office writing that feature you had a deadline for," he said.

"I finished the damned thing! Thank God. Got it in to my editor by lunch-time and told him not to give me such ridiculously tight deadlines again."

He moved over to her, placed his hands on her hips and kissed her on the lips.

"What did he say to that?" he asked.

"He promptly gave me another feature to investigate with an equally stupid deadline."

Paul laughed. She smiled at him and returned to stirring her cooking. After years together, he still thought Anna was a knockout. Her intelligent blue eyes were set in a wonderful bone structure, her body was long and rangy which suited the casual clothes she opted for, and her thick blonde hair was worn loose and slightly wild. He loved everything about her. Her looks, her casual charm, her caring personality, even her slightly husky clipped accent.

He looked at the dinner table, all set.

"This is just about ready," she said.

He took off his suit jacket and sat down as she came over and began to dish out the stew onto the plates.

"You know, I've been so wound up over that article we've hardly had a chance to chat," she said. "How's your week been?" She sat down opposite him.

"Same shit, different week. Sales not so good, staff problems. Nicola Newman in a particularly aloof mood."

"And Furstin?" She looked at him warily.

"The worst of them all."

"Oh, Paul!" She noticed the dark circles under his eyes. "That was him you were on the phone to at three in the morning last night, wasn't it?"

"I didn't want to wake you so I had my mobile on silencer and came downstairs to take it when it started vibrating."

"How dare he ring you at that time! What was his problem?"

"Wanted to talk about sales figures."

"At three in the morning!" she nearly screamed.

"Look, whatever you say about Furstin, he gave me the breaks along the way. He's made me general manager at Franklyns. What kind of a fantastic opportunity is that?"

"But you work so hard at it. And he uses these mind games. One minute telling you you're crap and no good at the job and then the next giving you ten grand in cash as a sweetener. I just don't think it's worth it any more."

"You know I hate quitting anything. I can't stand to admit defeat."

"It won't be admitting defeat. As you've said, you've been given a wonderful opportunity at Franklyns and established yourself and now it's time for us to plan your exit strategy – what do you say?"

"Okay, let's talk about it – but after dinner, okay?"

She smiled sympathetically at him. "Okay. So how're Gordon and Joanne doing with the new baby?"

"Met him for a drink the other night. Really delighted."

"Good," she smiled. Her eyes flashed something he couldn't read. Was it annoyance? They ate for a while in silence.

"Did you see what Brown said today on education? I mean, what the hell is he talking about? I'm going to a press conference tomorrow that he's giving and I'm going to challenge him on it. It's time this government realises that people don't care about wars. They care about schools and hospitals."

He nodded and stirred the food on his plate.

A text bleeped in his jacket pocket. He delved into the pocket for his mobile. He opened the text.

'Will you phone me? – Christine x'

"Who's that?" Anna asked.

"Just Christine asking something about work," said Paul, quickly turning the mobile off.

"I'm glad you're turning that off. Tell Christine she sees you enough during the day. If she wants to ask you anything tell her to ask you then."

Paul nodded.

"Bloody retail! Why did you have to pick a career in it? Your time is never your own. I mean, maybe it's just as well we don't have children because you'd never be here for them!"

They looked at each other in stunned silence for a while.

"Do you really think that?" he said.

"No, of course not. It was a silly thing to say." She got up quickly, picked up their plates and started to tidy them away into the dishwasher.

* * *

Paul stood looking at himself in the huge mirror in the large bathroom off their bedroom, wearing just his light-blue pyjama bottoms while he brushed his teeth.

He came out of the bathroom, wiping his mouth with a towel.

Anna was sitting up in bed looking through papers for work the next day.

"Busy day tomorrow?" she asked.

"A few meetings." He stood awkwardly, looking at her.

She put aside her papers, noticing a look of agitation on his face. "What is it?" She held out her hand to him. "Come here, love."

He went over and, taking her hand, sat beside her on the bed.

"What's wrong, Paul?"

"Did you give any more thought to what we touched on a couple of weeks ago?"

"Given it thought? It's all I've been thinking about. I'm thirty-seven. All I can hear is the clock tick-tocking. But it's not like a deadline for the newspaper. This is something I've no control over."

"So let's check if there's something wrong with us."

"But it doesn't stop there . . . what if they recommend IVF? I mean, physically it's such a lot to take on. Let alone the emotional side."

"I just feel we need to deal with this. We always expected to have children one day. And we have to decide what we're doing." He saw her face crease with worry. "I'm sorry." He started to rub the back of her neck. "It's just we never spoke about this through all the years and now it's all flooding out. But if you don't want to do it, I'll go along with what you want, of course."

"Of course, I want a child, Paul."

"So, we'll make an appointment?"

She nodded and brought her head close to his. They rested their foreheads together with their eyes closed.

"Agreed?" he asked.

"Agreed," she smiled back.

* * *

Leo was renting a terraced house near Stratford. It was a

slightly shabby street and the house was small. An open-space living-room downstairs with a kitchenette off it. Two bedrooms upstairs with a bathroom. He'd bought some expensive furniture and had managed to smarten the place up considerably but the place could not lose its slightly shabby look. One big plus the house had was a very secure garage out the back that he could keep his sports car in – the area had a very high crime-rate figure – and so he could sleep easy, knowing his car was safe.

He sat on the sofa, one eye on the television, one on his laptop on his lap as he typed away furiously, with music blaring in the background from the stereo. He was working on a new scheme involving people investing into a shopping centre in South Africa, which, of course, would never materialise.

He was expecting a pizza to be delivered and when the bell rang he jumped up, grabbed his wallet and unlocked the three locks on the door.

He saw his mother standing in the doorway. His face dropped.

"Hi, Leo," she smiled.

"You should have called first," he said. "I'm just heading out the door."

She looked pointedly at his T-shirt, torn jeans and bare feet.

The pizza delivery man arrived just then behind Stephanie.

Leo threw some money at the man, took the pizza and turned quickly to hide his embarrassment at being caught out in a lie.

"Just heading out, are you? So who's having the pizza?" Stephanie smirked.

He threw the pizza down on the coffee table, then went upstairs without a word.

Stephanie took the pizza into the kitchen and then went and sat in the living-room.

Leo came downstairs, having changed his clothes.

"I put your pizza in the kitchen," she said.

"I really do have to head out," he said.

"I'm not going to take up too much of your time."

He went to the laptop and snapped it shut.

"So how have you been?" she asked.

"Just great."

"I've left lots of messages on your phone."

"I know. Sorry I didn't get a chance to get back to you. I've been really busy with some projects I've been working on."

She smiled enthusiastically. "That sounds very exciting. Tell me about them."

He looked at her apologetically. "Would love to. But, as I said, I just don't have the time tonight."

She nodded and they sat there in an awkward silence.

"So who are you off meeting tonight?

"Tom. You know, who I used to work with."

"Ah, yes. He's keeping well?"

Leo nodded.

"Leo, I've really come over to have a chat with you about something in particular."

He looked uninterested. "Yeah?"

"I'm starting a new job next week. What I'm going to tell you, well, it's incredibly important you don't tell any of your friends – Tom or anybody. You know Franklyns? Well, it's going into receivership and I've been appointed as Brand Director."

He thought of Daniella and then Rachel and perked up.

That was all a bit too close for comfort.

"Right . . . well, congratulations. No doubt you'll be a big success there."

She heard a faint sneer in his voice.

"Leo . . . I'd like you to come and work at Franklyns." He looked at her, his face contorted in confusion. "As what exactly?"

"Well, that's what I want to talk to you about tonight. As anything you want. I mean whatever area you want to work in."

"What you mean is as a security man on the door!"

"Leo, I'm giving you *carte blanche* here. If you want to work in IT, accounts, marketing, management. I don't mind."

"Thanks, Mum, I appreciate the offer, but I don't think so."

She felt exasperated "But why not?" she demanded.

"I don't fancy working in retail for long hours and for poxy pay, thanks all the same."

"The pay might not be great at the beginning, Leo, but it's a chance for you to go anywhere you want. Look at me. Work hard and you'll be on the right track for life."

"I'm doing very well, thanks all the same. In fact, more than all right."

Stephanie's face clouded over. "Leo, I'm offering you a solid career with solid prospects. Not this topsy-turvy lifestyle you live, running from one scam to the next."

"I'm running a legitimate business!" He seethed with anger.

"Come off it. You've been doing scams since you turned thirteen!"

"Yeah, because you were out working all the time!" he spat back.

"I worked so hard in order to get you out of that hole we lived in!"

"We didn't move out of the flats until I was twelve! It was a bit late by then."

"I did my best, Leo." She remembered his childhood when they lived on income support before she went working. She remembered going without food to get him toys for Christmas. She softened her voice. "Leo, let's forget about the past and concentrate on the future. You're everything to me. And I worry about you."

"There's nothing to worry about. I'm on top of the world. Now, really, I have to go. Tom will be waiting."

She sighed and stood up and walked into the hall. She opened the front door and turned to him. "The offer is there and it's an open offer." She reached forward and kissed his cheek before walking out into the street.

He closed the door quickly after her.

Chapter 12

Paul was doing a cash run on the Wednesday of that week. Usually a member of the cash office would do the cash runs, with security. But Paul did one every second day, as the destination for this cash run wasn't the cash office.

Paul walked through the ground floor, with two security men one of whom had a briefcase handcuffed to his wrist.

When they reached the cosmetics department Paul saw that Rachel was busy selling. Calvin Harris was blaring from the sound system. She was a natural showwoman, her chutzpah drawing people over to her and then buying from her.

"How's that new product going along?" he asked her as he walked in behind the counter with the security men.

"Sold the last of it before lunch." She moved away from her till out of their way. He was taken aback.

"You've sold all of it?"

"Every last one."

He typed some numbers into the till and it opened. He started counting out cash. "You remind me of myself when

I started off in sales. I always had a crowd of customers around me."

Rachel saw he must have taken at least six thousand out of the till.

"That was a while back though, I'd say?" she said, smiling mischievously.

Paul raised an eyebrow at her as he put the cash into a float bag and, reaching over, shoved it into the security man's briefcase.

"See you later," he said and they were off to the next counter.

"I think he has a thing for you," said Daniella.

"Don't be daft!" snapped Rachel.

She was distracted by a stunning woman walking past, dressed in a fur coat down to the ground, her blonde hair swept back. Two men walked either side of her, dressed in Armani suits. The woman stopped abruptly at a counter and started testing the cosmetics on it.

"Who's that?" questioned Rachel.

"That's Elka Furstin," said Daniella slowly, almost reverently.

Rachel continued to examine the woman. Of course, she knew the name. Karl Furstin's wife was a figure on the London's social scene. She was always being photographed by the press as she attended a continuous stream of socialite events around the city.

"Nice work if you can get it," said Daniella. "Having this place as your own playground to pick out anything you want."

"She's in here a lot then?"

"Yes, her ladyship comes here to play Supermarket Sweep quite often."

"And who are the guys with her?"

"Security, I guess, bodyguards." Daniella was then distracted by an expensively dressed male customer smiling over at her. She flung back her hair. "Oh, here's that guy back who was in yesterday!"

Rachel watched Daniella flirting with the customer who was asking her advice. As he completed his purchase, he handed Daniella his card.

"I'm only in town for a short while, so call me today," he said, and then turned and walked off.

Rachel moved over to Daniella who was fanning herself with the card and fluttering her eyes.

"He tried to pick you up!" said Rachel.

"He certainly did," said Daniella, smiling.

"The cheek of him! What does he think this place is? That we offer a special offer of a girl with every perfume purchase?" Then Rachel noticed Daniella's cat-that-got-the cream look. "You're not serious, Daniella! You aren't going to call him?"

"Sure, why not?"

"Because he's a creep who thinks he can just pick you up like *that*!" She clicked her fingers.

"What's the big deal? He's very attractive and by the look of him very rich. Just my type."

"And what about Leo?"

"What about him?"

"I thought you were mad about him."

"Oh, look, what he doesn't know won't hurt him! Besides, he's closing a big deal today and he'll have the profit from that shoved up his nose quicker than you can say 'I like candy'."

Rachel was taken aback by this revelation. "I don't get you, Daniella. I thought you really liked Leo – why bother with him if you don't?"

"Darling, it's *you* that I don't get. Lighten up and enjoy life a little. As I told you when you started here – there's rich pickings out there. Do you think Elka Furstin got what she has by not being ambitious? I'm going to get a life of luxury and a man is going to be my key to getting it. I'm not going to be working in this shithole for the rest of my life. Leo is all well and good, but if someone better comes along – well, I'd be foolish not to, wouldn't I?"

"We obviously just have a different set of values," said Rachel, shaking her head.

Rachel tried to concentrate on work for the afternoon but found it hard to. She was angry at Daniella's attitude. She was no prude but she hated disloyalty. She had obviously misread the situation. She had thought that Leo was the one with the wandering eye but in actual fact there were probably two of them in it. Daniella was using Leo. Besides, Rachel hated that kind of bimbo mentality. If Daniella wanted to be rich, then she should go and bloody work to get there! And what was Daniella saying about him and nose candy? Was that true? If so, was all that cockiness he displayed just a cover? If he was a regular drug-user and had a girlfriend who was just with him for what she could get, and by the sounds of it no very close family, then he probably wasn't in a great place. He had been nice to her and sorted her out with a great flat. She felt herself start to feel sorry for Leo and hoped he would sort himself out.

* * *

After the cash run Paul and the two security men made their way to Karl's office. Outside the office, Paul took out a key, unlocked the handcuff joining the security man to the briefcase and took possession of the case himself.

Karl looked up from his paperwork as Paul entered.

"Is it busy?"

"Very busy today," said Paul, placing the briefcase on Karl's desk.

Paul watched Karl take out a key from a drawer, open the case and begin to count out money. Karl had been taking money from the tills since Paul had arrived there. Paul knew it was probably unethical in some way but then he figured Karl owned the store so he was only robbing himself, if you didn't factor in the small number of minor investors. It was probably some tax scam. He wondered how Karl explained away the gap in the company accounts but that really wasn't his business.

* * *

That evening Karl looked appreciatively at his dining companion across the table. Ingrid sat, her uneasiness obvious. She had spent the day with personal shoppers, beauticians and hairdressers. Her natural beauty had been polished and now she looked like a movie star from the fifties. She was dressed in a flowing white chiffon dress, her blonde hair piled high on her head, the loaned diamonds from Franklyns sparkling around her neck. They were seated in a chic restaurant in the city which was packed that night.

Karl reached over and placed his hand over hers which was trembling.

"Are you cold?" he asked.

"Eh, no . . ." She shook her head.

"Why do you shiver then?"

"No reason." She looked down at the beautiful food on her plate.

"You may eat," he sanctioned, releasing her hand.

She nodded, picked up her knife and fork and cut into the chicken on her plate.

The night was just a continuation of the bizarre and disturbing episodes that had occurred since she had joined Furstin's personal staff. One minute he treated her like a slave, the next he did something amazing for her. She had contemplated leaving but then he had informed her that a large sum of money would soon be deposited in her bank account and that dissuaded her.

He reached forward for his glass of wine and took a sip from it, his eyes still fixed on her.

"Is everything all right?" she asked, unnerved by his staring."

"I'm just admiring you, in the same way I'd admire a horse." He put down his glass of wine. "I like your look. You're a thoroughbred. You or your background aren't particularly interesting, but I like your look." He paused and sipped his wine again. "My wife, now *she* is something. Have you seen her in the store or maybe in the magazines?"

Ingrid shook her head.

"South African. A perfect woman. Intelligent, beautiful, excellent breeding. A champion show jumper in her day. Brought up to be a society princess. She not only fitted into London society, she rules it. A million miles away from your background."

Ingrid looked up from her food at him. She despised him and decided she would hand her notice in to Nicola Newman that week. And yet . . . she thought about the large amount she knew would be deposited in her bank account in the coming days. With that boost, she soon she would have enough to return to Stockholm and finish her university course.

"Would you excuse me for a minute, please?" Karl stood up and walked away.

* * *

Rachel turned off the television in her new flat. She stretched and got up to go to bed. She was looking forward to work the following day. Since she had decided to make the best of the shop floor, she was really enjoying it. She thought about Daniella, off out on her date that night with the customer. She was obviously a girl who knew what she wanted in life and went for it. Rachel couldn't help feeling bad about Leo, completely unaware his girlfriend was out with another man. As she looked around the flat, feeling content, she thought he really had played a blinder organising it for her. She had been quite abrupt with him when they had gone for a drink and felt a little guilty about this. She picked up her phone, found his number and sent a text: **"Hi Leo, Rachel here, thanks so much for the flat, you're a star."**

* * *

Leo was busy sending emails in his apartment when his phone bleeped. He picked it up and saw Rachel's name on the text. He was surprised – he hadn't expected to hear from her again, except through Daniella. He groaned to himself. He hoped there wasn't a problem with plumbing or something and she expected him to sort it out. He opened the text and was surprised by her niceness. He had almost been regretting setting her up in the flat because of her aloof manner the day they had gone for a drink. But then he wasn't that surprised by the text – it was a classy thing to do and she seemed a classy girl.

He picked up his mobile and sent Rachel back a text: **"No problem."**

* * *

Ingrid looked down at her watch. It was nearly midnight and Karl had been gone for two hours. Most diners had left the restaurant. She sat there feeling increasingly anxious. The bill had been left on the table half an hour ago.

The staff were beginning to look at her as they began to clear tables.

One of the managers approached the table, smiling. "Will there be anything else, madam?" he asked.

"I…eh…no," she said.

"In that case, would it be very rude of us to ask you to settle the bill?" The manager continued to smile.

"Eh, Mr Furstin will be settling the bill."

The manager looked concerned. "Mr Furstin left the premises over two hours ago."

"He left!" Ingrid was perplexed.

"He said you would settle the bill."

Ingrid glanced at the bill which came to over £1000. "But – I have no money on me, no credit card!" She didn't even have her mobile with her.

The manager looked very worried. "In that case, we have a very embarrassing situation."

Ten minutes later Ingrid was standing at reception, shaking, surrounded by management from the restaurant.

"I told you I was Mr Furstin's guest," she was nearly shouting. "I would never have ordered all that expensive wine and food without the money to pay it. I would never have come to this restaurant!"

"That's immaterial. There's a bill here that needs to be paid."

"If you give me till tomorrow, I'll go home and get my credit card and pay the damned bill!"

"I'm afraid that's not good enough," said the manager, picking up the phone. "I'm afraid I have to call the police."

"No, please!" begged Ingrid.

Karl's chauffeur suddenly appeared.

Ingrid gasped in sheer relief. She turned to the manager and noticed that he didn't seem at all surprised. In fact, he didn't register any reaction at all.

"I'm sorry," said the chauffeur. "There seems to have been a misunderstanding. Mr Furstin would like tonight's bill charged to his account."

Ingrid felt her whole body fill with relief and she allowed herself to draw in a deep breath.

"I see. That's no problem," said the manager in a cool manner, again with no hint of surprise. He took Ingrid's coat from the cloakroom attendant and held it out for her to put on. "Madam!"

Ingrid angrily slipped into the coat and stormed out. At the door she paused and looked back. The chauffeur was discreetly slipping the manager some money.

Ingrid walked down to the waiting limousine. The chauffeur hurried ahead and opened the door for her. She expected Furstin to be there and was surprised to find the car empty.

"Where's the bastard?" she spat as she got in.

The chauffeur said nothing and drove through the streets of London to Knightsbridge.

He pulled up outside a plush apartment block.

"You're to go the penthouse. The concierge will show you where the elevator is."

Ingrid got out of the car and walked quickly into the building, her fear of Furstin forgotten she was so angry with him.

The concierge led her to the elevator.

On the top floor the elevator doors opened and Ingrid stormed out and into the apartment

"What the fuck did you think you were doing leaving me like that?" she shouted in anger. But she was surprised to see the beautiful room was empty.

"Furstin!" she shouted. She went running into the next room but again it was empty.

She raced through the penthouse but couldn't find him or anybody.

"Where are you?" she shouted.

Slow classical music began to play in the background.

Her anger subsided and began to be replaced with fear. All her senses were screaming at her to leave. She hurried to the lift and pressed the button. The lift didn't come and she pressed the button again and again before realising it had been disconnected.

Shivering slightly, she went to sit down on the couch. The time went by slowly and she became more and more unnerved. After an hour she went to the phone and picked it up to dial a friend but realised it was dead.

And then suddenly she heard the elevator door open.

Chapter 13

Paul was walking down the bustling street of Knightsbridge to Franklyns, on his mobile to Anna.

"I just did it," said Anna. "I made the appointment at the hospital. Next week – Friday."

"Great. How do you feel?"

"Really nervous and scared – but glad I've done it."

"At least now we'll know what the situation is."

"Try not to be too late home tonight, Paul," she said before giving a little laugh. "I kind of want you around this evening."

He was touched by the vulnerability in her voice. "I'll leave work early, I'll be home even before you are."

"That'll make a change. See you later."

* * *

"How did your date go?" Rachel asked Daniella, genuinely interested in the answer.

"Not bad," Daniella said, then made a face. "But not great. Absolutely loaded. Yacht in the Med, apartment in New York, house in Florida."

Or so he says, thought Rachel. "Sounds like just what you're looking for."

"Only one little drawback. He's off to the States for six months, so I can't see anything developing there."

Rachel wondered if they had slept together. "And if he was staying in London, would you have dropped Leo for him?"

"Oh, I don't know. I'd have to have gone out on a few dates with him to see if there really was anything between us other than sex. I mean, Leo is a gem – I wouldn't drop him for just anybody, you know."

Rachel couldn't help giggling. "Glad to know your conscience is clear!"

"You know, I was thinking maybe I should ask for a transfer to the men's clothing department. I mean, it's logical that I stand to meet a rich man there much more easily than at the Chanel counter."

"What are you like, Daniella!" Rachel looked horrified.

Daniella became annoyed. "Get off your high horse, Rachel. You were the same the other day. If you don't like what I say, then I won't bother telling you things in future." She turned to walk away.

Rachel put a hand on her arm. "I'm sorry, Daniella. I'm only teasing. It's just I think you and Leo make a good couple. And I wouldn't like to see you throw it away just because something richer, but not better, comes along."

Daniella shrugged.

"Listen," said Rachel, "you've been great to me since I arrived here, and so has Leo, sorting me out with the flat and everything. I'd love to have the two of you over for dinner this week. You'd be my first guests!"

Daniella smiled. "Yeah, I'd like that."

"Maybe Monday night?"

"I'll just check with Leo but I'm sure that would be fine."

* * *

Paul was walking through the store with Karl, two security men behind them. They walked into the cosmetics department.

"I'm very pleased to say that cosmetics sales have hit beyond target over the past two weeks," said Paul.

"Good. We'll have to adjust the targets upwards in that case," remarked Karl.

Paul raised his eyes to heaven, unseen.

Rachel was loudly selling her perfume and Karl stopped in his tracks as she caught his eye.

"Who is that girl?" Karl demanded.

"Eh, she's a new girl from Dublin. Proving very good with customers."

As Karl continued to look her up and down, Paul began to feel agitated, recognising the look in Karl's face.

"I want her to join my personal staff. Go tell her she starts on the sixth floor immediately."

Paul felt stressed as his suspicion was confirmed.

"Eh, Rachel is actually a born saleswoman," he said. "I don't think she would be suited to admin work."

Karl turned quickly and fixed Paul with a steely look.

"I want her on my staff."

"Seriously, she is the main reason why sales have met targets in this department. I think –"

"I don't care what you think. Go and inform her she's joining my staff."

"Karl – "

"Enough!" Karl's face darkened with annoyance.

"There is a vacancy on my staff that urgently needs to be filled! That Swedish girl you recommended to me turned out to be incompetent and uncooperative. I've had to get rid of her – she's leaving this very morning. I need this Irish girl to replace her. Go tell her to get herself upstairs at once."

Paul paused for a second and then, sighing, turned and walked over to Rachel.

He didn't want Rachel to go up to the sixth floor. It was a different dimension up there. He had heard rumours of strange things. He wondered about the fate of the Swedish girl, Ingrid – she certainly hadn't lasted long. She must have seriously offended Furstin. Or he must have seriously offended her. In either case, she was lucky to have escaped from the sixth floor and Furstin's clutches. Karl's staff were broken down and mechanical, controlled. Rachel was too spirited to work in that environment.

"Rachel, I need a word," he said and drew her aside. "Eh – it's your lucky day," he said quietly. "You've been handed a promotion."

"A promotion?" She shook her head, confused, and smiled.

"That's Karl Furstin over there."

"Yes?" She glanced over. He was the man she had bumped into the street. The one who had made her feel so unnerved.

"And he's offered you a job in his private staff."

She immediately felt claustrophobic. Looking at Karl Furstin now he stirred the same reaction as before and she just wanted to get away from him. .She didn't want to be cocooned up on the sixth floor away from the main business of the store. Daniella had told her that when staff went to work on the sixth floor they weren't allowed to speak to anyone else.

Rachel thought for a few seconds before shaking her head.

"No, thanks. Very nice of him to offer, but I'll decline."

Paul looked at her, surprised. "It's a big pay increase. Cushy number. Don't have to deal with the public."

"You know, I'm surprising myself. I don't mind dealing with the public. No, you can tell Mr Furstin that I politely thank him but have to turn him down."

Paul looked around at Karl who was looking restless. He leaned forward to Rachel. "You don't have any choice, Rachel. He wants you up there and that's the end of it. You have to go."

"There's always a choice in life, Paul. And I'm saying no to this."

"Nobody has ever said no to Furstin before." Paul frowned with concern.

"I just have," she said firmly.

He looked at her, perplexed, and then, shrugging his shoulders, went back to Karl.

Rachel watched discreetly as Paul spoke to Karl.

Suddenly there was an eruption from Karl.

"Don't you ever tell me something is not possible!" he shouted, before storming off, followed by Paul and the security men.

A little while later Christine came up to Rachel and said: "You don't know what you've done."

* * *

A row of black Mercedes pulled up to the front of Franklyns. Stephanie and David Stafford got out of the first. Equally smart, suited people got out of the other cars and followed Stephanie and David into the store.

* * *

Nicola had Rachel's contract out on her desk and was perusing it. She had received a furious call from Karl insisting that Rachel Healy join his staff. And if she continued to refuse, he wanted her demoted to something so bad that she would willingly take the promotion. Why didn't the silly girl just take the damn promotion and stay out of her hair?

Paul came storming into the office.

Nicola looked up, surprised. "Paul?"

"Has Furstin talked to you about the Irish girl, Rachel Healy?"

She sat back in her chair and viewed him coolly. "I've heard there's been some kerfuffle about her turning down a job on the sixth floor. I'm quite surprised because she expressed an interest in building a career when I interviewed her."

"A career, yes. Not a soul-destroying experience as somebody's slave."

"I don't think any of us are in a position to say that. Anyway, why are you talking to me about this?"

"Because he's going to get you to do his dirty work. It's a free country. If the girl doesn't want to go upstairs to work, then leave her alone."

"I think it's you who usually recruits the staff for Karl, Paul, not me. It's a bit late for you to start feeling concern about the process now. I merely sort out personnel problems and am trying to get to the bottom of this one."

"Look, Nicola. For once in your life why don't you become a real person and stop seeing people as merely commodities. Every time you look at a person, you see what their value is to the store as opposed to the person themselves. And that's where we're going wrong. That's why the store is going down."

Nicola looked at him in horror. "I will not be spoken to in such a way by you or –"

Yvette came rushing in, looking distressed.

"You'd better come quickly!" she cried.

Nicola stood up and followed Paul out of her office, then looked around in confusion. A number of people she did not recognise were being directed by a smartly dressed woman and a business-suited man into the various offices, from which the Franklyns staff were emerging looking confused and almost frightened..

Paul stormed up to the woman, Nicola by his side.

"What the fuck is going on here?" demanded Paul.

"I'm calling security," said Nicola.

"My name is Stephanie Holden and this is David Stafford. We're from Barons Bank. I'm the new Brand Director for Franklyns and Mr Stafford is the new Financial Controller."

"I don't understand," said Paul, immediately recognising David from years ago at school.

"The store has been sent into receivership," explained David.

"Could you tell us where we could find Mr Furstin?" said Stephanie.

Paul was speechless for a moment before saying, "He's on the sixth floor."

Nicola could hardly concentrate on what was being said as she stared at David Stafford.

He was the man she had seen on the train and been following the morning she was mugged. The man she had fallen in love with.

Paul recognised Stephanie from photos in the newspapers, usually announcing dramatic new directions for the retail empires she reigned over or announcing huge profits.

"But there was no notice given on this, no warnings!" said Paul.

"There rarely are in receivership cases," said David Stafford.

"I think you'll find Mr Furstin was well aware of the danger Franklyns was in – it's a pity he didn't decide to warn his senior staff," said Stephanie.

"And what does this mean for us?" asked Paul. "For my staff?"

"I cannot say at the moment. I will obviously meet with senior management at the earliest opportunity. There will be a complete restructuring. If either of you feel an unbreakable loyalty to Karl Furstin then I must tell you he will be leaving the building today and not returning – if you feel you have to leave with him out of loyalty that's your option. If you stay, as I said, your positions are not guaranteed."

Nicola had been listening intently but saying nothing. She tried not to stare at David Stafford and tried not to show the very real shock she was feeling.

"You'll have to excuse me," she said in an even, nonchalant manner as if she was oblivious and unaffected by the chaos around her. "This sounds all very unplanned. I'm afraid I can't waste any more time listening to maybes and what ifs. I have a very busy afternoon. If you want to see me, please phone my secretary for an appointment."

She turned and walked confidently into her office, then closed the door behind her. She leaned against the door and started breathing hard. What did this mean for her?

Did it jeopardise her position? Karl Furstin gone? It was unthinkable. And yet through all her racing thoughts, she could not believe she had seen the man on the train again. And that he was coming to work at Franklyns. That she now knew his name. She repeated his name over and over. David Stafford.

Outside, Stephanie shrugged, deciding to leave Nicola to be dealt with later.

"He's on the sixth floor you said – Furstin?" Stephanie checked with Paul.

"Yes," nodded Paul.

"The financial director and his chief accountants are being dismissed immediately," said David to Paul. "I would appreciate it if you could accompany me to their offices."

Paul nodded.

"I'd better get up to Furstin and give him his bad news," Stephanie said, heading towards the lift.

Paul looked after her, concerned, and turned to David. "Actually, I don't think it's a good idea for her to go up there alone," he warned.

"The financial department is our main concern," said David. "We need to freeze all activity immediately. Let's face it, Furstin's just an old has-been – the only real damage that can be done is through the financial department."

"Yes, but –"

"She's Stephanie Holden. Believe me, she's the best equipped person to give Furstin his marching orders. The Financial Department?"

"Eh, yes, this way."

In the lift, the two men looked at each other for a few seconds.

"Long time no see," said David.

"Yeah, something like that," said Paul.

Suddenly years were stripped away and Paul was no longer a highly confident business boss, a married man well aware of his own appeal, but an A-level student, dying to get away from school and his classmates whom he didn't dislike but didn't like either.

"It's a pity we're not meeting under better circumstances," said David. "We'll catch up for a chat later but at the moment we'd better get on with the job at hand."

Paul nodded and led the way.

* * *

As Stephanie got into the lift, the words she had overheard David say echoed in her ear. *"She's Stephanie Holden . . . she's the best equipped person to give Furstin his marching orders."* It made her proud to be described in such glowing terms. That was her reputation. Fearless, strong, able to handle every situation or person. It's what had brought her to the top.

She always felt it was important that she be the one to give the former owners the news. It established her from the word go. The King is dead . . . long live the Queen. You had to be seen as the person doing the firing and that started at the top. It was the only way you could execute real power. Once she had been seen as the one getting rid of Furstin she would be respected, feared. She would have stamped her control on the store.

It was also an intensely personal moment for most people, she had found – telling them they had lost their business. A lot of people had spent their lives building up those businesses. Even though she knew it was inevitable that because things hadn't been run properly it was necessary for her to step in and take over, she didn't like to accentuate their humiliation by having other people present. Most crumbled on being told the news, often in tears. And suddenly she could find herself giving them comfort and even encouraging talk. She'd tell them 'You've done it once, you can do it again', urging them not to give up on their careers, just that particular business.

On the sixth floor, the lift doors opened and Stephanie strode out. She was struck by the hushed plushness. There was a woman sitting on reception.

"Karl Furstin's office?"

The receptionist looked up and pointed down a wide corridor.

Stephanie marched down the corridor. As she walked the place became more eerie to her. She had thought it would be the same as the fifth floor, a busy office environment. But she was high on adrenaline.

She entered a large reception area where there was a haughty-looking woman sitting behind the desk.

"You're Furstins's PA?" asked Stephanie..

"I'm one of *Mr* Furstin's PAs." The woman looked Stephanie up and down in disdain. "Do you have an appointment?"

"No, he's not expecting me." Stephanie held up a copy of the receivership notice.

"He's not expecting this either. Mr Furstin no longer owns Franklyns. He's through here, I take it?" Stephanie pointed to the oak-panelled door and approached it.

"Wait! You can't go into there!" Too late, the PA leapt to her feet.

Karl was busy readjusting the papers on his desk when

Stephanie stormed in, the PA in her wake. He looked up, startled.

"I'm Stephanie Holden. I'm representing Barons Bank. I've bad news for you, I'm afraid. The store has been sent into receivership." Stephanie put the receivership notice in front of Karl on the desk.

"I'm sorry, Karl," said the PA. "I've rung security but nobody seems to be answering!"

"Get out!" he shouted at her and she quickly exited, closing the door behind her.

Karl picked up the paperwork and examined it. He started twitching and looked up at Stephanie. "It's going to take my staff days to scrub this office clean after you've been in here," he said.

She was taken aback by his response. She gathered herself together. "I'm afraid this *isn't* your office any more. You're required to gather any personal items and leave the building immediately."

"You're *afraid*!" He sat back and laughed. "That's the only sensible thing you've said since you came in here. You're right to be afraid. By the time I'm finished with you, you'll be very afraid."

"Mr Furstin, I understand this must come as a shock to you but I don't take kindly to threats."

He stood up. "It's not a threat. It's just a fact."

She felt very uncomfortable as his grey-blue eyes bored into her.

"I know you. I know all about you." He walked out from behind his desk. "You're trash who made a name for herself by taking people's businesses from them."

"If they had run the businesses properly they wouldn't have lost them."

"You're a fucking vampire. Feeding off other people.

Look at you!" He came close to her and flicked her hair back.

"Please do not do that!" she snapped.

Feeling threatened, she began to back away from him, but he followed her, flicking her hair.

"When I'm finished with you, there will be nothing left. Cunt. Don't sleep at night because I'll come after you. Every taxi you take, be frightened, because the driver might be one of mine bringing you to your end. And what an end I'll arrange for you."

Fear engrossed her as she continued to back away from him.

"Every pizza you get delivered to the door, he might be one of mine sent for you. Still want the job here? You think you're so tough, so great. The cheek of someone like you coming and thinking you can take my store. I wouldn't even use you as a prostitute!"

Her heart was beating fast as he backed her into a corner. She went to walk away quickly but he grabbed her arm tightly and pushed her back into the corner.

"I'm going to enjoy watching you being destroyed. You'll end up doing things you never dreamed of for me. The word 'dream' is wrong – 'nightmare' is a better word for what'll happen to you."

Stephanie felt a surge of relief as the door opened and the PA came in with two of Karl's bodyguards.

"Have her thrown out in the gutter," Karl ordered.

The bodyguards came and grabbed both Stephanie's arms and escorted her out of the office.

"Get your hands off me!" she demanded as they marched her down to the lifts.

They hauled her into the lift.

"You're making a big mistake!" she said through

gritted teeth. "This store is no longer Furstin's – he no longer employs you. You answer to me."

The bodyguards looked at her coldly. The lift doors opened and again they grabbed her arms and moved her through the ground floor.

Stephanie spotted Paul in the distance.

"Paul!" she shouted.

Paul turned and walked quickly to her, taking in the whole scene.

"Let her go," Paul said. The bodyguards glared at Paul but didn't release her.

"Get your bloody hands off me!" she demanded.

"I said let her go!" Paul shouted..

They did as he said and walked back to the lift.

Stephanie felt herself go weak from the whole episode.

"Are you all right?" asked Paul.

She rubbed her face.

"You really shouldn't have gone up there on your own," he said. "I warned Stafford."

Stephanie was aware that her whole power base had been badly damaged with Paul having to come to her rescue. It been glaringly obvious to anyone who had witnessed the incident that Furstin had demolished her.

"I'm fine," she said, dismissing Paul's concern.

But who could handle Furstin? She had been petrified by the man.

She quickly moved to reassert her position.

"Are you free in the morning, ten o'clock, for a talk?" she asked.

"Yes, that's fine." He looked at her, confused. "Where will I meet you?"

She had planned to use Furstin's office – she always took over the previous boss's office. It was psychologically important to do so. She had not been allowed access to it. After her encounter with Furstin she didn't even want it now. This was a nightmare.

"We'll have the meeting over breakfast," she said. "I'll meet you in the restaurant."

Stephanie went into the store rest rooms and looked at herself in the mirror. She looked visibly shaken. She steadied herself, arranged her hair and reapplied her make-up. Then she emerged and made her way to the fifth floor.

There David had taken control and was sitting in the Financial Controller's office as his team of accountants went through files.

"I had the previous controller and accountants escorted from the building," he said. "Don't want them covering up anything. How did it go with Furstin?"

"He . . . eh . . ." Stephanie didn't know what to say. She didn't want David Stafford or Barons Bank to know that Furstin had completely outplayed her. That she couldn't handle the man. That he had dismissed her and the letter of the law as a nuisance and instead of having him escorted from the building, he had brutally kicked her out.

"It was . . . confrontational," she said.

"Uh huh," David nodded and looked back at the file opened on his desk.

He didn't doubt for a second that Stephanie had come out on top.

Chapter 14

Paul felt exhausted as he left work in the evening. The whole day had been a shock. All he had done was to get on with his job and ensure the store continued to run properly.

He was getting continuous calls from the new management, asking him questions that needed quick answers. He thought about that expression – new management. Did that mean he was the old management?

As he walked past The Blue Posts he bumped into Rachel going in.

"Hi," she said. "Sorry about this morning. I hope Mr Furstin wasn't annoyed I didn't take his job."

Paul remembered the drama of Rachel refusing Furstin's offer. How unimportant it seemed now! "No, I think I can safely say he's probably forgotten about it by now," he said slowly and walked on by.

She looked after him. He seemed distracted and worried.

She pushed the door open and walked into the pub. The atmosphere was electric with the crowd inside, nearly all Franklyns staff, talking excitedly and very loudly. It was very obvious something had happened.

She bumped into Daniella.

"What's going on?" Rachel asked.

"We've been taken over. Furstin's gone and Stephanie Holden is taking over."

* * *

"Hi, you really did take my request to be home early seriously. I thought you might at least stray into the pub for one!" said Anna, kissing him as he came into the lounge.

He sat down beside her and put his arm around her.

"Everything all right?" she asked, concerned.

"I'm not sure ... Franklyns has gone into receivership."

"*What*?" she almost shouted.

"Barons Bank are our new owners, well, main shareholders, whatever you want to call it."

"And when did this happen?"

"This morning."

"And did you have any indication it was going to happen?"

"No. I knew that there were big bank borrowings but I never thought this would happen."

"Furstin must be devastated."

"I didn't see him all day."

"And what does that mean for you?"

"I don't know. You know Stephanie Holden? They've appointed her as Brand Director."

"And what role is that?"

"Well, I think she's my boss basically. I think she'll be running the store."

"And if she's running the store, then what will you be doing?"

Paul looked at her and shrugged. "I'm meeting her tomorrow for a breakfast meeting, so hopefully I'll find out more then."

"This is the wrong time for you to be looking for a new job and for us to be dealing with the stress of change. If we start IVF it's going to have such a big impact on our lives that I need to know where we are."

He nodded and looked down at the floor.

"Look, I'm not being a bitch. I wouldn't give a shit normally. My main concern would be you – it still is. But it's not going to just be about me and you if we go ahead with these tests. We need to be able to offer a child a safe and secure home. Maybe it's the wrong time to start these tests."

"No! Look, it's now or never. We're getting older. We can't postpone it because I might lose my job.We've a small window of opportunity here and we can't fuck it up. Okay?"

She looked at him.

"I said *okay*?" he reiterated.

She nodded. "Okay."

"You just don't worry about anything. Look on the bright side – at least I'm rid of Furstin."

"Very true – no more phone calls at three in the morning – that's a plus." She hugged him.

"It's really strange but there's this guy I went to school with and he's the new Financial Controller."

She pulled back from the hug. "Really? Who?"

"A guy called David Stafford."

"Were you friends with him?" She was curious. She had lots of friends from school and college but all of Paul's friends were from work.

"Friendly, I suppose. Just a bit odd seeing him after all these years."

"And he's the Financial Controller – does that impact on you?"

"He's part of the new management, so effectively I guess I answer to him."

Anna nodded, aware how uncomfortable that would be for Paul.

"Maybe you should start looking for a new job?" she suggested.

"Nah! I'm sure it's all going to be fine. Besides, where am I going to get a position that pays what I get and with the perks I get? I kind of like that company BMW out the front."

* * *

Nicola parked her Renault in her driveway. She got out, walked up to the front door and let herself in.

"Hello!" she said.

"In here!" said Oliver.

She walked through the hallway and into the parlour where Oliver was sitting reading the paper and listening to classical music.

She turned off the music and poured herself a large gin, so wrapped up in the day's activities, she didn't care she was being rude.

"You look in good form," he commented with a smile. He was delighted to see her looking happy. Nicola, always serious, had seemed too serious recently.

"Do I? Franklyns has been taken over by Barons Bank." She announced the news almost gleefully.

"What?" He put down the paper, full of concern.

"It came out of the blue!" She sat down and took a swig of her drink. "Seemingly Furstin's gone, with the whole shebang! Out with the old and in with the new!"

"Well, you don't seem too concerned. I mean you rule that place. Furstin lets you rule it. Aren't you concerned about your position?"

"No. I won't be going anywhere."

"How can you be so sure?"

"Because I always get what I want, Oliver. Always. Changes are a-coming!" She raised her glass and took another swig.

Oliver tried to figure out his wife's mood and her reaction to what he saw as very bad news. But then he was still trying to figure out her schoolgirl run across the CCTV footage. He had decided not to mention it yet. He'd bide his time and hope to figure it out. And this certainly didn't seem the right moment to confront her about it.

His officers had interviewed countless people around the station. Local business people, taxi drivers, rail staff. They had shown them all photos of Nicola. Had anyone seen her or anybody acting suspiciously that morning? They'd got no answers. It was just another mugging in a city full of them.

* * *

Stephanie was never so glad to be home and close the door of her apartment behind her. The whole encounter with Furstin had unnerved and frightened her. She had been unable to regain her composure for the rest of the day.

She threw off her coat, sat down on the couch and started rubbing her face. Tears sprang to her eyes and she allowed herself a good cry. She knew Furstin's words were the rantings of an angry man but he spoke with such spite and there were so many rumours about him. The whole day had been a fuck-up. She usually marched into a place and stamped her authority on it immediately. But she felt she had failed to do it that day with Franklyns.

She tried to shake her negative thoughts off but failed. The encounter with Furstin had shocked her to the core. She had never had such a threatening experience in all her years of business. She had felt completely vulnerable; she *had* been completely vulnerable. And the worst thing was she was so carried away with her image – The Great Stephanie Holden – that she thought she could handle anyone and anything, And that had led her into a dangerous situation. She would have to rebuild her defences and take back control tomorrow.

But what was Furstin going to do next?

Before she'd left Franklyns that evening she should have left orders that Furstin should not be allowed back into the building the next day. But the memory of being manhandled by the bodyguards had still been with her. She'd felt that, even if she'd issued the order, she couldn't have done it with confidence. Furstin's grip on the place was so tight she feared that it would take some time for her to break it.

She didn't like the look or the sound of Nicola Newman but it was obvious she would need her to take control of the store. She wasn't sure about Paul. Although he seemed pleasant and his reputation as a general manager was impressive, what role could he have at Franklyns other than as her assistant? She doubted he would be comfortable with that position and he might even undermine her as people would continue to use him as a point of reference. And he was too associated with Furstin for his or Franklyns' own good.

She sighed loudly and opened a bottle of wine. She was glad the day was over and she had learned some lessons for the future.

You're not indestructible, she reminded herself.

* * *

Elka Furstin sat on the elongated sofa in the penthouse, talking on the phone while a manicurist filed her free hand and a hairdresser styled her hair.

"Yes, I'll be back in Cape Town next week and so we can go to the polo when I'm there . . . No, of course Karl's not coming . . . Phone me next week and we can confirm." Elka finished off the conversation and put down the phone.

The lift doors opened and Karl walked in.

He looked at his wife being attended to and, clicking his fingers, snapped "Out!"

The two women stopped grooming and quickly packed away their belongings.

He waited for them to leave, looking at his wife. She sat poised, wearing a long satin dressing-gown draped to the floor, her luxuriant blonde hair combed back. She could see something was wrong.

Karl sat down opposite her.

"What is it?" she asked.

"They've taken it away. The store. The bank have sent it into receivership. A team of them arrived in today. Some nobody stormed into my office and announced she was the new boss."

"What did you do?" Elka's exquisite face creased.

"I had her thrown out on her arse."

"Good."

"I spent the afternoon stripping my offices of files, anything personal or professional that could incriminate us. There isn't much left to do. I'll finish it in the morning."

"You can't go back tomorrow," Elka said sternly. "They didn't expect you to stand up to them today. If you go back, they'll have prepared. You can't give them the satisfaction of throwing you out of your own store. So what are we going to do?"

"I've contacted our lawyers and told them to do anything they can to block this takeover."

"Good. How did it come to this?"

"All the borrowings we took to revamp the store – we weren't earning enough to repay them." He glanced at the diamonds around her neck. "And then there's the lifestyle."

She reached over to a cigarette resting on the glass coffee table and lit it. He grimaced as she lit up and he got up to open a window.

Looking at his agitated face, she said, "Karl, this is no time for your nonsense. We simply can't lose the store. Where would we be without Franklyns? And we have to work quickly. If they have control of the store for long . . . things will be discovered . . . things will come out. We face ruin."

Karl looked irritated at the wafting smoke.

"For fuck's sake!" Elka snapped and stubbed out the cigarette. "Get onto the lawyers now and get them to work through the night. Have you spoken to Paul Stewart?"

"I was too busy trying to remove everything."

"Phone him now and see what's going on."

* * *

Paul was on the couch at home, Anna lying beside him, him stroking her hair. His mobile rang and he picked it up.

"It's Furstin," said Paul.

"Don't answer it, Paul. You can't afford to be seen communicating with him. He's history now. If Stephanie Holden sees you on his side, you'll be given your marching orders."

Paul switched the phone onto silence.

* * *

"It's going on to his voice mail," said Karl to Elka.

"Stewart, call me immediately. I need to discuss today's events with you. We can't co-operate with them. If I'm exposed you'll be destroyed with me. You have too much to lose."

Karl hung up the phone.

"I always suspected his loyalty was in doubt," said Karl.

"None of their loyalty can be relied on," said Elka. "All they care about is their pay cheques – that's all we are to them. That's why they deserve the contempt we show them. We'll get Franklyns back. You can do it, Karl. You weren't just born to win – you were bred to win."

Chapter 15

Stephanie had slept badly that night, and had got up early and headed over to the Chelsea Harbour gym for an early morning work-out. As she toned herself physically, she also prepared herself mentally.

As she left the gym she looked at the array of newspapers at the reception. The takeover had made some of the front pages. A large photograph of Elka Furstin dominated the *Daily Mail* with the headline *"Franklyns Taken Into Receivership"*.

She picked up the paper and read through the article.

'Knightsbridge emporium, Franklyns, last night faced bankruptcy as the rug was pulled from under the owner, Karl Furstin. The retail king, Furstin, dubbed the Baron of Knightsbridge, who has owned the fashionable people's favourite place to shop since the eighties, was unavailable for comment last night. A city insider revealed the store has been in financial trouble for some time. The news has come as a shock to all who know Furstin and his South-African-born society wife, Elka. The Furstins have certainly shown no sign of the financial difficulties they have been in as they continued their legendary lavish lifestyle. Elka, whose spending ability the Chancellor of

the Exchequer once jokingly blamed for the country's rise in inflation, is a former champion showjumper. The Cape Town beauty. . .'

Stephanie cast the paper aside as the she realised the article was just a rehash of gossip to feed the public's fascination with the Furstins and had no real news on the takeover to offer.

She walked through the main doors of Franklyns and, from the nonchalant look of the security and sales staff, realised nobody knew who she was. She had walked around the store enough yesterday and the fact nobody knew who she was by this stage was bad news.

She made her way up to the restaurant. Franklyns' top-floor restaurant was a renowned eatery. Very trendily furnished to minimalist taste, there were glass windows all around looking out over the city. It was the must-be-seen-in lunch-time and afternoon eatery.

The restaurant was quite empty with just a small group having a business breakfast and a few people eating at the counter of the long bar that stretched down the middle of the restaurant. She spotted Paul sitting at one of the glass-topped tables. She made her way over to him.

"Paul," she greeted.

He rose and shook her hand. They both sat down.

"I'm sorry we didn't get a chance to meet yesterday but I was up to my eyes," Stephanie said.

"It was quite a day for all of us," he nodded.

She studied him. He was very handsome in a well-groomed way. His manner and speech were very confident. She imagined he went to all the right schools and colleges. She imagined he was the type Furstin liked to surround himself with. She also suspected that Paul might be a case of style over substance. Looked good and was the right image for the store but wasn't at the cutting edge of retail. Which would mean there would be no place for him in Franklyns' future.

A waiter came over with a big smile and a notebook.

Stephanie took up the menu and glanced through it. "Just scrambled eggs for me and some orange juice." She folded away the menu.

"Some bacon and eggs and coffee," said Paul.

"And you want your bacon crispy and eggs sunny side up as usual, Paul," smiled the waiter and off he went.

Stephanie looked at Paul. She imagined that he probably ate at the restaurant regularly and, of course, it would all be on the house. She did not like employees taking advantage of their positions and she imagined Franklyns was rife with it.

"I'm going to be very honest with you." Stephanie sat forward and folded her arms. "I do not have any plans for Franklyns at the moment. But that will change very quickly. I have to see how the store is run and who is going to fit into its future. And that starts at the top."

"You're telling me that my job isn't safe?"

She nodded. "How long have you been here?"

"Eight years. I came in as assistant to the general manager and then was promoted."

Stephanie scrutinised him. In her opinion he had stayed too long at Franklyns. He was probably institutionalised and new employers would smell that off him. He was also too connected with Furstin and that wasn't a connection that would go down too well if he was looking for a new job. As the waiter served their breakfasts, she imagined Furstin's perks had made it too lucrative for Paul to leave.

"There are two important things I want done

immediately," she said. "Firstly, organise a meeting of all department heads for two this afternoon. Secondly, I want Furstin kept out of the store. He effectively is not in charge any more. By the looks of it, he's turned the sixth floor into some personal fiefdom. But that ends today. Contact the head of security and have extra security placed at all doors. Under no circumstances is he allowed access."

"That's a huge pressure on the security department – to expect them to obstruct Furstin like that."

"When is everyone going to realise he's no longer the boss man?"

Paul gazed at her. "And what if Furstin's already in the store?"

Stephanie ignored the question. "Just one more thing. Those two security men you saw me with yesterday. I want them fired this morning."

Paul looked at her, startled. "To be fair, Stephanie, they were only acting on orders. They didn't know who you were. Furstin ordered them to throw you out. You could have been somebody attacking him for all they knew."

Stephanie looked at Paul, slightly impressed with him for standing up for the security staff. And she certainly saw his point. But their fate was sealed. She couldn't exert her authority with those two security still in the building.

"Just make sure they have left by noon," she said.

* * *

Stephanie and Paul stood at the top of the Board table as Paul began to speak.

"I suppose the shock of what has happened is going to take a little while to get over," said Paul. He tried to come across as reassuring and yet he couldn't quite keep his voice from sounding very concerned. He knew everyone present was worried about their jobs and what change would bring. "I certainly had no idea that this was coming. I've worked closely with all of you, and with some of you for quite some time, and I like to think of you guys as friends."

Easy on the emotion, thought Stephanie. Obviously her breakfast talk telling him his position wasn't secure had unsettled him.

"So I'm urging you all now, for the sake of the company, not to be afraid of change but to embrace it. And let's start moving on." He turned and looked at Stephanie.

"I'm sure Stephanie doesn't need any introduction." He sat down.

Stephanie glanced around the table.

"Is everybody here who should be here?" she asked.

There was a general nodding of heads.

Then Stephanie spotted a noticeable absence. "Nicola Newman?" she asked.

There was a coolness around the table.

"Where's Nicola Newman? Was she not informed of this meeting?" Stephanie asked Paul.

"Er – yes, Nicola was informed along with everyone else."

"Where is she then?" Stephanie demanded.

Paul tried to think of an explanation. "Maybe she got delayed."

An anger started to burn inside Stephanie. It was very crucial for the head of HR to be present. But she decided to press on with the meeting.

"I have been appointed the Brand Director of Franklyns. That means effectively I'm your new boss. But being a Brand Director doesn't just mean making sure everything runs properly; it means ensuring that the whole organisation is establishing the right image, the right reputation. One of the biggest blocks to establishing the right image is not moving with the times. I had a couple of surveys conducted about what people perceived when they heard the word 'Franklyns' ... the results were luxury, glamour, excellence, yes ... but then moving on to expensive, overpriced, haughty, condescending, elitist. What may be our strong points can very quickly become our weak ones."

* * *

The meeting over, the Board table was clear of everybody except Gordon, the head of the marketing department, whom Stephanie had detained.

"Please believe me, it's nothing personal," said Stephanie, "but I always take control of the marketing and PR departments myself when I take over a business. So that's leaves no room for you. I'm sure we'll provide you with excellent references and whatever redundancy is owed to you."

Gordon looked devastated. "Well, I do think after all the dedication I've given to the store, it's an outrageous way to be treated," he snapped.

"I understand how you're feeling but there's nothing I can do. I have to put the store first."

"We'll see what Nicola Newman has to say about this!" said Gordon.

Stephanie's eyebrow arched. "Nicola Newman? Nicola Newman won't have anything to say about this."

"Nothing happens in this store without Nicola's say-so. And she's going to be very pissed off when she finds out what you've attempted to do."

"Attempted?" Stephanie managed to give a surprised laugh. "I'm not attempting to do anything. I've done it. You're out, love!"

A deflated Gordon quickly left. Stephanie shook her head in disbelief. What was with this reverence of Newman? Didn't they realise she no longer had the power? And why the hell did she not turn up for the meeting?

Nobody had been able to offer her an explanation as to Nicola Newman's non-appearance. She picked up the phone and dialled Reception.

"Put me through to Nicola Newman. It's Stephanie Holden here."

Yvette came on the line. "I'm sorry but Mrs Newman is in a meeting."

Stephanie sat back in her chair, her face creased, not sure whether to laugh or erupt at the audacity of the woman.

"She was supposed to be in a meeting with me this afternoon. Was she not informed?"

"Yes, she was, but she had a prior engagement." Yvette sounded uninterested.

"Put me through to her," said Stephanie abruptly.

"I'm sorry but it's impossible…and she's actually tied up for the afternoon. It's Friday now, so I can fit you in Monday morning at, say, eleven … if it suits, of course?"

"How very kind of you!" Stephanie slammed down the phone, and sat back and thought. There was always opposition when she took over a business, people resisting the new power structure in place. Human Resources was a pivotal department when a company went into receivership. Inevitably there was an element of people being let go and new people hired and so it was important to have Human Resources on side in her experience. There was obviously a bit of resistance from Nicola. She would wait until she met Nicola Monday in person and suss her out properly before she acted hastily.

* * *

Yvette replaced the receiver of the phone in Nicola's office.

"She slammed the phone down on me," she said. "She didn't confirm eleven would be all right."

Nicola swivelled slightly in her chair. "Oh, she'll be here all right. Eleven will be just fine for her."

Yvette smiled and walked out of the office.

Nicola sat back in her chair. Stephanie Holden would soon realise who really ran Franklyns. But it was David Stafford, not Stephanie, who was paramount in her thoughts. She had purposefully avoided any circumstances in which she could have met him, even though she was dying to see him again. She couldn't risk meeting him in a casual situation. He had to really notice her. He had basically fired everybody in the financial department. She had smoothed over his decisions, allowing the easy departure of the staff, sorting out their redundancies and making sure there was no legal comeback. She had got Yvette and her other staff to contact him or his assistants with plenty of queries to show him that Nicola was somebody to be reckoned with and that she was helping him. But she didn't pick up the phone to him herself. Much better to remain distant for now. For her to be an intriguing name for him, a name he respected. And what then? She sat back and looked at the ceiling. What did she want? An affair? How daft she was being! How could she have an affair, even if David was interested in her? The fact was she didn't know what she was doing – she was just going on a very powerful instinct. And it made her feel good.

Her phone rang.

"Yes?"

"Gordon needs to see you. It seems urgent," said Yvette.

"Send him in." Nicola sat up straight.

Gordon was obviously very upset when he came in.

"She's fired me!" He let it all out in one breath.

"I see." Nicola was surprised.

" Kept me in after that meeting and said she was letting me go."

"Did she give any reasons?"

"She just said she always gets rid of the PRs and marketing when she takes over a store."

"They fired most of the finance department yesterday," said Nicola.

"I told her you wouldn't allow it ... I mean, we've just had a baby ... this is the worst thing that could have happened!"

"I haven't met Ms Holden yet. I'm due to meet her Monday morning. Until I've spoken to her, I want you to continue with your job as normal."

Gordon managed to smile. "Thank you, Nicola."

Nicola watched him close the door behind him, then reached into the drawer, took out the day's newspaper and scanned through the feature about the Franklyns takeover. This Holden woman coming in could be awkward. She obviously wanted to make waves. Nicola knew all about her. Some woman who had fought her way up through the system, known for her straightforward talk and her – some would say flashy, Nicola would say trashy – rebranding and marketing. Nicola had a lot of friends throughout the industry and they all liked to talk. She knew the father of Stephanie's son was a mystery, she knew about her affair with Neil Blackthorn. And knowledge was definitely power.

* * *

As Stephanie walked out of Franklyns that night her mobile rang.

She glanced down and saw Paul's number had come up.

"Yes, Paul?"

"Just letting you know that Furstin didn't try to enter the building today."

She felt relief. "Good. Just make sure my orders stand, that security don't allow him access again."

"Sure. I've a few things I want to discuss with you on Monday," said Paul.

"That's fine. I'm meeting Nicola at eleven. So shall we say a breakfast meeting at ten again?"

"Sounds good to me."

"Eh, Stephanie, I've just had Gordon on to me – saying that you're letting him go."

"That's correct."

"He's a damned good Marketing Manager, Stephanie. I just think you're letting someone go without giving them a proper chance."

"Paul, I'm taking over the marketing initially. There's no room for Gordon. It's nothing personal."

"Good that it's not personal . . . because his wife has just had a baby, so I wouldn't want you to feel bad about that . . . I'll see you in the morning."

Stephanie closed over her phone. She walked to the taxi rank on one of the sidestreets near Franklyns. She tried to ignore Paul's remark. She knew he was trying to make her feel guilty. If she didn't take the tough measures she had to, then everybody would eventually be out of a job. It was called market forces.

Hopefully that was the end of Furstin and she could now concentrate on the job at hand: transforming Franklyns' fortunes. She went to the one taxi waiting at the rank and was about to get in the back when she remembered Furstin's threat of being careful about every taxi she got into. She suddenly shivered. She closed over the door and started walking instead back to her apartment. She could do with the air to help clear her head.

She would take it very easy over the weekend and try to put work out of her mind, so that she would be renewed and raring to go Monday morning.

Chapter 16

Stephanie sat outside Nicola's office and glanced at her watch for the tenth time. It was fifteen minutes past eleven. Nicola had kept her waiting fifteen minutes and her blood was beginning to boil.

"This is ridiculous! I have another meeting in fifteen minutes," Stephanie said, standing up.

"I'm sure she won't be too much longer," said Yvette.

"I know she won't – because she's going to see me right now!" Stephanie walked towards Nicola's office.

Her breakfast meeting with Paul had gone well. He had wanted to discuss sales targets with her and she liked the way he did business. He did try to put in a word to keep Gordon but she told him she had no choice. At the end of the meeting Paul had just got up to go but she had called the waitress over and asked for the bill. To Paul's blatant surprise, Stephanie had proceeded to pay for the breakfast. She wanted everyone to know that the day of freebies in Franklyns was over.

She had then been walking through the store when she was surprised to see Gordon busily organising a product launch.

She'd stopped by his side.

"Gordon, you spoke to HR about your departure?"

"I did." Gordon had looked dismissively at her.

"I obviously didn't make myself clear. I meant for you to leave your position immediately."

"Nicola told me to ignore you," Gordon had said confidently and got back to his launch.

The time had come to let Nicola know she was in charge. Stephanie opened Nicola's door and walked in.

Nicola was doing paperwork at her desk and looked up surprised.

"I'm sorry! She just marched in!" gasped Yvette, following Stephanie.

"It's fine, Yvette. You can leave us."

Yvette backed out of the office and closed the door.

"Stephanie! I've been so looking forward to having a proper chat with you." Nicola put out her hand in such a fashion that it appeared Stephanie was supposed to kiss it.

Stephanie quickly shook her hand and went to sit down.

"Won't you take a seat?" said Nicola.

Stephanie was halfway to sitting down. She paused, glanced at Nicola, and then continued to sit. Nicola sat and placed her hands together.

"Now, what can I do for you?" Nicola began. "My time is a little limited today, so you'll have to excuse me for keeping this meeting quite short."

Stephanie looked at Nicola, wondering what planet this woman was on.

Stephanie cleared her throat. "Nicola, first of all I would like to know why you didn't attend Friday's meeting as I asked for you to be there."

Nicola sat back. "But I never attend sales meetings."

"It was not a sales meeting. It was a department head

meeting and it was very crucial for you to be there."

"Why?" Nicola asked.

Stephanie laughed slightly. "Because I wanted to introduce myself to everybody and explain my plans for Franklyns."

"From what I heard you didn't actually have any plans. You hadn't decided what to do with Franklyns yet."

Spies in the camp, thought Stephanie.

"Nicola," Stephanie's voice became angry, "the fact is, I'm in charge here and so when I say I need you to be somewhere, I expect you to be there."

Nicola looked at her blankly. "Well, what was so important that you needed me there?" she questioned with a shrug.

Stephanie found herself beginning to hate the woman. "Well, I needed to talk to you about the number of personnel working in each department, the job descriptions people have, if they are performing well –"

"Well, actually, all that information is confidential. Were you expecting me to start discussing this stuff at the meeting yesterday in front of everyone?"

"No, not actually at the meeting but –"

"Well, then, it really would have been a waste of time for me to attend that meeting. I really am too busy to go to things that don't directly concern me."

"Nicola, as your boss, you do what I tell you."

"You do realise that I'm also a shareholder at Franklyns?"

"A very small one, yes. That has no influence in the play of things here."

The women sat in silence for a minute looking at each other.

Stephanie decided to move the meeting on.

"I bumped into Gordon this morning. He seems under the illusion that he is still working here."

"Well, he is still working here until we go through the proper procedures. And I wanted to talk to you about him. Since he came to work at Franklyns, I have found Gordon to be capable, courteous, directed –"

"I'm sure he is all those things. But as I explained to Gordon Friday, I take control of that department initially in any place I work as my background is in marketing –"

"Really?" Nicola interrupted and gave mocking smile. "I heard your background was in checkouts."

Stephanie glared. "I expect Gordon to be given his redundancy packages and to leave his position today."

Nicola sat forward. "You know, Stephanie, it really isn't that simple. Everything has to be done legally and above board. I have a responsibility to Franklyns that no action is taken that could end up with us being sued. The press would love it if we were brought to a tribunal court."

"I'm not asking you to do anything illegal. I want all my instructions carried out legally. In the case of the last retail group I was with, the HR department carried out all my instructions and everyone left with good redundancy packages and everyone was happy."

"Ah, yes, but the difference is that Franklyns' staff can afford lawyers. As I said, I can't do anything to jeopardise the store, or for that matter my own reputation."

"So effectively you are refusing to carry out my instructions? You're blocking me?"

Nicola sat forward. "If you forward me, in writing, any wishes you have and explain the reasons for them, I will give them consideration. If your explanations are good enough and I agree with them, then I will comply."

Stephanie threw her hands in the air and stood up.

"I'm sorry but I don't do business this way. I had really hoped that you could work with me, as your role is fairly crucial, but you're not going to be able to remain in your position with this bad attitude."

Stephanie turned and strode out.

"Oh, and, Stephanie, two security guards contacted me about you firing them."

Stephanie paused and looked back, her hand on the door handle.

"They were only acting on their then boss's orders when they were throwing you out," Nicola went on, "so I don't really think that's grounds for dismissal, do you? I've put them on duty on the front door."

"I know you have a busy day, Nicola, but I want you to take some time out to write up your own terms of dismissal." Stephanie stormed out.

"There are certain procedures," Nicola called after her, smiling broadly. "Shall I record that as a first verbal warning for me?"

She then picked up her phone and rang her father.

"Hi, Dad, it's me."

"I was going to phone you today, wanted to have lunch with you soon."

"Of course, name the day. Listen, I need a little favour, I need you to arrange something for me."

* * *

Rachel stood in her kitchen that evening, stirring the chicken dish she was preparing. She opened a tub of cream and gently oozed it into the pan and the sauce became richer. She was expecting Daniella and Leo any minute. She turned and checked the table, perfectly laid in the kitchen. She lit the candle and then opened a bottle of red wine and left it on the table to breathe. Going into the sitting-room, she lit another couple of candles on the mantelpiece and then quickly checked her appearance in the mirror.

It had been a very exciting couple of days with the store going into receivership. The whole store was buzzing with gossip, most of it contradictory, as news filtered down as to what was happening. Furstin was gone, and a new management team headed by one Stephanie Holden was in place. It was all hard to take in with such a dizzying supply of news.

Rachel went back into the kitchen and stirred the chicken dish. She wondered what would happen to Paul. She hoped he wouldn't lose his job – she kind of liked him. Having said that, from her own point of view the timing was perfect. It saved her from being whisked up to work for Furstin or at least the aftermath of having refused to work for Furstin. She had been the talk of the place for all of three hours. Everybody had been shocked at her refusal and people kept coming up to her and giving her worried looks as if she had committed some terrible crime that she would pay dearly for. And then Franklyns had gone into receivership and she was old news.

The doorbell rang. She went out to the intercom and pressed it.

"Come on up!" She pressed the buzzer. She opened her front door and watched them climb up the stairs to her.

"You found the place all right then?" she asked smiling.

"Er – I have been here before!" said Leo.

"I know, only joking." She gave Daniella a kiss on the cheek and then kissed Leo's cheek. He handed her a bottle of wine.

"That's none of your cheap shit," he said.

"I'm sure there's nothing cheap about you, Leo!" she said, closing the door after them

"Oh, I love this place!" said Daniella looking around.

As Rachel put on an Amy Winehouse CD, she said, "Yes, Leo, you played a blinder finding it for me. Dinner's actually just ready, so come on through."

They followed her into the kitchen and sat down.

Rachel noticed that Daniella was dressed as glamorously as ever. Overdressed for a quiet dinner at a friend's place. She wondered if Daniella ever relaxed her image. And then realised a wannabe WAG always had to look her best as she never knew when she'd meet the man who could give her everything she wanted.

"This smells and looks really good," complimented Leo.

"Better than what I could come up with. I can't even cook that proverbial egg," stated Daniella, "but when you've got an ass as good as mine, what need have you to cook?" She laughed.

Leo reached forward and held Daniella's hand. "Yeah, babe, but when the ass goes you might need a couple of extra talents to get through life."

"I'll be rich by then and that's all the talent I'll need," said Daniella.

Leo raised his eyes and laughed.

"I used to live around here when I was a model," commented Daniella. "I used to love it. Beats where I am now, living back with my mother while I save for a deposit to buy. She's driving me mad."

"You're half the time over in mine," accused Leo.

"Yeah, well, even you are better company than my mother!" replied Daniella and tickled him under his chin.

"I love it when she flatters me!" said Leo to Rachel, rolling his eyes.

Daniella played with her food as she studied Rachel.

"That was a lucky escape for you the other day, Rachel."

"Huh?"

"When you refused to go and work for Furstin."

"Oh, please, I don't want to hear another word about it," pleaded Rachel.

"What happened?" probed Leo.

"Furstin took a shine to our Rachel, and she said *no* to working for him, cheeky mare!"

"What's the big deal?" Rachel protested. "From what I've been hearing his offices are the last place I'd want to work!"

"Well, you were this close," Daniella put her finger and thumb close together, "to becoming a Stepford Wife, or Stepford Slut – and next thing all hell breaks loose and you get off the hook!"

"You mean when Furstin lost the store – I read about it in the papers," said Leo.

"Got it in one, babe, and our Rachel becomes the last of Furstin's worries." Daniella smiled at Rachel.

"How's it going – with the new management?" asked Leo, probing to see if his mother had started there yet.

"Nobody knows what's happening. Lots of rumours, nothing concrete, apart from the fact that Furstin is no more," said Rachel.

"Bet his wife will miss the shopping trips!" remarked Daniella. "But have you seen the new boss-woman, Stephanie Holden?"

"I saw her march by this morning, all very business-like," said Rachel.

"She's supposed to be some hotshot but I never heard of her before," said Daniella.

Leo listened, intrigued.

"Oh, I've heard of her all right. She was responsible for making Backthorns the really trendy place it became," said Rachel.

"I passed her at lunch-time," said Daniella. "Not a bad-looking bird for her age. I wonder who she's fucking to get this job – not Furstin anyway!" Daniella erupted in giggles while Leo glared at her.

"Would you say that about her if she was a man?" Rachel challenged.

"Well, it probably wouldn't be true if she was a man! I know a buyer who worked at Blackthorns. I was talking to her yesterday and she said Holden was sleeping with one of the Blackthorn brothers. Now you try and tell me the same hasn't happened at Franklyns!"

Leo started to feel a rage that he struggled to control. "Daniella, will you shut up? That's my mum you're talking about!"

"What the fuck do you mean?" Daniella put down her glass of wine unsteadily, spilling a little, as Rachel stared in amazement.

"Stephanie Holden." He picked up his glass of wine and took a drink. "She's my mother."

"Since when?" Daniella's face was in shock.

"Since I was born, you dozy cow!" Leo put his glass on the table.

"But you never said!"

"Never said what?" Leo sounded annoyed. "I told you my mother's name was Stephanie. You know my name is Holden. What was there to say? You said yourself you never heard of her before she came to work at Franklyns."

Daniella's shock was not subsiding. "But she's supposed to be really well known and respected."

"She is – despite some rumours that she's slept her way to the top!" Leo looked at Daniella accusingly.

"Sorry about that, babe, but how was I to know?" Rachel sat back and examined Leo, shocked by the revelation.

"But I always thought you grew up on some rough council estate!" said Daniella.

"I did, for a good part of my life. Mum's ambition has only paid off the past several years."

"I cannot believe this!" Daniella filled her glass to the top. "I'm going out with the boss's son!"

* * *

A couple of hours later Leo and Rachel were sitting facing each other on the two couches, while Daniella stood between them at the fireplace, having consumed a considerable amount of alcohol.

She raised her glass and drank from it.

"Rachel, you remember me in my Tia Maria advert, don't you?" she demanded.

"Sure," nodded Rachel.

"I was running down a beach in the evening sunset. You know we wrapped it up after only a couple of takes. The director said I was the best model he had ever worked with."

"Listen, I think we've had enough with your '*Whatever Happened to Baby Jane?*' routine, love," Leo advised and smiled over at Rachel.

"I'm still on the agency's books. They could be looking through their files and see me and think I'm perfect for some campaign and hey presto!" She clicked her fingers. "I'm back on TV tomorrow!"

"Hate to burst your bubbles, babes," said Leo, "but you were not running down the beach in that Tia Maria commercial. You were sitting in the background sipping a Tia Maria with about five others while the main model ran past you on the beach."

Daniella sat down beside Leo and slapped him playfully.

"Oh, put a lid on it! Maybe your mum knows somebody in the agencies – I mean, she's supposed to be a pretty powerful person in fashion."

"I doubt it, love." Leo didn't offer any false hope.

Daniella lay her head back and closed her eyes.

Leo stroked her hair. "She's conked out," he said to Rachel.

"She did have a bit to drink," said Rachel.

"She's not a bad kid," said Leo.

"I'm very fond of her," agreed Rachel.

He reached into his pocket and, opening a cigarette case, took out a joint. He put it to his mouth and took out a box of matches. He went to light the joint but, spotting the surprised look on Rachel's face, he paused.

"Do you mind if I – er –?" He pointed to the joint.

Rachel would rather he didn't but didn't want to come across as square. Besides, she was glad Daniella had passed out – with this new revelation about his parentage, she wanted to delve into Leo's life some more.

"No, go ahead," she sanctioned.

He struck the match, lit the joint and inhaled deeply. He held the smoke for a few seconds and then slowly exhaled.

"Nice way to round off a meal and a few drinks, I think," said Leo. "Some people like pudding wine, I like a spliff."

"Each to their own," said Rachel.

"You said it."

Rachel watched him for a few moments, then said, "I do think it's a bit bizarre you didn't let your girlfriend know who your mother was."

"She had never heard of her before she started working at Franklyns – you heard Daniella yourself."

"I know but . . ."

"But what?"

"You haven't been honest. You even lied to me. When we went for a drink around the corner that afternoon when you showed me the flat, you were staring off at the council flats saying your poor old mum lived there."

"No, I said she lived near – and she does – Chelsea Harbour!" he laughed.

"But your mother isn't a poor old anything – she's a high-flying, very respected businesswoman."

He drew on the spliff deeply. "Good for her."

Rachel was detecting a problem between the two and was intrigued but Leo didn't seem to be too forthcoming. She also thought it odd that he had made no reference to his father.

Leo reached forward and offered her the joint.

"I'm not really into it," she politely declined.

He looked at her and laughed. "You need to open up to new experiences, Rach – you need to live life to the full, investigate everything."

"I think I'm far too square for that."

There was a pause which gave Rachel an opening.

"And what does your father make of Stephanie's new position?" she ventured.

His eyes shot up to her. "He's not around."

"They're divorced?"

Leo studied Rachel and a warning sign went up.

Stephanie was her new boss and he knew his mum was a very private person. It suddenly dawned on him that he was exposing her.

"Why all the fucking questions?" he snapped.

"Oh, no reason, it's just –"

"You want all the juicy gossip on your new boss, is that it? Entertain the girls up at the canteen during lunch-time?"

"Of course not! I'm not like that! Why are you being so defensive?"

"What about you? Sitting there all perfect. Why don't you talk a bit about yourself for a change? I don't know anything about you and I bet Daniella doesn't either."

Rachel went red, feeling threatened by Leo's anger. "What do you want to know?"

"Who were you last with? What's your story? Who are you seeing?"

She cleared her throat. "I was in a serious relationship before I moved to London. We finished just before I moved over."

Leo sat back, took a drag from the joint and studied her, still on guard and also wanting to know more.

"Who was he?"

"His name was Simon … he was just qualified as a doctor."

"Did you go off him?"

"No." Rachel began to feel on edge.

"Did he go off you?" Now it was Leo's turn to want to know more.

"Maybe, I don't know. He wanted more than I could give."

"Like what?" He noticed the tears brimming in her eyes but didn't care.

"He wanted to marry me and I just felt I was too young. I felt I hadn't done enough to settle down and have children yet. I told him I wanted to live in London and pursue my career."

"And?"

"And he said it was stay in Dublin and marry him or go away and build my career. He had no interest in moving to London and he didn't want a long-distance relationship ... so we finished."

"And do you think you'll regret your decision?"

"Well, I'm very lonely after him, if that's what you mean. But I don't regret the decision, no. I want to experience life first before I settle down."

He sat forward and stared at her. "Well, then, you're fucking mad. You want to have it all? Have the fabulous career, then meet the wonderful man, and then have the brilliant family – it don't work like that, baby. You'll never have it all. And if you met someone that you're mad about and you decided to put your career first, then I'm telling you, baby, you are going to regret that decision one day." He continued to stare at her and then sat back. "My mother thought she could have it all. She thought she could be the big businesswoman and be a good mother at the same time. You can't. Something's got to give."

They sat in silence for a while. Rachel could almost feel his bitterness. "That's very cynical and a bit bitter."

"Cynical is cool, sweetheart. Cynical means you never get disappointed."

They were silent for a while.

"It's nearly midnight!" She said, glancing at her watch and getting up quickly. She began to clear away the empty wineglasses.

He watched her walk into the kitchen with them. He nudged Daniella awake beside him.

"Come on, darling. Time we went home."

Daniella struggled awake and stood up. Rachel went and got their coats.

"Thanks for a l-l-lovely evening. See ya tomorrow," slurred Daniella.

At the door she gave Rachel a kiss on the cheek.

Leo smiled at Rachel. "See ya around, baby."

Rachel smiled back at him but her expression was wary. "Yeah, good luck, Leo."

She closed the door after them.

She went and stacked the dishwasher, then checked her mobile.There were a few texts from her friends and one from her mother. She closed over the phone and sat back on the couch. That had been a strange turn of events. Leo being Holden's son. She thought back on his defensiveness when she had probed his background. And his attack on her for making the decision to follow her career. He had been quite cutting. She had been trying to forget about Simon since arriving in London. She hadn't been sure if she had made the right decision, and she didn't need to hear Leo express his opinion that she hadn't.

Now she felt very sad and lonely for Simon as she made her way into her bedroom and, turning off the light, got into her warm bed.

Leo seemed to be damaged for some reason, and she found damaged people hard to be around. She had thanked him for the flat now by having him over to dinner and she wanted to give him a wide berth from now on.

Chapter 17

"David Stafford on the phone for you," said Conrad Richardson's secretary.

"Put him through," said Conrad.

"Conrad?"

"David, how are things going?"

"This place is a bloody mess, Conrad. So many basic accounting practices were just ignored. Expense accounts that would put the House of Saudi to shame. This is only the tip of the iceberg. One of my men just discovered an expense account that was being paid for by the store for Furstin's wife's make-up and hair for half a million a year. Think about that – *half a million*! The Furstins used the Franklyns' private jet like everyone else uses buses. They spent, spent, spent – regardless of the fact that the company was sinking further into debt. And broke every company law while they were at it, treating company assets as if they were their own."

"Continue to keep me informed. I'm due to meet Nicola Newman in a few minutes. Have you met her yet?"

"Only on the first day."

"How did you find her?"

"It was the briefest of meetings, I couldn't really tell. But I have to say she has been nothing but absolutely helpful to us. Anything we've asked for she's done immediately. I thought we might run into trouble with getting rid of the whole finance department in one swoop – remember the legal trouble we ran into at that fund-management company? But Nicola executed it all for us without a hitch. Why are you meeting her?"

"She has requested a meeting with me. You know her father is Roger Knightly, the MP?"

"No, I didn't actually." David was surprised.

"The request came through his office. She's quite a connected lady all round from what I hear."

"She has quite a reputation here in the store as well. She's one of those people whose power goes beyond her position."

* * *

Nicola sat outside Conrad's office dressed in a smart beige business suit. The meeting with the head of Barons had been very easy to organise. A couple of calls from her father had seen to that. Stephanie Holden might be under the illusion she was now running Franklyns but she would soon realise this was not the case. Nicola had decided to go right to the top.

"Now, Mrs Newman, if you'll follow me through," said the secretary.

Nicola smiled and, taking her briefcase, got up and followed her to the double doors of Conrad's office. Nicola walked in and smiled as Conrad rose up from his desk.

"Nice to meet you, Mrs Newman," said Conrad.

"Please call me Nicola, and you're so good to meet me at such short notice." She sat down opposite him.

"My pleasure. Please tell your father I'm very grateful for the lobbying he's doing on that new finance bill."

"I will. We're a very business-friendly family. Anything we can do to help business tick along is our pleasure though it's getting tougher all the time."

"Yes," Conrad smiled, his eyes not wavering from the woman. She cut an impressive figure, the way she held herself. "David Stafford has been singing your praises since we took over Franklyns, said you were a huge help to him."

She felt herself go red at this news, feeling a little thrill at David's recognition.

"I felt all David's decisions were correct ones. I've been under the impression that the old finance department hasn't been pulling its weight for years and I advised the previous owner to take drastic action."

"I see," Conrad said, warming to her all the time. He had feared she would be hostile to the takeover when she was obviously content with it.

"Nobody obviously wants to see a situation get to the stage where a business goes into receivership but when it's inevitable there's no other option. I am slightly surprised by your choice of – what title has she given herself – Brand Director?"

"Stephanie Holden?"

"Yes, I met the girl yesterday. I know we shouldn't judge on appearances but we do – don't we? I just didn't think she was the image required for an establishment like Franklyns."

"She has the best name in retail."

"Perhaps I'm speaking out of turn but she's done nothing since she's arrived except go around like a headless chicken. Firing people on whims, threatening people. She's the type who unfortunately lacks a natural authoritative air and so people have not been listening to her. I believe two security men were actually throwing her out of the store on her first day and Paul Stewart had to intervene."

"What?"

"I believe they thought she looked like a shoplifter."

Conrad leaned forward and rested his head on his hand in confusion.

"Unlike David Stafford who has carried out his end of things with impressive ability, Stephanie has come across as just out of her depth," said Nicola.

"Nicola … I'm obviously hearing what you're saying but this doesn't sound like the Stephanie Holden I know."

Nicola shrugged and sat back. "I have a great loyalty to Franklyns, Conrad. I've been running HR there for several years. I suppose you know that somebody with my reputation could find a similar position tomorrow with no trouble if I so desired but I want to be there for Franklyns during this, its rockiest period. I can guide and assist the new management with their plans. And also warn if any procedures risk legal action against us or could damage Franklyns' reputation in any way."

"And we are very grateful for that offer."

Nicola looked at Conrad and felt she still wasn't getting through to him.

"Also, the shareholders are very concerned at the recent developments. As a shareholder I can reassure them and give them a sense of continuity. I'm telling you now, Conrad, Stephanie Holden will not inspire confidence in them and you could end up with a worse situation than you had before."

Conrad sat forward and half smiling said, "Mrs Newman, er, Nicola, what would you like me to do? Are you suggesting that I get rid of Stephanie as soon as she's in the door?"

"No, I'm offering my help. I'll keep an eye on everything for you. With me at Franklyns, I can assure you, you'll be kept informed of everything going on."

"But Stephanie and David will be doing that."

"I think it's always good to have another perspective, don't you? After all, they have been employed to sort out the mess so they are bound to give you glowing reports, whereas I'll tell you exactly what's been happening."

"Well, you can never have enough information."

Nicola picked up her briefcase, opened it and took out a contract.

"I've taken the liberty of drawing up a new contract for myself."

"A new one?" Conrad was confused.

"Yes, due to the fact I'm going to be of such assistance to you, well, I need a little reassurance in return."

"And what is in this contract?" said Conrad, his look of contentment changing to concern.

"Nothing that wasn't in my last, apart from the fact that this contract is with Barons Bank and not the previous owners of Franklyns. You can get it looked through by your own HR people – in fact, I'd advise you to."

"Stephanie should be involved in this decision," said Conrad, taking the contract and glancing through it.

"I don't speak to the monkey, only to the organ player."

Conrad looked at Nicola. He was completely impressed by her and what she was saying made a lot of sense. They did need somebody of her standing to remain at Franklyns. If she worked with them, as reiterated by David Stafford, the whole process could be considerably less painful.

* * *

It was a beautiful sunny afternoon and Oliver was outside, working by the swimming pool at the back of the house. He was seated at the garden table on the patio, his laptop open before him.

His officers had made some progress on the mugging. A shop premises leading on to the sidestreet where Nicola had been attacked had found a tape that had mistakenly been marked erased. The shopkeeper, who had previously been interviewed by Oliver's men, discovered it contained footage of the morning of Nicola's attack and contacted them. The tape gave a clear view of the sidestreet and part of the attack. Oliver had the footage copied onto his laptop and was now watching it for the tenth time. It showed Nicola following the two businessmen down the side-street. It was much clearer than the previous outside footage. You could see the expression on Nicola's face. It wasn't the look of a normal morning commuter on their way to work. Her expression looked happy, almost excited, as she looked down the street after the men. Then suddenly there was a quick glimpse of the hooded attacker as he pushed her to the ground and both of them went out of shot. It was very unfortunate that there was no view of the attacker's face.

Conrad paused the tape on a good image of Nicola's face. He stared at the take. He had never seen his wife look so animated.

As he heard a car pull into the front driveway, he quickly turned off the laptop.

"Oliver?" called Nicola as she made her way through the house.

"Out by the pool!" he answered.

She emerged from the French windows onto the patio.

"This is nice – both of us home early!" she said. She was smiling as she came up to him and kissed his cheek.

She looked across the pool and the manicured gardens to the rolling countryside beyond it.

"I came out here to work – the maid was making so much noise cleaning the house today. She's prepared dinner for us and left it in the oven. What has you home?"

"I just came from that meeting at Barons Bank I was telling you about." She turned from admiring the view and sat down at the table, reaching over to the decanter and filling a glass with water.

"How did it go?"

"Very well. I met the head man, Conrad Richardson. Dad arranged it for me. I think he'll agree to everything I want. Once I have the contract signed, it'll be business as usual for me. I'll have Stephanie Holden out of there fairly quickly."

Oliver smiled at her. "She doesn't know what she's up against."

"It might be all for the best in the end. Furstin never got in my way but he did own the store. What has Holden got compared to that?"

Oliver reached forward and took her hand. "I've got a present for you."

She smiled at him "Really? You shouldn't have bothered."

He reached into his pocket, took out a ring box and opened it.

She looked down at the wedding ring. She couldn't stop her face from falling. No, you *really* shouldn't have bothered, she thought.

"I got it from the exact same jeweller's we bought your wedding ring from all those years ago. I had photos blown up of your hand wearing the ring and I asked the jewellers to make as exact a copy as possible."

"Yes, the resemblance is remarkable," she said dourly.

"I know it can never replace the original but it's the best I can do," said Oliver and he took her finger and went to put it on.

Her mouth was set in a thin line as the ring began to slip on her finger.

"It's too tight, Oliver. It won't fit," she said and began to squirm away.

"Nonsense, it's a perfect fit." He continued to slide it on.

"It's far too tight!" She fought against it going on any further.

"It fits like a glove!"

"I said it was too tight! You're hurting me!" she almost shouted and pulled her hand away.

Stunned, he sat back. "I'm – I'm sorry. I didn't mean to hurt you. It seemed to be fitting perfectly."

"Well, it didn't!" She rubbed her finger and looked angrily at him. She didn't want the damned ring. She never asked for it. She had lost the original and that was too bad, but now she had got used to not wearing it and she didn't want to start wearing one again.

Seeing he looked upset, she began to feel bad.

"It was a lovely gesture, Oliver. But no, it will never replace the one that was stolen. But why don't you give it to me and I'll get the size adjusted properly tomorrow."

He nodded and handed her the ring.

She got up from the table and went inside.

Chapter 18

Stephanie had arranged to have dinner with Malcolm Blackthorn and his wife Donna at The Ivy. Blackthorn was a widespread chain of clothes shops that could be found on every high street throughout the country. Blackthorn was the company that had given Stephanie her first real break. Blackthorns at that time was in trouble, with their products perceived as dated and expensive. Malcolm and his brother Neil had met Stephanie at many trade fairs and, impressed by her style, had asked her to come and work for them. She became their head buyer and tore up the rule sheet. Out went all of Blackthorn's tweeds and pleats, and in came a sexy catalogue of clothes that were much better value but still carried the cachet of Blackthorn. It was a runaway success. The Blackthorns had become good friends of Stephanie, and Neil and Stephanie had become involved for a while. Stephanie hadn't had many relationships – in fact he was one of only three men she had dated since Leo was born, none of them that important to her. She and Neil had had a very enjoyable affair, while leading independent lives from each other. She never introduced him to Leo who as a teenager had been impossible to control at the time. Then the relationship had fizzled out. She suspected that if she had wanted more, Neil would have been happy to have given more. But like her, he didn't wear his heart on his sleeve and so they had just drifted apart. They spoke on the phone every so often and met up for dinner every month or so.

"Neil was asking after you," said Donna.

Donna and Malcolm were a handsome couple in their late forties. They were both very fond of Stephanie and grateful to her for saving their empire. They would have liked nothing better than if Neil had settled down with her.

"How is he?" asked Stephanie.

"Good, you know. You should call him," advised Donna.

"I will," Stephanie nodded. "Are you going to the London Fashion Awards tomorrow night?"

"We can't," said Donna. "It's our daughter's birthday so we're going out to dinner with her. I take it you're going?"

"Yeah, I've been asked to present an award."

"As usual," said Malcolm in his booming voice. "So, how's the wonderful world of Franklyns doing?"

Stephanie sighed. "Difficult so far. I've never been in an environment like it before. All the people are so set in their ways."

"Nothing you can't manage though?" Malcolm looked concerned.

"No, now that Furstin's gone."

"You met him?"

Stephanie nodded and cut into her steak. She didn't want to go into the unpleasant details of the encounter.

"He's a nasty bastard all right," said Malcolm. "But, now he's gone, you shouldn't be up against too much?" He searched her face for a reaction.

She put down her fork and looked at her friends. She felt the need to confide.

"Who am I kidding? It's been a disaster. First of all Furstin practically physically attacked me in his office and had me flung out. Then nobody seems to be acknowledging that I'm the boss. There's a PR Manager who's still going around organising events in the store regardless of the fact that I fired him a few days ago. Nobody is taking me seriously. I have to issue orders through Paul Stewart all the time. If he stopped co-operating with me as the HR Director has I don't know where I'd be."

"The HR Director?" said Malcolm. "You mean Nicola Newman?"

"Yes. She refuses to co-operate with me. Was downright insulting and a bitch." Stephanie rubbed her temples.

"And have you told the Bank about this?" asked Donna.

"No. How can I? They've put an in-control superwoman in charge of the store to turn it around. How can I say I can't manage it? I might as well hand in my notice, and my reputation would be destroyed."

Malcolm reached out and gripped her arm. "I know what Newman is like. You need to get her out of there. You'll have no authority until you get rid of her. She's your problem. She's working against you."

Stephanie looked up, grateful for someone to be thinking with clarity for her. "I've already threatened her with the sack, even told her to draw up the terms of her dismissal."

"No, you need to actually sack her, Stephanie. Get her out of the store altogether. "

"You're saying I should just go in there and fire her tomorrow?"

"Absolutely. You've no choice," said Malcolm.

"And what if she starts bringing legal action or something?"

"Stephanie, think straight. The company has gone into receivership. It's just a redundancy due to change of business operation. There's not a thing she can do."

Stephanie nodded and smiled.

Chapter 19

"Listen, thanks for dinner the other night, I really enjoyed it," Daniella said to Rachel. They were standing at the cosmetics counter. It had been a busy morning but there was a lull in the past half hour.

"My pleasure. As I said, just a thank-you to the two of you for being so good."

"I'm still in shock over Leo's being Stephanie Holden's son. Can you believe it? I haven't seen him since and I tried speaking to him on the phone about it last night but he didn't have anything to say about her."

"Like what? What did you expect him to say?" Rachel was perplexed and then realised she was as guilty a Daniella for trying to use Leo to get information.

"I don't know. I mean here could be my break under my nose. I mean she could help me move up the ladder. I'm riding her son, you know! I suggested to Leo that he should introduce me to her and we should go out for a meal together but he started grunting something about being too busy."

Rachel studied Daniella. She seemed so wrapped up in herself that she would be blind to any signals Leo was giving out.

"Daniella, have you ever talked to Leo about his family before finding out who his mother was?"

"Not really – it never came up in conversation."

"I think Leo is dealing with some issues from the past and I think his mother is central to it."

"What makes you say that, Ms Freud?"

"Just a feeling I get. Just go a bit easy on him about Stephanie, okay?"

"Look, there she is!" squealed Daniella as she saw Stephanie walk down the stairs with Paul. "You know what? I'm going to go over and introduce myself!"

"As what exactly?" Rachel demanded.

"As her son's girlfriend, what else?"

"You can't just go over there and say that, Daniella!"

"Oh, no? Just watch me!" Daniella shook off Rachel's restraining hand and marched across the floor.

* * *

Stephanie had felt very confident coming into Franklyns that morning. Having dinner with the Blackthorns the previous night had done her a world of good and they had given her sound advice. She had rung Yvette, Nicola Newman's secretary, that morning and told her she would be up to the office at twelve whether Nicola was free or not.

Stephanie was walking through the ground floor with Paul, discussing sales figures, when Daniella approached them boldly and walked straight up to Stephanie.

"Stephanie?" said the girl.

"Yes?" Stephanie looked at the salesgirl, slightly annoyed at being interrupted.

"Hi, my names's Daniella – Leo's partner."

Stephanie stared at Daniella. "Leo?"

"Yes, I didn't realise you were coming to work here until the other day, otherwise I'd have said hello before." Daniella beamed a big smile.

Stephanie glanced at Paul who looked very confused. "Eh, sorry, excuse me a minute, please, Paul?"

"Eh, sure!" Paul sidled off and went over to Rachel's counter.

"He hasn't mentioned me?" Daniella eyes widened in astonishment.

Stephanie's voice softened "I haven't really had a good chat with him for a while. How is he?"

"Just great. You know Leo, always happy!"

"And you work here?"

"Yes, over there at the Chanel counter."

Stephanie didn't know whether to feel delighted to touch base with somebody in Leo's life or very threatened that the connection was through work.

"Maybe you could ask him to give me a call for a proper chat soon?" she said.

"I'm going to make sure he does!" said Daniella.

* * *

"How're sales on that new product?" Paul asked Rachel.

"Really well, up twenty per cent on last week."

"Using your usual pushy sales technique," he smiled at her.

She thought he looked incredibly tired and worried. She could imagine the pressure he must be under with the new management.

Both of them were staring at Daniella and Stephanie.

"Who's Leo?" asked Paul.

Rachel decided to be diplomatic. "Er, I don't know."

They stood in silence for a little while.

"How's everything?" observed Rachel.

"I've had a lot on my plate," said Paul.

"I can understand that. Look, I know I'm talking out of turn here. But no matter what happens or how bad this Stephanie Holden or the bank is, they can't be any worse than Furstin, can they? He gave me the creeps when I first saw him and I don't know how you worked so closely with him. Just think, that's over now. I know I'd be delighted if I was you."

"Yes, Rachel, you are talking out of turn." Paul looked pointedly at her and raised an eyebrow.

Rachel was embarrassed and felt herself go red.

As Daniella made her way back to them, smiling happily, Paul walked quickly away.

* * *

As Stephanie made her way to her meeting with Nicola Newman, her mind was distracted by the meeting with the salesgirl, Daniella. Leo never discussed his personal life with her and so Daniella just coming up and introducing herself like that had come as a bit of a shock. She seemed like a pleasant enough girl, very glamorous. A bit forthright coming up to her as she had. But in a way she admired her honesty. There was no point in their working in the same building and her not knowing. Funnily, she did feel a little exposed from it and prayed that the girl wasn't gabby or indiscreet.

The lift door opened and Stephanie walked over to Yvette.

Firing somebody of Nicola's stature was a little

daunting. But Malcolm Blackthorn had been correct: it was the only option. She had a busy day and wanted to leave early so she could prepare herself properly for the awards ceremony that night and she was in no mood to hang around in Nicola's reception until she deemed herself ready to meet her.

"I'm here for my appointment with Nicola," Stephanie said in a no-nonsense manner.

Yvette looked up and smiled. "She's waiting for you – you can go straight on in."

Stephanie nodded, walked to the door and without knocking walked in.

Nicola was standing there, smiling.

Both women sat down.

"And what can I do for you?" Nicola asked, putting her hands together in temple form on her desk.

"There's no easy way for me to say this, Nicola, and it isn't my style to beat about the bush, so I'll just come out with it. After our previous meeting it is very obvious that you're not willing to co-operate with me. And I simply can't have a department head working against me and undermining me. I told you at our first meeting that your position was no longer tenable. Today I'm confirming that you've been made redundant."

Nicola sat back and nodded. "I see."

Stephanie hadn't expected Nicola to be the type of woman who would become hysterical but she had expected *some* reaction.

"I would prefer if you vacated your position today. We'll obviously be giving you a very generous package as a reflection of the dedication you have shown Franklyns over the years."

"Very kind of you, I'm sure." Nicola sat back and her

face creased in discomfort. "Stephanie, I feel that you coming here today and saying what you just have is just another reflection of the chaos that has ensued since you arrived here and how you just don't seem to be on top of the job ... of what's going on."

"That's really none of your concern any more."

"But, you see, it is," said Nicola, reaching into her drawer and taking out a document. "I've just signed a three-year contract directly with Barons Bank to continue my position here as HR Director at Franklyns."

Stephanie looked at the contract as it was put down in front of her, not believing what she was being told.

"And who authorised that contract?" she asked harshly.

"Conrad Richardson – and I believe David Stafford seconded it. They were very frightened of losing me to a rival firm and so got in quickly. Must say, I'm a bit surprised they didn't tell you though."

Stephanie picked up the contract and flicked through it.

"You'll find it's quite in order. I drew it up myself. After your outburst, I do think this puts our relationship on a very negative footing. I really did want to work with you, Stephanie, and help you all I could. I even broke the news to Gordon this morning that he had to go. But after you've put your cards on the table, I am going to find it very – very – difficult to work harmoniously with you."

An anger swelled from deep inside Stephanie and she chucked the contract back down on the desk. She stood up abruptly and, frightened of what she might say, stormed to the door.

"And, Stephanie, do give me plenty of notice next time you have a departmental meeting. I think I should like to attend it after all. I think I could have quite a lot of things to say."

Stephanie slammed the door after her.

She shook with fury as she marched through the fourth floor. She could hardly punch in the Barons Bank number she was so angry.

"It's Stephanie Holden here. Put me through to Conrad Richardson urgently," she told Barons Bank reception.

"I'm sorry, Ms Holden, Mr Richardson is out of the office today."

"Will you please leave him a message to contact me very urgently." She closed over her mobile and angrily snapped, "Bastards!"

She made her way into the finance department. All Barons Bank staff were at the desks poring over files and computer data.

She went to David's office and without knocking barged in.

David looked up from his paperwork, startled.

"Nicola Newman has just told me she's signed a new contract with Barons Bank to remain in her position."

David nodded. "I believe that's correct, yes," he answered her coolly.

"And did nobody think to talk to *me* about it first?"

"I presumed Conrad had. He asked my opinion and I had no objection."

"The bastard! I should have been consulted over such a major decision."

"What's the problem anyway? She's the best you can get in HR. She's a great asset to us in trying sort out this place. I'm about to schedule a meeting with her to ask about this long list of people on the company's payroll who don't seem to have a job title –"

"She's a bloody bitch who I cannot work with! She has tried to obstruct me every step of the way in any dealings I've had with her."

"Nicola Newman?" David looked cynically at her. "Nothing has been too much trouble for her as far as I'm concerned."

Stephanie realised she was handling this wrongly. She could see the look of surprise on David's face. Surprise was about as animated as David could get, she suspected, with his cool in-control manner and groomed good looks. She knew he would be straight back to Conrad telling him she had come in like a madwoman and she knew that she was probably damaging herself. But she didn't care. How dare they go behind her back like that? She started pacing up and down the office.

"She's a nasty bitch and from what I can see since I've arrived at Franklyns, she represents everything that's wrong with this place. The problems start at the very top and work their way down. I've seen the salaries that these managers and directors have been paid. It's unbelievable! They've been looking on this place as a slush fund rather than a business!" She gave a laugh.

David coughed slightly. "Stephanie, you seem a little overexcited. Why don't you calm down?"

"You said Newman has a reputation for being the best in the business? I've met all the department heads and I've never heard of such strange personnel decisions. She promoted a store detective to being the head of security, even though he had no management training or experience. Her last secretary obviously did something right, because she went from secretarial duties to being head buyer with one wave of Nicola's magic wand. Again no experience required! Nepotism is alive and well in this joint and that's what has it the way it is!"

"There's nothing wrong with allowing people the opportunities to better themselves," remarked David. "In fact, if I'm not mistaken, you built your own career from nothing."

She felt annoyed that her background was again being pointed out to her. "Of course, there's nothing wrong with it. But people have to earn their stars. I worked bloody hard to get to where I am and I gradually climbed up the ladder. Anything else is just bad business, David. And I'm telling you, Newman is bad business for this store."

"Well, you should have been more vocal in your thoughts before a new contract was signed with her. There's very little that can be done now."

"I didn't make myself vocal because I thought I didn't have to! I'm in charge here and my decisions are what goes. I was going to give Nicola Newman the push today, only to be told I'm now stuck with her. You've undermined my position here and I'm really pissed off about this, David."

She turned and stormed out.

Chapter 20

Leo pulled his car up next to a bank link and, leaving the engine running, hopped out. Taking his wallet from his pocket he inserted his card into the machine. He punched in his pin number and checked his balance.

"Shit!" he muttered, seeing that there was only £100 left in the account. He pressed a button and withdrew it. He then took out another card and inserted it. Punching in another pin he waited, chose an amount and waited for the cash to come out. A notice saying 'Insufficient Funds' came up on the screen. He swore quietly to himself, cancelled the request and took back the card. He then jumped into his car and took off. His mobile rang. The number that came up was a contact of his called Tommy. Tommy was a great mate who was in with everybody from drug lords to detectives and always knew what was going on.

"Yo, Tommy, how you keeping? Haven't heard from you in a while!"

"I'm cool, man. Just thought I'd better give you a call to tip you off."

"About what?"

"That fake Spanish property scam you were pulling

has left a bad taste in a lot of mouths. It was too big a scam for you. There's a lot of angry investors who have lost their money and are baying for blood. The police are doing everything to track down the person behind it . . . i.e. you!"

Leo felt very uncomfortable. For Tommy to be calling him, it must be serious.

"There's no way they can track me down. I covered all bases. Closed down the office, the phone lines, the bank account. They don't know my name or anything about me."

"True, but they are doing everything they can to trace you and they will throw the book at you if they nab you. You need to lie low for a while. Don't get involved in anything dodgy, and I mean *anything*. You need to keep your nose very clean. Maybe go abroad for a while until this dies down."

Leo was silent on the other side of the phone.

"Leo?"

"Yeah, I'm still here. Listen, thanks, mate, for the tip-off. I've taken it on board."

Leo pulled up outside his house, his mind racing, and let himself in. He picked up the post from the floor and started opening it. It was credit-card bill after credit-card bill. And they were all maxed out.

He went into the kitchen and threw the bills on top of a pile of other bills. He took a beer from the fridge and, opening it, went back into the living-room. His outgoings had been much more than his income. He had expensive tastes, an expensive car, an expensive girlfriend. He had no money left. He could quickly pull a few scams to bring some cash in but now with Tommy's news he would have to lie very low. He reached into his pocket and pulled out the diamond necklace he had bought from Joseph and flung it on the coffee table. He had arranged to meet Joseph in the Chamber the previous night and had handed him the fifteen thousand in exchange for the necklace. He knew it was a good buy and the necklace was worth much more, but he should have checked his cash flow before he handed over the money. He actually couldn't afford to buy the necklace and should have held on to the fifteen grand. And now he couldn't risk selling the necklace after Tommy's advice to lie low. He took a drink from his beer, sat back in the couch and rubbed his eyes, wondering what the hell he would do.

* * *

Stephanie was consumed with anger after her meeting with Nicola as she prepared herself for the awards ceremony that night. What the hell had Conrad been playing at? David had seemed innocent enough but she was sure Conrad would have known he was breaking all business etiquette employing Nicola like that. She had dropped into the hairdresser and beautician on her way home and now, as she put on her Roberto Cavalli gown, she tried to put the problem to the back of her mind so she could enjoy the ceremony in The Savoy. She checked her appearance in the mirror and was happy with what she saw. Her long sleek black hair had been piled up on her head and her slinky beige dress stretched down to the ground. She poured herself a glass of wine and waited for the car organised by the Awards Committee to arrive.

* * *

Leo lay on his couch deep in thought. Everything was

flashing through his mind. From the weekend in Paris Daniella wanted them to go away on next month to the next rent due soon. For the millionth time he wished he was still working in the city.

What had he ahead of him now? No money to pay the rent.

He suddenly sat up as he thought of his mother's offer of a career at Franklyns. Due to the fact he could no longer do any scams till the coast was clear it would be a way of earning money. And, as she had pointed out to him, a way to get a proper career going again. Maybe even something that might lead back to the city. He would also be near Daniella and even have an opportunity to get to know Rachel a little better. The downside was he would be working for his mother and all that entailed. But it looked as if it was the only game playing in town.

* * *

The car arrived on time for Stephanie and, as it drove her through the London evening streets, she was excited about the night. These gatherings were a great opportunity to meet friends from the industry, have a few drinks and a laugh. Also it was her first official night out since taking over the reins at Franklyns. Really it should be her moment of glory, her crowning as one of the most important people in retail. Everyone there tonight would be aware of that. A pity everyone working at Franklyns wasn't aware of it as well, she thought wryly.

The car pulled up outside The Savoy and the back door was opened for her by one of the many security men outside the hotel. A red carpet led to the entrance and on either side were gathered the press and the public anxiously gathered to spot a model or star. Stephanie made her way inside and was greeted by a PR who kissed both her cheeks and presented her with a glass of champagne. Stephanie mingled effortlessly amongst the crowd, as people approached congratulating her on her new post and wishing her luck. She was bumping into lots of acquaintances and her diary quickly began to fill up for lunch and dinner appointments for the next few weeks. Designers carefully went out of their way to have private chats with her, all trying to leave a good impression. *This* was why she worked as hard as she did, she reminded herself. She loved the recognition, the power and the respect.

As she chatted away to an Italian designer, she became aware of a disturbance at the entrance of the lobby. She glanced over to see what the commotion was. And she was shocked to see Elka Furstin arrive into the lobby. She was surrounded by four personal security men and was with a woman friend. Members of the press were vying for her attention as she quickly strode through the lobby dressed all in white and looking a knockout. Her security made sure nobody got near. The Furstins had not been seen since they were ousted from Franklyns and this unexpected appearance was causing much excitement as the press had continued to speculate where they were and as revelations emerged about their extravagant lifestyle.

Stephanie watched as Elka glided quickly through the lobby, making a beeline for the function room where the awards ceremony was to be held.

There was something familiar about the female companion who strolled behind her. Something disturbingly familiar. As Stephanie continued to look she realised with a fright she was Hetty Barrington – now Hetty McKay – the wife of Stephanie's old lover Danny

McKay. The woman he had dumped Stephanie to marry.

Stephanie supposed she shouldn't be too surprised by a friendship between Hetty and Elka as they mixed in the same small circle but, as she made her way into the function room, she felt unnerved by their presence. The press had rumoured that the Furstins had gone to South Africa. And after Stephanie's encounter with Furstin and his threats, she had hoped it was true.

As the PR showed her to her seat in the front row at the side of the stage ramp, she realised she was seated right across from Elka and Hetty on the other side of the ramp. The two women noticed her immediately and Elka started whispering into Hetty's ear while the two stared over.

Two chief executives of retail empires sat on either side of Stephanie and were chatting amiably to her. But she found it hard to concentrate on what they were saying, she was so aware of the two women opposite staring and whispering.

She had met Hetty when she had been Danny's girlfriend all those years ago. She had imagined that neither Danny nor Hetty would even have remembered her. But as Hetty continued to glare at her and give her dagger looks, it was clear that she remembered her all too well. She felt intimidated by the two women. One whose husband she had gone out with and the other from whose husband she had taken his business away.

* * *

The night was in full swing. Awards were being given out with many standing ovations, interspersed with models displaying fashion as they stalked up and down the catwalk ramp.

The time came for Stephanie to announce the award she was giving and she was quickly beckoned by a PR to follow her backstage. She stood nervously behind the curtains as the presenter announced: "Ladies and gentlemen, here to present the award for Best British Designer is a woman known to you all as simply the most powerful woman in British retail – Stephanie Holden!"

Smiling, Stephanie strode confidently onto the stage and up to the stand where she adjusted the microphone.

"Ladies and gentlemen, I thank the organisers for the opportunity to present this award tonight. I feel tremendously honoured to present an award which recognises, celebrates and encourages the best of our native talent and . . ." Stephanie glanced around the function room as she spoke and when her eyes fell on Elka and Hetty, her words dried up. Elka was smirking up at her. Then she leaned over to Hetty and started whispering into her ear. Hetty put a hand to her mouth as if to stifle a giggle but then laughed out loud.

Stephanie started to shake slightly and decided to cut to the chase and announce the winner. She opened the envelope and said: "And I'm very happy to announce the winner as Jayne Kilroy!"

Applause erupted around the room and, as the designer came on the stage Stephanie gave her the award, kissed her cheek and quickly walked off backstage.

"Are you all right?" asked the PR. "You looked a bit on edge out there."

"No, I'm fine thanks. Actually – I do feel a bit funny – would you mind ordering my car. I think I'll call it a night."

* * *

The car left Stephanie off at Chelsea Harbour and she wearily entered the building.

As she walked down the corridor to her apartment, she searched in her bag for her key, her thoughts troubled.

So, she had gone running off, unable to face Elka and Hetty. She really needed to sort herself out. She could usually stand up to anyone. But since she had started in Franklyns, starting with Furstins's attack on her, her confidence had been knocked and, like a house of cards, it kept crumbling down. Now she couldn't even hold her own against the spendaholic former owner's wife and the wife of a boyfriend from twenty-odd years back. Although, if the truth be known, she had never been able to hold her own against Hetty. Every time she saw her photo she had scrutinised it, wondering what she could offer the love of her life that she didn't have. They had certainly tried to intimidate her tonight – but worse of all they had succeeded.

Letting herself into the apartment, she locked the door behind her and walked through the hall and into the lounge.

There was a figure sitting in the armchair and she screamed.

"It's all right, Mum. It's only me!" said Leo, leaping out of the seat.

"Leo, what the hell are you doing here?" she cried as her hand jumped to her chest to settle her heart that had skipped a beat.

"I wanted a chat. You weren't answering the intercom and so I let myself in with my key."

"You scared the shit out of me! Don't ever do that to me again!"

"You're always saying drop by!"

"I know! But you never do! How was I to know you'd be sitting here in the near dark?"

She sat down on the couch..

"Maybe I shouldn't have bothered coming over!" he sulked.

"I'm sorry – I'm just under a bit of pressure at the moment and you really gave me a fright."

She got up again, went to him and kissed his cheek.

He looked her up and down. "Somewhere nice tonight?"

"Just at an awards ceremony."

"You're always out somewhere posh."

"I go out somewhere nice a couple of nights a week. The rest of the week, I'm on my own here either recovering from a hard day's work or even worse still working – taking calls and doing reports."

"You don't have to explain yourself, Mum. I'm not judging you for going out. Fair play to you. You should get out and enjoy life a bit. You worked long hours long enough."

Stephanie looked sharply at him. "Leo, I take it that's your usual sarcasm."

"No, I –"

"Look, I'm just really not in the mood for one of your judgemental conversations. I'm under a lot of pressure."

"Aren't you always?"

"Do you want something to eat?"

"No. There's no point in messing around. I want to know – were you serious about offering me a job at Franklyns?"

Stephanie looked at him, very surprised. Maybe his girlfriend Daniella had made some headway where she never could. She thought better than to mention Daniella to him, in case she scared him off.

"Yes – yes, of course I was serious. I would love to see you settle into a good career."

"Well, I have been giving the offer a good bit of thought ... and maybe I want to give it a try. Would that be okay?"

Stephanie smiled at her son but her mind was screaming that this was the worst thing that could happen to her at Franklyns. She was barely in control of the situation and it was the riskiest job she had ever had. The idea of her wayward son coming to work there could only jeopardise her more.

"Of course, it would be all right. I'd love you to come and work with me," she said.

He looked at her nervously. "That's cool then." He stood up quickly. "I'd better head. I'm supposed to be somewhere."

She stood up too and walked him to the door. He seemed in such a hurry to get away.

As he opened the door, she reached forward and kissed his cheek.

"Right then, I'll give you a call," he said. And he rushed off down the corridor.

Chapter 21

Nicola sat at her desk looking at the photo of Stephanie taken at the awards ceremony the previous night. Then she flung the newspaper in the wastepaper basket and sat back to think about David Stafford.

She had decided that her next move should be to do nothing. She needed to sit back and wait for an opportunity to present itself where he would need to speak to her. Her whole days were taken up with the anticipation of the call. She had to let him come to her. She had become nervous to even venture out around the store in case she bumped into him and her first conversation with him would be reduced to a casual few words and she wouldn't be able to make the impression she wanted to.

She glanced at her watch: it was nearly three. She sighed, realising the call wouldn't come through that day. She closed her eyes as she realised how daft she was. She knew nothing about the man. What if he was married? Had a live-in partner? Had several children? It was as if all the above were unimportant to her in this obsession she had developed. She sighed again as she realised they were as unimportant as Oliver was in her feelings for David Stafford.

Her phone rang.

"Yes, Yvette?" she snapped.

"Nicola, I've just had David Stafford on – wanting a meeting with you. He asked would eleven tomorrow morning be suitable?"

Nicola was overcome with excitement as she contemplated the news.

"Nicola?" pressed Yvette as no reply was forthcoming.

"Eh, yes, eleven is fine."

"His office or yours?"

"Eh … mine, of course."

Nicola hung up the phone and rubbed her mouth, feeling nervous but excited.

* * *

Paul was walking through the fourth-floor corridors on his way to Gordon's office. The door was opened and he walked in to find Gordon packing files into boxes.

"So, it's official then. You're definitely leaving?" asked Paul.

"Sure is," sighed Gordon, barely looking up as he continued packing. "I'm been thrown out on my arse."

"I thought there might be a possibility you could stay on."

"Nicola Newman tried a last-ditch effort to have me kept on but even she failed. Goes to show you how much control Holden has, when even Nicola is sidestepped."

Paul nodded. He felt cynical about Nicola's attempted intervention. He knew Nicola very well. Although she could often be perceived to be helpful to people as she catapulted careers high without substance or reason, she was often just on a power trip. He felt she often saw people in the way a chess player saw pawns. Considering how she had got rid of the whole finance department without a backward glance, he suspected there was something else behind her trying to help Gordon.

"You'll be inundated with offers – you won't be out of work for long," he encouraged.

"Yeah, but will they offer the salary I'm on here? Despite all Furstin's many horrendous faults, he bloody paid fantastically."

"That's why we all stayed, mate," said Paul.

"It's just the timing with the new baby and everything. You know, we're up all night with her – this is the last thing we needed. And Joanne's worried sick ..."

Paul nodded, completely understanding. He felt the uncertainty of his own position couldn't come at a worst time with his and Anna's situation.

He put out his hand. "If you need anything – references, whatever – just give me a call."

Gordon shook his hand. "Stay in touch." He grabbed the box he had filled and his briefcase and headed off.

Paul's mobile rang and he saw Anna's number come up.

"Hi, love, what's up?" he said.

"Everything's fine. I'm just phoning to remind you we have the doctor's appointment tomorrow."

Damn, he had completely forgotten! He had a couple of meetings he would hastily have to reschedule.

"That's fine," he said.

"Okay, listen, don't be late tonight, all right?"

There was an edginess in her voice. She had been slightly unsettled since they agreed to go down the medical route to try and have children. He knew it was only the beginning.

He reassured her that he would be leaving soon and closed over his phone. He made his way to the lift and went down to the next floor.

As he walked through the busy shop floor to his office, he heard his name being called. He turned around to see Stephanie Holden.

"Paul, I left a couple of messages on your mobile," she said.

"I haven't had chance to check my messages yet, sorry."

"Paul, I want to call a department head meeting tomorrow at two, if you could organise it for me."

"Tomorrow?"

"Yes, in the boardroom."

"It's a little short notice," he ventured.

She looked at him coolly. He seemed to give a little dig whenever he got the opportunity. Same when he said about Gordon just having a baby when she got rid of him. She imagined he would never have spoken to Furstin in the same manner.

"It's a Board meeting of department heads who all work in the same building, hardly a dinner party where everyone needs to check their social diary weeks in advance," she snapped sarcastically.

"It's just that tomorrow is my day off."

"Well, can't you reschedule it?"

"No, I've something important on."

"Do you know something, Paul, I'm getting a little sick of everyone working against me in this fucking place! No wonder it's gone into receivership as everyone seems to put everything ahead of what the place is actually about – making a profit. I'm very sorry to inconvenience you but the meeting is scheduled for tomorrow at two and I expect to see you there. And when I say in the boardroom, I mean

Furstin's old boardroom on the sixth floor. That's where I'll be holding meetings from now on."

As much as she disliked the whole ambiance of the sixth floor and its unpleasant connotations since she was treated so ignominiously there, she felt it was important that she reverted to her first intention and took over Furstin's office. It was psychologically important to be working from the old boss's throne. It would immediately give out the signal she was the undisputed new boss. And she desperately needed to start giving out that signal. And that's why she must overcome her repugnance for Furstin and hold all her meetings in his boardroom.

Stephanie turned her back abruptly on Paul and walked away. Did nobody realise that she was trying to save a business here? That nobody was going to get paid anything if they kept going the way they were because there would be no business to pay them. They were all too interested in maintaining the status quo, to keep their salaries, their perks, their power. This business had to be transformed into a sleek lean operation, where there was no room for nepotism, no favoured people in unnecessary jobs. She thought wryly of the idea of Leo coming to work here.

She looked at her watch. It was now nearly four. She might as well go up there now.

She went to the lift. She remembered the hushed atmosphere up there the day she first arrived and the receptionist and PA looking at her haughtily. She had nearly asked Paul to accompany her today but again felt she couldn't show weakness. She mentally prepared herself for meeting Furstin's old staff. Surely even they would have heard of her by now and not give her any trouble? She was in no mood for them. And if even one of them gave her trouble she would erupt in temper.

The lift door opened and she marched out into the reception area. She was surprised to see nobody there. She glanced around the opulent interior. Slowly she walked down the corridor that had led to Furstin's office. Some of the office doors were open and she could see the offices were empty. As she continued walking down, she opened other doors, only to find that all the plush offices were empty. She walked into one and, opening a filing cabinet, saw it was empty. She got an eerie feeling and forced herself to continue down to the huge area where Furstin's PA had been. Again, her desk was empty.

She moved towards Furstin's door and, pushing it open, entered. Remembering her encounter with Furstin there made her skin crawl and she fought a desire to run away. She walked around the huge office and opened a door leading off it. She was surprised as she entered a gigantic marble bathroom with a sunken bath.

"What the fuck is this place?" she asked loudly. There was an echo around the room.

She approached his desk and sat behind it. She felt very small in the grand surroundings. Where had all the people gone? All the staff seemed to have disappeared.

* * *

Anna was very on edge that night when Paul arrived back from work.

"You know I haven't been able to concentrate on this feature that the editor gave me all week," she said. "I've just told him I need another few days. He was a bit taken aback as it's the only deadline I've ever missed. Hopefully I'll be able to concentrate better once we've tomorrow over and done with."

"Uh huh," he nodded. "What time is the appointment again?"

She gave a small laugh. "Do you ever listen, Paul? I've told you before – two o'clock."

"I guess there's no way they can see us a bit later?"

Her face showed annoyance. "What are you talking about? The appointment is for two, end of story."

"It's just that Stephanie Holden has called for a meeting tomorrow at two, said I had to be there."

"Oh, for fuck's sake, Paul!" Anna raised her voice. "We can't cancel this appointment! We're *not* going to cancel this appointment. I'm completely hyper about it. I can't stand putting it off any longer. I'm all psyched up for it." She started pacing the floor.

Seeing she was getting upset, he went to her and said, "Of course, we won't miss the appointment."

"Good!"

She went to put the kettle on as Paul sat down at the kitchen table and opened up the newspaper.

"Have you seen much of that friend of yours from school, the accountant?" she asked.

"He was hardly a friend – we just used to be in the same class. I guess we hung around together a bit but there were always lots of other people there."

"Shall I take that long-winded answer as a no?" she queried.

"No, I haven't seen him. He's up in his lofty office saving the company, no doubt."

It had actually very much unnerved Paul that David had come to work there. He felt very exposed having him there and certainly hadn't gone out of his way to meet him. He wasn't Paul Stewart, GM of Franklyns, to David – he was Paul Stewart, average at academia, average at sports, average at friends and below average with the opposite sex.

"I'm detecting hostility from you towards him," Anna said, sitting down at the table next to him.

Paul sighed, folded over the paper and put it away from him "No hostility towards him. He was always very pleasant to me in actual fact."

"So what's the problem then?"

"Are you bloody blind? He's effectively over me."

"But he's not lording it over you, is he?"

No, Stephanie Holden is, though, he thought. "Course not, David Stafford was never the type to lord it anyway – he's much too confident in himself to have to lord it over anyone. It's just, well, you know, he's seen my salary, he knows how much tax I pay. He's looked through my files, he had to, it's his job – but I feel weird about it."

"Hmmm, I think I understand." She gave his hand a comforting squeeze. "But don't worry. It'll all be fine."

* * *

Nicola spent the evening looking through her wardrobe excitedly, trying on different outfits and studying herself in the mirror. She wouldn't wear one of her usual business suits to meet David. She needed to wear something a bit different. She settled on a very light brown sixties-style suit. The skirt came to just above the knees, the jacket was a good cut and reached just to her waist, while she wore a plain satin cream blouse underneath.

"You seem in very good form," commented Oliver, coming into the bedroom and watching her look at herself in the mirror.

She turned and smiled at him. "What's not to be happy about?"

Chapter 22

Nicola held her breath as Yvette opened her office door and held it open for David to walk in. Nicola stood as David entered and approached her.

She had wondered so much if he would have the same effect on her when they were alone and close. The effect was even more powerful.

"Thanks for meeting me, Nicola," said David as he stretched out his hand.

She smiled back confidently at him and shook his hand. Her hand seemed to melt into his.

She watched him sit down and then did the same.

He looked at her, quickly sizing her up, and then smiled.

"First of all, thanks for all the help you've given me with the finance department. It can be very messy stuff getting rid of people at short notice like that."

"I'm glad I was of some help. Actually, I've thought the finance department here has been a mess for years. I'm glad it's been sorted out at last."

He smiled crookedly and looked down at the paperwork in his hands. She took the opportunity to quickly check his fingers and was thrilled to see no wedding ring there.

"There are a lot of things in this place that are a mess." He looked up at her and smiled "I was hoping you might help me get to the bottom of a few things?"

His smile caught her off guard and she forced herself not to blush.

"Anything I can help you with, just ask."

It was the fact that he had never before met Nicola Newman that prevented David from realising how differently she was acting towards him compared to her normal brisk aloof manner.

He placed the paperwork on the desk.

"This is a list of personnel being paid salaries by Franklyns. The ones I have ticked I can account for by their job descriptions – the ones un-ticked, I have no idea what they are employed as. I wonder if you could shed some light?"

She took the paperwork and glanced through the pages and pages of names.

"I'll go through this list in more depth and check against our personnel files. But a lot of these names would have been on Karl Furstin's personal staff."

"And what did he need this army of staff for? What did they actually do?" David enquired, a bewildered and bemused look on his face.

Nicola could tell from his manner that he was a man everything came easy to. She shrugged. "One of life's mysteries, I'm afraid. To be honest, I had very little to do with his staff. Paul Stewart might be a little more informed."

"There has been a development with his staff. This week's salaries paid to all of Furstin's staff bounced back.

The normal payments were not accepted by any of their accounts."

Nicola was surprised. "I'm sorry, I don't undertstand."

"Well, all their accounts must have closed or changed or something because none of their payments were accepted. They stayed in the Franklyns account. Also, Stephanie Holden informed me today that the entire sixth floor is empty. All his personal staff have left Franklyns by the looks of things."

Nicola sat back and frowned. "How very odd!"

She took up the file and started looking through it again. She felt he was studying her intently and that, combined with her own feelings, made the atmosphere tense.

"These names here at the back – I've never even heard of these people," she said. "As far as I'm aware they do not even work in the store. But I'll check it all out for you."

"Thank you, Nicola. I really don't know what was going on but I would really like to straighten it all out. There's one salary payment that I'm particularly perplexed about. A monthly salary paid to a family living in Latvia. What's that all about? Why would a family in Latvia be paid a salary from Franklyns? What work can they possibly be doing?"

Nicola placed the file down and looked at his confused face. She wanted to help him.

She sat forward and her voice became so gentle that nobody else would have recognised her.

"David … Karl Furstin and his wife were very … individualistic people. I didn't have much to do with them outside work. I hardly met Elka Furstin at all. I tried to keep Franklyns running as smoothly and professionally as possible in, I'm sure you'll agree, very difficult circumstances. And, yes, there's a farmer's family in

Latvia which has four daughters with the most beautiful hair and their hair is cut regularly and fashioned into wigs for Elka, hence the payments . . . I've heard Elka travelled the length and breadth of Eastern Europe looking for the perfect hair for her wigs." She sat back and smiled as she saw the look of disbelief on David's face. "Would you like me to write to the farmer and tell him that Franklyns no longer requires his family's services?"

Still looking shocked, he nodded. "I think that might be a good idea." He glanced down at his watch. "I'd better go. I've another meeting to attend." He stood up. "Thanks, you've been very informative."

She noticed his mood had changed. "I'll get working on these files and phone you when I've a full report done."

David nodded. "Have a nice weekend," he said without a smile. He turned and left the room.

* * *

Anna and Paul walked hand in hand to the clinic.

"I'm so nervous, I'm trembling!" said Anna but she was smiling broadly.

"First step for us to get our little family," said Paul, leaning forward and kissing her lips before they entered the building.

* * *

Stephanie looked around the Board table at the sales managers. She glanced at her watch. It was ten minutes after two.

"Does anybody know where Paul is?" she asked.

There were a few coughs and the managers glanced at each other.

"Well?" she snapped.

Christine spoke up. "Paul isn't in today."

Stephanie contained her anger.

"I see – well, since the General Manager doesn't think he's important enough to attend the meeting, I don't think he is either. I've been looking at the sales figures of all your departments …"

Christine sat back as Stephanie droned on.

* * *

That evening Nicola and Oliver sat out at the pool. He was reading through police reports while she stared out at the rolling countryside, almost in a trance. She had been like that since her meeting with David. She had re-run the meeting over and over in her head and the more she thought about it the more she realised how stupid it was to talk about that Latvian family and Elka Furstin's wigs. She remembered how his expression had gone from warm to slight disgust as she informed him of what the Latvian family's use was. Now she feared that he would judge her by association. She had been so anxious to impress him with her knowledge and how useful she was that she had lost her better judgement. By her very knowledge of such an arrangement, was she not coming across as bizarre herself? And what would happen when he discovered the further excesses of the Furtsins' lifestyle?

Oliver looked up from his reading and studied his wife. He could hardly fathom her. She had been as excited as a schoolgirl all last night and again this morning, and then since she had come home today she was distant, not too happy-looking.

"Everything all right?" he probed.

She didn't hear him as she continued to stare down the fields.

"Nicola?" he snapped.

She awoke from her thoughts and turned to him.

"Sorry – what is it, Oliver?"

"You seem a bit distracted – everything all right?"

"Eh, yes – everything's fine, I guess. Just a lot on at the moment at work since this takeover."

"Nothing you can't handle, I'm sure."

"I had a meeting with the new financial controller today – David Stafford. I don't think the meeting went too well." She sighed.

"You didn't get on with him?"

"I just didn't handle the meeting well ... started going on about Latvian hair."

He looked at her, confused. *"What?"*

"Oh, it's a long and daft story, I'm not going into it. I've a bit of a headache, I think I'll go for a lie-down." She got up and walked inside.

His eyes followed her in. He was becoming more and more worried about his wife.

She went from happy to upset over nothing. The other night she was overjoyed over nothing and now she looked so down and again no explanation. She wasn't the contented happy old Nicola. He was still trying to understand her reaction to the ring he had bought her. He was still trying to understand why she just didn't get the Tube to work as normal the morning of her attack. He was trying to understand why she was running around Liverpool Street station. And yet she had put a wall up against him and he was frightened of her reaction if he pushed. The investigation had effectively came to an end. If he looked at that CCTV footage any more he feared he would go mad. Looking for something that wasn't there. Ever since he had met Nicola he had always put her on a pedestal. He always just wanted to make her happy. He always, deep down, felt she could have done better than him. He was so surprised and delighted when she agreed to go out with him. Ever since he felt he'd been trying to fit into her world. To prove that he deserved her. And he was almost frightened of upsetting her in case that would be proof that she wasn't happy with him.

Chapter 23

Anna was looking at herself in the mirrored wardrobes in their bedroom that night. She had a cushion pushed up her nightdress at the front. Paul came into the room and laughed.

"I'm just checking what I'd look like pregnant," she said as she continued to examine her reflection. "Would you still fancy me looking like this?"

He came and put his arms around her and she allowed the cushion to drop.

"I'd fancy you looking any way."

She turned and walked over to the bed. "You say that now. I wonder if you'll say the same thing when I'm throwing up in the mornings and then become as big as a whale."

"I can't wait for you to be like that and I'll be running around doing everything for you."

"Hmmm, I'll have to keep a close eye on you to make sure you don't go eyeing up any young girls!" She hugged him tightly and laughed.

Paul smile didn't falter for a second. He knew she was only joking and would never suspect him of being unfaithful. And she would never find out about Christine. Or the girl from the Christmas party the year before. Or the girl on the graduate management course. He joined her on the bed, stretched out on his back and put his arms behind his head looking at the ceiling.

"So – you're happy after today?" he asked.

"Very much. Thanks for forcing the issue with me. You know me, I can face any issue except the ones that directly affect me. I was so scared to think we couldn't have children and I thought it was so final. But, as the doctor said today, nature needs a little help now and again. It's quite simple the way he put it."

"Very straightforward."

"You know, it makes total sense for our generation. We really are the first generation who can have it all. We don't have to be slaves to nature or our bodies. Why should women have to have children in their twenties? Let's face it, we're younger for much longer. Being in your thirties now is what being in your twenties used to be."

"Forty is the new thirty?" said Paul, smirking. He loved it when Anna rationalised everything.

"Exactly! I mean, let's face it, Paul, we weren't ready for kids until now."

"I thought you said the other night that we put our careers before having a family and you regretted it?"

"I was just feeling apprehensive. But the fact is, Paul, we did put our careers first, but why the hell shouldn't we? Now we've done everything we wanted to do, are now financially stronger, and we can concentrate on being the best parents in the world. If we had had a child a few years ago, it wouldn't have been our priority, whereas now he or she will be. The fact is, Paul, our generation has beaten time. Science is helping us until evolution catches up with our lifestyle change. People used to have children young because they weren't around as long. We have science to stop us from having children when we aren't ready for them and we have science to restart things when we decide we want them."

"I've a feeling I'm getting a preview of your next Sunday's column," he said, smiling.

She rested her chin on his bare chest and looked up into his face. "Maybe you are."

"We might be younger mentally for longer but do you think we older parents will be able to cope physically?" he asked.

"Of course," she said excitedly. "Because we eat better food, go to the gym, stay much fitter – and we know so much more about being healthy – so again we've beaten time. And, because we concentrated on our careers, we can afford help whenever we need it."

He stroked her hair. "And how will you feel if in a few years' time at Sports Day all the mothers are much younger than you?"

"Well, that's just it, they won't be because it's becoming so common for women older than me having children. It's the norm." She started stroking his chest. "And if I do start looking older, science can again rescue me – the first Botox is on you, mate!"

He laughed. They looked at each other.

"So we're very positive about all this then?" he asked.

"As positive as we could be."

As she continued to stroke his chest, she pulled herself up, lay fully on top of him and began to kiss him.

She opened her mouth and his tongue slipped in, gently probing and playing with hers. She sat astride him and he reached forward and unbuttoned her nightdress, revealing her slim rangy body. He cupped her breasts in his hands and massaged them gently as she began to stroke him. She fell back, lay out on the bed and he moved on top of her.

Later they slept soundly in each other's arms.

Suddenly Paul's mobile started ringing, jolting them both awake.

"Who the fuck is that?" Anna mumbled. "I thought Furstin was out of our lives!"

He looked down at the private number and, jumping out of bed, went into the bathroom and closed the door.

"Who is it?" he snarled down the phone.

"Paul, it's me," said Christine's slurred voice.

"What the hell are you ringing me for? It's nearly one in the morning."

"I just wanted you to know that Stephanie Holden was really pissed off with you today for not showing up at the meeting. I can't believe you didn't show up. She'd get rid of you in a moment – look what she did with Gordon."

"You're pissed, Christine – go to bed and don't ring me again."

"Paul, why don't you come on over to mine. I've a bottle of champagne in the fridge and –"

"Christine – will you fuck off!"

"Don't talk to me like that! Who do you think you are? You're not going to be GM at Franklyns much longer, Paul. You're so stupid, you can't even see you're being used until Holden settles in. And what will wifey say then? I might break the news to her myself – in fact maybe there's quite a few things I should inform Mrs Stewart about."

Paul switched off the phone and slammed it on the counter.

He came out of the bathroom and saw Anna sitting up in bed.

"It was nothing – just one of the managers telling me that my absence from that meeting today didn't go down too well." He climbed back on the bed and lay on his back, looking up at the ceiling.

She looked at his concerned face.

"You love that place, don't you?" she smiled.

"Franklyns? It's a living."

"No, you love it. You love the whole pizzazz of the place. The glamour, the money. You even in a strange kind of way loved the Furstins and their excesses. You liked being part of their world. "

"I'm not sure about that," he objected.

"You like all the good things in life and you like the money and position Franklyns has given you."

"Nothing wrong with that, is there?" he asked, perplexed.

"No, nothing at all. But you know I've been on at you for years to leave that job. And even though you agreed with me, you never had any intention of going. You loved it too much. Even with Furstin being such a bastard, you loved the window he showed you into his world full of money and power. It's just when you wrap your life around one thing like that, it's very hard to move on when sometimes life forces you to move on. Do you understand what I'm saying, Paul?"

Paul continued to stare at the ceiling and nodded.

Chapter 24

Paul had been steadfastly avoiding Stephanie all day but now, as he saw her march across the shop floor towards him, he braced himself.

"Where were you on Friday?" she demanded.

"I took the day off, as I explained to you."

"That sales meeting was very important. I was setting out the new sales targets for the next six months. I expected you to rearrange your day off to attend such an important meeting. Now you are completely uninformed about what those targets are. You're supposed to be the general manager."

"You should have given me a little more notice. I had something on Friday that I really couldn't get out of."

She stared at him. If it was in different circumstances she might be a little more understanding. But she felt her whole position had been so undermined since she started at Franklyns that she couldn't show any weakness.

"If Karl Furstin had told you to be at that meeting, would you have attended?" she challenged him. "Would you have dared not attend? Of course, you bloody wouldn't. I don't like the way Furstin did business – in fact, he seems like a despicable man – but if he ruled this place through fear and fear is the only thing you all understand, then I'll run this place the same way. It's bad enough that Nicola Newman thinks she's a law onto herself. I'm not having a general manager thinking the same way. If you ignore an instruction from me again, don't bother showing up for work the next day."

* * *

Stephanie seemed to spend the next couple of days in meeting after meeting with department heads, going through sales figures and the activities that were planned for Franklyns for the next few months. She didn't get out of the store until nine on the Monday night, ten on the Tuesday night. By the time Wednesday came she made sure she was home at the half respectable time of seven. She ran a hot bath and, slipping out of her robe, stood into the bath and sank down into the water. Allowing the water to glide over her skin and relax her tense muscles, she thought about Paul Stewart. No doubt he thought her the biggest bitch in the world, dictating what day he could have off. She would prefer to run the place in a progressive and fair way, but she was beginning to realise that was impossible.

Her mind slid to Leo. She had been avoiding thinking about him, putting off contacting him about coming to work in Frankyns. She had made the offer before she had begun actually working at Franklyns. Little had she known then what a mammoth task it would be running the store. To be honest, the last thing she needed was her unpredictable and wayward son coming to work there. She knew it would undermine her further. And here she was, trying to stamp out all the old system in Franklyns: the lavish expense accounts, the nepotism, the undeserved promotions. Now she would come across as a huge hypocrite handing out a big job to her son. That certainly wasn't leading by example.

Coming to work for Franklyns was proving to be one of the most difficult periods of her life. But as her mind drifted back through the years, she knew she had seen worse times . . .

* * *

The money that Stephanie had put aside while singing for The Yell quickly began to run out after she quit the band. When she had walked away after her final performance at Live Aid, she had half expected Danny McKay to come and find her. He knew where the tiny flat she rented in Clapham was. She expected him to come to realise that he was just as much in love with her as she was with him and that he would dump Hetty and all would be great between them again. But as she continued to see Danny and Hetty photographed in the papers or in lifestyle magazines at his fabulous home or at her family's stately pile and being described as one of the eighties' most glamorous couples, her dreams slipped away from her. She realised Danny had never had any intention of staying with her. As he said himself, they were from the same place. He wasn't impressed by her or where she was from. He wanted to move up in the world; she was a step down.

She hadn't been confident enough in her burgeoning singing career and kept putting off contacting people she knew in the music industry to ask them for another break after she had walked out on The Yell. Her confidence had been knocked, full stop. She was nursing her broken heart and living simply on the little money she had put by. And just when the money started running out and she knew she would have to make a move to start singing again, she realised she was pregnant. The shock was immense for her. Not just the shock that she was pregnant but that she was pregnant by Gary Cosgrave, a man she could barely stand. And a man she had only gone with as some kind of stupid revenge on Danny McKay, that as it turned out Danny neither knew about or if it came to it would care about. She contemplated contacting Gary Cosgrave but just the idea of meeting him again made her skin crawl.

So faced with no money, no career and no father of the child, she went home to Mum. Stephanie knew that nobody ever did or ever would or could love her as much as her mother did. Her parents had done everything for her under difficult circumstances bringing her up. She had hoped to return home one day as a star. Instead she arrived home, with a battered suitcase, broken dreams and in tears.

Things had also changed a lot where she had grown up in the East End. All the thriving businesses had closed down. The arrival of the huge shopping centres nearby had meant there was no need for all the little shops, the kind her parents ran. They still did a bit of trade but customers were few and far between. Her brother was secretly delighted when their shop closed down as it freed him to do what he really wanted to do – to become a stage hand for bands he knew. He took off, touring Europe and finally becoming a stage designer. She envied his freedom. There was to be no freedom for her.

"What'll I do?" she asked her mother as she recounted the whole story.

"You'll do what people always do – we cope," said her mother.

Stephanie applied for a council flat and, after being placed on a waiting list, managed to get one in a high rise. Leo was born, and something changed in her as she realised that he was the most important thing that would ever happen to her. But her joy in her new son was quickly replaced by the pain of the reality of the situation. She would lie out on the floor in her flat, unable to stop crying as Leo slept in his cot. Her worst day for crying was the day when Danny and Hetty got married in a fanfare of tabloid publicity at a marquee at Hetty's family home. Was this what her life would be for evermore, a bleak council estate and grinding poverty? She would get depressed at the memory of her life in the music industry, the parties, the glamour and the excitement. Now she just felt so alone, except for her family who tried to support her as best they could. But they didn't have much either and were now living quite a distance away in the East End. She remembered her mother's words – "We cope" – and that was what she tried to do. As her son developed into a wonderful toddler she took great pride in him and smothered him with love and attention. They did everything together. The council estate was very rough and so all her time was spent ensuring that Leo was protected and didn't come to any harm. Time went by and she was always trying to compensate for him not having a father and hardly any money.

By the time Stephanie was thirty and Leo was becoming a teenager, she took stock of their lives. Apart from a few years on the road with The Yell, she hadn't really done anything with her life except for bringing up Leo. She couldn't help feeling that she had wasted years and was now anxious to get on with her life.

Leo was now getting a bit older and so she could allow him a little more independence. She was so sick and tired of eking out a living and literally watching every penny. She wanted to live in a nice home and be able to give Leo nice things.

If Leo hadn't come along, she could have the world conquered by now. She had believed in herself once and she could do it again. She wanted money. She wanted her son to want for nothing and she was prepared to work very hard to achieve that. Apart from music, the only other thing she knew was retail as she had worked in her parents' shop and on Oxford Street as a teenager. So it made sense to go back to that area. She was taken on as Christmas staff at a department store in the West End in the ladies' fashion department. She worked like a Trojan for the whole Christmas period, literally shocking her bosses with her sales achievements. They asked her to stay on after Christmas and she gratefully accepted. It was great to be earning a wage again and to be able to buy stuff for Leo. The hours weren't great for a mother on her own with a young son but he was old for his years and she felt she could trust him. Once she started working again all the pent-up desperation to be somebody and get a good life came flooding out and she literally worked non-stop. She was made a Sales Manager within six months. She continued to outperform and was inspired by the money and the power that was coming her way. She had to make up for a lot of lost time, which pushed her further. Her bosses were impressed by her commitment, and her looks made her good for the store's reputation. She could afford a glamorous wardrobe. She possessed all the ingredients for a clear path to senior management. When she was offered a job in the marketing department she jumped at it.

She had become intrigued by sales culture. She had learned that people spend money to buy happiness and the trick in selling was letting people believe that what you offered would give them the elusive happiness everyone sought. She started doing a business management course at night, which took her further away from Leo. She soon became the Marketing Manager and after a year she was poached by a rival retail group.

She wasn't sure exactly when Leo started hanging around with the wrong crowd.

But she did remember the day she got a call from the principal of his school and she was summoned to hear that Leo was being expelled for having pot found in his locker and for extorting money from younger kids. She went ballistic. He promised to reform. She tried to get him into a better fee-paying school but he steadfastly refused and so he was enrolled into another school with barely a better reputation than his previous one. At least he was in school – he had threatened not to go at all if she forced his hand. She at least managed to get him away from the council block as she took out her first mortgage on a house nearby. But his school reports continued to get worse and their relationship continued to disintegrate. She wanted to have the time to put him on the straight and narrow. But as she was headhunted for more powerful jobs she literally didn't have the time. And she felt that whatever chance Leo had, if they slipped back to the state they were in previously, he'd never make good. The harder she worked the more she resented that he didn't appreciate all she did for him and all she gave him. He wouldn't come home at nights and their screaming matches were scary. By the time he was eighteen, she felt their relationship was based on resentment.

As the bath water cooled, she slipped out and wrapped her robe around her. She was dwelling on the past recently and she knew it wasn't a healthy thing to do. But she needed to understand where things had gone wrong with Leo so she could put things right. After school Leo had talked himself into a job in the City and the wheeling and dealing had suited him perfectly. He was exceptionally bright and she knew he could make good if he just got the right break and played by the rules. He got the break in the City but hadn't played the rules and was kicked out. What made her think he would play by the rules in Franklyns? Nothing, she admitted to herself. But she still had to give him the break.

Chapter 25

Nicola finished work at midday on the Thursday and made her way down Brompton Road for her appointment at her hairdresser's. As she walked down the street she spotted David driving by in a navy soft-top Maserati. He had his sunglasses on and was looking straight ahead. She turned and watched the car as it headed towards Franklyns. She thought the car looked fantastic.

"Your usual?" asked her regular hairdresser as Nicola sat down in front of the mirror in the busy large salon.

"No, actually, I was hoping for something a little different." Nicola smiled up at the woman.

* * *

Nicola drove into the driveway, got out of the car and let herself into the house.

She looked at herself in the large antique mirror in the hall. For years she'd basically had the same hairstyle, a shoulder-length bob which was easy to care for. But this time she had asked for something completely different. As she studied her new sassy, retro, flicked style she was delighted with what her hairdresser had done.

She was smiling as she walked into the lounge.

Oliver was, of course, looking through paperwork. As he looked up at her he started.

"Oh! Well, that's a bit different!" he said.

"Isn't it?" She crossed over to the fireplace and began to toy with her hair in the large gold-framed mirror over it. "Do you like it?"

"Well, eh, as I said, it's different!"

She felt annoyed by his lack of enthusiasm. "For fuck's sake, Oliver! You could sound a bit more enthusiastic."

He coughed. He didn't like it when she swore. "No, I'm sorry. It's very nice. Just will take a while to get used to. It's just you've had the other style for so long."

"You know what your problem is, Oliver? You're such a stick-in-the-mud. You're terrified of change. You need to lighten up a little." She ignored his slightly injured look as she walked past him. "I'm going to change."

At the door she stopped and swung around.

"Oh, and my car is playing up, incidentally."

"Is it? I'll make an appointment to take it to the garage this week."

"No, don't bother. You know, I was thinking I might just change it. I've had it a couple of years now and I never really liked that model." She smiled at him and continued out the door.

Chapter 26

Stephanie had sheets of fashion designs spread out all over her desk. When she had headed the Panther Fashion Group she had given the first break to a young fashion designer called Veronica Carter. Veronica had gone on to great things and had recently been appointed the creative designer with a top fashion house. She had approached Veronica last week and, having reminded her of the favour she owed her, asked if she would exclusively launch her summer designs at Franklyns. Veronica had seemed interested and had couriered over some stuff she was working on. She trusted Stephanie's opinion and was nervous about her new role at the haute couture fashion house. The designs were spectacular, Stephanie thought, and was excited about Franklyns getting an exclusive with them. This was the kind of stuff they needed to re-establish themselves at the cutting edge and not just be seen as a rich wives' and tourists' playground. She pushed the designs away.

She had been putting off the call long enough and decided to take the bull by the horns. She dialled Leo's mobile.

"Yeah?"

"Leo, it's your mother here."

Silence on the other end of the phone.

"I'm just ringing you about the job here at Franklyns. I think the best thing is for you to start on the management programme. It's considered one of the best around and you can find your feet and decide what area suits you best."

"Cool, when do I start?"

"Er – just let me put a call through to HR and sort it out. I'll give you a call back this afternoon."

"Fine," Leo said and the phone went dead.

Stephanie sighed as she stared at the phone, contemplating how to approach it with Nicola Newman. What was this? Was she nervous of talking to somebody who effectively worked for her? She picked up the phone quickly and rang through to Nicola's department. As she expected Nicola's secretary kept her waiting nearly five minutes before putting her through. She tapped her taloned nails on her desk impatiently.

"Ah, Stephanie, and what can I do for you?" Nicola's assured voice finally came on the line. "Any more sackings you want arranged for you?"

Stephanie ignored the sarcasm. "Actually, no I'm hiring somebody and I want to organise an appointment for you to meet them and go through the necessary paperwork."

Silence on the other end of the phone.

"Nicola?" snapped Stephanie.

"Yes, I'm still here. It's just, well, all hirings usually come through HR. We advertise the role both internally and externally, interview, check references etc. There's a huge procedure we go through to ensure Franklyns hires the very best."

"It really seemed that promotions were given out on

merit in the past!" Stephanie said, matching her sarcasm.

"Well, actually they were. If you're referring to any promotions authorised by Karl Furstin, that was up to him. But hiring of staff was always meticulously carried out by my department."

Stephanie raised her eyes to heaven, realising that this was going to be as difficult as she had feared.

"Nicola, I want this person hired." Stephanie's voice was ice.

"Well, as you know, I am trying to help the new management to the very best of my capabilities. If you want to send this person in to me, I'll go through the normal procedures with them. What's the name of the person and what role are they applying for?" Stephanie thought Nicola was being very clever by not directly challenging her authority but also ensuring that her own stamp of approval was on the new person's appointment, so reinforcing her position.

"Leo Holden is his name and he's joining the Franklyns' management scheme."

There was a pause and then Nicola said coolly,

"Holden?"

"Yes, he's my son," Stephanie acknowledged, preparing herself for the row that was bound to follow as she was attacked by Nicola for nepotism. "Have you a problem with that?"

"Ah, no, none at all. Tell him to be at my office at eleven on Monday morning."

Stephanie hung up the phone and felt worried. She was expecting Nicola to be hostile – it was more worrying that she hadn't been.

* * *

Rachel and Daniella watched Paul as he swept past their counter looking tired and hassled.

"He looks like he's under an awful lot of pressure," said Rachel. "Not at all his usual in-control, suave self."

"Smug is the word you're searching for. I'm not surprised. The rumour is that his days are numbered."

"Really?" Rachel was surprised and slightly sad at hearing this. She couldn't imagine the place without him.

"Well, with Leo's mum now in charge, what's there for him to do long-term? He's kind of surplus to requirement."

"I wonder what he'll do then."

"Get a job somewhere else, I imagine." Daniella shrugged. "His wife's got a good job so they won't be down on their uppers anyway."

"His wife?"

"Yeah, she's the journalist, Anna Stewart. You know, she's on the breakfast shows commenting on things every so often and she has a column in one of the Sunday newspapers."

Rachel racked her brain and vaguely could recollect her. "Oh, yes. I didn't realise he was married to *her.*"

"I don't think he realises it himself half the time."

"Huh?"

"I told you before about his affairs. He's the store's ladies' man."

"Yeah, but how much of that is true?" Rachel protested. "There's always gossip about people in power."

"It's true all right. I was quite friendly with a buyer who used to work here. Lovely girl. He was screwing her for a few months."

"And what happened to her?"

"I think she left when she realised there was no future in it. Didn't want to hang around. I think she had fallen for him. Then there's Christine. She got drunk over in the pub one night and said a little more than she should have to me. She's very bitter about him. And she's such a bitch he'd want to watch his back, because she won't let him just walk off without paying. Christine is a very good saleswoman and she believes a price has to be paid for everything. And Paul will pay the price for messing with her."

As Rachel looked at Daniella's judgemental face, she thought better than to remind her of her own indiscretion against Leo.

"Why doesn't he just leave his wife?" Rachel asked in an exasperated manner. "They don't have any children, do they? I can't stand that kind of messing around."

"Who knows what makes people tick?" shrugged Daniella.

Chapter 27

"I've got the lovely new range of Renaults in, Nicola – that's what you have at the moment, isn't it?" said Jeremy Jones who owned the local dealership near the Newmans'.

Nicola and Oliver were walking around the luxurious car salesroom in the dealership on Saturday afternoon.

"Hmmm. You know, I'm looking for something a bit different," said Nicola as she walked past the different-coloured Renaults without a second look.

"Are you?" asked Oliver, surprised.

"Yes, I've had three Renaults in a row and I'm a bit bored with them."

"You always said you were content with them. You said they were a sensible choice."

"Hmmm, a little too sensible. Fine for popping down to the market but nothing else really."

Jeremy laughed. "Why don't you take a look at our new Mercedes convertible, Nicola? You'll get more fun out of that than popping down to the market." He nodded over to the soft-topped red SLK two-seater Mercedes taking pride of place in the extensive windows.

"Oh, that is lovely, Jeremy!" Nicola gazed over to the

vehicle in admiration and walked slowly towards it.

"It's a fine car all right," laughed Oliver, following his wife.

She touched the bonnet of the car and ran her hand along the body.

"Why don't you sit in, Nicola?" smirked Jeremy, opening the driver's door for her. She sat into the comfortable cream leather.

"It's fabulous!" she sighed.

"Take her for a spin!" encouraged Jeremy.

She glanced up at him with a mixture of 'wanting to' but 'frightened to'. Jeremy threw her the keys. Then he pressed a remote and the window of the garage rose up in front of the car.

"All right, I will!" She put the key into the ignition and took off.

"She seems to like it!" said Jeremy laughing.

"She's wasting time – she's just going to end up buying a Renault in the end," said Oliver. "Well, might as well take a look at the new Range Rovers while I'm here!" Oliver clapped Jeremy on the back. Like most business people in the area, the Newmans had befriended Jeremy and his wife over the years and they often attended social occasions together.

Nicola drove quickly through the country roads, a smile beaming across her face. She felt free and empowered and young as the beautiful countryside whizzed past her on the sunny day. She didn't ever want to go back to the garage but at last reluctantly stopped and turned.

"Smashing, isn't it?" beamed Jeremy on her return. "You can dream, can't you? Did you ever think of a Volvo, Nicola? I've got a nice new range in." Jeremy thought he'd better get the conversation back on proper selling ground.

"No need. I don't need to look any more. I've found what I want." She tapped both hands on the steering wheel.

"You want to buy *this*?" Jeremy was incredulous.

"Definitely, there's no doubt in my mind," Nicola confirmed.

Oliver unfolded his arms quickly. "Don't be daft, Nicola!"

"I'm not being daft at all. Why should you get the glamorous car, while I get stuck with a family saloon?"

"The Range Rover suits our needs which is why I have it. And you always loved the Renaults."

"I didn't love them. They did me. There's a difference!" she snapped back.

Oliver shot Jeremy a look and Jeremy quickly said, "I'll leave you two to have a word about it. I'll just be in the office when you've made up your mind."

Oliver waited until Jeremy walked off before speaking.

"Are you absolutely crazy, Nicola? Look at this flashy car – it's just not you!"

"Who says it's not me? It feels very me when I'm behind the wheel."

"But it's so flashy and loud and obnoxious – everything we're not!"

"I love it and I want it and we're going to buy it. We can afford it."

"Of course, we can afford it but that's not the point, Nicola. I hate everything this car is."

"As I was saying to you the other night, you've become such a stick-in-the-mud! I'm not going to slowly wait for old age visiting antique fairs and attending boring dinner parties, Oliver. I want to live a little!"

"Nicola, I'm seriously worried about you. You're not

yourself recently. I've been ignoring it but when you want to land this monument to bad taste in our driveway then I have to say something."

"Oh, Oliver!" she snapped. "Why are you making a song and dance about everything? It's really very simple. After the attack, I'm not comfortable commuting in on the train any more. Silly, I know, but I can't help how I feel. So I want to drive to work more so I can feel safe. The Renault is fine for driving down to the market here but, Oliver, I'm the head of Franklyns – I can't be seen arriving up every day in a family saloon! Can't you see where I'm coming from?"

He stared at her, at the mixture of anger and excitement, an expression he wasn't used to seeing on her face. There were so many things about her recently that he wasn't used to. And it must all be because of that mugging – she had just said it herself. The incident was obviously making her re-evaluate her life.

"Who do I make the cheque payable to?" Oliver asked in Jeremy's office.

Jeremy looked at them from behind his desk, not quite comprehending they were buying the Mercedes convertible. Oliver looked plainly unhappy while Nicola looked ecstatic.

* * *

Rachel had had so few Saturdays off since she had started working at Franklyns that she really treasured them. She had got up early and gone shopping. She got the bus up to Oxford Street and bought some new clothes in Selfridges before continuing her way to Bond Street. Then she went into the tube station at Bond Street and caught the tube to

Sloane Square where she started walking down Kings Road. She admired the fashion on display in the sunshine.There was a procession of flash cars that were grinding along very slowly with their flashier owners sitting behind the wheels.

"Hey, Rachel!" shouted a man's voice. She turned around to see that the speaker was Leo, seated in his sports car, the top down, dressed in a tight white designer T-shirt, with Daniella beside him dolled up in designer gear, both of their faces hidden behind huge Dolce & Gabbana sunglasses.

"Hi, darling!" Daniella waved over.

Rachel walked over to them, smiling, laden with large shopping bags.

"Ohhh! Been shopping?" cooed Daniella excitedly.

"Yeah, needed to get some new clothes."

"Us too!" Daniella nodded at the back seat which was crammed with designer shopping bags.

"Nice to have somebody waiting on us for a change, isn't it?" said Daniella. "We're going to the pub for the rest of the afternoon – why don't you join us?"

Rachel glanced at Leo, his even teeth shining in the sun. She still sensed danger from him. "No, you're fine. I've a load of things to do but thanks anyway. See you Monday!"

"Suit yourself – phone my mobile if you change your mind."

The traffic began to move. Leo revved up the car and began to move forward.

Rachel waved goodbye and walked on.

* * *

"She wasn't very friendly," said Leo.

"Rachel? I thought she was fine."

"She is fine with you but – I don't think she likes me."

"Don't be stupid. She sang your praises for finding her the flat. She likes you fine. She's just a bit reserved."

"I'm telling you she doesn't like me," Leo snapped. "I don't know what her problem is."

"We forgot to tell her you're starting work in Franklyns on Monday."

"Don't tell her – let it come as a surprise for her!"

She reached over and tickled his chin. "Now, not only am I going out with the boss's son but the boss as well!"

He smirked. "Not the boss yet, love, but give me time."

He glanced at all the shopping in the back seat and was very grateful for the new job. He had coaxed a credit-card company to up his limit on the strength of it.

* * *

Rachel went down to the local newsagent's on Sunday morning as usual and made sure to get the paper Daniella had said Paul's wife had a column in.

Back in her flat, she poured herself a smoothie. Then she settled down on the sofa and flicked through the paper, scouring for Paul's wife column. She spotted Anna Stewart's name and paused. There was a photo of Anna at the top of the article. Rachel studied the image intently. Rachel thought she was classically attractive and imagined the two of them made a very handsome couple. Sitting alone in her flat in a huge city where she knew just a few people she felt herself become slightly envious of them. She imagined they lived in a lovely home and the two of them seemed to be at the top of their careers. They had everything going for them. She hoped when she got to their age she was as settled and successful as them. She reminded herself what Daniella had said about Paul having affairs and that his job was on the line and not to romanticise their lives. If what Daniella had said was true their lives must be far from ideal under the surface. If Daniella could be believed. People always gossiped about people in power, not caring whether it was true or not.

Chapter 28

It was Monday morning. Leo glanced down at his watch. It was a quarter to eleven. He looked up at the Franklyns building, consumed with nerves at the idea of going in. He was usually full of confidence but this was different. This was going into his mother's territory. He usually liked to keep his life very separate from his mother's, and now they were coming together. Daniella had informed him how she had gone up and introduced herself to Stephanie. He had cringed at the thought of it and, when he berated her for doing it, she asked him what else was she supposed to do – wouldn't it be odd if she hadn't, with them working in the same building? She had a point, he supposed. He really just hated the closeness of it all. And yet, with the state of his finances, he had no choice.

He marched through the front doors.

* * *

"I thought this meeting was supposed to be for eleven?" snapped Leo to Yvette as he looked down at his watch and saw it was now half past.

Yvette looked up at him from her desk, surprised.

"This *interview* will take place whenever Mrs Newman can fit you into her very busy schedule," she said in her plummiest voice.

She had been studying him out of the corner of her eye, intrigued to see what Stephanie's son would be like. She decided she loathed him. He had swaggered in wearing his Armani suit, full of cockiness and what he thought was charm.

"What's with all this interview shit?" he asked, puzzled. "The job's already been arranged, I'm just going through a formality here."

"Well, I think Mrs Newman might have something to say about that," said Yvette and smiled at him condescendingly.

Leo was just about to deliver a retort when the phone on Yvette's desk rang.

"Hmm hmm," Yvette said, giving her thumbs-down signal to Nicola before saying, "I'll send him in." She hung up and looked over at Leo. "You can go in now."

"'Bout time," said Leo, getting up.

As he walked past Yvette's desk, she said: "Word of advice – lose the attitude."

Leo stopped abruptly and, putting his two hands on her desk, leaned forward and said, "I'll do a deal with you – I'll lose my attitude if you lose your condescension." He winked at her and went on to Nicola's door and without knocking entered.

* * *

Nicola took one look at Leo as he strode towards her and knew that under normal circumstances she would show this young man the door in a matter of seconds. His whole demeanour was not what Franklyns wanted for any position.

He smiled at her and shot out his hand for her to shake. She looked down at his hand, slowly reached out and limply shook it.

"My mother said you'd sign me up and do whatever you have to do," said Leo, pulling up a chair and sitting down.

She looked at him with cool eyes and a slight smile.

"Allow me to introduce myself to you, Mr Holden. My name is Nicola Newman, I'm the HR Director here at Franklyns and I decide who gets employed and who doesn't, contrary to what you might believe."

He looked at her with a bored expression. "So you're saying you don't want me, is that it? Because I really cannot be bothered with this bullshit. There either is or isn't a job for me here. If there ain't, then let me know now and stop wasting my time." His eyes challenged her.

She sat back and studied him. She thought him common and uncouth, and just what she imagined Stephanie Holden would have reared. What was to become of Franklyns now that it had fallen into the hands of these people?

After speaking in such a disrespectful fashion to her, she would normally have the likes of him escorted off the premises.

But he had the kind of arrogance that nothing could diminish. She felt he would very happily skip out of the store and not give a damn if she told him that he was unsuitable. And she would have the satisfaction of angering Stephanie Holden further and rubbing it in that she really wasn't in charge. But as she looked at this flashy young man, she knew that he was Stephanie's Achilles' heel. The fact was Stephanie Holden had to go, there was no question about it. Nicola wanted her out. And her son could very well be the key to getting her out. And so it was to Nicola's advantage to have Leo begin work at Franklyns.

Nicola sat forward. "Of course, there's a position for you at Franklyns. Your mother wouldn't have wasted your time otherwise. But I still need to put a file together for you. Unfortunately, I have absolutely no details yet. Did you bring a CV with you?"

"No."

She looked at him in amusement. "I see." She sat forward and, taking up her pen, prepared to make notes.

"Which university did you attend and what degree did you get?"

He looked at her and she spotted the first flicker of vulnerability on his face.

"I didn't go to university."

"I see." She sat back in her chair and toyed with her pen. "Right. Your mother didn't specify a role for you. So I think that, without any qualifications, putting you in sales is the best idea. Maybe in the shoe department?"

"I'm not working in any shoe department."

She shrugged. "And you have how many A-levels?"

"Pass."

Nicola nodded and made some notes. "What have you been doing with yourself since school?"

He yawned. "I was working as a broker up in the City."

"Ahh," she smiled, "now we're getting somewhere. The firm you worked for?"

He stared at her blankly, not wanting to give the name.

"The firm's name?" she pushed.

"Fleishmans."

She scribbled down the name.

"And you're still there?"

"No, I left some time ago?"

"And can I see your references?"

"I don't have any."

"I see." Nicola twiddled with her pen. "Martha Harkman – is she still the HR over at Fleishman's?"

Leo became very uncomfortable and coughed.

"Was that a yes?" she asked.

"Yes, she's still there."

Nicola nodded and made a note. "And your present employer?"

"I'm working for myself."

"As what exactly?"

"In commodities."

She smiled sarcastically at him "Business must be good as you're coming to work at Franklyns."

He scowled at her.

"Right, I think we know where we are," said Nicola. "You have no further education to speak off, no references, no retail experience – but I think you're probably just what we're looking for. I'll have your contract drawn up today and Yvette will contact you later to sign the contract and take bank details etc." She started writing further notes on her pad.

After a short while she looked up and said, "You may go."

He stood up and hovered.

"Where do I go now?" he asked.

"Do you know, I'm really not sure, Leo. You're such an exceptional case. Best for you to find your mother and see what she wants to do with you." She smiled up at him and he abruptly walked out.

As advised he phoned Stephanie after leaving Nicola. To his surprise she told him to meet her up in the restaurant. She was such a workhorse he expected she would be mad busy with no time to spare him..

She was waiting for him, seated at one of the tables situated beside the large glass wall offering views across Knightbridge.

"I thought we might have a bit of brunch," she said as he approached the table and sat down.

"Good idea," he shrugged and took the menu to look at it.

"How did it go in HR?" She held her breath for the outcome, almost waiting for Leo to say Nicola gave him his marching orders.

He yawned. "Went okay. Met some toffee-nosed twit who seemed to be full of shit."

Stephanie laughed. She liked that description. "Nicola? But there were no major problems?"

"No, I have to go back this afternoon to sign a contract."

"Good." She allowed herself to breathe again. She wasn't sure what she would have done if Nicola had been obstinate and refused to employ him. "Welcome to Franklyns!"

The waitress came over. Glancing at her watch, Stephanie decided to have something substantial now as she would probably have to skip lunch because of meetings..

"I'll have the salmon," she said.

Leo looked the menu up and down before smiling up at the waitress. "I'll go for that Franklyns Gourmet Hamburger to see what it's like, and the fries with it of course." He waited until the waitress had left before asking, "So what am I supposed to do in this joint?"

Good question, thought Stephanie. There wasn't really a role for him, but the main thing was he had started and she would figure out what to do with him in soon enough.

"Just for now I want you to get used to the feel of the store. Walk around the different departments getting familiar with everything. If you see something that particularly appeals to you then let me know. Okay?"

The food arrived.

"Sounds good to me," shrugged Leo, reaching forward for the Franklyns Gourmet Burger which just looked like a cheeseburger laden down with different relishes to him.

"You know, the sixth floor has a lot of spare offices from Furstin's old staff who've all left, so why don't you pick an office there that suits you?"

"Cool."

She looked at him happily eating and felt relieved and delighted he was there.

"You know, this is the first meal we've had together in quite some time," she said.

"I guess," he grunted.

She reached forward and put her hand on his. "I can't tell you how delighted I am you're here working with me."

* * *

Rachel had arranged to go to lunch with a couple of girls she had befriended from other departments. She now stood at one of the back entrances of Franklyns waiting for them.

There was a line of Limousines and Rolls Royces parked along this quiet street, bumper to bumper, the chauffeurs waiting either in the cars or on the pavement for their employers to return from shopping in Franklyns. A steady stream of cars continued to pull up with more clients emerging – a lot of them Arab, some Oriental – and proceeding into the store where the doormen greeted them and where often a personal shopper had been prearranged to meet them. She had seen the kind of money they would be spending.

Her thoughts drifted to her career. She remembered her first meeting with Nicola Newman when she had been told Franklyns didn't recruit straight into the press office. She wondered how long would be considered acceptable before she applied internally for a promotion. She hadn't been there that long but from what she had heard the entire press office and marketing departments had been got rid of since the takeover. So they were bound to be employing new people soon. She didn't want to miss this opportunity to get where she wanted to be. She made her mind up to make an appointment to see Nicola Newman, much as the thought didn't appeal to her.

* * *

Paul prepared himself in his office for Christine's arrival. He had paged her to come and see him urgently.

His office door opened and she strode in confidently. He could tell from her half smile that she was hoping he had called her to discuss 'them'. And he had, but not in the way she wanted.

"Christine, what you did the other night was extremely dangerous and stupid," he said.

"What I did?"

"Ringing me at three in the morning, pissed out of your

head. This drink and dial has to stop. Anna was there and she was suspicious."

Christine laughed lightly. "Ah, you mean dangerous for *you*!"

"And I do *not* take kindly to threats. You were out of order threatening to tell Anna about what happened between us. Christine, I've asked you before, but now I'm telling you – you're to stop all this nonsense from right now. I'm a married man and you need to respect that and move on with your own life."

"You really take the biscuit! I need to respect the fact you are a married man? You didn't respect that when we were in the throes of passion, did you? And now because you want to reinvent yourself you want me to disappear! But I'm not running away with my broken heart like the last mug you went out with!"

Paul stood up and raised his voice. "I'm warning you, Christine. Fuck off out of my life!"

"No!" she spat back and smiled.

"I wish I'd never met you, let alone gone to bed with you."

"But you have and you did. I'm not going to let you treat me like this, Paul. You picked the wrong gal when you picked me!"

"Christine!"

"And another thing – it's a bit different around here now if you hadn't realised that. You're no longer the boss man, you're the puppet – or muppet might be a better description. Everyone on the shop floor is taking bets about how long you'll last. Furstin might have turned a blind eye to your dalliances with staff – in fact, that creep probably approved. But I doubt Stephanie Holden will. And I'm going to let everyone here know just what you're like. Your wife is the last of your problems, mate!"

* * *

The phone rang on Nicola's desk.

"Stephanie Holden has just left the building, Mrs Newman." It was Jim, the Security Manager on duty. It was six thirty on Monday evening.

"Thank you, Jim."

Nicola hung up the phone and got up from her desk. She made her way to the third floor where she found Mabel waiting for her as arranged. Mabel was the store's top personal shopper and stylist.

"Let's get on with it," said Nicola.

"Maybe we should start off with you telling me what you want? What kind of thing are you looking for?"

"Well, I'm not that sure." Nicola felt very exposed meeting Mabel and asking for her advice. It was like admitting a weakness. "I just want a change from the tailored business suits I seem to live in. I feel they are ageing me somewhat. I want something younger ... sexier."

Mabel's eyes widened at the thought of Nicola wearing something considered sexy.

"I see – well, let's take a walk through the store and start picking out things that I think would suit you and that you like as well. How – eh, sexy – do you want to go?"

Nicola was scheduled to meet David the next day for a follow-up meeting. She was racked with nerves and wanted to look great but be comfortable as well.

"I don't know. Maybe nothing too shocking – to begin with."

Mabel was deep in thought.

"If you look at Stephanie Holden," said Nicola in a begrudging fashion, "she manages to combine looking business-like and fashionable and individual at the same time."

Mabel nodded in agreement and smiled. "Yes, I think I know what you're looking for now. You admire Stephanie?"

"No, I don't admire the woman," snapped Nicola. "I'm just trying to give you an example of what I'm looking for."

The two women set off.

Then Nicola stopped abruptly and looked at Mabel glacially.

"And Mabel – nobody is ever to know about this."

Chapter 29

Nicola was glad that Oliver had an important appointment and had left the house early the next morning. She wasn't due to meet David until later in the day but she was taking the morning off to prepare herself fully and didn't want Oliver being in the way for any longer than he had to.

She opened her wardrobe and looked through the selection of beautiful new outfits chosen with the help of Mabel Hunter. She selected a cream outfit, an elegant one-piece that came to just above the knee with a matching short blazer to be worn over it. She took her time showering, then did her hair and make-up before slipping into her new outfit complete with high-heeled shoes. She stood back and looked at herself in the mirror. She was very happy with the results. Very chic but very sexy.

Smiling to herself, she grabbed her handbag and, leaving the house, walked across the gravel driveway. She looked around and breathed in the fresh air. It was a beautiful morning with the birds singing in the trees. She pressed a button on her car keys and the roof started to fold back on her new car.

She took off her blazer and threw it in the back of the car, placing her handbag on the floor in front of the passenger seat. Sitting into the front seat, she started the ignition and sped off. By the time she was driving through Knightsbridge, she was feeling very confident and very happy with the changes she was making in her life. As she pulled into one of the sidestreets behind Franklyns, she spotted Leo Holden in the rear mirror, driving behind her. She discreetly observed him. He was so cocky she couldn't stand him. Luckily, she was confident nobody else would be able to stand him as well. She was surprised that Stephanie had allowed him near her workplace. But, as Nicola knew only too well, people were blind when it came to their own.

Suddenly Leo pulled out and overtook Nicola. He smiled falsely and waved at her as he passed. She ignored him. He sped off down the road, breaking the speed limit and, indicating, pulled into the carpark entrance under Franklyns.

Nicola had been surprised and annoyed that Leo had been given a parking space – they were only supposed to be for very senior management. Obviously Stephanie had organised one for him or just given him hers. She pulled into the carpark, waving to the security man, and drove over to her parking space. To her annoyance she saw that Leo had parked in a haphazard fashion, nearly taking up two spaces. There was no sign of him around. She parked in her parking space beside Leo's car and looked in annoyance at his slapdash parking. Reaching into her glove compartment, she took out the large notebook and pen she kept there. In big letters she wrote: '*Why don't you learn to park properly?*' Then crossing over to his car she placed it under the windscreen wiper.

* * *

Nicola decided to meet David in his office. She wanted to see him in his own territory this time. She prepared herself as she made her way to the finance department, carrying the files she had prepared. As she walked through the large open-spaced area, she didn't recognise one face as all the old staff had been replaced by people from Barons Bank who were now painstakingly working on the mammoth task of going through Franklyns' accounts. David's office had a wall of glass which allowed him to look out at his whole department. She saw him swinging slightly in his chair behind his desk while he sat back talking on the phone. She was consumed with butterflies as she approached his door. Keep a hold on yourself, she demanded – don't start twittering about Latvians – you need to impress him.

He saw her and beckoned her in with his free hand. She smiled, opened the glass door and, entering, closed it behind her.

"Yep, I'll try and get those accounts over to you by tomorrow. It'll mean me working on into the night though – you owe me one!" He hung up the phone, then looked up at her and smiled. He did a double-take for a second as he took in her new appearance.

She began to blush and willed herself to stop as she sat down opposite him.

"So, how did we do with those files I gave you?" he asked confidently, sitting back and putting his hands behind his head.

"Er, very well I think." She opened the files on his desk. "As you said when we met, all of Furstin's personal staff who worked on his floor no longer seem to be in Franklyns' employ. I haven't a clue what has happened to them but their salaries were not accepted into their accounts. Their banks won't give out any information. It saves us having to get rid of them is how I look at it."

David nodded. "Very strange though. They must have all left with Furstin and gone to work in his direct employ. I'm don't know how he's paying them though – he's not supposed to have any money."

Nicola nodded. "It does seem the most likely possibility. The names that you ticked here – these women who all have Mayfair addresses – some of them are ex-salesgirls. Some of them I know worked on the sixth floor, others I've never heard of before. As far as I'm concerned they had left our employ. I honestly don't know why they continued to be paid these extravagant wages."

David looked worried. "Is there any way we can find out what all these people did? I have to produce a report for Barons. I have to account for everything and everyone."

Nicola shook her head lightly. "I'm sorry."

"Maybe Paul Stewart might know something?"

"I doubt it. As I explained to you before, Karl Furstin operated the sixth floor in complete privacy. There would be no paper trail. I would file them all under administrative jobs, if I were you. And you can just say you've let them all go – cost-cutting." Let sleeping dogs lie, was her opinion. And besides, she was speaking the truth: David would never be able to uncover anything.

"It all leaves a rather bad smell, doesn't it? What was going on?"

"I'll stop these salaries from going through to these people from today, shall I?"

"Yes, do that."

There was a pause as David studied the files.

"Another thing, Nicola, the sales management seem very top heavy. There are so many managers. You've got product managers, then department managers, then assistant floor managers, floor managers, then more managers over two floors. There seems to be too many chiefs and not enough Indians. In my opinion we could slash the management by half. I'm about to talk to Stephanie Holden about it."

Obviously from the Thatcher school of economics, thought Nicola. "I've been saying for years that there is too much management," she said.

David nodded. "Good."

This time she managed to hold his eyes.

The door opened loudly and Stephanie walked in.

"Sorry, David. I've been run off my feet today so only getting to you now."

Nicola turned around, surprised. The woman had just barged in without the good manners to knock. She hated her breezy 'cut through all red tape' style. She'd felt she was just getting somewhere with David and, of course, Holden had to thunder in!

"If you're busy, I'll pop back later, shall I?" said Stephanie and she glanced down at Nicola. "Oh, sorry, Nicola, I didn't recognise you for a second." She gave Nicola a quick look up and down. "You've changed your hair – I like it." She was in fact quite taken aback by Nicola's change of image.

Nicola went bright red, furious with the woman for pointing out the change.

"No, I think we're just about finished, aren't we, Nicola?" said David.

"Eh, yes," said Nicola, standing up quickly. She turned to leave the office and knocked against the corner of the desk by mistake, sending paperwork that was near the edge of it flying to the floor.

"Oh!" said Nicola, going redder and bending over to pick up the papers.

"It's all right – no harm done," said Stephanie, bending over quickly, scooping up the paperwork in a flash and putting it back on the desk.

Nicola stood there awkwardly for a moment before quickly turning and leaving as Stephanie took her seat and started to talk loudly about deadlines.

She made for the safety of her own floor and office. Holden had just come in and dismissed her as if she was some salesgirl! Having the cheek to comment on her hair! Her whole manner towards her hadn't an iota of the respect she was used to. And then Holden had caused her to stand up abruptly and send that paperwork flying like some fumbling idiot. She had completely undermined her with David. And on top of it all Stephanie seemed to speak to David with such blasé familiarity.

Back on her own floor, Nicola walked past Yvette, spotting Rachel Healy waiting for an appointment with her. She went into her office, took off her blazer and put it behind her on her chair. Picking up the phone, she said to Yvette, "Send her in."

A few seconds later, there was a knock on her door and Rachel entered.

"Thank you for meeting me," Rachel said, smiling and taking a seat.

Nicola looked at Rachel sourly. "What can I do for you?"

Rachel had forgotten how intimidating Nicola was but she forced her nerves to play second fiddle to her ambition.

"I just wanted to say I'm very much enjoying working with Chanel. But as you know I really want to work in the press office or marketing department, and since I've now been working in store for a while I was hoping I might be able to apply for a position in either of those departments, as we originally discussed at my interview."

Nicola viewed her coolly for a few seconds. "Highly unlikely. I'm afraid there's nothing suitable available for you there."

Rachel felt crushed, shot down. "But I heard both departments had been let go and that all those positions are soon to be refilled."

"Franklyns is full of all sorts of gossip – you'd be a silly girl to pay any heed to it."

"Well, could I at least put myself forward for anything in those departments when you do start recruiting again?"

Nicola looked at Rachel.. She half smiled. "But, Rachel, I believe you've already been offered a promotion that you subsequently turned down."

Rachel looked confused. "A promotion?"

"Yes, I believe Mr Furstin offered you the chance to join his personal staff?"

"Yes, but I didn't want to work there. I wanted to be at the cut and thrust of retail."

Nicola's expression dripped cynicism. "Oh – you didn't want to work there, didn't you? What a lovely luxury, to be able to turn down the chance of a promotion! I think you should feel lucky you're still in a job when you had the audacity to turn Mr Furstin's offer down!"

"I had heard stories about his staff and didn't feel that environment would suit me."

"You heard stories? By the sounds of it all you do is stand around and gossip all day. Be careful what you wish for. You want to be at the cut and thrust of retail – well, I think that aptly describes where you are right now: the Chanel counter on the ground floor. Is there anything else?"

Rachel felt tears stinging her eyes but refused to let this woman see how much she had upset her. She stood up. "That's about all." Rachel walked to the door before turning and saying, "Is there any point in me applying for a promotion in the future?"

Nicola said curtly, "Your face doesn't fit."

Rachel nodded and quickly left.

She angrily got the lift down to the ground floor. The woman had made her feel like a nothing. There she had been, knocking herself out, working as hard as she could to make an impression so she could move on in Franklyns and get the career she wanted and she was wasting her time. At least now she knew – she had no future here. She would start looking for a new job straight away. But she felt crushed. She had admired Franklyns for so long and had really wanted to establish herself here. But her face didn't fit.

She made her way to the Food Halls. She walked through the chocolate department. Counters were filled with row after row of fabulous chocolate: handmade chocolate designed into different shapes, squares of white chocolate with cream centres, rectangles of dark chocolate wrapped around praline, circles of milk chocolate with all kinds of centres. Truffles. Melted chocolate gurgled down a huge centrepiece fountain. Rachel stopped in front of one counter where all the chocolate was wrapped in red, gold, silver and orange foil wrappers and put in her order. The sales assistant placed her selection in a Franklyns bag.

"Ten pounds when you're ready," smiled the sales assistant.

Rachel opened her handbag, popped the bag of chocolate in and handed over the money. She then walked through the large open doors into the main Food Halls. The area was filled with different counters offering every delicacy a heart could desire. The same Victorian tiles had been in place on the floor since the store had been built and the whole Food Hall had the feeling of a giant Victorian pantry. An abundance of pheasants, quail and gammon lay enticingly roasted on the different counters. Ducklings and goose cooked to perfection were being eyed by the passing shoppers. Pots of mousaka, cottage pie, shepherd's pie were enticingly arranged behind the glass counters.

The glossy patés looked too good to pass.

As Rachel tried to make up her mind which she wanted she heard her name being called.

"Rachel!"

She turned around.

There were different eateries in the corners of the Food Hall. People were sitting up on high stools at the counters being served the specialities of each particular café. One such eatery was the Oyster and Champagne Bar and up at the counter sat Leo on his own save for a glass of champagne and a plate of oysters. Rachel waved and made her way over to him.

"Hello there!" she said when she reached him.

Leo tapped the empty stool beside him. "Hop up there and have a glass of champagne with me."

"If only I could! And those oysters look divine – but I'm working."

"So am I!" said Leo, taking an oyster and swallowing it before downing his glass of champagne.

Rachel glanced around. "Are you with clients or something?"

"No – I mean I'm working here – at Franklyns!" He savoured the confusion on her face.

"As what exactly? Champagne-tester?"

He bellowed a laugh. "That would be a great job all right! No, I've joined the management here. Bit of a bore, but – hey – couldn't let the old woman down when she asked me to help her out."

"I see!" Rachel couldn't hide the shock on her face. "And what department are you managing?"

"I'm a kind of floater. You know, just looking around and seeing what needs improving or not. I'm going to be like a big suggestion box." He brought the tips of his fingers to his mouth and kissed them. "Have to say, champagne and oysters are excellent. No improvement needed here! You sure you won't join me for just a glass?"

"Eh, no!" Rachel glanced at her watch. "I'm very late back for work, I'd better run or Christine will kill me."

"Well, see you later. We'll be seeing a lot of each other from now on." Leo winked at her.

She smiled and quickly made her way from the Food Halls.

* * *

Paul was pacifying a customer on the second floor. The customer was a formidable woman in her eighties. Her family had been immensely wealthy and she had grown up coming to Franklyns. To her it was her local draper's and grocer's. Although her fortunes had declined through the years, she still wouldn't think of shopping anywhere else.

"I do hope, Mr Stewart, that this is not the end of Franklyns as we know it with this bank now owning the store," said the old woman.

"I can assure you that it's business as usual. No changes whatsoever," said Paul, smiling at her.

"I don't know about that, Mr Stewart. I can't bear to come through the front doors any more. All that paraphernalia in the cosmetics departments. Blaring music, flashing lights, it's like entering a circus."

"Well, even Franklyns has to give a nod in the direction of changing times."

"Anyway, as always a pleasure to speak to you, Mr Stewart." She nodded and walked slowly off.

Stephanie had observed the whole interaction.

"Nice touch, Paul," she said, coming up behind him. "I'd say you kiss babies when the need arises as well."

He wasn't sure if her smile was faintly mocking. "Well, you have to make people feel they're special, don't you? That's why they keep coming back here, because they feel special. Her family have been coming here for generations."

Stephanie watched as the woman cautiously got on the escalator.

"And I'd say she's spends no more than a fiver here every week. Unfortunately it's not about making the customer feel special any more. It's about making them feel unhappy. The more unhappy they feel, the more they will spend to try and buy happiness. From the moment people step inside here they need to be overawed – they should feel that their own lives are shit in comparison to what's going on here and that should make them spend a fortune here to try and emulate the lifestyle we offer. Unfortunately, that old dear feeling special is Franklyn's past."

As the old lady went down the escalator, a group of young girls of around twenty came up the corresponding escalator. They were extremely loud and dressed in expensive but tacky clothes, carrying big designer bags.

Stephanie pointed to them. "And that is Franklyns' future."

"It all sounds a bit depressing to me," said Paul.

Stephanie handed him a file. "And now I've something even more depressing for you to do. Here's a list of all the sales managers. The decision has been made that the management needs to be cut by a third. Here's a list of the people who, with the help of Accounts and Personnel, have been chosen to be made redundant. Because you know them better than anyone else, I want you to go through it and give me your feedback about whether we're making the right choices."

Paul reached out and took the file, almost frightened to do so.

"Don't look so worried, Paul – your name isn't on it." Stephanie turned to leave.

"Oh, and Stephanie?"

"Yeah?"

"Tomorrow is my day off. Just want to check you've got nothing you need me for tomorrow?" There was a hint of sarcasm in his voice.

Stephanie shrugged. "No, that's fine."

Chapter 30

Rachel swung around the counter at Chanel, her face flushed.

"I've just met Leo quaffing champagne and oysters in the Food Hall!"

"I know! He's been recruited by Franklyns. Fab, isn't it?" Daniella squealed.

"But what experience has he got of working in management here or anywhere else?"

"Well, none directly, love. But somebody with Leo's life experience, well, he'll be nothing but an asset here."

"You were right in what you said about this place when I started – they like to keep the power to themselves upstairs. Cover me, will you? I'll be back as soon as possible."

* * *

Leo glanced at his Rolex. It was nearly five. Nobody had come near him all day since he finished lunch with his mother. He was still relishing the look of surprise on Rachel's face. Maybe he was going to enjoy being at

Franklyns after all. He decided he would head home early. His mum had his mobile number if she wanted to ring him.

He went down to the underground carpark and made his way over to his car. He was about to get in when he spotted the large sheet of notepaper on his screen. He picked it up. *'Why don't you learn to park properly?'* somebody had written in big letters. Fucking idiot, he thought, somebody had nothing better to do. He crumpled up the paper and threw it on the ground. He was about to sit into his car when he spotted the SLK Mercedes parked next to him. It hadn't been there when he had come in and he remembered seeing Nicola Newman driving it earlier when he had overtaken her. There was a very good chance it was she who had written the note after she parked there. Condescending bitch!

He picked up the paper, uncrumpled it and smoothed it out. He reached into his briefcase in his back seat and took out a big black marker. Then, on the other side of the paper he wrote in big black letters: *'FUCK OFF, YOU DOG!'* Then he got some sellotape from his briefcase, walked over to her Mercedes and stuck the notepaper on the wall over Nicola's car with the tape for all to see.

Then he got into his car and drove away.

* * *

Rachel steadied herself as she walked off the shop floor to where she knew Paul's office was. As always Paul's door was wide open and she saw he was at his desk perusing some paperwork. She knocked on the door and he looked up.

"Can I have a word for a minute, Paul?"

"Sure." He waved towards the seat opposite him. "Fire ahead."

She looked up at all the monitor screens giving different views of the store before focusing on Paul again.

"I can keep an eye on everything going on," he smiled, observing that her cheeks were flushed.

She nodded. "When I came to work here I wanted to have a career at Franklyns. I have a degree and had been working in the press office at Brown Thomas. I came here for the opportunity to make something of myself."

"That's good. Franklyns likes commitment."

"Well, that's just it. I'm not sure if it does. I've been working like a Trojan since I've arrived here and I think my sales figures speak for themselves."

"You're one of the best sales assistants we've ever had working here," he said truthfully.

"Well, that's just it. I've been working hard to prove myself so I could get a promotion into the press office."

"Why don't you apply for it then?"

"I did ... and Nicola Newman said my face didn't fit."

"Ahhh!" Paul sat back, realising what the conversation was about.

"I was just wondering if there was anything you could do?"

"Me? I'm afraid there isn't. When Nicola Newman makes her mind up on something or someone there's no changing it."

"But that's so fucking unfair! Just because I said no to that creep Furstin, she's holding it against me – she told me so! I would work twenty-four seven if given a break here. I've left so much behind in Ireland for the sake of my career and I've just been wasting my time here –"

"Whoa!" Paul's face clouded over and he put his hands

in the air. "Steady on! Did anyone tell you when you started here you would be guaranteed a promotion into the area of your choice?"

"No, but I was told I couldn't work in the press office until I accepted a lower position."

"And now you're sulking like a spoilt child because you fell down at the first hurdle?"

"It's not the first hurdle! I've been told outright that's there's no future here for me."

"I tell you who there's no future here for." He picked up the papers on his desk. "This is a list of managers who are to be told this week that they're being let go and it's a long list. Some of these people have given years to this place and it will crush them. You're young and relatively are at the beginning of your career. You've invested a little time in a corporation that doesn't love you back. Believe me, you'll get over it quickly. But for these people who are about to be let go – well, it's a different matter. You know, Rachel, I had you down as many things: a bit cheeky, spirited, ambitious and with a big future ahead of you. But I never had you down as feeling sorry for yourself."

Rachel stared at him for a few seconds:

"I'm sorry. I've spoken out of turn," she said before turning and leaving quickly.

* * *

"Will Paul approve of the names on the list?" David asked Stephanie as they left work that evening .

"He knows he's got no choice. I gather he's a bit sentimental, has a huge loyalty to Franklyns and the staff."

"It's a wonder he put up with Furstin then."

"The salary Furstin was paying and we are still getting

was a bit too big to walk away from, I imagine. Besides, I'm sure Paul went around undoing Furstin's damage wherever he could. You know, between ourselves, I think Paul is very capable but I'm actually finding him hostile to our takeover in a passive way. He might be different with you, since you know each other."

"That was a long time ago and, looking at the Paul who's been the General Manager here, I wonder if I ever knew him at all. I keep meaning to catch up with him but I've been snowed under with work."

"Maybe you should catch up – you might be able to iron out that thorny attitude he has. Anyway, I'll see you tomorrow." She moved off to flag down a taxi.

"You live in Chelsea Harbour, don't you?" David called after her.

"Yeah."

"Come on, I'll give you a lift. I'm going past there for rugby practice in Fulham anyway."

"Are you sure?"

"Positive."

* * *

The lift doors opened. Nicola walked out and crossed the underground carpark to her car. She stopped abruptly as she looked up at the note saying, *'FUCK OFF, YOU DOG!'* stuck on the wall over her car. She froze. She heard laughing and talking and turned to see Stephanie and David walk round the corner.

She stared at them, taken aback at their being there together.

"Hello, Nicola," nodded David.

"Hi!" she managed.

As they continued to walk, they looked up at the note over Nicola's car in amazement.

"Fan mail, Nicola?" said Stephanie with a smirk as she went to the passenger door of David's car parked nearby.

Nicola quickly went to her car and opened it.

David started his ignition and out of the corner of her eye Nicola saw them drive off, laughing and talking together. When they had safely driven out, she marched up to the note, grabbed it off the wall and saw that it was written on the back of the previous note she had left on Leo's car.

"That little bastard!" she screeched.

* * *

Nicola tore into the driveway and got out of her car, slamming the door behind her. She marched towards the house, quickly wiping away the tears that had been falling down her face for the past half hour.

She could hear the television on inside the lounge as she marched past the open door and ran up the stairs.

"Nicola?" Oliver called out after her.

She went into the en suite and closed the door behind her. She stared at herself in the huge mirrors around the bathroom.

She felt humiliated and demeaned. For that bastard Leo Holden to have had the audacity to stick that note over her car in the first place was bad enough – but then for it to be seen by Stephanie and *David*! Why had he called her a dog? Did he think she was ugly? Did people think she was ugly? Did David? Her whole confidence had been dashed. And there was Stephanie Holden, so confident in her looks and her sexuality, and men going ga-ga for her. She even had David under her spell. While she herself had been hiding in her office and nervously fantasising about him, Stephanie had built up a rapport with him. The two of them heading off laughing and joking together – for dinner maybe or a night out! Was there something happening between them? The thought nearly caused her to scream. She stripped off the chic outfit she had been wearing and put on a satin nightgown. The tears were threatening again.

There was a knock on the door. "Nicola? Are you all right?"

She cleared her throat and wiped her face. "I'm fine!" she called out.

Oliver opened the door and came in. He got a start when he saw her.

"What's wrong? You've been crying."

She walked past him into the bedroom and lay down on the bed.

"I'm fine," she insisted. "Just a headache."

He sat down on the bed beside her. "Nicola, tell me what's wrong?" His face was determined and full of concern.

She knew he wouldn't let it rest. "Nothing ... and everything. Everything's just been so difficult recently. You just don't know what I've been put through. First the mugging – and then work's been so hard. There's been this takeover and everything's different. There are these horrible people in charge now. First they tried to get rid of me and now they're making my life hell."

"This Holden woman?"

"Yes, and now her rotten son has started. And they think they are *it* but they are just so *common*!"

He started stroking her hair. He had never seen her like this and his heart went out to her.

"Why stay there? Leave tomorrow – you don't have to put up with it."

"Oh, Oliver! Don't be so stupid! Why should I leave a job I love and I've worked so hard to succeed in, because of them?"

He admired the fight still in her. He continued stroking her hair. "You know I'll do anything to help you," he said reassuringly.

The Nicola of old would have destroyed them all in a single breath, he thought, the Nicola before the mugging.

Chapter 31

Oliver paced up and down his office as he waited for the two officers investigating Nicola's attack to arrive. He had had hardly any sleep all night, he had been so consumed with worry. All his fears had been confirmed. The attack had left a terrible mark on his wife and that was why she had been so hard to fathom recently. Everything from her new hairstyle to the Mercedes sports car was a reaction to her attack. She had said it last night. Nicola was the strongest person he had ever met – nothing fazed her – and to see her crying like that had broken his heart. As she spoke about the problems at work, he knew that usually she would squash any opposition like flies. This was the woman who had Karl Furstin eating out of her hand. If she could deal with the likes of him without a problem then she could certainly deal with this Stephanie Holden woman. No, it was all down to the attack. And he who had spent his life fighting crime should have realised the impact it would have on her. He shouldn't have listened to her when she dismissed it as a minor event, a nuisance – he should have realised it had affected her much more deeply. He loved her very much.

As was the destiny of most London Commissioners, he was working hard towards one day being knighted. At forty-three he had achieved a lot in his career. He loved their life together and was very happy. And he couldn't wait for her to become Lady Newman, one day when he received his title. It was such a steady road ahead that he was truly shocked to find Nicola having a meltdown and their perfect lives in jeopardy. He would do anything to get things back to where they were.

A knock sounded on the door and the two officers came in.

"My wife's attack – what's happening?" Oliver demanded.

"Er. . . we've come to a dead-end, sir. We can't get a proper visual of the attacker from the CCTV. Nobody saw anything. Your wife can't remember anything. It's difficult to see where we can go from here." The policeman felt exasperated. Any other attack and it would have been filed away by now as unsolved but the Commissioner wouldn't let it drop and there was nowhere else for them to look, no one left for them to interview.

Oliver took up a file and slammed it on the table. "You're trying to tell me that we have absolutely no leads?"

"We've carried out exhaustive interviews and again nobody is of any use. That sideroad is very quiet. It's rarely used except by people trying to skip the taxi queue by waving down a taxi on the way back to a rank. Nobody saw –"

"Now, you listen to me! What chance have we got to save this city from crime when we can't even find who attacked my wife! You get back to Liverpool Street station and you leave no stone unturned until you get the bastard that did this. Get undercover police officers in the station looking out for anything suspicious. Anything!"

* * *

Nicola felt embarrassed by her display in front of Oliver the previous night. In all their years of marriage she had never cried or shown weakness in front of him. Her continuously deepening feelings for David just made her feel so confused and vulnerable. She had explained away how she had felt to Oliver by blaming the mugging. She could scarcely tell him that the main reason she was so upset was because she had been shown up in front of the man she had fallen in love with.

Now at work, Nicola checked her emails. There was one from Stephanie Holden. It was a group email to all department heads telling them to attend a Board meeting the next day at three.

She sat back in her chair. She had really underestimated Stephanie Holden. She had thought a few quick outmanoeuvres would finish her off. But from what she could see and what her spies around the store told her, Stephanie was now very much taking control after her disastrous start. And now that her son, who was a bastard in every sense of the word, had come to 'work' at the store she needed to move swiftly to get rid of them. It wasn't enough that Stephanie knew Nicola was boss and didn't interfere with her. She needed her gone. And if she had her eye on David Stafford, the sooner the better. She wouldn't get the chance to laugh at her again.

Yvette came into her office and left some papers on her desk.

"What do you want me to get you for lunch, Nicola?" asked Yvette.

Nicola had looked at herself in the mirror that

morning. Her figure was good, she was slim, but she felt that maybe she should try and lose a few pounds. She would start a diet immediately.

"Will you get me a chicken sandwich," she said to Yvette, "and actually leave off any mayonnaise or any dressing or butter."

Yvette nodded, recognising the signs that Nicola was on a diet, but she dared not comment.

Nicola reached over to the file she had created for Leo and opened it.

"Get Martha Harkman, Head of HR at Fleishman Stockbrokers, on the phone for me, will you?"

"Sure." Yvette walked out.

A minute later the phone rang.

"Hello, Nicola?"

"Yes, Martha, and how are you?" Nicola purred. They knew each other from being members of a couple of businesswomen's organisations together.

"I'm really well. Usual problems, you know."

"Only too well. We have to do lunch soon and you can tell me all about them. I'm just looking for a reference from you for somebody who used to work at Fleishmans."

"Sure. Who is it?"

"Leo Holden."

There was silence for a bit and then a hollow laugh.

"You know it's illegal for me to give a bad reference, Nicola, so I think I'll just choose not to give a reference at all."

"That bad?"

"Uh huh."

"Do go on."

"Are you asking me to speak in an official capacity or as a friend wanting a gossip?"

"As a friend wanting a gossip."

"In that case – Leo Holden is trouble, and spell that with capital letters. He certainly started off showing promise. He's very bright, very enthusiastic. But perhaps he's a little too bright and a little too enthusiastic." Martha paused.

"I'm listening."

"He was impossible to control. Refused to take direction, took massive gambles, terrible risks, hid mistakes etc etc. But then there were other things. We heard back from very reliable sources that he was supplying clients with cocaine. Now I know a bit of that can go on but this was too big and too indiscreet to turn a blind eye to. But he's very clever – it was hard to pin anything on him even though we knew what he was up to. We finally got him on insider trading and we got rid of him very quickly I can tell you. He left quite a mess behind him. We discovered that he had ignored his clients' instructions and they were really furious when they discovered, especially as they made a loss."

"A bit of a loose cannon then?"

"More of a loose army. Take my advice – bin his CV and show him the door."

"I will. Thanks for that, Martha."

"Any time."

* * *

Paul and Anna had been at the private clinic in Wimbledon and now silently got into the car. Anna's face looked slightly red but she seemed happy. Paul's lips were set in a thin line as he put the key in the ignition and drove off.

"Wasn't too bad, was it?" said Anna cheerily.

"No, I guess not."

She leaned over and stroked his face. "Ah, did you find the whole thing a bit embarrassing?"

"It's just it's bad enough dealing with doctors and hospitals when you're sick, rather than bothering them when there's nothing wrong with you." Paul aggressively turned a corner.

She sat back and smiled. "Mr Big Man at Work doesn't like being told what to do!"

Mr Big Man at Work is very much getting used to being told what to do, Paul thought wryly.

"Anyway we may as well get used to it," she continued, "because depending on these tests we might be starting IVF soon and that's when the fun really starts."

Paul nodded. Why couldn't life be simple, why couldn't they just have a baby as everyone else did, rather than messing with all this nonsense?

"Don't mind me," he said. "It will be all worth it when we have kids."

That night Paul studied the list of names Stephanie had handed him for dismissal. They were all good friends, people who had been in his life for a long time. It devastated him to have to sign off the list. But he knew his approval was only a courtesy – they would get rid of these people anyway.

He was stretched out on the couch in the lounge in jeans and a white shirt. His bare feet gently rubbed Anna's leg as she sat at the end of the couch typing on her laptop, her glasses on.

"You know, here I am writing about the education system again and the funny thing is, I actually don't really care. Can you imagine that? I just care about what we did today and that we're taking the first steps to having our own children. And, you know, when we do have them I won't give a shit about the education system because I'll want ours to have the very best and I'll be sending them to the best private school. There – I'm a self-declared hypocrite after all my years of talking about the need for a good public education system."

He looked at her and laughed. "Have you checked out the price of the best private schools recently, my love?"

"Well, that's just it. I want them to have the very best, no matter what."

Paul hid the sharp twang he felt over the insecurity of his job.

He thoughts drifted to Christine and the trouble she was causing him with her threats. With her big mouth she could seriously undermine him at work and, from what he could sense, they were looking for an excuse to get rid of him. He looked down at the list and saw the name Greg Hudson on the list. He was a good Sales Manager, always willing to go the extra mile. Paul picked up the pen resting beside his tea on the coffee table beside him and drew a line across Greg's name and then he wrote Christine's name in its place.

Chapter 32

Stephanie put up her umbrella as she came out of the Tube station at Oxford Circus. It was nearly one and she had arranged to meet Neil Blackthorn for lunch. Her mobile rang and she paused to answer it as she made her way to Argyll Street.

"Stephanie, Conrad Richardson here," said the smug voice on the phone. "All set for the meeting this afternoon?"

"Yes, I've all the department heads lined up and so it's a good opportunity for you to meet everyone."

"And check on progress."

"Indeed. Give me a call when you're approaching Franklyns and I'll come down and meet you."

"Very kind, see you at three."

Stephanie turned into Argyll Street and walked the few metres to The Argyll pub. When she had been Brand Director of Blackthorns she had been based at their flagship store on Regent Street. When she started going out with Neil, they used to come up to The Argyll for lunch or drinks after work regularly.

She walked in and down the corridor into the main pub which was furnished in traditional brass furnishings.

She walked up the stairs and into the restaurant where the tables for two were all laid out for lunch with white linen tablecloths. It was only half full and she spotted Neil sitting at a table in the corner beside one of the long open windows. She waved over to him and walked across to greet him.

"You're late!" he accused, standing up and giving her a quick kiss on the lips.

"Can I remind you that you are working just a stroll down the street, while I had to get the Tube from Knightbridge?"

They both sat down.

"So, how's tricks?" he asked as she took up the menu and looked through it.

"Good, I suppose."

"Just suppose?"

The waitress came over with her notebook. "Are you ready to order?"

"Yeah, I think so," said Stephanie. "I'm going for the bangers and mash with gravy."

"Hmmm, that sounds tempting. I'll have the same and a pint of Heineken please ."

"Just a water for me," ordered Stephanie.

"Don't be daft! She'll have a red wine."

"I can't! I've a big Board meeting with Conrad Richardson this afternoon," Stephanie objected.

"She'll have a red wine."

The waitress nodded and smiled.

"I really do need a clear head this afternoon, Neil."

"I always find a glass of wine clears the head brilliantly!"

She smiled at him. Neil was a big handsome man in his late forties. He always had a glint in his eye and a smart mouth and she loved his mischievous ways. As she looked out the open window at the rain pouring down on the fruit stalls beneath them in Argyll Street and the people hurrying by she felt very cosy and safe and nostalgic for her time working at Blackthorns.

"Malcolm and Donna say hello," said Neil. His permanent mocking grin could be annoying at times but she also found it irresistible.

"I had dinner with them recently."

"I know," he nodded and raised his eyebrows.

"You could have come too," she said defensively.

"And I know that too."

"Well, why didn't you then?"

"Because I would have to listen to Donna going on for the next two weeks about what a great couple we make and why we should never have broken up!"

She smirked at him. "We didn't actually ever officially go out in order to have broken up, if I may say."

"Well, whatever we had then. A shag every couple of weeks, if you want to call it that."

She felt he was teasing her – he teased everybody. She decided to change the topic. "So how's everything at Blackthorns?"

"Very good, everyone says hi."

"Give them all my love. A great bunch of people, I miss them a lot."

"Well, you didn't have to leave them. Nobody forced you out. You had a job for life with us. But you had to conquer the world and go and become a big hot-shot. Congratulations – you've got it all now, running Franklyns – don't come any higher than that."

The waitress brought over the drinks.

"Why do you say it as if I did something wrong? I

never made any secret of my ambition. I wanted to get to the top."

"Are you happy now you're there?"

She nodded and smiled sarcastically at him. "Blissfully!" She raised her glass and took a drink.

"Now . . . here's your food," said the waitress, putting the plates in front of them. "Enjoy!"

They began to eat.

"I have Leo working there with me now," Stephanie said after a few moments.

He looked surprised. "The mysterious Leo! Are you sure or is that just another figment of your imagination?"

"Oh, shut up, Neil!" Neil always teased her that Leo didn't exist as she had never introduced them.

"I still think it's the strangest thing you kept him hidden away."

"I didn't keep him hidden away. I just didn't want Leo being the kind of kid who was used to having his mother's boyfriend around."

"Better to leave him alone in the evenings while you came back to mine then?"

She shot him a harsh look and warned, "Overstepped the mark, Neil."

He held up his hands. "Sorry!"

They ate in silence for a minute.

"Anyway, I'm glad I never introduced you to Leo," she said then. "What would be the point? Nothing was ever going to be serious between us. I knew it and you knew it, and that's the way we both wanted it. Why bother mixing up a kid's head getting him used to someone who isn't going to be around for long?"

"I'm still around, aren't I?"

"Yeah, as a friend in my life, but not in his."

"I'll never fathom out your relationship with your son."

She shrugged. "What's to say? I know I'll never win Mother of the Year." She sat back and drank her wine. "I was so very young when I had Leo and I wasn't ready for him. When you come from where I come from, you want a lot in life, you know.

"I wanted wealth and power and to be famous, and nothing was going to stop me. I really thought my singing career would bring me to where I wanted to be. Then I was a teenager with a young baby and had to shelve all my plans. And there I was again, in the never-ending cycle of being poor and powerless. And I felt stuck and, of course, I loved my son but I hated my life. And then the years went by and I got the chance to make something of myself again in a new career. And I guess I wasn't going to let anything get in my way this time. So maybe I neglected Leo but I'm really going to try and make it up to him now."

She put down her wine and started eating again.

"You neglected yourself as well," said Neil.

"How?"

"Not letting yourself get too close to anyone. In case it got in your way."

She laughed. "Are you trying to talk about us? As if you were ever going to remain faithful to me! Of course I was never going to get serious about you, Neil, much as I adore you. You were out in casinos every night! You love your life and your space too much, and so do I. Let's leave it at that, shall we?"

"Maybe," he laughed. "At least I know that you would have been the same with anyone. Work always came first."

She leaned forward and chinked her glass against his. "You just keep telling yourself that, if it makes you happy."

* * *

The rain was spilling down as Stephanie hailed a taxi on Oxford Street.

"Can I drop you down Regent Street?" she asked Neil as she folded away her umbrella.

"No, a walk will do me good."

She stepped under his umbrella and gave him a big hug.

"Give me a call, and we'll meet up soon again," she said as she quickly got into the taxi and it pulled away.

* * *

Nicola had toyed with the idea of not attending the department head meeting. Of just not turning up, like she had done the last time, and enraging Stephanie by showing her that she was still unimportant. But she realised that her boycott strategy was shooting herself in the foot. She needed to be present so she could have a voice. She also needed to show David that she was a force to be reckoned with. And she needed an opportunity to get to know him more. That morning she had selected one of the new outfits Mabel had chosen for her and self-consciously did her make-up and hair. She liked the result in the mirror. She looked in control and sexy – she hoped.

* * *

As Stephanie went down to greet Conrad Richardson after meeting Neil for lunch, she felt very nostalgic about her Blackthorn days. They really had been like a family to her at Blacthorns and no other place had the same effect.

Certainly not Franklyns with its gigantic problems and cold and snobby ways.

Conrad Richardson's car pulled up to a side entrance of the store.

"Good to see you again, Conrad." She shook his hand.

"How is everything going?" he asked as he walked alongside her into the store and they made their way to a private elevator to bring them up to the top floor.

"It's actually going very well, Conrad. I've learned a lot about the store and I see where we need to go now. I thought it important for you to meet the department heads and listen to what progress we've made and where I see the store going."

"Naturally. I'm very much looking forward to hearing all."

* * *

Paul spotted Stephanie walking over to the Boardroom with an older man, presumably Conrad Richardson.

"Stephanie, can I have a word with you for a moment?" he asked.

"Sure. Conrad, you go in and I'll follow in a second."

Paul drew her aside and handed her the list of names for redundancies.

"Just letting you know I've approved the names you gave me – except one."

She glanced down at the sheet and looked up at him, surprised. "You think we should keep Greg Hudson?"

He nodded. "I think it would be a mistake to get rid of Greg – he's far too committed to the job. I've given you a replacement name."

She glanced down at Christine's name and shrugged.

"Okay, it's much of a muchness to me who goes as long as we pare down the management."

He nodded and walked into the Boardroom with her. Inside sat David with seven other department heads and Conrad. Paul closed the door behind him and sat down, leaving the top space free for Stephanie.

"Hi, Paul." David nodded over to him.

Paul nodded back at him. This was the first time he had seen David since their initial encounter and the first time they had attended a meeting together. David seemed to never leave the finance department, which suited Paul fine. He studied David as he chatted to the woman beside him. He would not allow himself to be intimidated by him. He was still the General Manager at Franklyns and as such he would speak with that authority.

Stephanie stood there and glanced around the table. She saw Nicola wasn't present. That suited her fine. The woman was an irritating bitch and maybe the more she stayed out of the way the better.

"Ladies and gentlemen, may I introduce to you Conrad Richardson from Barons Bank. Conrad is here to observe what progress we've been making here at Franklyns and listen to some of our plans."

The door opened and Nicola walked in.

"Sorry I'm late, everybody. I got held up."

She looked around the Board table and smiled at everyone.

Paul wasn't sure if he was more surprised to see Nicola turn up or to see her looking so chic and glamorous.

"And Conrad! Good to see you again and welcome to Franklyns!"

Conrad stood up and shook her hand. "Nice to see you again, Mrs Newman."

Nicola flinched for a second as he used her surname. She sat down beside him. She looked around the table and smiled at David who smiled back at her.

Stephanie was looking decidedly sour at her arrival.

"I'll continue, shall I?" snapped Stephanie.

"Please do," Nicola nodded.

"We're about to make some big changes with personnel and I'm going to let David talk about that but first of all Conrad has something to tell us."

Conrad nodded around the table. "As you all know, when Franklyns went into receivership, Karl Furstin was the majority shareholder and we took over his shares. There are number of much smaller shareholders who are naturally very concerned about their investments." He turned and smiled at Nicola, fully aware she was one of the small investors.

"I've never had any doubt that Franklyns would survive this bumpy patch, Conrad, and I'm sure the other shareholders feel the same way," Nicola reassured him.

"Let's hope so, because we are calling a general meeting in two weeks' time, firstly to reassure them and secondly to listen to them."

Nicola saw David looking at her. She thought he looked impressed.

"I want to tell the shareholders that basically I want to democratise Franklyns," said Stephanie. She looked pointedly around the table.

"Democratise?" Nicola laughed lightly. "You make the store sound like a banana republic in the Caribbean."

"In many ways this place has been run like one," Stephanie countered. "I think everyone present is aware of the overstaffing and vast perks that have been going on around here. All that is stopping from now on. I'm stopping all expense accounts from today." Stephanie could see looks of horror around the table but nobody was brave enough to say anything.

"And quite right too," Nicola spoke up. "I've been saying for years there's been far too much excess here."

An unexpected vote of approval, thought Stephanie.

"My plans for Franklyns are to drag it kicking into the modern world. I have been studying intently who is coming in to shop here and there are certain types: the old moneyed class, the Arabs, the tourists. That's all very well. But you know luxury brands are now opening up to everybody. Everybody can afford or aspire to afford luxury items these days. Everyone has Crystal champagne in the fridge, Cartier watches. People want luxury brands and what we should now do is open Franklyns up to the masses who, okay, are not millionaires but have big disposable incomes and want to buy a bit of luxury."

Nicola creased her face in worry. "Please! You're not opening the doors to the chavs, are you?"

Stephanie didn't hide her irritation. "What do you mean by chavs, Nicola?"

"I mean exactly that. Chavs, isn't that the expression for them? These trashy people who spend a fortune trying to buy class."

"That's exactly my point: *spend a fortune*. I want to reach out to everyone who wants designer goods and make them feel they are welcome to buy it at Franklyns. I want everyone to have Franklyns shopping bags. I want people to think when they are out with a Franklyns shopping bag that they are making a statement about themselves. We have to get away from the stuffy image Franklyns has."

Paul cleared his throat and quickly glanced over at

David. "I just think when you dilute a brand like that you're risking losing it altogether. If every slapper in town is seen having been shopping in Franklyns, then we are going to lose the elite name we have and scare off our regular buyers."

Stephanie raised her eyes. "This is the very snobbery that I'm trying to fight here. We're scaring away customers who could turn around this store's fortune."

"You know you did this very same strategy with Blackthorns," said Nicola. "Lots of my friends used to wear Blackthorn and now they wouldn't be seen dead in it. You completely cheapened the Blackthorn brand."

Stephanie kept her temper in check and glanced at Conrad who was attentive to every word.

"I'm sorry if some of your friends don't like wearing Blackthorn any more but for every Home-County middle-aged housewife we lost as a customer, we gained ten new young customers who actually buy more than just a Blackthorn scarf once a year. And Blackthorn's profits are doubled – and at the end of the day it's all about money."

Nicola glared at Stephanie, furious with her comment about her friends and implying she was a middle-aged housewife by association.

"So you're talking about a whole new brand for Franklyns, a less exclusive direction?" asked Paul.

"I want a lot more people through the doors of this store spending a lot more money and that's the way to do it," asserted Stephanie.

"Well, I for one would like it to go on the record that I disapprove of this course of action and think it will badly backfire," stated Nicola.

Paul felt you could cut the tension around the table with a knife. He thought quickly. Should he take the safe option and say nothing? He felt David look at him curiously.

"I want to second what Nicola has said. I think cheapening the Franklyns' name is a bad mistake," Paul said loudly and clearly.

Stephanie looked at Paul in surprise.

There was silence as she looked around the table for any support but there was none coming. David gave her a sympathetic smile. It was a smile that said he was Finance and not willing to voice an opinion on an area that didn't directly concern him.

"There seems to be some difference of opinion," said Conrad who was studying Stephanie intently.

Stephanie felt her heart beating quickly as all eyes were on her. If she weakened now the game was lost.

She spoke clearly and slowly. "I am the Brand Director of Franklyns and I will direct the store's image as I see best. My record has spoken for itself, otherwise I wouldn't be here. I thank you for your opinions but what I say goes and if any of you have a problem with that I suggest you leave now."

She could almost hear her heart beat.

Nicola sighed and sat back. "I hope you're right, I really do, because the consequences may be disastrous."

"Right, shall we move on?" said Stephanie, trying to disguise her relief. "Unfortunately, we have had to make some big cuts with the sales management team. It's not what any of us want but we have to do it to ensure the store's survival. David, do you want to take over?"

Nicola had been dying to look at David and now had the opportunity.

David nodded and his deep cultured voice said, "I'm afraid as Financial Controller the first thing I had to look at was the salaries and, having checked with HR, we are going to slash the Sales Management team substantially."

Paul observed David speak with the easy confident manner he always had. It was as if nothing had changed and Paul felt his whole power base slipping away. He felt fired up from his earlier revolt. "Although I've given my approval to the names of those who are being made redundant," he said, "I do want to point out that I think it will greatly reduce the customer service and quality of management that Franklyns is renowned for."

Stephanie was very surprised by Paul's outbursts. He really was doing himself no favours obstructing all changes, especially in front of Conrad.

David's forehead creased in surprise at Paul's interruption. "Well – I – I think the whole store is top heavy and I think things can operate just as efficiently with less management, maybe even more so."

"Couldn't agree with you more, David," Nicola said cheerily. "Now this is a change that needs to happen and I think you're very brave to instigate it."

The old bitch was nailing her colours to every mast going, thought Paul, and he felt left out on a limb.

"Come on, Paul, you know well we don't need all that management," said Nicola. "You're just being sentimental. Change is hard, but necessary." She addressed him as one would a child.

"I want to make these redundancies from this week," said David.

"Leave it to me, I'll sort it all out," Nicola smiled at him and he smiled back appreciatively.

"Some progress at least," said Conrad.

Nicola sat forward, placed her hands together and slowed her speech. "I really have to say … in the midst of all these redundancies in sales management … I'm very surprised that we have recruited a new member of staff."

"Sorry?" David was confused.

Nicola looked at Stephanie. "Oh, does nobody know?"

Stephanie froze as she stared at Nicola.

"We've just recruited Stephanie's son, Leo. I believe he's coming in at management level, though I haven't a clue what he's supposed to be doing."

All eyes shot to Stephanie. Stephanie sat speechless.

Nicola looked at Stephanie, enjoying every second. "Maybe I'm mistaken? Is Leo Holden not your son?"

Stephanie bit her lower lip. "Yes … Leo's my son."

"And he has started here in management, has he not?"

Stephanie could see Conrad's look of surprise and Paul's look of anger.

"Yes, he has."

Nobody said anything for a long while.

David looked at Stephanie who seemed to be able to offer no explanation and decided to help her out.

"I think that's everything for today then, if nobody has anything left to add?"

There was a general shaking of heads.

"So nice to see you again, Conrad," Nicola said as everybody got up from the Board table and started to leave.

"And you too, Mrs Newman," Conrad smiled at her.

"Nicola – please call me Nicola. You know, my father is having a drinks party over the next month. I would love to introduce you to him." She made sure to say it loud enough for David to hear.

"Yes, I'm an admirer of his and I would love the opportunity to meet him."

Stephanie waited at the head of the Board table, glaring at Nicola who was busy chatting to Conrad and trying to impress him. She was waiting for her opportunity to nab her as everyone dispersed. As Stephanie watched Nicola and Conrad exit behind the others, she stood up to follow them, ready to pounce on Nicola. Suddenly Paul reappeared and closed the door behind him.

"Paul, I can't talk right now," Stephanie said, walking past him and going for the door.

He blocked her. "Your son is working here?" he demanded angrily.

"Yes, he is. What of it?"

"What of it?" He was aghast. "Firstly, I am the General Manager and until you make the decision to fuck me out of here, then I am still directly in charge of management and I should have been consulted before you took someone on. Secondly, how can you justify employing someone when you've just given me a long list of people to get rid of? And thirdly, he's your son! I thought you wanted to end nepotism in this store?"

"I didn't get the right moment to tell you about Leo. I was going to say it to you today but Nicola pre-empted me." She stared at him but couldn't think of anything to say to counter his accusations.

"You know something, Stephanie? That really stinks. You can tell all those people on that list that they are being dumped yourself, I'll have no part of it. And yes, you can see that as a direct and flagrant disobeying of your instructions." He turned and left.

"I wasn't going to ask you to tell them …" She trailed off. He was gone.

She quickly made her way out of her office to look for Nicola. She didn't have to look far. She was positioned at the end of the corridor by the lifts, still talking to Conrad. Stephanie approached them.

"Nicola, a word, when you're finished?"

"Yes, give me a second. Conrad, so nice to see you again. Be in touch."

"I certainly will." He turned and nodded at Stephanie before getting into the lift. "I'll talk to you later, Stephanie."

"Thanks for coming, Conrad."

Stephanie waited until the lift doors closed. She knew she was the only person who still had an office on the sixth floor and so there would be nobody else about, but she was so angry she wouldn't care if there was.

"That was a lousy trick bringing up my son in the meeting," she spat.

"It was no trick at all. I thought everyone knew."

"Don't bullshit me, Nicola. You knew what you were doing. You tried to undermine me at every opportunity."

"If I can remind you, you were the one who insisted I attend these meetings. I just like to voice my opinions."

"Don't play the innocent, Nicola!"

"I'm not playing the innocent. You know it's usually quite good to have a veneer of niceness but I don't think there's any point between us, is there? Why shouldn't I shout from the rooftops about your son coming to work here amidst a sea of redundancies? If I wasn't three times cleverer than you, I would be gone too. You did try to give me my marching orders, didn't you?"

"Only because you were so hostile to everything I was trying to do – you gave me no option –"

"Of course I was hostile to you," said Nicola in a cool and relaxed way. "As far as I'm concerned you represent everything that is wrong with this country. I actually happen to care a lot about what happens to Franklyns. It's been a big part of my life. For you, it's just something to rebrand, mark up and sell on. Your plans for the store made me shudder. You might as well take down the Franklyns sign at the front and put up a new name – 'Chavs-R-Us'! Twenty years ago you wouldn't even be allowed in here to shop, let alone run the place along with your bastard son!"

Stephanie fought back the tears. She would not allow this woman to see how much she was upsetting her.

"As you pointed out, there plainly is no reason to keep a veneer of niceness any more. I'm not leaving, Nicola. I'm here to stay. And I'm going to turn this store around and make it attractive enough for buyers to come in and buy it when it's launched on the stock market. You might not like it, but you're the past here and I'm the future. Franklyns needs to be at the cutting edge with somebody savvy enough to bring it there. You're old-fashioned, Nicola – your thoughts, your life and, despite a recent improvement, your style – that's why there's no future for you here."

"We'll see." Nicola's voice was ice and she hit the button for the lift and quickly entered it.

Chapter 33

Rachel walked into the staff restaurant which was at the back of the store and offered views across the mews houses of Chelsea.

Daniella was reading a copy of *Hello* on her own in a corner table. Rachel got a coffee and headed over to her.

"Oh, hi!" Daniella closed the magazine. "You'll never guess the latest – they've only gone and put up the prices of all the food here. It's not subsidised any more."

"You're joking?"

"Part of all the cutbacks. You look a bit fed-up. What's wrong?"

"Oh, it's just this place. You know I really wanted to make something of myself here and now the door has been firmly slammed in my face."

"I did warn you," said Daniella sympathetically.

"I know. More fool me to believe I could get anywhere here. You know, I actually feel like going out tonight and getting pissed – are you on?"

"I'm always on for that, love. It's usually me dragging you to the pub!"

"Well, I fancy a few drinks tonight, so off we go to The Blue Posts!"

* * *

Paul looked at all the television monitors on the wall of his office. He was glad he'd spoken up at the meeting and glad he'd told Stephanie Holden what he thought about her son's appointment. They were railroading over everything and everyone. Furstin might have been many things but at least he left the running of the store to Paul and he made sure things were run smoothly. Of course, he had to defer to Furstin and Nicola when they were being petulant or when they wanted their whims agreed to. But as a rule he had enough power to run a good ship. He felt powerless now and these people weren't just petulant – they were just interested in profits.

There was a knock on his open door and he swung around. He was startled to see David Stafford standing there.

"Hi, Paul, do you mind if I come in?" said David who had already entered. "I've been meaning to drop by and have a catch-up with you, but I can't believe how busy it's been."

"I can imagine," said Paul.

"How crazy is this, working in the same place after so many years?"

"Pretty crazy all right." Paul felt very uncomfortable.

David coughed. "I might as well get the unpleasantness out of the way first."

Paul had felt that it was something more than a social call. "If it's about what I said to Stephanie, I totally stand by it. This is Franklyns of Knightsbridge and we should be very careful about interfering with the brand. I believe –"

"Wait!" David put his hands in the air. "Not my department, Paul, luckily. No, all that side of things has nothing to do with me. I'm the Finance."

"Well, what is it then?" Paul couldn't keep the impatience out of his voice.

"It's the Beamer."

"What Beamer?"

"Your Beamer … your BMW."

"What about it?"

"Well, you heard how all perks stop from today. I'm afraid your Beamer is one of those perks. We're taking back all company cars."

Paul was speechless. He wanted to shout and kick something.

"Paul?"

"Oh, yeah sure." Paul took out his car keys from his trouser pocket and tossed them through the air.

David grabbed them. "Thanks, Paul. Listen, I would really love to catch up with you, find out everything that's been going on in your life. Let's not leave it any longer. What you doing this evening after work?"

"Well, I was –"

"Excellent, let's go a across to The Blue Posts for a drink – that's where everyone seems to hang out around here, isn't it? I'll meet you down at Door 7 at six." David smiled, tossed the keys into the air and caught them again as he walked out.

* * *

Rachel and Daniella made their way across to The Blue Posts after work.

"You know, I've been looking forward to this all day," said Rachel happily.

"Oh, meant to tell you, Leo's joining us – that's okay, isn't it?"

"Oh!" The smiled dropped from Rachel's face but she quickly replaced it. "Of course it's fine." Damn, she was looking forward to a bit of relaxed fun for the night. Leo's presence meant she would be on guard.

* * *

Paul had been apprehensive all afternoon about meeting David for drinks. Why was David bothering? What point was there in trying to revive a friendship after twenty years, especially when there hadn't been much of a friendship there in the first place? Just because they now worked together didn't mean they would have anything in common. They didn't then, why should they now?

David was waiting outside Door 7, smoking a cigarette.

"You still haven't managed to kick them then?" asked Paul as they strolled across to The Blue Posts.

"I never bothered trying to give them up. Why bother? You know, this is really weird – it's like years ago after school when we used to all go playing footie or go off drinking or whatever, remember?"

Paul gave a little shallow laugh. "Just like old times."

* * *

Nicola came out of the building and saw Rachel and Daniella disappearing into The Blue Posts. Then she spotted Paul and David also going in. It certainly hadn't taken David much time to settle in. One minute heading off with Stephanie and the next off drinking with Paul. She felt very excluded. She was surprised he would go into The Blue Posts, as it might look bad for his position. Nicola always maintained bosses should stay separate from workers. David obviously didn't care or was confident enough in his position. She turned and walked away. She had been very happy with her day's work up to a point. She had completely put Stephanie in her place. But then, just like a drowning horse coming up for a last breath, Stephanie had got her back by describing her as old-fashioned. The insult had cut deep. Did David see her as old-fashioned in spite of her recent revamp? Maybe it hadn't been just the way she had been dressing or her hair – maybe it was something coming from within. Maybe she didn't have that free-and-easy attitude that the likes of Stephanie had. Maybe he wouldn't see her as the type of person to go for a drink with. Well, if the truth be known, she actually wouldn't be the type of person to go for a drink with, because she never went after work. It was almost unthinkable for her to go to The Blue Posts.

* * *

Leo was already waiting at a corner table when the girls arrived and he waved over to them.

"You're late!" he accused, standing up and kissing Daniella.

"We're not all the boss's son, you know," said Daniella. "We can't all clock off when we feel like it."

Leo reached forward to Rachel, put his arm around her waist and kissed her cheek. She took the kiss awkwardly.

"What are you two drinking?" he asked.

"Two white wines," said Daniella, sitting down.

Rachel sat down and spotted Paul over at the bar talking to a man she didn't recognise.

"I see that bastard is over there." Rachel nodded in his direction.

"Paul? I thought you had a soft spot for him," said Daniella.

"You're sadly deluding yourself."

* * *

David hadn't changed that much, Paul decided, as the two of them sat up at the bar.

He had aged very well – if anything he was more handsome than he had been years ago and attracted even more female attention from what he could see as they entered the crowded pub. And he was oblivious to it, as he had been years ago, almost as if the attention was his birthright. When David went out with the best-looking girls, it was taken for granted. He never made a fuss about it. David sat at the bar in the same self-assured confident way he always had and Paul felt himself growing jealous of him. It was a feeling he despised in himself.

"So you're married anyway." David nodded at Paul's wedding ring.

"Yeah, to Anna. We're married a few years."

"Good for you. Any kids?"

Paul felt on edge again "No, not yet. She's a journalist – you might have read her columns – Anna Stewart?"

"Oh, sure, yeah, think I've read her once or twice. She gets a quick look in between the business section and the sports section." He didn't seem overly impressed.

"You?" Paul asked.

"No, still looking."

"Where are you living?"

"Hampstead, been there a while. No plans to move just yet. You?"

"Wimbledon. So you became an accountant – that's what you wanted to be, wasn't it?"

"Yeah, always knew exactly what I wanted," said David. "Well, I suppose Dad being an accountant paved the way. I went to the London School of Economics from school if you remember, then after qualifying went to work at a few city firms. Got sent out to work in Dubai for three years. Then came back and started working at Barons Bank."

"Two and two equals four."

"Huh?"

"No setbacks along the way – everything worked out perfectly for you."

"Yeah. I guess I was lucky."

As if you would be anything else, thought Paul.

"You're not in touch with anyone from school, are you?" quizzed David.

"No … you?"

"Yeah, loads of them. I still play rugby with most of them or meet up for drinks. I'm still friends with Rob. Remember him?"

That twit, thought Paul.

"And Rupert, remember him?"

That twerp, Paul thought.

"Then there's Josh."

Asshole that he was, and probably still is.

"Then there's Ben. I was his best man last summer."

And another reminder why I didn't keep in contact with any of them.

"What Uni did you go to again?" David questioned.

"Eh, I didn't hang around college for too long. It kind of bored me. Wanted to get out into the real world." "Oh ... did you always want to work in retail management? I can't quite remember what you wanted to be."

"I wasn't really sure, David. It was trial and error for me. But I found my niche and I'm very happy with where I am."

"Good for you. We all take different routes to get where we want to go."

If David was nasty, pretentious, insulting, it would be easier for Paul to know why he didn't like him. But he wasn't, which made it harder to understand.

"Don't mean to talk shop, if you'll pardon the pun, but it's a funny old place, Franklyns, isn't it?" said David.

"In what way?"

"Well, the things I'm uncovering you would not believe. When I make my final report I don't think the folk back at Barons Bank will believe it all. It reads like a fairy tale. Furstin and his wife Elka sound like they were cuckoo."

Paul felt himself become defensive. "They weren't that bad. Just very rich. Very rich people can sometimes let it go to their heads."

"Well, that's just it – they weren't very rich. It was all borrowed, some of it maybe illegally."

Paul's face became creased with worry. He wished he hadn't agreed to going for drinks with David. He might be trying to get information out of him for all he knew.

David looked around the pub. "So go on, fill me in on all the gossip. Who's who here and who's shagging whom?" He gave a little laugh.

"There isn't really anything to tell," Paul said defensively.

David's blue eyes bored into him as if just realising the situation. "You can relax, Paul. I'm not here to pick your brains or trip you up. I genuinely just wanted to meet an old mate for a drink or two."

Paul said nothing for a while and then visibly relaxed. David wasn't a devious person – that was one thing he remembered distinctly about him.

"Yeah," sighed Paul. "It's just that it's trying times and I suppose everyone's on edge."

David gave an understanding nod and then leaned forward. "So, go on, who's shagging whom?"

* * *

Paul looked at the clock on the wall behind the bar and was it was half past eight. He hadn't told Anna he was going out that night and felt he should make tracks, but he was finding David's company oddly compelling. The fact he hadn't changed that much was astonishing for Paul, considering he felt he had changed so much himself. And he had this ridiculous desire to impress David even thought he knew deep down David was the type of person who never got too impressed.

"Nicola Newman is an interesting woman, isn't she?" said David, as two more pints arrived in front of them.

"Is she?" Paul raised an eyebrow.

"Yeah, she's just so in control and capable."

"Oh, she's that all right."

"Impressive."

"That's one word for her, I suppose. I guess I'm not surprised you are impressed by her. Didn't you have Margaret Thatcher up on your bedroom wall while most kids had Madonna?" Paul laughed.

"That's a bloody lie!" David laughed too.

"We used to stay out of each other's way when I used to run the store –" He stopped abruptly, thinking of what he had just said, and corrected himself. "She used to stay out of my way while I ran the store. She thinks she's above everyone because she's an MP's daughter and married to the Police Commissioner."

"What's her husband's name again?"

" Oliver Newman's her old man. I'll tell you one thing – you'll never get the better of Nicola Newman."

"I think you might be right on that."

A tall blonde girl walked past Paul and gave him an obvious cold look. She was the girl he had had a fling with on a management course the previous summer.

"She doesn't seem to like you," observed David.

Paul raised his eyes to heaven. "Hmmm."

"What's wrong with her?"

The drink was having its effect on Paul and he felt loosened up and needing to impress David. "Nothing. She just doesn't take rejection easily." Paul gave a knowing look.

It took a while to sink in. "You mean – you and her?"

Paul nodded.

"And when was this?"

"Oh, a couple of years ago."

"Paul, you dirty dog!" He got up and took his cigarette packet from his blazer pocket. "I didn't think you had it in you! Just popping outside for a smoke." David shook his head and, laughing, went outside.

Paul swung towards the bar smiling to himself. That would give David something to think about. Let him carry that story back to the old gang.

To his right he spotted Rachel waiting for her order. She

was looking straight ahead.

"Hi there," he said.

She glanced at him quickly and said "Hi," before looking straight ahead again.

"Bit of a chill wind around here," he said with a smirk.

She glanced at him again and looked away.

"Ah, you're not talking to me after our chat the other day," he said.

"There's nothing wrong with me, Paul. Just waiting for my order."

"I didn't think you'd be the type who sulked."

"Well, you didn't think I was the type to feel sorry for myself either. So there you have it. You got me all wrong!"

"*Ewe!*" Paul laughed. "You *are* prickly!"

She turned and looked at him. "Well, now you know how a cold shoulder feels. When I came to you looking for a bit of guidance you shot me down and showed me the door."

He was a little taken aback. "Is that the way to address your boss?"

"I don't really care, Paul, because you're not going to be my boss for much longer. I'll be starting to look for a new job next week."

"You are taking this setback seriously."

"When I have been told that my face doesn't fit, there really isn't any point in me hanging around. I want to build a good career for myself and Franklyns obviously can't provide me with it. So I'll go elsewhere. I think I've a lot to offer, even if nobody else does."

"I never said you hadn't a lot to offer. Look, if I was a little brusque with you then, I'm sorry. I've been under tremendous pressure recently. I actually do think you could have a big future ahead of you and –"

"You only have a big future ahead of you if people allow you to have one."

Her drinks arrived and she took them and began to walk back to her table. She halted then and turned back to him. "Apology accepted, Paul. I can imagine what pressure you're under. And, you know, everything that's going on is very unfortunate but I can't lose sight of why I came to London and that was to build my career and I have to go where I get the best chance to do that." She walked off.

David came back in from outside.

"Is that another of your conquests?" he asked laughing.

"No – not at all," Paul stopped looking after Rachel and turned back to the bar and his drink.

* * *

Rachel had been so wound up and in need of a good night out that she began to let her guard down in front of Leo as the night wore on.

He came back from the bar with three glasses of wine and also three shots of sambuca. He placed a glass of wine and a sambuca in front of her and another wine and sambuca in front of Daniella's empty chair. Daniella had had a quick succession of drinks and was now up at the side of the bar singing.

"I'm not drinking any shots, thanks very much anyway," said Rachel, looking suspiciously at the sambuca.

"Why not?" Leo took up his sambuca and downed it in one.

"Because I have work tomorrow and I know I'll have a bad head, but a shot of sambuca might push me over the edge."

"In for a penny, in for a pound – that's always been my motto," said Leo.

"I can't imagine you doing anything by half measures, all right." Rachel looked over at Daniella who was hitting a high note. She picked up her glass of wine and chinked it against Leo's glass. "Well, congratulations on your appointment!"

"Thanks, I think I'm going to enjoy working at Franklyns more than I thought I would."

"I thought you said to me before that you didn't like working for other people and that's why you left the City?"

"You've a good memory," he accused in a surprised tone. "I'm not going to say no to an opportunity when it presents itself like this – I'd be mad to. Give me a few months in there and I'll be upstairs with the big boys. Board of Directors, the lot."

She both admired and was irritated by his confidence. "I suppose I could say something like it might help that your mother is the boss."

"*Ohhh!*" He grinned and slapped his hands together. "I like your style! I knew it wouldn't take you long to get cynical. As I told you before, being cynical is good. You don't get disappointed."

"Hmmm ... the last thing I want to be is cynical. Just had a bit of a disappointment in work recently and I have to snap out of it."

"Don't snap out of it, baby. Go with the flow. Get fired up from what you're feeling and do something about it. Your trouble is you play life by the textbook. You should take that textbook and tear it up and realise the rules are there *are* no rules. It's not how hard you work but what you're seen to be doing; it's not what you know it's who you know. You want something, you take it."

"It's not in me to be some ruthless bitch."

"Lighten up and enjoy life, Rachel, and stop feeling dutiful and guilty about what the right thing to do is all the time."

She sighed and shrugged. She took up the shot of sambuca. "Down in one?"

He nodded. "Down in one!"

Rachel held her nose and tossed the liquid to the back of her mouth.

* * *

Paul put his keys into the front door and let himself in. Anna was curled up on the sofa watching a film.

"I didn't hear you drive in," she said, before spotting he had been drinking. "Oh, you've been to the pub."

"Yeah," he sighed and sat down beside her. "Went with David Stafford."

"The guy who you were in school with. How was it?"

"Stimulating!" He threw his eyes to heaven and she giggled. He began to rub her feet "Being in the pub isn't the only reason I don't have the car. They've taken back the –" he pulled a face and imitated David's accent, " *Beamer.*"

"What?"

"The BMW – gone. All part of the cutbacks, no more perks."

"I'm sorry, Paul! I know how much you loved that car."

He sighed again. "We better go looking for a new car next week. Not sure we'll be getting a BMW with the IVF costs though."

"The BMW might have had to be changed anyway.

When we have children, you'll need a more practical family car."

"I guess – you're always so positive." He smiled at her and she smiled back. He was furious with himself for intimating to David that he had had an affair. He was so intent on impressing the bastard he had bragged and ended up shooting himself in the foot big time. Firstly, he had been desperately disloyal to Anna. Then he probably had undermined his position as opposed to strengthening it by showing he had slept with one of the employees. And lastly he had portrayed his marriage as being not so great.

Paul threw his head back against the back of the couch and groaned loudly. "I'm such a pratt!"

"Hey – what's brought this on?"

"I'm such a vain, easily flattered, egotistical show-off – why do you stick around?"

She smiled. "Because at least you realise you're all of those things. And they're only a small part of you. Anyway, it's endearing when you are like that – you make me laugh."

Chapter 34

The middle-aged businesswoman got off the train at Liverpool Street Station and briskly walked along the platform to the main concourse. She stopped off at the newsagent's and picked up a morning newspaper. She looked at her watch and, realising she was late for her meeting, hurried towards the steps that led outside. She sighed as she saw the queue at the taxi rank and quickly made her way to a sidestreet where she had often managed to flag down a taxi returning to the rank.

As she turned into the quiet sidestreet she kept alert, looking for any approaching taxi. Then she was suddenly struck on the side of the arm and sent flying to the ground. Dazed and confused, she looked up in horror as the youth who had struck her reached down for her earrings while at the same time grabbing the watch off her wrist.

Suddenly the youth was pulled away. She watched petrified as two men pushed him up against the wall. Then, as one of the men continued to restrain the youth, the other came towards her.

"You're all right. You're safe," he said reassuringly, seeing her panicked face.

* * *

"I feel there's a very good chance this could be the same guy who attacked your wife," said the police officer to Oliver. "The way he operated was exactly the same."

"Good work," said Oliver. The two officers investigating Nicola's attack had been scouting around Liverpool Street station in plainclothes, trying to make a breakthrough.

"Get me a photo of the bastard," said Oliver.

* * *

That morning Nicola had chosen the sexiest outfit that Mabel had selected for her before coming to work. Since the previous day her mind had been occupied by the thought of David going to The Blue Posts. He was obviously a social creature and she needed to be one too if she was to get near him.

Yvette came into her office and put some papers in front of her.

"What do you want for your lunch?" she asked.

"Ah, just a salad, no dressing, small piece of chicken on the side."

"Uh huh," Yvette nodded. Nicola had been rigidly sticking to a strict diet regime every day.

"Eh, Yvette . . . do you fancy going for a drink?" Nicola asked.

"Sure," said Yvette. "What do you want, a coffee or a tea?"

"No – I –"

"Soft drink?"

"No . . . I mean go for a drink . . . with me . . . after work?"

Yvette took on the appearance of the proverbial bunny caught in the glare of a headlight.

"A drink?" Yvette's voice seemed to have risen an octave but her smile looked set to crack her face. "Eh . . . yes . . . that would be lovely."

"Good," Nicola nodded.

"Eh, where shall we go?"

"The Blue Posts. Doesn't everybody?"

* * *

"That boyfriend of yours is a very bad influence," groaned Rachel. Her head had been thumping all day from a hangover and wasn't being helped by the loud music and never-ending progression of customers.

"Oh, you get used to dealing with hangovers after a while," said Daniella.

"I don't want to get used to this, thanks very much. I would have been fine if I'd stuck to the wine but he started ordering shots."

"He's great, isn't he?" grinned Daniella.

"Hmmm . . . Listen, we're out of stock on that new perfume – I'm just heading up to the stockroom to get some more. Give me a welcome chance to get off this bloody shop floor."

Rachel made her way up to the stockroom on the third floor. She walked out through the double doors of the shop floor and past Paul's office door which was, as ever, open. She didn't even glance in.

* * *

Paul was sitting at his desk pressing the buttons on the remote control, changing the different views of the floors on the television monitors on the wall.

He heard a slow clapping in his doorway and looked over to see Christine standing there.

"Got to hand it to you, Paul, well done!" Her voice was harsh as she walked in and up to his desk. "You managed to get rid of me at last, didn't you?"

"If you're talking about your redundancy, Christine, you're just one of a lot of managers being let go. It's nothing personal."

"Nothing personal! You had control over who went and who stayed."

"No, I didn't. The list was drawn up by the new management."

"Don't lie to me!" Christine nearly shouted.

Paul stood up. "I do think this is for the best all round. I never promised you anything. We had a bit of fun and you couldn't let it go. It's not a healthy situation. I need to get back to my life and you need to get on with yours. The redundancy package is very good and I'll give you an excellent reference –"

"What, that I was a great shag? You're filth, Paul. You used me for a little diversion from your fucking boring marriage and life and then just dropped me."

"I never wanted it to get this bad between us!"

"No, you wanted me to go off quietly with a lovelorn look on my face, your ego fed. Well, fuck you, Paul! I wish I'd never set eyes on you. And I pity that poor stupid wife of yours that you can't come clean and just say your marriage is a sham."

"That's the whole thing, Christine – it isn't a sham. I love her very much."

"I don't understand you, Paul . . . and, you know, now I don't want to any more."

She stormed to his office door. Then she turned and fixed him with a steely glare. "Oh, and Paul . . . watch your back."

"Christine!" He walked out from behind his desk and went quickly after her but Christine had already stormed through the double doors back on to the shop floor.

He turned around to go back into his office.

And there was Rachel, standing there carrying several boxes of Chanel, her face embarrassed and anxious.

"I . . . eh . . . . . ." She didn't know what to say.

Paul glared at her, feeling exposed and guilty. He walked back into his office and closed the door.

* * *

That evening, Yvette and Nicola walked across the road towards The Blue Posts. Nicola felt apprehensive. In all her years at Franklyns, she had never dreamed of going into the pub. She had strange feelings towards the place, a mixture of contempt punctuated with jealousy.

"Have you been to The Blue Posts much?" she enquired as she opened the front door.

"A few times," said Yvette, looking uncomfortable.

Nicola walked in, followed by Yvette. She looked around the traditional interior. "It's larger than I thought it was," she said.

As they walked through the crowd, which was mainly composed of Franklyns' employees, people began to spot her and suddenly whispers were rushing around the pub. Nicola felt herself blush and wished she could spot Paul or somebody who could give her moral support.

"Eh, what do you want to drink?" she asked Yvette.

"A chardonnay would be divine," said Yvette.

"Two chardonnays," Nicola said to the barman. She took her purse out of her handbag and paid him as he served them their drinks.

Whispers continued to circulate then suddenly everyone was talking normally again.

"Where shall we sit?" asked Nicola.

"How about over there?" Yvette nodded to a free window table.

"Yes, that looks fine."

Sitting down, the two women exchanged a quick awkward smile before lapsing into quietness.

* * *

Nicola looked at her watch. It was now half eight and she was keeping one eye on the door, wondering if David would walk through, while Yvette twittered on. She was willing him to walk through the door, hoping he might be working late.

"I have such a problem with food," Yvette was saying.

Nicola cast an eye over Yvette's slim frame.

"I just can't put on weight – no matter how I try. It's terrible. I can eat anything and never put on a pound. I went to the doctor and he said I was actually underweight. He devised this high-fat diet for me, but did it work? No. I actually had to keep forcing myself to eat all this fattening food but to no avail. I would be sitting at home with a huge bowl of carbonara in front of me, having already eaten loads of other food, and I was actually stuffed but still had to eat. I gave up in the end – some people are just naturally skinny, and what can you do?"

Nicola sat stony-faced. She was starving after her light diet lunch. And all Yvette seemed capable of talking about was food.

Nicola looked at the door again and realised David wouldn't be coming in that evening.

"Shall we go?" she said eventually, cutting in on Yvette's description of the aromatic duck she'd had the previous night that had failed to add an ounce to her figure.

"Oh, yeah, that's fine," said Yvette as Nicola stood up and put on her coat.

* * *

Oliver was waiting expectantly at the kitchen table when his wife came in. She looked a bit dejected. He could hardly contain himself.

"Sorry, I meant to call you to say I would be a bit late," she apologised.

"That's fine. Just come over here a minute and sit down," he said.

"What is it, Oliver?" she said snappily. She was in no mood for any of Oliver's long-winded stories.

"Just come over here a minute," he insisted.

She tutted and went and sat down.

"Now, I want you to prepare yourself for this. I'm going to show you a photo and I want you to tell me if it jogs anything in your memory from the mugging."

"Go on, Oliver! Just show it to me – I want a bath."

He opened the envelope and put the photo in front of her. She froze as she looked at the photo, remembering the fear she had felt at the moment of the attack.

"Yes, that's him," she said. It was strange but the

mugging had happened so fast she had no image of him in her mind, but being presented with his photo, the memory was all too real.

Oliver smiled and sighed. "Excellent. We have him in custody. He attacked another woman near Liverpool Street station today." He reached over and took her hand. "This means we can finally put this behind us. I'll be able to track down your jewellery and your wedding ring and we can start getting back to normal."

He smiled at her. She looked at him blankly.

Chapter 35

Stephanie spotted Leo chatting in an animated fashion to two salesgirls on the second floor. Whatever story he was telling was obviously hilarious as the two girls were in stitches. She spotted Paul Stewart glaring at him, arms folded. She frowned and, turning, made her way to the lift to go back to her office.

She took out her mobile and dialled Leo's number.

"Mum?" he answered right away. At least now he took her calls – which was one good thing.

She kept her voice light. "Leo, if you have a spare moment, could you pop up to my office? I want to have a quick chat with you."

"Sure. I'm free now. I'll head up to you."

She closed over her phone. Free now? He was free all the time from what she could see. And he seemed to be making no headway in finding a role for himself at Franklyns. It had been two weeks since he had started and she had thought, had hoped, he would have an idea of what he wanted to work at in the store by now. Since the disastrous board meeting where Nicola had informed everybody that Leo had come to work at Franklyns nobody had mentioned her son to her.

The series of redundancies was now nearly complete. She had handled them herself. Never a pleasant experience, she had gone home and had a good cry after doing them. Paul Stewart continued to give her a look which was a mixture of anger and disappointment when she was dealing with him. Nicola Newman she had avoided like the plague. Only David Stafford continued to treat her in a professional and courteous fashion. She knew the Thatcherite in him would obviously not approve of Leo's appointment but she guessed he had much bigger fish to fry. Besides, he was an outsider like her. She went into her office, turned on the computer and checked her emails. There was one from Conrad Richardson. She opened it.

Stephanie,

We had a board meeting here at Barons and have heard that the remaining shareholders are very concerned about Franklyns' future. We feel it is imperative to reassure the existing shareholders. When Franklyns is launched on the stock market, if these shareholders feel a lack of confidence they will rush to sell their shares. However, if they feel confident about the store's future they will be the first to buy and the share price will immediately start to accelerate.

We feel we need to launch a public relations offensive to reassure the investors. I'm suggesting a function, sooner rather than later, where we can unveil our plans for Franklyns and also provide an opportunity for them to meet the new team. I'll leave the arrangement of the function in your very capable hands.

Conrad

Stephanie frowned. She certainly saw Conrad's point.

It was just that she had more than enough on her plate trying to sort the place without having to organise a party for a bunch of investors. And since she had got rid of the PR department, there was nobody she could delegate it to.

The door opened and in swayed Leo. He glanced around at the grandeur of Karl Furstin's old office.

"Wouldn't have thought this was to your taste," he said, going to one of the windows behind her and looking out at the view.

"Believe me, it's not. I'd like to do a refurbishment but I could only imagine the reaction of David Stafford if I suggested something so frivolous. I'll just have to put up with it for now."

He went and sat down opposite her. "I suppose there's worse things you have to put up with."

"I guess." There was an awkward silence. "I just wanted to check in on you really. How are you enjoying it, working here?"

"It's not bad – I'm enjoying it more than I thought it would."

"That's good. I was wondering if you had decided what department you felt you wanted to settle down in yet?"

"Not really."

Another awkward silence.

"I see . . . .. You know, with your personality you'd be great in sales. Doesn't Sales Management appealed to you?"

"Definitely not. Listening to all those old ones moaning all day. Nah, I think I'll rule that one out."

"Pity – it's a great start for somebody in retail."

"Not for me."

"Hmmm . . . How about finance? I could have a word

with David Stafford. With your experience from the city, I'm sure you'd be a great asset, and you love working with money."

"Nah, I've seen that David Stafford guy around. I really don't think he's my cup of tea – too much milk and not enough sugar. I don't fancy working with him."

Stephanie felt herself becoming deflated. She chose her next words very carefully. "Leo . . . we have a lot of enemies here."

"We?"

"A lot of people would like to see us fail . . . be kicked out."

"*You* have a lot of enemies, you mean."

"If you like . . . but they might try to use you to get at me, if you know what I mean."

"No, actually, I don't."

She sighed and sat back. "I'll just have to spell it out then. It really looks bad for you to be swanning around the store all the time with nothing to do."

"It was you who said to take some time out and get acquainted with the store!"

He was so impossible to argue with, she thought. He had an answer for everything.

"I know I did and now I'm saying it's time to settle down to something, so the likes of Paul Stewart and Nicola Newman can't say you're only here because of me!"

"But I *am* only here because of you."

"Leo! Try and help me out here!"

"Look, if you don't want me here – then just say it!" He threw his hands in the air.

She massaged her temples. "Leo, I'm not saying I don't want you here. Of course, I want you here. I wouldn't have asked you otherwise. Why does everything have to turn into an argument with you? I'm just saying I don't own this place, I just run it. And I really don't want people thinking that we're taking advantage of the situation."

He sighed, sat back and folded his arms. "I'll tell you what – since I haven't decided what I want to do, *you* give me something to do."

"I would prefer for you to do something you actually enjoy rather than me just giving you something that you mightn't like."

"As long as Nicola Newman is happy, that's the main thing." His voice dripped sarcasm.

She racked her brains trying to think of something that might suit her son. Her eyes fell on the email from Conrad. A smile broadened across her face.

"Actually there is something that you could do, and something really important – and you'd be doing me a big favour as well."

"Go on."

"They want to have a function, a party for all the shareholders at which we'll unveil our plans for the store. "Could you organise it for me?"

"Well, what kind of a party?"

She sat back and smiled. "That's what I'm employing you to do. Organise the location, banqueting, music, invitations. You think you could do that?"

He shrugged and nodded. "It doesn't sound too taxing."

"Great. I'll talk to David Stafford to sort out a budget and, as I said to you before, choose one of the offices on this floor to work from. Let's face it, there's enough of them free after the departure of all of Furstin's staff. Then you can get to work. Deal?"

"Okay," he nodded and got up. "See you later."

As the door closed behind him, she sighed and sat back in her chair. At least he would be seen to be doing something rather than wandering around chatting up sales assistants and drinking champagne in the Food Hall.

* * *

"Okay, baby, that's fab news, delighted for you – see you after work!" Daniella blew a couple of kisses down her mobile and tucked it under the counter.

"You're going to get into terrible trouble if you're spotted on that mobile all the time," warned Rachel. Since Leo had started at Franklyns, Daniella was forever on the mobile to him.

"Who's going to spot me? They got rid of Christine. The other manager is too stretched to keep a close eye on us."

Paul Stewart walked by quickly, eyes focused straight ahead.

"Even he doesn't come near us any more," said Daniella.

"Well, I think that's more my fault than anything else," sighed Rachel.

"How so?"

"I overheard him having a row in his office and I think he's embarrassed."

"What row? With who?" demanded Daniella.

"Oh, it doesn't really matter."

Daniella pinched Rachel's arm.

"Oww! Daniella!"

"You tell me the gossip! I tell you everything."

"He was having a row with Christine just after she had been let go. It was fairly heated. It was obvious they had had an affair."

"I told you! That's probably why she was let go."

"Hardly. He didn't have an affair with all the management they let go, did he?"

"I wouldn't put anything past him. Anyway, Leo had some good news."

"Really?"

"He's been given the job of organising a big party for the shareholders to unveil Franklyns' plans for the future."

Rachel's face creased with displeasure. "And his experience in Public Relations is?"

"You know, if you don't lose that bitterness, you'll age prematurely."

Chapter 36

Oliver braced himself as he made his way to the interview room. It would be the first time he had seen his wife's attacker in person. The guy's name was Jason Cody, a violent and vicious thug who had been in serious trouble since he was fourteen. He'd had spells in youth detention centres for theft and assault. He had graduated to burglary. Most worryingly, although theft was the motivator, there was always a degree of violence attached to his crimes. He had served prison sentences in the past and had gone underground when he had recently been released on bail for a particularly vicious assault. In fact, Oliver had felt that Nicola got off lightly when he read the details of that last crime.

There was a young police officer on duty outside the interview room.

"Have you had your lunch yet?"

"No, sir."

"Go take it now."

"Yes, sir." The policeman nodded and walked away.

Oliver opened the door, entered the interview room and closed it behind him. Jason Cody sat behind a desk, arms folded, looking bored. Oliver leaned against the door, studying him. He couldn't have been any more than twenty-two. He had that hardened rough look but only when you really looked closely at him. Other than that, there was nothing about him that stood out. And this gave him the ability to come out of the crowd unseen, attack his prey, and then disappear quickly back to where he came from.

"I want my solicitor present for any more interviews," stated Cody.

Oliver approached the table slowly. "I don't give a fuck what you want. You have been charged with the assault of Doris Bailey outside Liverpool Street station."

Jason Cody pursed his lips and looked away.

"I'm investigating other attacks on women in the vicinity that have a remarkable resemblance to the attack on Mrs Bailey. Do you know anything about those attacks?"

"No." Jason continued to stare at the wall.

Oliver opened a large envelope he was holding and took out a photograph of Nicola. He looked down at his wife and felt nauseated at the idea of showing a photo of her to this scum. He put the photo in front of Cody.

"Ever seen this woman before?"

Cody refused to move his stare from the wall.

Oliver sat down opposite him. "We can either do this the easy way or the hard way. Now look at the fucking photo!"

Cody paused for a while and then gave a quick glance down at the photo before looking quickly up at the wall again. "Never saw her before."

"Well, she says she saw you. She says you attacked her one morning coming out of Liverpool Street Station. You viciously threw her to the ground and robbed her jewellery – earrings, necklace, engagement and wedding rings as well as her bag. Ring any bells?"

"The stupid bitch needs glasses. I said I never saw her before." He concentrated on the wall.

Oliver's leg lashed out under the table and knocked the chair from under Cody, sending him flying to the ground. Quick as a flash, Oliver was around the other side of the table, bending over Cody, his hand around the back of his neck.

"I want my solicitor!" Cody shouted.

"And I want that jewellery back. I've cleared my schedule for the rest of the day and you and me are going to get to know each other really well."

* * *

Leo surveyed the view across the Thames to the South Bank in the early evening sunshine from the deck of the yacht moored at the embankment. The yacht, the King Charles, had recently been refurbished to an excellent standard and only recently re-opened. The venue's manager was called Sam and he was trying too hard to look cool and trying too hard to sell the yacht as a venue for the Franklyns' shareholder party.

"We actually had the Storm party here last week. It was great, with models packed in here, paparazzi desperately trying to get on board. I had to have extra security on to keep them at bay."

"Hmmm . . . well, I think this function will be a little more sedate than that – these are serious business people who will be attending."

"Hey, we had a City firm have a do here the week

before. Wall-to-wall with stockbrokers. They absolutely loved the place."

Leo half-expected Sam to start a tap dance and start singing, "I can sing, I can dance – I can do anything!"

Leo sensed that the King Charles hadn't been as successful as the owners had hoped since its reopening and no doubt Sam was under a lot of pressure to bring in the business.

"I remember this place before it closed down," said Leo. "There used to be discos here every Friday night."

"Yeah, that's right. Were you ever here?"

"A couple of times. It was a bit tacky."

"Well, you certainly couldn't accuse it of being tacky now since the refurb," defended Sam with a sniff.

"Yeah, it looks good."

These words of praise were enough for Sam, and as if by magic he produced a diary and started flicking through the pages.

Leo could see there were a lot of blank pages in the diary. "How about the 26th?"

"Yes, we've nothing on that night. I can fit you in then."

"Hmmm," Leo stroked his chin and began to walk up and down the deck. "I'm just not sure."

"Not sure about what?" Sam's face continued to sport a smile that threatened to crack it.

"I don't want the night to be regarded as a booze cruise."

"It won't. I'll make sure the event is oozing with class." Sam spoke with certainty.

"I'll tell you what . . . I'm going to have a little think about it. You're definitely in the running but I've seen some other really impressive venues as well. I'll give you a call over the next couple of days."

Leo turned and started to walk away.

"Wait!" called Sam. "I'll give you a twenty-per-cent reduction. Final offer, that's the best I can do."

Leo stopped and turned around, looking pensive. "I'll tell you what . . . give the company a ten-per-cent discount and give the other ten-per-cent to me – cash – and you've got yourself a deal."

Sam's smile had disappeared but he spoke eagerly as he threw his hands in the air. "Fine! Deal." He started scribbling in his diary.

"I'll give you a call tomorrow to discuss details. Just one more thing. I'll be supplying the champagne for the night – the rest of the bar will be yours."

Sam looked up, irritated for a moment. Supplying the champagne would be very lucrative but he was in no position to argue.

He nodded. "Whatever you want – you're the boss."

Chapter 37

Rachel looked around the big crowd of revellers in the Mexican restaurant in Notting Hill. One of the girls was leaving and a big gang of them had come out for her leaving night. Daniella had declined to come. Daniella was funny like that, Rachel thought. One minute she would fit in with the gang and the next she would do her own thing. Trying not to be cynical, Rachel reckoned Daniella basically suited herself. If she fancied a night out with the gang that was fine, but if a better offer came along then she'd be off. In fact, ever since Leo's mother had become the new boss, Daniella had not been endearing herself to her work colleagues in the least.

The girl who was leaving seemed to be very happy with her move. It should be me who is leaving next, thought Rachel. She wanted to go but didn't seem to be able to motivate herself to look for a job or even get out her CV. She knew she was wasting time in a place that wasn't going to offer her a career but in a strange way she was being pulled further into the place. The longer she was there, the more attached she was becoming to Franklyns. Maybe it was just as simple as that: she was in a new city and Franklyns was the only thing that was familiar to her and she was reluctant to let this safety net go. Or was she intrigued by all the people she had met there and all the changes the place was going through? She was intrigued by Daniella and her cocky boyfriend. She was fascinated by the new boss, Stephanie Holden, as she swung around the store making her changes and letting everyone know she was in charge. She was absorbed by Paul Stewart whose power base was slipping away while he juggled his complex life of mistresses and wife whose intelligent columns she hungrily devoured every Sunday. She was even captivated by Nicola Newman, whose manner she despised. Apart from Daniella and Leo, she knew she probably wouldn't be given a chance to get to know these people better but she would love the opportunity.

"Fair play to her for getting out," said the security man who sat on her left as he took a sip from his bottle of Corona.

"Huh?" Rachel asked as she turned to him.

"Janet." He nodded over to the girl who was leaving. "Always had her down as a bit of a lifer."

"A lifer?" she quizzed.

"Yeah. When someone comes to work here, me and the guys always take bets on whether they will end up staying here for years – lifers."

"Oh, I never imagined anyone staying here for years!"

"Oh, they do, loads of them do." He turned around and looked at her pointedly. "We have you down as a lifer."

* * *

Leo and Daniella sat on the couch in his house eating a Chinese takeaway while the Kaiser Chiefs played in the background.

"I thought there was a big group of your friends heading out tonight," said Leo as he tucked into sweet and sour pork.

"Yeah, there was – that girl Janet is leaving. But I prefer to be curled up inside with you for the night."

"Ah, babe!" Leo leaned towards her and gave her a quick kiss on the mouth.

"Besides, I was never overly gone on Janet," she said. "She always got on my tits after a while." She took a mouthful of chicken satay.

"Has Rachel gone with them?"

"Yeah, of course she has. She wouldn't miss an opportunity to be Miss Popular."

He glanced at her "Is she? Miss Popular?"

"Well, she tries hard enough to be."

Leo looked at her curiously "I thought she was your mate."

"Oh, she is ... don't mind me. I love her to bits. It's just ... I don't know ... I find her a bit too ... *right* ... sometimes."

"What do you mean?"

"Just, you know, everyone likes her, she never puts a foot wrong ... I mean, she should live a little. You know what I mean? When I'd been in Franklyns as long as she has, I'd ridden half the security!"

He looked at her and his face clouded over.

"Joke!" she almost yelled. "I'm only joking!" She leaned forward and kissed him quickly on the lips.

"Hmmm ..." He returned to his sweet and sour.

"I think London has been a bit of a shock to her," commented Daniella. "I think she led a charmed life back in Ireland and is a little shocked to find the streets of London were not paved with gold for her. She's had a few knock-backs at Franklyns and I think it's a little damaging to her ego . . . she's dead jealous of you, babe."

"Of me?" Leo looked at her quickly. "What do you mean?"

"Well, that you just waltzed into Franklyns and took over."

"Not quite . . ."

"It's so exciting you organising this big party on the yacht. What am I going to wear?"

"Wear?" He looked at her perplexed. "Doll?"

"Yeah, babe, what am I going to wear on the night? Something that will knock them dead."

"I hadn't thought you'd have wanted to go, doll." He was filled with dismay at the thought of Daniella coming along.

"Babe, I wouldn't miss it for the world!"

Chapter 38

Stephanie sat at her desk swinging slightly from side to side while she spoke to Miranda St John on the phone. Miranda was a young English designer who had risen quickly through the ranks of several French fashion houses and had now become a force to be reckoned with. Stephanie had already achieved a coup for the store by securing Veronica Carter, and now she was after Miranda.

"So what are you suggesting, Stephanie?" Miranda asked.

"I'm suggesting a partnership between you and Franklyns. That you launch your next season of clothes here at my store."

"*Your* store?" Miranda allowed herself a little laugh. She was going to say something cutting like 'Karl Furstin might have something to say about that!' but thought better of it. "I don't know, Stephanie, I really don't. I just don't think Franklyns is the right image to launch my designs."

"But why?"

"Because it's Franklyns! A bit too traditional, full of American tourists, and Arabs who might buy the designer frocks, but really, when do they ever wear them? No, you're just not the image I want to ally my designs too closely with."

Stephanie decided to play hardball. "Maybe you don't want us to stock your designs full stop? Maybe I should order the buyers not to buy anything from your house any more, if that's the case."

"Nonsense. Of course I value you as a client."

"Well, you'd be a fool not to, considering the amount of orders we give you each year. We're good enough for you to take our money but not to give us an exclusive?"

"Look, if I gave you an exclusive, I could seriously damage my brand. You're just not cool enough for me."

"But you don't know what I've planned for the store. You'll be begging to have your launch with us soon."

"Well, get back to me then," said Miranda.

"It'll be too late then. I want you now!"

"I forgot how bloody dogged you can be . . . let me think about this. There's a lot to consider . . . and it's not just me who makes the decisions here, you know."

"Bullshit! From what I hear they're all scared to say boo to you in that fashion house!"

"As I said, let me think about it."

"Great. Call me as soon as you can and we can start organising dates for the launch."

"Stephanie!" Miranda shrieked in exasperation.

"Byyeee!" Stephanie hung up the phone and smiled to herself. It would be quite a coup to get Miranda to launch her season at Franklyns.

The office door opened and Leo walked in. He was smiling broadly.

"Afternoon," he said and sat up on her desk beside her.

"What has you looking so happy?" Stephanie quizzed smilingly.

Leo threw a brochure in front of Stephanie.

"That is where we're having the shareholders' party," he announced.

She took it up and started glancing through the glossy brochure.

"Looks pretty impressive," she nodded, loving the idea of having it on a yacht.

"Have a date booked and everything," said Leo. "The 26th."

She looked up, slightly alarmed. "That's quite soon. Will it give you enough time to organise everything?"

"Of course it will! Not a bother to me."

"Okay, I'll send Conrad Richardson an email now informing him. He'll be delighted – he wanted it soon. I'll give the Finance Director a call to sort out a budget for the event."

"Don't worry. I already spoke to David Stafford this morning and the whole thing is sorted. He was quite generous with the budget actually."

She sat back, surprised. "How did you know who to speak to?"

"What do you think I've been doing since starting work here? Finding out the lie of the land – who's who, who makes the decisions."

"I see." Stephanie was impressed and annoyed with herself for judging her son too harshly. "We'd better contact all the shareholders quickly and let them know about the party."

He got up, went behind her and started massaging her shoulders.

"You just relax and leave everything to me. I'll sort everything."

She allowed herself to relax. "Okay."

"Now where can I get the contact details for these shareholders to send out invitations?"

"I guess Nicola Newman will have all the details. No, best leave her alone – Conrad will have them. I'll phone him this afternoon."

"Will you relax! Don't bother Conrad. I'll get Nicola to give them to me."

"Well, she won't give you them, Leo. She'll take great pleasure in turning you down and make you feel this small ..." She put her thumb and forefinger close together.

"Leave her to me," Leo assured her and, with another smile, strolled out of the office.

* * *

Nicola drove through Knightsbridge towards the store, the top of her car down. She had gone to meet a couple of friends for lunch and was now heading back to work. Oliver had been very focused since the arrest of the man who had attacked her.

He was spending much time interviewing the culprit, trying to crack him. She felt relieved her attacker had been caught. She didn't want anyone else to go through what she had. But if Oliver thought that finding this man and getting back her wedding ring would – hey, presto! – turn her back into the wife she had been, then he was sadly mistaken.

From what she could see it was he who was obsessed about the mugging. Maybe it gave him something to focus on other than their deteriorating marriage. And as for her – she was obsessed with David Bloody Stafford! And maybe both their obsessions distracted them from their usual marital obsessions – antique fairs and farmers' markets and friends' dinner parties. What a marriage! She drove into the underground carpark, got out and made her way to the lift.

She was making her way through the store when a voice said, "Hey – Nicola?"

She turned to see that the speaker was Leo Holden. She glared at him frostily and said nothing.

"Just wondered if you could help me?" he ventured.

She maintained her frosty glare.

"I'm looking for all the shareholders' contact details, addresses, phone numbers, that kind of thing."

She laughed derisively. "You're the last person in the world I would give such details to." She turned and began to walk off.

He watched her go and then followed her quickly, walking alongside her.

"I could always get them from Conrad Richardson.

""Well, I suggest you do then . . . I'm sure you'll get the same reaction from him."

"You're a shareholder, aren't you?"

"What business is that of yours?" Nicola snapped.

"Well, when I get the details from Conrad, I'll just make sure to leave you off the guest list, since you don't seem interested."

She stopped abruptly and fixed him with a cold look.

"What are you talking about?" she demanded.

"Conrad has asked me to organise a big shareholder party – you know, to introduce my mum and David Stafford and all the new team. A kind of get-to-know-you party."

Nicola's mind went into overdrive. "This is a social event?" she quizzed.

"Yep!"

"And *you're* organising it?"

"Sure am!"

Nicola thought for a moment. "The mind boggles . . . I'll leave the details with my secretary. You can collect them later today. And all those details are to remain strictly confidential."

She marched off, her mind swimming with thoughts. A social event where David would be – just what she had been waiting for.

* * *

David Stafford had left three messages on Paul's answering machine suggesting they do lunch. Paul had chosen to ignore all three requests. He was not eager to resurrect non-existent friendships. However, when David walked into his office at twelve thirty with a big smile, insisting they have lunch that day, Paul couldn't get out of it. And as they made their way across Brompton Road to a Burger King, Paul realised that David was not so much somebody who didn't take no for an answer but someone who had received so little rejection in his life that he just didn't recognise it.

"Oh, incidentally, you need to get your answering machine checked out – don't think it's recording your messages," said David as they sat down at a window seat with their trays of Whoppers and fries.

Paul nodded and managed a smile. "Thanks, I'll check it out."

"So, all set for the 26th?" asked David as he unwrapped his burger.

"The 26th?"

"The shareholders' party."

Paul shook his head casually. "It's the first I've heard of it."

"We're organising a big shareholders' party. There's a lot of unrest in the ranks, so we just want to settle nerves, make them feel at ease. Make sure they don't rush to sell their shares the moment we go on the stock market."

"Makes sense, I guess."

"I had young Holden in to me today, Stephanie's son, eagerly discussing the details. He's hired a yacht for the night. He's been put in charge of the event."

"Give him something to do other than chat up salesgirls," said Paul.

David smirked at him. "Worried your reputation as the Franklyns' ladies' man is being threatened?"

Paul quickly looked down at his food and started eating fries. How fucking stupid of him to give Stafford details of his private life!

"Listen," David went on, "I know you were a bit raw about Stephanie bringing in her son when all the old staff were being let go but you know that's what happens in these situations. The new management will always bring in their people. I'm as guilty as Stephanie. All the old finance department were wiped out and replaced with my foot soldiers. It always happens."

"How many receiverships have you actually been involved in?" Paul was curious.

"Too many to count."

Paul let the disdain creep across his face. "It's a dirty job to be involved in. Taking away people's businesses, their livelihoods."

David was surprised by his reaction. "I don't see it that way." He put down his burger and looked pointedly at Paul. "Look, Paul, take some advice from an old friend.

I've seen who survives these situations countless of times. It's the people who can adapt, who forget about the past and fit quickly into the new management structure, who survive. They are the ones still standing when everyone else falls. Adapt. So Stephanie has employed her son, big deal. From what I know that's a pretty small crime compared to what went on under Furstin. Stop walking around looking injured by what's happening. Instead, walk around looking like you're a *part* of what's happening . . . yeah?"

Paul looked at David, filled with anger and confusion. He was angry at him giving him advice, making him feel inadequate. And yet he was confused as to why he *was* giving advice. What did he care what happened to Paul?

Paul took a drink from his Coke. "I probably won't even be invited to that party."

"Of course, you will. You know all the shareholders, don't you?"

Paul nodded.

"Well, then you're an integral part of a smooth takeover."

An integral part of being used to smooth over the takeover, thought Paul. He felt like saying it but held back.

"You know – really work the party, Paul – make sure you talk to everyone who's important, get yourself known to Conrad and everyone on our side . . . Okay , enough said." He picked up his burger and bit into it.

Paul searched for something to say.

"Hey, I was out with Ben and Rob the other night," said David. "Remember them from school?"

Unfortunately, Paul thought as he nodded.

"Was telling them all about you . . . stud."

Paul felt himself go red. "David, what I said about that affair was in confidence. I'm a happily married man."

David put his hands in the air. "Sure you are! You should come out with us one night."

Paul nodded and looked at his watch. "Better rush back. I've a meeting in ten minutes."

Chapter 39

Paul held Anna's hand as they sat listening intently to the doctor talk about IVF at the clinic. The doctor had a kind face, with curly hair swept back in a bun. Her name was Karen.

"I think the biggest mistake so many couples make when they start IVF is they look at it through rose-tinted glasses. And in a way I don't blame them, because the IVF process could be an answer to all their prayers. But the word *could* is the crucial word here. It could work and then again it might not. Sometimes it can take many goes before it works, and sometimes it might never work."

Anna squeezed Paul's hand. "We're aware of that, doctor. But it's the only chance we've got."

"There's the physical hardship of it, Anna. The hormone injections every day in the build-up period. Then the actual process. I need you to be fully aware of what will occur."

"We have already been advised of the physical implications," said Paul.

Karen put her hands together. "And I want you to be aware of the emotional implications. This will put huge pressure on your marriage. It has torn many couples apart, especially if the outcome isn't the desired one. However, I do know a lot of couples who have found it has brought them closer together. You need to be patient and work at it together."

Anna squeezed Paul's hand even more tightly and smiled at him. "We just feel very lucky we've managed to get this far."

"That's good. My advice to you is to try to keep the rest of your lives relatively normal as we begin the process. Try to avoid any unnecessary complications or troubles so that if the IVF starts putting strain on you, you're not already overburdened."

* * *

It was early evening when they left the clinic and made their way to the West End to have a bite to eat in a restaurant near Leicester Square. The doctor's advice kept going through Paul's mind. He wished they had done IVF a couple of years ago when everything at work had been smooth. Now, he found he was unable to think about anything else but the burdens of work.

Afterwards they strolled over to Regent Street arm in arm.

"I'm so excited about this," said Anna. "I can't wait to get started."

He nodded and smiled at her. "Me too."

She squeezed his arm affectionately.

"Went to lunch with David Stafford today," he said.

"Oh? How did that go?"

"Duty call. He seems to be insisting that we should be friends. Doesn't get the message."

"And is that so wrong – being friends with him?"

"We have nothing in common."

"No, Paul, you *had* nothing in common. Now you both work in the same place, you have a great deal in common."

"He's an arrogant fuck. Started to give me advice about how to fit in in Franklyns. I've been there years. He's only in the door and he's giving me advice!"

"What did he say?"

"Started bullshitting about adapting to the new management. Working with them."

Anna stopped abruptly and faced Paul as they reached the top of Regent Street.

"Which obviously means you *haven't* been working with them?"

"I've been doing my job the way I've always done it. I don't see any reasons to change."

"Well, I can see the attitude written across your face so the new management must be painfully aware of it. Paul! Can't you see what David Stafford is doing? He's throwing you a lifeline. He's not advising you. He's warning you. For whatever reason he has to feel warm towards you, he is trying to warn you that your days are numbered if you don't get your act together."

"I feel they're just using me anyway. They'll dump me as soon as they can so why should I make it easier for them?"

"Because you're bringing about a self-fulfilling prophecy. You believe they want to get rid of you. And your attitude will force them to!" She sighed. "Come on. Let's go home." She grabbed his arm and they walked into Oxford Street Tube station.

* * *

Paul lay awake in bed. He reached over and glanced at his watch and saw it was three in the morning. He climbed out of bed and made his way downstairs. In the kitchen he put on the coffee maker. Never in his wildest dreams did he ever expect he would be going through IVF. Life never turned out as you expected – he should have known that by now.

Time can distort memories but Paul knew his childhood was idyllic. Maybe it wouldn't have been idyllic for everybody but he wouldn't have wanted it any other way. He grew up in a northern town. His mother Catherine and father Tony had met when they were still in their teens. Catherine had worked in a solicitor's office as a secretary after school while Tony had gone to work in the giant steel plant that dominated the town. They married young and Paul, their only child, arrived a year later. Catherine gave up work to stay at home to mind Paul and Tony worked extremely hard at the steel plant. He applied for every promotion going and caught the eyes of his bosses who realised they could depend on him to do anything without question or complaint. Whereas a lot of Catherine and Tony's friends were applying for council houses or at best buying small terraced houses, they managed to buy one of the new semi-detached ones on the outskirts of town. And as time in the seventies passed by, they had a very happy marriage, a very happy social network and Paul had loads of friends. By the time the eighties dawned Tony had risen to the rank of middle management at the plant and as Paul entered his teenage years he was almost unaware of the growing recession that was gripping the neighbouring towns and cities. All that concerned him as he hit fourteen was his very active social life. His parents were fairly liberal and so he was allowed out a lot to go to music gigs and discos with the large group of friends he had.

He remembered walking back from a party one night. His housing estate was on a hill and as he walked up the road home the town was stretched out in front of him. All the great new music sounds that he'd heard at the party echoing in his head, he strolled up the driveway and put the key in the front door, then straightened himself up so his parents couldn't see he had drunk too much.

They were curled up on the sofa together in the front room watching a film.

"I thought I told you to be in by twelve," said his mother in her sing-song cheery voice, her eyes not straying from the screen.

"Is it after twelve? I didn't realise," said Paul, trying to sound convincing. "Anyway it's Friday, so there's no school tomorrow, so it doesn't matter." He walked down the hallway into the kitchen and started fixing himself a sandwich.

"Are you wearing aftershave?" his father called after him.

"No," said Paul, feeling confused as he sat at the table and looked at his parents through the open double doors.

"I think you are," insisted Tony. "It's that new brand . . . Eau de . . . Heineken!" And he and Catherine erupted in giggles.

"Very funny," said Paul, but as he looked at his parents he felt very safe and content.

Tony's happy-go-lucky expression began to be more concerned as the recession began to creep closer and closer. There were rumours that there would be a wave of redundancies at the plant. In school, Paul's friends' fathers began to join the dole queue one by one. Finally the rumour became reality as it was announced that half the staff at the plant would be made redundant. As middle management, Tony's job was safe for now, but who knew what the future would bring? With news of the redundancies the trade union mobilised and before anyone knew what was happening the whole plant was out on strike.

For the first time Paul saw the carefree expressions of his parents vanish and soon they looked permanently worried. Tony went into the factory to work every day, crossing the abuse of the picket line. And when he got into the plant there was nothing for him to manage as no work was being done.

"I'm going to have to join them," Tony said to Catherine over the kitchen table. "I can't go past them every day. I worked alongside them until a couple of years ago. They're my friends."

"But when the strike is over, you'll have lost your management position. You'll be demoted."

"I've no choice, love."

"But how will we pay the mortgage, Tony? What will we do?"

"What does everyone else do?"

Tony joined the strike and it continued and as the months went by it became fiercer as the strikers became more desperate. Often riot police would be called in and violent battles were flashed across the television news. Tony's face became more hopeless every day while Catherine's became more fraught. Paul thought his mother's face was too pretty and too kind to look so stressed.

Paul felt guilty years later but at the time his youth protected him. Even though he knew the seriousness of the situation he still went about his business as any fifteen-year-old would. And as the summer dragged on against the background of the strike, he was enjoying life. Out swimming in the dam, playing football in the park, parties at night.

The strikers finally gave in and there were mass redundancies. By then Tony was very much top of the list to be let go. And it was only then that it really hit Paul, because until then Tony still had a purpose. He still went out every day. He still hoped they might win. But now the bleakness of the situation sank in as he realised there was no hope of another job with the tides of unemployment about. He and his wife had borrowed money from their parents to keep going during the strike but now, with all their savings gone, she took matters into her own hands and managed to get a secretarial job in the old legal firm where she had worked before. Her salary wasn't much but it kept them going.

And Tony began to drink regularly all day long. Catherine would arrive home late from the office and Tony would be in a drunken stupor, feeling sorry for himself. She wasn't an arguer. It wasn't in her nature. She just got on with it.

But Paul saw their home life slowly fall apart.

When he came home from school one afternoon Catherine sat him down and explained very gently that she couldn't go on living with Tony and that she had found somebody new. She had started a relationship with one of the solicitors at work and he had asked her to marry him. He had got a job offer in a big city firm and so they were all going to live in London.

"But what about Dad?" Paul demanded.

"Your dad's is at the end of the line, Paul. He's going to

have to sort himself out. We can't do any more for him."

"You go to London. I'm staying here with him."

"Paul, you're coming with me and Les. It'll be wonderful. I've already been looking up really good schools for you. You deserve a better education than the one you're getting now."

"I can't leave here. I can't leave my friends and Dad."

"We often have to do things we don't want to. I'm really sorry about this, Paul, but one day you'll understand why I'm doing it."

But he didn't.

His father let them go without a fight. They moved to a lovely house in London. He thought it might be worth it if his mother recaptured the carefree face she used to have but it seemed to be gone for good. But she was happy with her new husband Les. And Les was very nice. He was mad about her and did all he could for Paul.

Paul was sent to an expensive fee-paying school and it was a complete culture shock as the kids there were so different from back home. These kids had never wanted for anything. They all had their lives planned, whereas Paul still hadn't a clue. They were all pleasant to him although he was sure he was an oddity to them. He knew he didn't really like them but he put up with them, pretending to be their friend. He would join them socially or for sports but looked for the earliest opportunity to leave. He'd make the journey home by train to see his father every couple of months. Tony just seemed to get worse all the time. He lost the house and was now living in a flat in town. Paul was troubled by it all for a long time. And then he left school, headed to college and got on with his own life.

* * *

A hand gently nudged him awake.

"Paul? What are you doing sleeping down here?" Anna gently asked.

Paul sat up quickly and looked around. "Oh, I came down for a drink. I must have dozed off."

"Breakfast?"

"I'll just have a cereal," he said and he headed up for a shower.

As he stepped under the hot shower he thought about his father's life. Maybe that was why this whole receivership of Franklyns was hitting him so badly, stirring up bad memories. Tony had allowed the loss of his job to destroy him. Maybe if he had handled it all differently his life might have worked out differently. All their lives might have worked out differently.

He stepped out of the shower, dried himself and put on his dressing gown. He headed down to the kitchen and poured cereal into a bowl.

"I meant to say to you that there's a big shareholder party on the 26th. Kind of unveiling our plans for the future. It's on some yacht seemingly. Do you want to come?"

Anna put down her newspaper, surprised. "Me?"

"Sure." Paul joined her at the table.

"But you never invite me to any work do's."

"Well, I'd like you to come to this one."

She smiled. "Well, then, okay."

Chapter 40

Stephanie yawned and looked at her watch. It was nearly nine and she was still at her desk. She was busy making notes after her series of meetings during the day. She had met with most of the buyers. As she looked at a list of the suppliers they were working with she drew a series of lines through a number of them. A lot of these designers were not cutting edge and there would be no room for them in Franklyns' future.

This shareholders' party was an extra pain in the ass she could do without. She knew she would have to have a few announcements to impress them on the night. She was due to meet interior designers the next day to discuss a revamp of some of the store. Standing up, she decided to call it a night.

She felt a little uncomfortable being on her own at Franklyns. Even though she knew there was security around, there was still an eerie feeling when the place was empty. Maybe it was just up there on the sixth floor which she felt still had Furtin's stamp on it.

She left her office and walked down the corridor towards the lifts. She pressed the button and waited. She could hear somebody talking somewhere and got a start. The voice was coming from one of the offices down the opposite corridor. There shouldn't be anyone on the floor and certainly nobody in the building at that time of day. She took her mobile out, ready to ring security, and cautiously made her way down the corridor.

She saw a door ajar and gently opened it. To her relief she saw Leo sitting behind the desk, feet up, chatting on the phone.

Spotting her, he waved at her to come in. "Sure, and I want you to email me a selection of menus for the night. I want something a bit different, so be adventurous." He hung up the phone. "Just on to the caterers there for the party."

"You're working late," she said.

"So are you," he responded.

"You gave me a start."

"You suggested my taking one of the offices," he said, almost defensively.

"I know I did. There's no problem with it. You seem to have everything under control."

He felt it was a question as opposed to a comment.

"Yep. I heard back from most of the shareholders and they can nearly all make it."

"Good. Well then, I'll see you tomorrow." She smiled at him and left.

As she made her way back to the lift, she couldn't dispel the feeling of nervousness that he would fuck up the party. After all, he had no public-relations or event-organisation experience. When she suggested he organise the party, she hadn't thought he would take it over completely. She thought she would guide him and he would report back every step to her. She should have known Leo would want to do it his way. She had no choice now but to trust him.

* * *

"I have to look a million dollars on the night," Nicola explained to Mabel as they walked through the rows of designer dresses in Franklyns. Nicola had arranged to meet Mabel very early before the store opened to allow her the privacy she needed.

"How daring do you want to go?" Mabel enquired.

"I've been pushing myself a little further each week and I think I'm ready to go pretty daring at this stage," said Nicola.

Mabel stopped and took out a very eye-catching but risqué gown

"Maybe something like this?"

"That looks like something Liz Hurley would wear to one of those premieres," said Nicola.

"If it's too much –" Mabel went to return the gown.

"No, wait!" Nicola took the dress studied it. "I'll try it on."

Nicola made her way into the dressing-rooms and, taking off her suit, slid into the gown. She gasped when she saw herself in the mirror. Could she be brave enough to wear such a dramatic dress? Hearing her mobile ring, she reached down into her handbag and seeing it was Oliver phoning raised her eyes to heaven.

"Oliver, I'm just in the middle of something right now, so make it a quick one."

"Oh, it's nothing important. It's just you left so early this morning – you were gone by the time I got up."

"Yes, I had an early meeting."

"Right. Well. I'll see you tonight then."

"Okay, bye. Oh, Oliver, meant to tell you – next Thursday night we're having a big work do. I'm expected to go naturally. It's going to be a very late one and so there's no point in me heading back home at that time. I'm just going to book into a hotel."

"Oh, well, I don't mind driving in and picking you up."

"That would be ridiculous. Much easier for me to stay at a hotel. See you tonight." She hung up.

* * *

Oliver put the receiver back on the phone on his desk and rubbed his hand to his face.

He was due to meet Jason Cody again in the interview room. He was a tough nut to crack. So far Oliver was sure that Cody was no longer in possession of Nicola's jewellery or indeed any of the items he had stolen from his victims. From what he could establish, Cody quickly sold the jewellery on to a third party. But it was here that Oliver was coming up against a brick wall. Try as he might, and he was trying everything, Cody would not give him the name of the person who was his buyer. This led Oliver to believe that this buyer must be pure scum, someone Cody was too afraid of to reveal. But Oliver was breaking him down bit by bit.

* * *

Leo walked into his mother's office.

"Just need your signature on this," he said.

"What is it?" she asked, looking up from her paperwork.

"An advance for the band I've booked for the party night."

"What kind of band are they?"

"A good band."

"Yes, but are they a classical band? Or even a jazz band? Now remember, Leo, most of these shareholders are going to be older – most of them will never have heard of the Arctic Monkeys. We don't want to frighten them too much!"

"I did try to book the Arctic Monkeys but they were busy that night."

"Leo! I'm being serious here!"

"Trust me – please!"

She took the pen and signed at the bottom of the page.

* * *

Rachel and Daniella stared over at Stephanie as she directed the interior designers around.

"This big shareholders' party is the first time I'm going to be out socially with Leo's mum," Daniella said. "It's a good opportunity for us to get to know each other."

"So who's going to be at this party?"

"Everybody who's anybody. You should see the plans Leo has organised for the night!"

"How're my favourite girls?" asked Leo as he appeared at the counter.

"Great. I was just telling Rachel all about the party."

"It's going to be a great night!" Leo winked at Rachel.

"So how about Rachel coming as well?" said Daniella.

"Oh no – I couldn't possibly –" began Rachel.

"Sure, why not? I could always do with an extra pair of hands," said Leo, and winking again he walked off.

Daniella grinned. "That's great now! A good opportunity for you to mingle with the right people!"

"Daniella, it's really kind of you to include me but I don't think I should."

"Why not?"

"Because what would I be doing there? It would be full of shareholders' and Nicola Newman and Paul Stewart would be annoyed to see a salesgirl there."

"Well, I'll be there."

"But you're Leo's girlfriend. I would have no reason to be there."

"You know, Rachel, you're really letting this place take you over. When you first arrived you were all fired up about having a big career here and now you're listening to them telling you to know your place."

"Well, I'm not going to force myself where I'm not wanted."

"Oh, come on, Rachel! You might meet a big shareholder who fancies you on the night and gets you promoted into the press office!"

"That's not how I want to get ahead, thanks. If I was like that I would have just accepted Furstin's offer to join his staff."

"Well, maybe you should have! If you can't get ahead on your terms, Rachel, get ahead on any terms that are offered to you."

* * *

Rachel was on the phone to her mother.

"Are you all right, darling? You don't sound yourself."

"No, I'm fine," Rachel assured her.

"How's work going for you?"

"Fine!"

"I meant to tell you I bumped into your friend Melissa the other day. She was mad asking after you."

"I have to send her an email."

Her mother paused for a few seconds. "You know if you're not happy there, Rachel, you can come home any time. We all miss you so much. If things aren't working out, then just come home."

"Really, everything's fine. I'd better run. Thanks, Mum."

Rachel sighed and then went over to her laptop and opened it up. She really had to catch up and send emails to all her friends. As comforting as her parents' words were, in a way they didn't make it easier for her to forge her new life in London. Not when she had such an inviting opt-out clause. In a way she'd had opt-out clauses all her life. She didn't grab opportunities in the way Daniella shamelessly did. Because of her comfortable background she'd never had to. But maybe she did have to compromise herself if she was going to get ahead in London. Maybe it took more than hard work and talent. Maybe you had to push doors open – the way Leo lived his life. She picked up her mobile and texted Daniella.

"Would love to go to the party, and thanks x"

* * *

Leo sat on the floor in his house with dozens of bottles of champagne around him. He was carefully sticking labels to the front of the champagne bottles one by one. He had got the champagne from a mate who knew somebody who worked in one of the top vineyards in France. They had sold him the lot at a knockdown price. It hadn't been hard to get fake Bollinger labels and now he was sticking them carefully on. He had bought some real Bollinger as well, at a reduced price, from somebody it was better not to ask too many questions of, and he would mix all the bottles up.

The crowd wouldn't notice the difference at the party and he was doing up a fake invoice charging premium rates for the champagne for Franklyns. The end result was a neat profit for Leo. Nice work if you could get it.

Chapter 41

Nicola looked at herself in the mirror of her dressing-room, wearing the gown that Mabel had picked out for her. Here, on the day of the party, the dress didn't look so much risqué as downright shocking. A slash right up to her thighs, a plunge right down to her waist and backless to boot, it was like one of those outfits a soap starlet would wear to a tacky awards ceremony, intent on being the one who gets most photographic attention. The handle turned on her dressing-room door.

"Nicola?" called Oliver as he realised the door was locked.

She turned quickly around, glad she had locked the door.

"What, Oliver?"

"Just wanted to check what time you're home tonight?"

"I'm not. I told you. It's the night of the shareholder party. I've booked into The Dorchester for the night."

"A shareholder party? I thought you said it was a work do?" He was surprised.

"What's the difference?"

"Well, if it's a shareholders' party, I might have liked to have gone, since we are shareholders."

She sighed quietly and quickly wrapped a long flowing bathrobe around her, succeeding in hiding the gown. She unlocked the door and popped her head around it to him.

"I'm there in my role as a director not a shareholder," she explained.

"It's just – I might have been interested in going to it – find out if I think our investment is in safe hands."

"Of course, it's in safe hands. I'm on the Board of Directors, aren't I?"

"Yes, but –"

She quickly changed the subject. "Any luck cracking that bastard?"

"Eh, yes, we've managed to get some names out of him, eventually."

She adopted a hurt look and rubbed her ringless wedding finger. "I think you've got more pressing matters to attend to than some silly party, don't you?"

A determined look came over him and he nodded. He reached over and kissed her.

"Just relax and try and enjoy the night, love. It might do you some good," he advised.

She managed to look slightly happier. "I'll try."

He kissed her again and walked away. She closed the door of the dressing-room again, locked it and removed her robe.

She stared at herself again. There was no way she could show up in front of everyone that night wearing such a get-up. Sighing, she quickly removed the gown and hung it up. She then rifled through her clothes and selected a long midnight-blue floaty gown.

* * *

David glanced through the figures that Stephanie had presented to him in his office.

"Nothing too outrageous there to give you a heart attack," said Stephanie.

"Hmmm, no . . . for what you're proposing it all seems very reasonable." David closed the pages over quickly and sat back, putting his hands behind his head. He smiled. "That's if you can stick to your budget."

"I'll stick to it," she said. "Just wanted to make sure there's nothing you disagree with there before I start announcing this stuff to shareholders at the party tonight."

"All set to meet your public?" he asked smirking.

"Our public, David, our public. They'll want to meet you as much as me. In fact more so, since you control the purse-strings."

"Bring it on!" he laughed. "What time you arriving there?"

"Leo's invitations said nine thirty so I guess I'll be there a little before, to greet the guests as they arrive."

"Good thinking. I'll swing by Chelsea Harbour on my way there and pick you up in a taxi."

"Fine," smiled Stephanie. "I'd better get moving. I've quite a few things to prepare for tonight."

* * *

Rachel's mobile rang and she spotted Daniella's number come up on the ID. Daniella had called in sick that morning.

"Daniella! Are you all right? Such a day to get sick – you must be so pissed off you won't make the party tonight."

"I'm not sick, darling! I'm at the beautician's."

"The beautician's?" Rachel was aghast.

"Yes, I took the day off to prepare myself for the party tonight. I want to look my best."

"But, Daniella! Are you mad? Paul Stewart and everyone else will see you there tonight and they will all know you pulled a sickie!"

"So? What can they do? Report me to my boyfriend's mother? I don't think so . . . Where are you getting ready this evening?"

"Up in the locker rooms."

"Does the glamour ever stop?" Daniella's voice dripped sarcasm. "I'm going to be down on the boat having a drink with Leo before the crowd arrives, so come straight down after work and join us."

* * *

Nicola had thought up a pretence to visit David, concerning an ex-member of staff and redundancy.

David picked up the phone and had the problem sorted out in thirty seconds.

"There – you shouldn't hear from them again," he smiled, returning the receiver to the phone.

"Thanks for taking care of that, David."

"Not a problem."

"Big night tonight," she ventured.

"Certainly is. I'm looking forward to meeting all the shareholders."

"I know most of them personally over the years . . . I'll introduce you to anybody you need to know . . . if you like." She smiled at him.

"Thanks, Nicola. I appreciate your help." He nodded sincerely at her.

"What time are you aiming to be there?" she asked.

"A little earlier than the invitation says. I'd like to meet them as they arrive."

She stood up and smiled. "Well, I'll see you then."

At the door she stopped and turned around. "I'm getting a taxi to the party . . . can I collect you anywhere?" To her dismay, her voice sounded a little shaky. She forced a little laugh. "No point in wasting two taxi journeys to the one event. They're always telling us to be economical with cars, aren't they? Save the planet?"

He looked surprised and she felt herself go red.

"That's kind of you," he said, "but I've already arranged to go with Stephanie."

"Oh, that's no bother then." She forced herself to smile and exited quickly.

That bloody Stephanie Holden!

She looked at her watch and decided to call it a day. She needed to get to the hotel and the hairdresser's.

* * *

Leo was on the yacht. He looked at his watch. It was nearly eight and the staff of the boat were running around, making sure everything was ready. The band was on the stage setting up. He was relieved it was a warm dry evening and so everyone could avail of the decks. He felt slightly nervous as adrenaline coursed through him.

* * *

Paul was fixing his tie in the mirror of the lounge at home. He was thinking of his strategy for the night. He would be charming and helpful to everybody. He would make himself known to Conrad Richardson. He would have a supportive talk with Stephanie before her speech.

"Will I do?" asked Anna as she walked into the sitting-room.

Paul stopped fixing his tie in the mirror and turned to view her. She was dressed in a simple black trousers and top, and was wearing a long flowing black cape. Her long hair was tied back at the nape of her neck and her make-up was minimal with a gloss of lipstick. She did a little twirl.

"You look gorgeous." He went and kissed her. "We'd better make a move or we'll be late."

* * *

After a trip to the hairdresser's Nicola had got back to The Dorchester early and relaxed in a long hot bath. Then she had a cool glass of white wine before changing. She looked good. She wasn't sure about the midnight-blue floaty gown. She wasn't sure if it was sexy enough. She wasn't sure if it was sexy at all though it did show a little cleavage. This was the night. She thought about David – she might never be in a close situation socially with him again.

David and Stephanie had obviously got close. She had spotted them around the store a few times, having what looked like intense conversations or simply having a laugh. She wondered was there something going on between them. Though, despite Stephanie's looks and glamour, she really couldn't see somebody like David going for somebody as lowbrow as Stephanie.

She also had a bit of work to do regarding Stephanie that night. She had to convince the shareholders that Stephanie needed to be replaced immediately.

She continued to apply her make-up as she schemed.

* * *

Rachel had changed into a simple cream cocktail dress in the locker rooms and touched up her make-up. She then got a taxi to the Embankment. She strolled down the Embankment, looking out across the Thames, passing the many moored yachts that served as bars and restaurants. She had chosen a simple dress as she didn't want to appear to be looking for attention on the night. She supposed Paul Stewart would get a shock to see her there, not to mention Nicola Newman. They might be pissed off that a salesgirl was at such an important event. Daniella was right: so much for her dream of getting to the top – now she felt embarrassed even being in their company. Finally she arrived at the King Charles and looked up at the majestic craft. She walked up the steps, down the sturdy gangplank onto the deck and in through a wide double door that led to the reception hall.

In the gigantic bar Daniella and Leo were sitting up at the bar enjoying a glass of champagne. She remembered from working in the press office at Brown Thomas the excitement and pressure before a big event and how she would run around with the team doing last-minute checks. She had expected to see Leo running around organising things. But instead he was perched on a stool, looking relaxed and carefree.

"Hello!" Daniella called to her and beckoned her over.

Rachel made her way over and saw that Daniella had, as expected, pulled out all the stops on the glamour side of things, wearing a green gown with slits up the front and a deep plunge down the back.

"You look amazing," complimented Rachel as she sat up on a stool beside them.

"I'm just so looking forward to tonight," said Daniella, pouring Rachel a glass. "We've just been talking about Leo having a word with his mum about me becoming a buyer for the store."

* * *

"Thanks so much for collecting me," said Stephanie, getting into the back of David's taxi.

"You scrub up well," said David, casting an eye over Stephanie's elegant but very sexy dress.

"You don't look too bad yourself," said Stephanie.

The taxi took off.

"We nearly had a third party join us," David said, smirking, aware of Stephanie's negative feelings towards Nicola.

"Really?"

"Nicola Newman was offering to share a taxi with me. I was going to suggest that we should collect her and then I remembered you two don't exactly see eye to eye."

"To put it mildly." Stephanie made a face.

She was glad David was arriving with her. She felt quite nervous about the night, especially as Leo hadn't answered his phone all day.

Chapter 42

Nicola looked at her watch and, seeing it was nearly nine, gave herself a quick once-over in the bathroom mirror. There were always taxis waiting outside the hotel so she knew she would have no bother getting one.

She went to open the bathroom door and, as she gripped the door handle, it came away in her hand. She looked at the handle in surprise. She tried to put the handle back into the socket but it wouldn't go. She tutted, threw the handle on the floor and tried to pull the door open but it wouldn't budge. She got on her knees and tried to pull the door out from the base but it was too close to the floor for her to get a grip. Then she tried the top of the door but met with the same problem. With increased panic she began to try to open the door in any way she could think of.

* * *

Paul held the taxi door open for his wife as she stepped out onto the pavement.

He held her hand and they walked confidently up the

steps and down the broad gangplank. His confident swagger hid the nervousness he really felt. He wasn't sure if he was more nervous that Anna was there with him and would meet all his work colleagues, or if he would be more nervous without her.

"Funny this, walking the gangplank," he said. "I feel I am really walking it and will be thrown to the sharks at the other end."

"Well, I for one am looking forward to the night. I can't wait to meet this David Stafford and Stephanie Holden, not to mention Nicola Newman."

"You've met Nicola before," said Paul.

"But only in passing. I'm going to study them all tonight."

He squeezed her hand as they stepped onto the deck.

"These are my work colleagues, not something for you to analyse and pick apart for your next Sunday's column, okay?" He gave her a warning look.

"Would I?" She pretended to look horrified.

They continued into the boat.

"Looks like we're nearly the first to arrive," said Paul as they walked into the bar.

They came face to face with David.

"Ah, there you are!" said David, giving the impression he had been looking for Paul.

He looked at Anna and beamed a smile. "And this must be your wife Anna?"

"Eh, yes." She smiled broadly back at him and shook his offered hand.

"David Stafford, I used to go to school with Paul."

"Yes, he's said. Coincidence, isn't it? How are you finding Franklyns?"

"So far so good. Lots of teething problems but we're muddling through it all, aren't we, Paul?"

"Eh – yes."

"You're the journalist, aren't you?" said David.

"For my many sins. I'm just going to pop to the ladies' – back in a mo." Still smiling, she headed off.

"She's lovely," David said earnestly, watching Anna head off. "What the fuck were you doing messing around with scrubbers from Franklyns when you had somebody like her at home?"

"Eh, listen, David, that night in the pub when I told you all about that stuff, I was exaggerating."

"Exaggerating? But how can you exaggerate something like that? You either fucked somebody else or you didn't."

"I admit I have not been faithful in the past but that's my point – it's all in the past. It was a mistake and I regret it. I'm actually very happily married, we both are."

David was nodding. "Well, that's good then . . . I admire your bottle though, bringing your wife to a work do when you've screwed around there."

"I think tonight is different from bringing her across the road to The Blue Posts for a drink. There are only senior people here tonight and, apart from Nicola, who doesn't mix with the great unwashed at Franklyns anyway, they are all new people like Stephanie who doesn't know and cares less about my past."

David nodded. "And apart from those two salesgirls over there with Stephanie's lad – they work at the store, don't they?"

Paul glanced over and saw Daniella and Rachel. He groaned to himself.

* * *

Leo spotted his mother walking over to them at the bar.

"Hmmm, here's trouble." He put his champagne glass behind the bar and jumped off the bar stool.

"Everything under control?" asked Stephanie.

She was surprised to see Daniella there and some other girl who looked vaguely familiar, probably another salesgirl from the store. She wished Leo hadn't brought them. She wished he'd kept his private life out of this.

"Everything's cool," said Leo.

"Hi, there!" Daniella slid off her bar stool and came up to Stephanie, giving her a kiss on each cheek.

Stephanie froze slightly and felt awkward.

"This is a great opportunity for us to get to know each other better," Daniella said, smiling brightly. "This is my friend, Rachel – she works in Franklyns too."

Stephanie nodded over to Rachel.

Rachel said hello and smiled at her. She was cringing as she realised it had been a mistake to come. Stephanie obviously hadn't expected them to be there and probably didn't want them there either. Rachel knew where she was coming from. Daniella was going to stand out in the crowd and draw undue attention to Leo.

"Daniella and Rachel are doing some free work for Franklyns," said Leo. "I thought it would be a good touch that when the shareholders arrive they are escorted over here to the bar or out to the decks – rather than their just finding their own way around. Daniella and Rachel volunteered."

"Oh, that's a nice touch – thanks, girls," said Stephanie and her face relaxed. She spotted Paul Stewart talking to David. "Everything's under control so?"

Leo gave her the thumbs-up.

"Good. I'll catch up with you later." She made her way over to Paul and David.

Daniella turned and looked at Leo, her face a mixture of confusion and anger.

"What's all this about me and her working here?" she demanded.

"Well, I had to give some explanation as to why you're here!" said Leo.

"I'm your fucking girlfriend! That's enough reason, isn't it?"

"Look, I'm here in a work capacity, so I had to say you are too. Just look busy for the first hour or two. Just greet the shareholders when they arrive and bring them over to the bar, or out onto the decks to the food."

"I'm not a fucking hostess!" Daniella's voice was too loud. "I'm here to have a few drinks, a laugh and enjoy myself!"

"Well, sorry, babe, but I'm here to work."

"You are crossing a very fine line and are on very thin ice!" spat Daniella. "Me meet and greet a load of snobby old bastards? You can think again!"

"Come on, Daniella!" Rachel intervened. "It's only for an hour or two! We can relax and have a few drinks afterwards."

"I serve ignorant fuckers all day long. I don't need to come here to do it as well!"

One of the band members came and patted Leo on the shoulder

"Leo, have you got a minute, I just want to check the music schedule with you."

"Sure," said Leo, grateful to be offered an escape route from Daniella's wrath. He followed the man out to the decks.

"Can you believe the cheek of that bastard?" snapped Daniella, reaching for her glass of champagne and downing it in one.

* * *

Nicola stood at the bathroom door, hammering it for all she was worth.

"I'm trapped in here!" she screamed at the top of her voice. "Help me somebody!"

She looked at her watch and saw it was nine thirty.

She started hammering and screaming again.

* * *

"I feel a bit like the Queen or something!" Anna whispered into Paul's ear. They were standing beside Stephanie and David, greeting shareholders as they arrived.

"Just keep smiling," Paul whispered as they continued to shake the hands of the arrivals.

"Ah, Mrs Harrison!" Paul said to a middle-aged woman as she came up and greeted him. He shook her hand and gave her a kiss on the cheek at the same time. With a big smile he said, "And may I introduce you to our new Brand Director, Stephanie Holden, and our new Financial Controller David Stafford."

Stephanie and David greeted the woman warmly.

"And this is my wife, Anna."

As Anna and Mrs Harrison shook hands and exchanged a few words, Stephanie whispered into David's ear. "He's being very co-operative. He almost looks happy to be here!"

"Paul?" David murmured. "He's proving to be quite an asset for the night."

"Just as well, since Nicola hasn't bothered to turn up.

We're relying on him for personal introductions to everybody."

Rachel and Daniella stood a little way inside, waiting to escort the arriving guests.

"Rachel!" said Paul. "Can you make sure Mrs Harrison gets a comfortable seat, maybe out on the deck? And order her favourite tipple – Bacardi and Coke, isn't it, Mrs Harrison?"

"God bless your memory, Paul!" laughed Mrs Harrison as she was led away by Rachel.

* * *

Nicola finally stopped banging the bathroom door. She gave it a vicious kick and screamed out of frustration. She turned and, putting down the toilet lid, sat down on it in despair, her dress spread out around her. Was she to be stuck in the bathroom for the night? She was missing the party. She felt like crying. She imagined Stephanie and David going around the yacht talking to everybody, having a great time, while she was stuck there. Her imagination drifted to them drinking into the night and she suddenly imagined them rolling around a bed together. She buried her face in her hands. What was she doing? What was becoming of her life? What was she allowing to happen to her life? She should be home safe in her lovely home with her caring and loving husband, instead of fantasising about a stranger. From the moment she had seen David Stafford he had caused her trouble, from being attacked outside Liverpool Street to being stuck in a loo in The Dorchester. What had she even been planning should happen at this party tonight? She didn't even know. Suddenly the door opened and in walked a

Hispanic-looking maid holding a stack of neatly folded white towels.

The maid took one glance at Nicola, screamed and quickly left the bathroom apologising, "So sorry, *senora*, so sorry!"

The maid went to pull out the door behind her.

"No!" shouted Nicola, jumping up. "Don't shut that door!"

She grabbed the door and tried to pull it open, while the maid tried to pull it shut from the other side. There followed a tug of war until the shocked maid dropped her stack of towels and ran screaming from the hotel bedroom.

Nicola glanced at her watch and, seeing it was nearly ten, grabbed her purse, gathered her dress up around her knees and raced out of the bedroom.

* * *

"I'm going to make him pay for this!" spat Daniella to Rachel, having just escorted another shareholder out on deck. "What the fuck does he think I am? An unpaid skivvy?"

"Look, will you calm down? It's only for an hour or so!"

"No, Rachel, he's crossed a line. Inviting me here as his partner and expecting me to show leery old men to the bar!"

Would have thought you wouldn't have minded that too much, thought Rachel.

"And did you see his mother? She wasn't exactly excited to see me, was she?"

Rachel glanced over at Stephanie who was busily engaging a couple in conversation.

"She looks like she's under a lot of pressure," she suggested.

"Fuck her and fuck her son! Or rather, I'd prefer not to. I'm her son's partner – she should be putting me before all these old fools."

"I guess she didn't expect to see you here."

"Well, she can fuck off!"

Stephanie finished talking to the couple and glanced around.

"Daniella, would you mind showing Mr and Mrs Peterson out on deck, please?" she requested loudly as she directed the couple over.

Daniella stood glaring. "You'd better go to them," she hissed at Rachel. "The way I feel now I'll fuck Mr and Mrs Peterson over the side into the river and Stephanie along with them!"

Rachel moved quickly forward. "If you'll follow me, I'll show you the way," she offered, smiling.

"Thank you," said Stephanie before turning her attention to another group of shareholders.

* * *

"Can you not go any faster?" Nicola demanded of the taxi driver.

The unimpressed driver gave her a filthy look through the rear-view mirror. "No!"

She was sure he then drove even slower out of spite.

* * *

Conrad Richardson had arrived and was speaking with Stephanie and David out on the deck.

He looked at the throng of people around them. "How are we getting on?"

"It's going very well so far," confirmed David. "We're being hit with many questions about the store's future. To be honest, they all seem very concerned about everything that's been going on."

"Which is what tonight is all about – calming the nerves. Excellent choice of venue and everything looks superb." Conrad surveyed the delicious banquet of food laid out on tables and being served by an army of chefs.

The band had started to play. They were positioned on a higher deck looking down on the crowd. They were a jazz band and their music oozed over the chatter and into the warm London night.

"It was actually Stephanie's son Leo who organised the event and I don't know how he managed it all on such a low budget," said David.

"Really? Well done to him then," said Conrad. Stephanie flashed David a grateful smile.

* * *

"You know, I think I could get used to this role of corporate wife," Anna said as she browsed through a buffet of food on the decks.

"If I'd known you'd be so good at it, I'd have used you before," said Paul.

"So why didn't you?" she asked him curiously.

"Because I had no need for a corporate wife. Karl Furstin wasn't running a corporation – he was running a personal fiefdom."

"I suppose. But I knew I'd come in useful some day to you! Incidentally, you're playing a blinder. You're charm itself, schmoozing in a way that would put Bill Clinton to shame. Proud of you!" She blew him a kiss.

Rachel deposited a guest at the table beside them.

"Now, please help yourself to whatever you fancy," she said. "And if you need anything, just ask me."

She turned around and came face to face with Paul and Anna.

"Hi, Rachel," Paul said.

"Eh, hi!" Rachel immediately recognised Anna from her photo over her newspaper columns.

"Rachel, this is my wife, Anna."

Anna put down her plate of food, put out her hand and smiled warmly. "Hello, Rachel, very nice to meet you."

Rachel was taken aback by the warmth and friendliness of the woman. She shook her hand and smiled back.

"You work at Franklyns?" said Anna.

"Yes," Rachel smiled.

"Oh dear! You have to put up with him all day then, do you?" Anna said mockingly and nudged Paul.

"He's not a bad boss really!"

"You have to say that now when he's here but you can tell me the truth later." Anna winked at Rachel and picked up the plate again.

"What has you here tonight?" Paul asked, looking and feeling uncomfortable.

"Eh, Leo Holden asked me to help out. He's organising the night, as you know."

"Paul, have you got a minute?" David called over.

"That's Conrad Richardson with David," said Paul to Anna. "I'd better introduce you."

"No rest for the wicked!" Anna put down her plate of food again. "I was really going to enjoy tucking into that as well! I'll chat to you later, Rachel." Anna gave a little wave and followed her husband.

* * *

As Nicola hurried down the gangplank onto the yacht, her mobile rang. Seeing her home number, she pressed the off button and put her phone away. As she made her way into the bar she saw all the shareholders had already arrived. The night was ruined. She had wanted to be the first there to greet everybody, with David. She scanned the crowd to try and spot him. She grabbed a glass of champagne from a passing tray being held aloft by a waiter and took a good drink from it.

"Nicola!" said a woman's voice beside her. "How are you?"

She turned to see some shareholders she knew. A further delay, she thought, as she smiled at them and began to engage them in conversation.

* * *

"I've been thinking about office space recently," said Paul.

"You want a bigger office or something?" said Conrad.

Stephanie and David laughed at his expression.

Paul laughed and shook his head. "No, not at all. In fact, I've been thinking that we've got too much office space, now that Karl Furstin and his army of staff are no longer occupying the sixth floor. The whole floor is empty, save for Stephanie. Why don't we move all the office staff from the fifth floor up to the sixth and convert the fifth floor into extra retail space?"

There was a moment of quiet while everyone digested the idea.

Stephanie shrugged. "Makes perfect sense. I might have a reputation of being difficult to work with but there's no need to isolate me on a floor on my own!"

"It would probably take a great deal of money to convert the floor," said Conrad.

"But it would be increasing our floor space by a sixth and possibly our turnover by a sixth." David gave his seal of approval. "And it's profit and turnover that will impress all these people here."

"Hello, everybody!" said a slightly out-of-breath Nicola as she arrived.

"Ah, Nicola! We had you written off!" said David.

"I had a slight problem at work which delayed me and which I'm not going to even begin to bore you with!"

"Always the consummate professional," said Conrad with an approving grin.

Stephanie had seen Nicola leave the building very early in the afternoon and it looked like she was going for the day. She didn't believe the delayed-at-work story for a moment.

"So good to see you again, Conrad," said Nicola. She nodded to David. "And David, Paul and Anna. I must have a catch-up with you later, Anna – it's been a long time – we see so little of you."

Anna was taken aback at the transformation in Nicola's appearance, even if the dress was a little 1950s debutante.

"You look great, Nicola, really good," Anna complimented her.

Nicola just smiled.

Stephanie was seething. Nicola had purposefully greeted everybody but her. She had passed over her as if she wasn't there. She would teach her a lesson later, when she was making her speech.

"And aren't we blessed with the weather!" Nicola went on. "With an open-air venue like this it could have been a disaster if it was raining. I think it was a bit of an unnecessary risk when there are so many excellent venues that don't rely on good weather."

Stephanie realised she was making a dig at Leo's choice. "In case you didn't realise, that was a large indoor bar you just walked through to get out here. We could have just stayed indoors."

Nicola refused to look at Stephanie but continued to address everybody else. "But that would have been even more depressing, cooped up in there while the rain pelted down on the decks!"

Stephanie rolled her eyes. "Excuse me, please. I need to talk to the shareholders." She walked away from them.

After a while Conrad left the group and headed off to take a phone call.

"I guess we'd better mingle," said Paul then. "That's what we're here for, to make the shareholders feel at ease." He took Anna by the arm and guided her indoors.

"Talk to you all later!" said Anna with a wave.

At last, thought Nicola as she was left alone with David.

"Well!" she said, holding her wineglass in front of her with her two hands.

"You live in the country, don't you?" David asked. "Did you come straight from home?"

"No, I actually booked into The Dorchester for the night. It was a bit too long a journey to be heading home so late."

"Oh, is your husband not here?" David looked surprised.

Nicola didn't know what to say. She wished she could just airbrush Oliver out of the equation. "Eh, no, he's not."

"I suppose he was too busy with his own work."

She stared at him blankly.

"Isn't he the Police Commissioner?"

She had never thought that David would have found out about her from others. She decided to change the subject but the only subject that sprang to mind was Stephanie Holden and she didn't think David was the proper audience to hear the venom she longed to spew out about her. Then she thought of Anna.

"Paul's wife is lovely, isn't she?"

"She seems very nice. I always wondered what kind of a wife Paul would end up with."

Nicola was confused.

"We were in school together," David explained.

Nicola looked even more confused. "Were you? I didn't know that. I always thought Paul had gone to some comprehensive in the north somewhere."

"No, no, we were school-mates," said David.

They stood in awkward silence while Nicola racked her mind to try and think of something else to say.

"Nicola Newman!" said a loud voice beside her.

Nicola recognised the speaker as a shareholder called Mary Castle.

"Hello, Mary, good to see you again."

"And where's that wonderful husband of yours?" asked Mary.

Nicola glanced at David. "He's – eh, not here."

"What a pity, I do so enjoy talking to him. He's such a gentleman."

David put his hand gently on Nicola's arm. "Nicola, if you'll excuse me, I need to have a talk with Conrad."

As David walked off, Nicola stared after him while Mary Castle rattled on about share prices. Nicola put down her empty glass and grabbed another one from a passing waiter. She observed as David made a beeline, not for Conrad, but for Stephanie and the two of them were suddenly laughing together.

"I've been saying to everyone tonight that as long as Nicola Newman is still at Franklyns then our investments are as safe as houses," said Mary Castle.

"Thank you, Mary."

"I've said to everyone that Nicola will keep an eye on everything and protect our shares!"

"Mary, you can certainly rely on me to do that. However, there is one serious problem that I think you and all the other shareholders need to be aware of."

"Oh?" Mary looked stressed.

"Can I rely on your discretion?"

"Of course!"

"It's that new Brand Director, Stephanie Holden. She completely lacks the experience, talent and class to be in charge of Franklyns."

"Really?"

"I'm afraid so. I don't know how we're going to get rid of her but we simply have to!"

* * *

Stephanie allowed herself to relax. The night was proving to be a big success. Everything was very much under control and as she looked at Leo working through the crowd, she felt very proud of him. He hadn't stopped all night, running around making sure the catering was right, the drink kept flowing, that the shareholders were being looked after. And he seemed so relaxed while keeping everything under control.

Maybe a career in public affairs beckoned for him at the store. She turned around to start talking to some more shareholders who were looking for her attention when suddenly her eyes became transfixed.

She stared in disbelief as she saw Danny McKay walking slowly through the crowd. He was smiling at her and walking straight to her. She was suddenly transported back over twenty years to when she was a backing singer in his band, to when she was in love with him. She came sharply back to reality when she spotted his wife Hetty walking alongside him, also smiling at her.

Suddenly she became aware of the loud music and the crowd around her again and she shook her head quickly. Danny and Hetty were then standing in front of her.

"Stephanie," Danny said simply, smiling warmly at her, then giving her a tender kiss on the cheek.

"Hi, Danny," she said quietly.

"Stephanie!" Hetty cried loudly and embraced her.

"How many years has it been?"

"It's been a long time," said Stephanie. "What has you here?"

"We're shareholders at Franklyns," said Hetty. "Didn't you realise? My family have been shareholders at Franklyns for generations!"

"I see," Stephanie nodded, making sense of it.

"But look at you!" Hetty's voice was too loud. "You look marvellous! You really are gorgeous. Who'd ever have thought? And you've done so well for yourself! When I saw a photo of you in the paper saying a Stephanie Holden had taken over at Franklyns, I couldn't believe it. I said to Danny, surely this couldn't be our little friend from years ago?"

"It's me all right," Stephanie shrugged.

"We often wondered what had become of you," said Danny.

"Well, now you know."

"And who'd have thought, really, who'd have ever thought you'd end up running a big company like Franklyns," said Hetty, her eyes wide in amazement.

"Are you living in London?" Stephanie enquired. She was trying to look at both of them as she spoke but her eyes were being drawn to Danny.

"We have a place in London but we spend a lot of time down on our estate in Wiltshire."

Stephanie nodded. She had seen their house featured in *Hello* many a time. Eighties pop icon and his aristocrat wife showing off their perfect life.

"What about you? Are you married?" asked Danny.

"No, it managed to avoid me."

"Ahhh!" Hetty's face oozed sympathy. "And I always thought you'd make such a good wife and mother."

"I do have a son. Leo. That's him over there, actually." Stephanie pointed at Leo who was busy charming a group of people.

"How gorgeous!" Hetty remarked.

"What does he do?" asked Danny.

"He's actually working in Franklyns," said Stephanie.

"Keep it in the family, eh?" said Hetty. "But you look too young to have a son that age!"

Danny stared over at Leo. "How old is he?"

Stephanie's mind went blank as she thought of what to say. "Eh . . . he's . . . twenty-two . . . What about you, any kids?"

"We certainly do," said Hetty. "Four daughters who keep us on our toes. All teenagers. We've got Penelope, she's the environmentalist. Then there's Camilla, she's the vegetarian and big on animal rights. Then we have Pru, she's the great beauty. And finally we've got Tilda who's trying to decide whether she's going to be a communist or a capitalist. She's given herself until the end of the year to decide. I'm kind of hoping she opts to be a capitalist – I couldn't bear to listen to her constant disapproval of our lifestyle."

Stephanie realised Hetty still spoke in a tone that made it hard to figure out if she was being serious or amusing.

Danny's face had a curious expression as he observed Leo and then flicked back to looking at Stephanie.

"Listen, I'm afraid I have to make a speech," she said hastily. "It's been really nice to see you again."

"Well, we just can't not meet again," said Hetty. "We must meet up and do a big catch-up after all these years – wouldn't that be fun?"

"Yes, I'll talk to you later in the evening." She nodded to them and made her way through the crowd.

Chapter 43

The band stopped playing out on the decks. Leo approached the microphone.

"Ladies and gentlemen, if I could have your attention please," he said into the mike. The crowd chatter slowly died down. Other guests began to move out from the bar inside.

Stephanie looked on, trying to ignore the jitters she was feeling, but feeling very proud of Leo.

"On behalf of Franklyns –" Leo began.

"Ha!" came from the audience. It was Nicola.

"– I would like to welcome you all here tonight. And I'll now introduce Stephanie Holden to say a few words to you." He smiled at his mother and held out his hand to her.

She felt overwhelmed by the kindness radiating from his face as she walked out of the crowd and taking his hand stepped behind the microphone. He adjusted it for her height and then walked away, standing at a distance behind her.

"Thank you, Leo." She looked around at all the faces staring at her. "I'm sure the past while has been a very confusing and worrying time for you. I suppose the simple way to explain what has been happening at Franklyns is to say that, to protect your investment and Barons Bank's investment, Barons have stepped in and taken charge of the store. We believed that if drastic action wasn't taken immediately, there wouldn't have been a Franklyns in one year's time."

There was a general mumbling through the audience.

"As if!" Nicola whispered to a couple beside her. "Franklyns was here decades before she arrived, and it'll be here decades after she's gone!"

"You all are very important to Franklyns' future and as we are on a journey to change Franklyns' fortunes around, you are important to us. We have many exciting innovations underway at the moment. We are making many changes, from upgrading our personal shoppers to refurbishment and rebranding the store."

"She sounds like a British Airways commercial," Nicola whispered to another couple.

"We're making huge changes in our buying department," Stephanie continued. "We're getting exclusives for the store from top designers and are stopping stocking some brands that are no longer fashionable. We want to open the store to make it a place where everyone can shop, for it to be *everybody's* favourite shop. I would love to talk to you all personally tonight, so please approach me with any questions you may have. I've a great team around me – David Stafford in finance – and I think you all know Paul Stewart who is acting as a wonderful bridge from the past to the present and the future. And of course Conrad Richardson, a safe captain to head any ship. We're all here tonight and we all look forward to meeting you personally."

She stepped away from the microphone as the crowd clapped.

She turned around and smiled at Leo who was clapping for her as well. She mouthed "Thank you" to him.

* * *

Nicola was holding court with a small group. She was seething that she had not been mentioned in the speech – a deliberate omission on Stephanie's part to further undermine and ostracise her.

"I have faith in the new management. I think Franklyns has been crying out for change for a long time. It's been forced on us now and maybe that's not a bad thing. I have full faith in Conrad Richardson, David Stafford and Barons Bank. However, I'm very doubtful about Stephanie Holden – I think she's a mistake, and a big one."

* * *

"Leo, isn't it?"

Leo turned around. The speaker looked familiar and he tried to place him.

A smile crossed his face. "You're that geezer from that band back in the eighties."

"Danny McKay."

"I should have recognised you straightaway. There have been photos of you and Mum and other members of that band up on our sitting-room wall since I can remember."

"Really?"

"Sure. I was brought up listening to Mum's old war stories from her days with your band."

"It was a great time for us all."

"And then I came along and put a stop to all that!" Leo laughed.

Danny stared at Leo intently.

"You've aged a bit since then!" Leo remarked.

"Thanks, Leo! It comes to us all, you know. You'll find that out yourself some day. But you're only a young man now. How old are you?"

"Twenty-three."

Danny's eyes bored into Leo more intently. Then he looked over at Stephanie who was at the bar.

"Your mother is a remarkable woman, Leo."

"So everyone keeps telling me."

Danny looked at Leo and again and clasped his hand on his shoulder.

"Good to meet you. Hopefully I'll see you again."

Chapter 44

Although Rachel hadn't expected to be working on the night, she was really enjoying it. She loved the buzz of being at an event and it reminded her of her old days at Brown Thomas. After escorting a shareholder out to the dessert table, she went to look for Daniella.

She found her perched up at the bar, glass of champagne in her hand, talking closely with a middle-aged handsome man.

"Daniella, what are you doing?" Rachel asked.

"I'm doing what I came here to do, bloody well enjoying myself! And if I can't enjoy myself with Leo, then I'll just have to do it with somebody else." She turned and flashed a seductive smile at her male companion.

"But seriously, there are some shareholders still arriving . . ."

"Well, you show them where the loos are. I've run around after enough old fogeys for one night, thank you very much!" She indicated the man she was with. "Rachel, this is Giovanni. He's from Rome."

Giovanni stood up and took Rachel's hand, kissed it and breathed, "Enchanting!"

Once Rachel had managed to get her hand back, she said, "Daniella, can I have a quick word with you?"

"I'll be back in a tick, Giovanni. Keep my seat warm." She winked at him and followed Rachel to the end of the bar.

"What is it?" Daniella snapped.

"Daniella, you are flirting outrageously with that man in front of all your bosses, Leo's mother and, worse of all, Leo himself."

"So what? At least Giovanni knows how to treat a lady, unlike the rest of them. He's absolutely minted, Rachel! Big shareholder at Franklyns, villa in Rome. I think he mentioned something about a private jet as well, though the language barrier was causing a bit of a problem, so I'm not sure about that one."

"Come on, let's go and find Leo and have a few drinks and a laugh," Rachel encouraged.

"Forget it! Give this lot another couple of hours and they'll be throwing a dishcloth in our hands and asking us to do the washing up! I think Giovanni can offer a girl a little more fun than that." With that, she turned and went back to rejoin Giovanni.

* * *

Nicola had been keeping one eye on David all night, waiting for any opportunity to speak to him. At last she spotted him alone, coming in from the deck into the main bar.

She hurried over to him, grabbing two glasses of wine en route.

"Wine?" she offered, holding out a glass.

"Oh! Yes, all right." He took the glass and smiled.

"There's a lot of people here speaking very highly of you tonight," said David.

She blushed. "The shareholders? I guess I've known them a long time."

"They've a lot of respect for you."

"It's nice to be appreciated."

He smiled awkwardly at her. She always seemed to be trying to be very friendly with him. He wasn't sure if it was her reputation, or her slightly unnatural manner, but he felt uncomfortable with her in a way he didn't with Stephanie.

"You know, we've been working closely together but I don't know that much about you," said Nicola.

David didn't think they had worked that closely together.

"There isn't that much to know about a boring accountant like me."

"I doubt that. Where do you live?"

"In Hampstead."

"House, apartment?" She needed to put the pieces of the jigsaw together.

"House actually."

"That's a lovely area to live in."

"I like it." His phone suddenly rang and he reached into his pocket to answer it.

"Excuse me, Nicola." He turned and walked out onto the deck.

She waited anxiously for him to finish. But as soon as his phone call ended, Conrad grabbed him and led him off to talk to some people.

* * *

Rachel ventured away from the main deck down the quiet side of the boat. She wanted to get away from the crowd and take a ten-minute break from the party. She looked across the river as the sun began to set over the South Bank. She breathed in the evening air and closed her eyes. Then she continued walking down the deck and saw Anna Stewart on her own, gazing across the river while smoking a cigarette. She looked so serene and lost in her thoughts, Rachel didn't want to disturb her. She quickly turned to walk back but in doing so knocked over an empty bottle of champagne which had been left on the deck.

Anna looked around, startled. "Oh, hello!"

"Oh, sorry, I didn't mean to disturb you!" Rachel walked back to her.

"Just crept away for a few minutes for a sneaky fag." Anna looked guiltily at her cigarette. "You won't tell Paul, will you? He thinks I've given up – he hates the habit."

"I won't say anything!" Rachel laughed.

"Thanks. Do you want one?" Anna held out the pack.

"No, thanks." Rachel shook her head.

"It's Rachel, isn't it?"

"Yes." Rachel was impressed that she remembered. She was sure Anna would have met many new faces that night.

Anna took a deep drag from her cigarette. "To be honest, I hardly ever smoke any more. Just the odd one every so often. Or on stressful nights, like tonight."

"You look the most relaxed person here. I doubt anything would make you stressed." Rachel meant what she was saying.

Anna held up her cigarette. "Well, now you know why!"

Rachel laughed again.

"Where do you work in Franklyns?" Anna asked.

"I'm down at the Chanel counter." Rachel pulled a face.

"You don't enjoy it?"

"It's all right."

"I started in retail myself years ago. I worked in the press office at Selfridges – in fact, that's where I met Paul."

"Really?" Rachel was intrigued and moved a little bit nearer. "I worked in the press office in Brown Thomas in Dublin. I'm hoping to end up in a press office again some day." Rachel pulled a face, indicating it wasn't going according to plan. "It's what I wanted to do at Franklyns but I was told I had to start on the shop floor."

"You might do better to move out of retail. I moved on as fast as I could. I wanted Paul to as well but he seemed to love it. And when Paul makes up his mind, it's hard to shift him."

"He has a strong personality," Rachel agreed.

"You're from Dublin?" asked Anna.

"Yes, I'm not over that long."

"Ah, I was over there a couple of months ago covering a story. Had a great time. How are you finding Franklyns in general?"

"It's good. The social life is great. Everyone out to the pub every night. It's a good network of friends, especially when you're not from London, like me."

"Ah, yes, the famous Franklyns' social life! My husband is one of its leading lights. Out till all hours every night." She laughed.

Rachel's face dropped for a second when she thought of Paul's alleged affairs with Christine and the others.

"Anyway –" Anna threw her cigarette down on the deck and stamped it out, "better head back to the party."

"And I'd better get back on duty!" said Rachel.

The two women strolled back to the main deck, each feeling they had made a friend.

Anna was quickly taken aside by a shareholder when they re-entered the yacht. Rachel spotted Daniella who was now outrageously flirting with her Italian at the bar.

She sighed in exasperation but realised she could do nothing about it.

Paul came up to her.

"So how did you get roped into working here tonight?" he asked quietly.

"It's a long story – I won't bore you with the finer details."

It was the first time she had the chance to speak to him privately since she overheard his row with Christine. She felt she needed to clear the air.

"Paul . . . that afternoon when I was outside your office, I wasn't eavesdropping. I know it looked like it."

Paul looked very uncomfortable. "So you didn't hear anything we said then?"

She nodded. "I did hear, but I didn't mean to, or want to. I was coming back from the storeroom and as I approached your door I heard what was going on. So I stopped. I couldn't pass your door because you'd see me. Then, as I was hesitating, you two came bursting out. I felt very awkward. I know you've been odd with me since and I would like to clear the air."

He looked at her sharply. "I thought we weren't on good terms anyway since I wouldn't overrule Nicola Newman and promote you?"

"True . . . I guess it was a little unfair of me to expect you to do anything, given all the changes and pressure at the store at the moment."

"To be honest, Nicola has always had final say on personnel. If she didn't want something to happen, it didn't."

"I can see that," agreed Rachel.

They were both watching Anna talk to a shareholder in the corner. She was smiling and laughing.

"I was chatting to Anna outside," said Rachel.

"Were you?" He looked concerned.

"She's very lovely," complimented Rachel.

"I know that."

"Well, try not to forget it either."

* * *

Stephanie was making her way through the crowd when her arm was suddenly grabbed by Nicola and she was spun around.

"Well, that was a really nice trick not mentioning me in your speech!"

"I mentioned the people who were helping me, not working against me."

"Well, your little stunt will backfire. Most people here admire and respect me, and leaving me out will only work against you," Nicola warned, her eyes dancing with anger.

"I'll take that risk," Stephanie looked defiant.

"I think you're taking a few too many risks!"

"And how's that?"

"Trying to take over at Franklyns for a start. Of course, women like you try to take out a little insurance to help them succeed." Nicola suddenly looked smug.

"What are you talking about?"

"Well, it wouldn't be the first time you screwed somebody to get ahead. Everybody knows about you and Neil Blackthorn."

Stephanie's face became serious. "I don't appreciate being the object of tittle-tattle."

"Well, keep your legs together then."

Stephanie glared at her. "Nicola, what are you talking about? What is your fucking problem? I really can't fathom you!"

"It's just that it's quite obvious that you've set your sights on David to secure your position at Franklyns, the way you used Neil Blackthorn before."

"David? David Stafford? Are you accusing me of shagging David?"

"If the cap fits."

Stephanie flicked back her hair and roared with laughter. "Oh, Nicola, you're delusional! Whatever gave you that impression?" She laughed again. "Wait till I tell David!"

Nicola suddenly leaned forward, her face furious. "If you tell David anything I said, then I'll kill you!"

Stephanie studied Nicola's anger and the penny dropped. Nicola had feelings for David!

"Nicola, I think you've had a little too much to drink – maybe you should go home."

"Don't you dare presume to condescend to me! Don't you –" Nicola stopped and her eyes widened as she stared at something over Stephanie's shoulder.

Stephanie swung around to see Leo over at the exit, confronting Daniella and a dark-haired man.

* * *

"Daniella, what the fuck is going on?" Leo was demanding. He had just caught up with her and Giovanni as they reached the exit, arm in arm.

"I'm leaving the party. I've had enough."

"But we haven't spent any time with each other," Leo protested.

"And whose fault is that?"

"Well, I'm finished work now, so we can go and relax."

"Too little too late, I'm leaving with Giovanni."

"Him? You're not going anywhere with him!"

"Oh yes, I am. In fact, he's invited me over to his villa in Rome."

"Don't be so fucking stupid! He's just using you!" Leo looked incredulous,

"We'll see!" She turned to walk out.

He grabbed her arm and swung her around.

"Hey!" shouted Giovanni "Leave the *laydee* alone."

"Fuck off, Mussolini, and stay out of this!" Leo shouted at Giovanni, his face a mask of anger.

"Get your hands off me right now, Leo! I'm leaving and that's the end of it. You blew your chance." Daniella's temper was rising too.

People around became aware of the commotion and began to stare as Giovanni tried to release Daniella from Leo's grip and Leo flung him away.

"Inviting me over here to work!" Daniella yelled. "Who the fuck do you think I am?"

Stephanie knew it had been too good to be true as she made her way over to the disturbance. In her heart she had known something would go spectacularly wrong during the night. Leo would fuck up and she would end up humiliated in front of everyone.

"You can't just walk out like this. Not with him!" Leo was insisting.

"Watch me, Leo. I can do whatever I fucking want!" Daniella blazed.

"Leo, what's going on?" demanded Stephanie.

"Stay out of it!" he snapped.

"Leo, you're making a show of yourself and me –"

"I said stay out of my fucking life!" he hissed at her.

Shocked by his reaction, she stepped back.

* * *

"What's the fuck's going on over there?" said Paul to Rachel.

"Oh no!" said Rachel. "I thought something like this might happen."

"I'd better get over there and sort it out." Paul began to walk over to the rowing couple.

"No!" Rachel grabbed his arm and pulled him back. "You'll only make it worse. Let me deal with this, I know them."

She hurried over.

Leo was still grasping Daniella's arm aggressively while she pulled away from him, and she had begun crying. Giovanni was in close proximity, swearing in Italian but no longer trying to come to grips with Leo.

"Will you just both calm down!" Rachel insisted as she moved between them.

"He won't let me go, Rachel! He invites me here, ignores me for the night and then won't let me go when I want to leave with Giovanni!"

Leo glanced at Rachel. "She's not leaving with that Eurotrash!"

"Okay. Just keep your voices down," said Rachel calmly as she firmly pulled Leo's hand from Daniella's arm. He didn't resist. "Now, Daniella, just leave quickly."

"But –" began Daniella.

"Just go, Daniella! You two can sort this out tomorrow when you're less hot, less emotional and less drunk and when you've no audience. Now, just go!"

Daniella wiped her eyes and, turning, took Giovanni's arm and walked out.

"Wait!" Leo exploded. "She's not going to walk out on me like that!"

Rachel caught his arm and held it tightly. "Leo, you can sort it out tomorrow. This is not the time or the place. You can never keep somebody from going if they want to go. Now come on, let's find a quiet spot and calm down." She led him through a nearby exit and they found themselves on an empty section of deck.

Inside, Stephanie turned around and faced the large group of onlookers.

"Sorry about that, everyone! Everything's okay now. Just a misunderstanding." She forced herself to smile as she made her way through the crowd. She spotted Danny and Hetty who were staring at her, having witnessed the whole scene. She turned away from them and started walking in the other direction only to come face to face with Nicola.

"Well, I must say, that little show just proves to me what I've always known. You can't buy class!" Nicola was holding a near-empty wineglass and her voice was ever so slightly slurred. "You come here thinking you're somebody and you put that twit of a son of yours in charge of a big event like this. Of course it had to be a disaster and everyone has seen you for what you are-"

Stephanie sighed loudly. "Oh, just go home, Nicola!" She pushed past her and walked away.

Chapter 45

Rachel marched up and down outside the gents' toilets waiting for Leo to come out. He'd been in there for ages. She took out her mobile and tried ringing him but it just went into voice mail. What a night! What a horrible scene! She was furious at Daniella, but not surprised. Her heart went out to Leo and she was now very concerned about him. He had been very stressed out after the episode.

She went to the toilet door and knocked loudly.

"Leo, are you all right?" Her voice became pleading. *"Leo?"*

Suddenly the door swung open and Leo came out, looking more relaxed and in control. He walked right past her.

"Leo? Where are you going?" she asked as he walked towards the main exit. "Leo?" She followed him as he swaggered down the gangplank. He took off his jacket, crumpled it up and threw it over the railing into the water. As he marched down the Embankment, she managed to keep up with him.

"Leo, where are you going?"

"As far away from that fucking party as I can get," he announced.

"Your mother will be worried about you," Rachel insisted.

"Oh sure!" He went to the edge of the pavement and looked up and down the road, trying to spot a vacant cab.

"Leo, stop and talk to me, please!"

"Why?" His eyes were concentrating on the passing taxis.

"Because I'm worried about you."

Spotting a free taxi, he hailed it and it swung over to the edge of the pavement.

"Take me to Mahiki," Leo ordered as he sat into the back.

As he went to close the door, Rachel made a lightning decision and suddenly she was climbing into the back of the cab as well.

"What are you doing getting in here?" demanded Leo as the cab took off.

She was about to say she was worried about him again but realised this would anger him.

"I . . . want to see what London has to offer," she said confidently.

"You've seen what London has to offer . . . a kick up the arse! Now get out of the cab, Rachel, and go on home to that cosy little flat and cosy little life of yours!"

"But that's just it. I don't want to go back to my cosy little world – I want to see . . . more. You told me that everything's there for the taking, you just have to reach out and take it . . . so show me life!"

He stared at her intently. "You shouldn't believe all the shit I come out with."

She reached out and gripped his arm. "Just show me your world tonight."

"Okay. But you're either in or out. You can't jump off

halfway because the ride gets a bit bumpy."

She nodded.

"Okay," he said.

Rachel felt relieved that he hadn't insisted she leave. Even though he had now resumed his full cockiness, she had seen the state he was in earlier and didn't want it on her conscience if something happened to him.

She could kill Daniella.

The cab pulled up across the road from Mahiki. Leo threw a fifty at the driver and got out. Rachel followed him as he strolled across the road.

"Are we going to get in here?" Rachel asked as she spotted a couple of celebrities go in and a young royal leave at the same time.

"You just say nothing and just look as confident as possible," he said. "Leave everything to me."

Rachel had read somewhere that Mahiki was Members Only. And unless you were a major-league Hollywood star you didn't stand a chance of getting in. She braced herself for the humiliation of being rejected from the door. She really did not need this.

The two surly doormen viewed them coldly, while the manager hovered behind them.

Leo was beaming a big smile and looked at all three of them as if they were old friends.

Rachel cringed, waiting for the rejection.

"Hi, boys!" said Leo. He focused on the manager and, stepping past the doormen, quickly took his hand and shook it warmly. "Hi, good to see you again. You're looking good. Did you enjoy that party last week?"

"Eh – yes?" The manager looked confused.

Rachel made sure to play along too and slunk in behind him.

"Is John here yet?"

"Eh, don't think so, not sure, haven't seen him," said the manager.

"No doubt already holding up the bar!" Leo gave a little laugh and then clapped the manager on the back and continued walking into the club. Rachel hardly breathed as she followed him. As she passed all the famous faces, she said nothing, frightened she might somehow give the game away.

"A bottle of rum and two Cokes," Leo told the bartender.

"Don't you mean a bottle of Coke and two rums?" suggested Rachel.

"I know what I mean," said Leo as the waiter unscrewed a full bottle of Jamaican rum and placed it along with two glasses and two small bottles of Coke in front of them.

Rachel arched an eyebrow. "We can't drink all that!"

"Shhh! You'll give the game away," warned Leo.

"What game?"

He poured two hefty glasses of rum and diluted them with the Coke.

"The game of pretending to be somebody you're not."

"I don't want to be somebody I'm not," she said.

"Then you shouldn't be in here."

Chapter 46

A lot of the crowd had left as Nicola walked around the emptying bar. The band had stopped playing. She was searching for David but couldn't find him anywhere. She sighed as she realised he must have slipped off home. She looked at her empty glass and deliberated about having another drink. She decided against it and put the glass down. She ran her hands through her hair and headed for the exit.

"Where can I get a taxi?" she asked the waiter.

"There's a steward outside with taxis waiting," said the waiter.

She nodded and walked out of the bar, feeling dejected. She felt like crying. David had barely noticed her all night. She had walked out of the main entrance and started down the gangplank when, out of the corner of her eye, she spotted a figure. Then she saw it was David, on the deck down towards the front of the yacht, smoking a cigarette and talking on his mobile. She stared for a while and then quickly turned around. She walked down the deck and hid behind a lifeboat, waiting for him to finish talking.

"Yeah, okay, that's sorted then. I'll see you tomorrow, Conrad," he said, finishing the call and closing over his mobile.

Nicola steadied herself and emerged from behind the lifeboat.

"Nicola!" He was surprised to see her.

"Sorry, I just spotted you having a cigarette and . . . well, I've been craving for one all night!"

"Oh!" he laughed and searched in his pocket for his packet. Opening it, he offered her one.

"Thank you." She reached forward and took one and placed it between her lips.

He fumbled for a lighter and ignited it.

She leaned forward with her cigarette and rested her hand on his to steady the lighter. She took her time lighting the cigarette, finally pulling away.

"Thanks, you've saved my life!" She smiled and inhaled, then coughed. She hadn't smoked since her college days. She inhaled again, forcing herself not to cough.

"It was a good night," she said.

"Yeah, I think Conrad was happy enough. The shareholders are very nervous though – it's going to take a lot of work to calm them."

"Well, that's what we're here for." She moved slightly closer to him.

"They gave me a lot of good suggestions. I'm going to work on their ideas."

Fuck the shareholders! she wanted to scream.

"Really?" she smiled.

"A few of those guys are stockbrokers, so they gave me lots of new ideas for the stock-market launch."

"Excellent."

She was staring into his face. He seemed immune to her.

"I think I was overestimating the share price we were going to launch at. I might have to revise my estimates."

Nicola suddenly lurched forward and started to kiss him passionately, dropping her cigarette.

"Nicola!" He pulled back quickly, shock written across his face. "What the fuck?"

"I – I –" She was lost for words.

"What the fuck was that about? Are you drunk?"

"No. I –" Her hand shot up to her mouth as she realised what she had done. "I'm sorry!" She turned quickly and began to run away.

"Wait – Nicola!" He ran after her.

Suddenly she slipped and fell. "*Owww!*" she yelled as she sprawled out on the deck.

"Nicola!" He got down on a knee beside her. "Are you all right?"

"I'm fine," she insisted, her eyes filling up with tears.

He helped her to her feet and kept an arm around her shoulders to support her.

"What was that about?" he asked.

"I don't know," she said blankly.

"You're married," he said, staring at her.

"I'm not!" she snapped. "Not any more."

"But you're Nicola Newman!" he exclaimed.

"Is that so bad?"

"No, it's just . . . I never thought of you like that. I don't know what to say."

Their faces were inches from each other.

"You don't have to say anything," she whispered, putting her hand around the back of his neck. She inched her face closer to his and they began to kiss.

Chapter 47

Leo and Rachel were seated at a table, zipping through the rum at a fast pace as they looked down at the crowd. Will.I.Am and Cherly Cole's 'Heartbreaker' was playing loudly.

"I have to admit, I was impressed," she stated.

"Huh?"

"The way you handled yourself out there at the door. I take it you didn't meet that manager last week?"

He shook his head. "Never saw the guy before in my life."

"And I guess there is no mutual friend called John?"

"Got it in one. Nice touch though, huh?"

"You managed to convince all of them that you belonged in this celebrity hangout."

"Nearly all of them. The doorman to the right didn't believe me but he was too frightened to voice his opinion in front of the other two. As they say," Leo chinked his glass against hers, "two outta three ain't bad! Everything's an illusion. I just created an illusion I was something I wasn't. They wanted to buy it, so they bought it. Everyone here is creating an illusion. In the same way the perfume you sell to people every day is giving them the illusion that they are something they're not. Quite literally, your work is selling a sweet smell to disguise the real smell of life."

She had heard him being cynical so many times before that she now expected it.

She coughed and took a drink. "But when Daniella walked out on you tonight, that wasn't an illusion. I saw how you reacted. That looked like real despair to me."

"You're mistaken. You're mixing anger up with despair."

He looked out at the crowd. They sat in silence.

"Do you wanna get outta here? Do you want to get away from this illusion and see what life is really about?"

"What now?"

"Right now."

She was intrigued by him and his attitude. What had scared her about him before was now drawing her closer to find out more.

She nodded. "Okay."

* * *

David and Nicola sat in the back of a cab.

He looked at her in a slightly awkward way. "Eh . . . your place or mine?"

She thought for a second. Her heart was thumping so hard she didn't know what to say. She thought of the hotel. She didn't want to bring him back to a hotel.

"Yours – if that's all right?"

He nodded. She turned and looked out the window as he gave the driver his address.

As the cab took off, she turned and looked at him. He

gave her a very awkward smile and she did the same. Then they both sat, stony-faced, looking ahead.

The cab drew up outside David's house. It was a Victorian terraced house on a leafy street. Nicola spotted David's Maserati outside it. David paid the driver and she followed him to his front door. The drink from the party was beginning to wear off and now the seriousness of what was happening was hitting her.

"After you," he said, holding the door open for her.

She tentatively stepped in and he turned on the lights. She realised the house was cleverly designed on different levels on the inside. Oak stairs led up from a large hallway. She glimpsed a bedroom to the right on the ground floor. She followed him down some steps that led to a large sitting-room area, with a kitchen to the rear.

"Drink?" he asked.

Fuck yes, she thought. "That would be lovely, thanks."

The kitchen area was separated from the sitting-room by a large breakfast bar. He stepped around it and went to the fridge.

"What do you want to drink?"

"Champagne, if you've got any."

He nodded. As he got the glasses out and began to open the champagne, she looked around the large room. It was how she imagined it would be. Large white sofas on dark walnut floors. A modern white kitchen, again contrasting with the walnut floors. Lots of expensive-looking music systems, DVD players and a giant flat-screen television on the wall. There was no clutter – everything had its place.

"Lovely house," she commented, taking off her shawl and throwing it down on the couch.

He came out from the kitchen with two glasses and the

champagne in an ice bucket, placing them on the coffee table.

"Thanks."

He poured the champagne.

"Have you lived here long?"

He handed her a glass. "I bought it about five years ago."

"It's nice." She took a sip.

"Do you want to sit down?" he asked.

"Eh, yes." She sat down on the couch.

He joined her on the couch but a little distance away from her.

"You live in the country, don't you?" he asked.

"Yes. Not that far really. The commute can be a little boring but I try to avoid rush hour."

He nodded and took a drink. "That's good if you can manage it."

They both took another drink and lapsed into silence as they looked straight ahead.

* * *

Paul and Anna walked quickly and happily arm in arm across the pedestrian bridge that brought them across the Thames to Waterloo.

"You did absolutely great tonight," said Anna.

He was glad to hear her words of approval. "Thanks for being there for me."

"I enjoyed it."

"So what did you think of them all?"

"Nicola's how I remembered her – looks great though. Stephanie seems tough but fair. I'd say she takes no prisoners."

"And Stafford?"

"To be honest, Paul, he's seems really nice. I can't really fault him."

Seeing his unhappy expression, she said, "It's a just a silly male pride thing, Paul. Get over it – he seems to like you."

"I know. He just makes me feel unaccomplished."

"Well, that's just stupid. And you don't know what's going on behind closed doors. Just because he comes across as all suave and successful, it doesn't mean he's happy. He's strikes me as the kind of man who'll end up alone surrounded by lots of expensive toys."

"Doubt it somehow."

"I like that Irish girl."

"Rachel?"

"I was pretty impressed with her."

"Yeah, she's nice. Don't think she'll be with us for long though."

"Why?"

"Nicola doesn't like her so won't give her a promotion and she's pretty ambitious."

"Isn't there anything you can do to help her?"

"Darling, I can barely help myself in there."

* * *

"I saw your father being interviewed on the news a couple of weeks ago," commented David.

"Yes?"

"I've always admired him a lot. He's got real economic insight."

"He's a great man," said Nicola.

They had been lapsing from bouts of conversation to silence.

David turned to her suddenly. "Did you say you were booked into The Dorchester tonight?"

"Eh . . . yes. It's a long way to get a taxi home, so I booked into the hotel."

"Oh, makes sense . . . What's your house like?"

"It's a restored farmhouse."

His eyes studied her. "The old marital home?"

She looked down at her drink. "Yes."

"And you live there on your own now?"

She stared down at the bubbles seeping to the top of her drink.

"You live there with your husband, don't you?" he asked eventually.

Nicola continued to stare at the bubbles.

"I think I'd better order you a taxi to take you back to your hotel, don't you?"

She said nothing as embarrassment and shame swept over her.

He went to get up off the couch.

"Please don't!" she said, suddenly reaching out and grabbing his arm.

"I don't mess around with married women," he said.

"I'm only married in name. Our marriage is over, honestly."

"This is all very bizarre, surreal . . . I don't think you know yourself what you're doing here. It's probably best you go."

"I do know what I'm doing here. I've never been more sure of anything."

"A married woman booking into a hotel for the night, looking for a drunken casual shag at a work do? I don't really like the sound of it."

"You've got me all wrong. I do not sleep around. I've

never done something like this before . . . But believe me, my marriage is over."

They stared at each other. She lunged forward and began to kiss him hard. He was slightly taken aback but began to respond. Suddenly she was on top of him, kissing aggressively. As he kissed back, they rolled off the couch, knocking over the coffee table. The champagne bucket and glasses went crashing onto the walnut floor. Almost oblivious to the fall, they rolled around, undressing each other urgently as they began to violently make love.

Chapter 48

"Where are we actually going?" Rachel asked Leo as they were driven into the East End. They had left Mahiki thirty minutes before.

"I told you – to see real life."

"You can pull up just here," Leo instructed the taxi driver.

They got out. Rachel looked around the area which was fairly run down. There was a lot of activity with people coming out of takeaways, Chinese restaurants and pubs that were still open even though it was long past closing hours. She felt unsafe and held her handbag a little tighter. A car pulled up across the road and the driver spoke to a girl standing in the street. They discussed terms and the girl got in and the car drove off. Down the street two men were having a fierce argument and one threw a punch at the other.

"Leo, what are we doing in this place?" she asked, full of concern.

"You asked me earlier to show you what London had to offer … to show you life."

"I know but this place is dangerous."

"I warned you it would be a bumpy ride. Come on." He started walking across the street.

She hesitated for a few seconds and then followed him. They walked across to a huge club. She saw name The Chambers over it. Leo greeted the doormen as old friends, with a handshake and a quick hug. There was no act here like at Mahiki, she observed – they really did know each other. They looked at her with curiosity as she followed Leo in. Inside the reception area there were doormen giving body searches to other customers as they entered. Leo was waved through without a search.

"Are they searching for drugs?" asked Rachel.

Leo laughed out loud. "No, if they were looking for that, nobody would get in! They are searching for guns."

Rachel shook her head in amazement.

He went to the bar, ordered two bottles of beer and handed her one.

"I don't drink beer," she said, taking the bottle anyway.

He smirked at her. "Come on."

She felt she stood out a mile amongst the people there and she was attracting a lot of unwanted attention.

Goldfrapp's 'Ooh La La' was playing loudly as they got a booth and sat down.

She observed the crowd. She saw people openly trading drugs. She saw people doing deals. She saw cash and jewellery being exchanged. While all about them the music blared and people partied.

"What kind of a place is this?" she asked.

"It's a place I've been coming to for years."

"But why? It's so dodgy!"

"Well, business isn't just done in swanky places like Franklyns, you know. This is their shop floor. In fact, I learned much of my technique here for when I worked as a trader. There isn't much difference between here and the stock market. People trading stuff, making money, no difference."

"The difference is that everything traded here is illegal."

"Just because society says one thing is illegal and one thing isn't doesn't make it right or wrong. Believe me, there are more people working in the stock market that would rip you off than are here tonight."

"You know, Leo, you're a very bright guy, with a very interesting perspective on the world. If you wanted to, and applied yourself, I really believe you could get anywhere in life."

He stared at her, taken aback by her compliment. She seemed to mean it.

She looked around at the crowd and inadvertently shivered.

"Relax, nothing will happen to you here. Nobody is going to come near you because I'm with you."

"And if you weren't here?"

"You probably wouldn't last two minutes."

"Leo, my man!" a voice suddenly boomed.

Leo looked up to see Joseph, the contact he bought the necklace from.

"Hi, Joseph," Leo nodded.

"Got some interesting things on me tonight, if you're buying?"

"No, I don't want anything. See you later."

Joseph looked at Rachel and sneered. "Maybe then ... you're selling?"

Leo looked up alarmed. "No sale. Get out of here, Joseph."

Joseph continued to stare at Rachel. "I'll offer a very good price."

Leo became angry. "I said get out of here!"

Joseph shrugged and left.

"What the fuck was that all about?" demanded Rachel.

"Nothing, just ignore it." He took a gulp from his beer.

Rachel continued to glare at him.

"I shouldn't have brought you here," he said. "It was a mistake. Come on. Let's go." He got up abruptly.

* * *

They seemed to walk through the streets for ages. The area became quieter than the strip The Chambers was on and more residential, but it was still an area Rachel would not feel comfortable being in on her own. Finally they got to a small terraced house.

"Home!" said Leo, taking out his key and letting them in.

She looked around the trendily but cheaply furnished house. She always imagined Leo in a swish apartment somewhere and was surprised to see where he lived.

He put on some music.

"I'm sorry I brought you to that place."

She sat down. "Don't be sorry. In a way I'm glad you brought me there. I've never seen anything quite like it. But what I can't understand is what you're doing there, Leo – you're worth so much more than that."

He looked at her, amazed by her words.

"Seriously, Leo, don't sell yourself short by going to places like that. I'll be honest with you ... I was really wary of you for a long time. I'd never met anyone like you before, with your attitude to life. And I really didn't like it. But the more I spend time in London, the more I realise you're right. If you play by the rules, you get nowhere and shit does happen."

"You really shouldn't pay that much attention to what I say."

"I meant what I said earlier, Leo. I really think if you applied yourself you could go places . . . I mean, look at that wonderful party you organised tonight."

"Seriously – don't mention the war." There was a warning in Leo's tone.

"But you'll have to face the music tomorrow."

"Then I'll face it tomorrow."

Chapter 49

Rachel woke up with a start. She quickly looked around and realised she had fallen asleep on Leo's sofa. She couldn't remember falling asleep. She remembered she had lain out on the sofa while they talked into the night and she must have just dozed off. She had been covered with a blanket – Leo must have put it on her before he headed off to bed. She glanced at her watch: it was nearly six thirty. She would have to hurry if she was to get to work in time. It was too early to wake Leo and she figured he could do with as much sleep as he could get before he ventured in to work. She would have to get home and shower. She got up from the sofa, slipped into her shoes and then headed to the front door. She gently opened it and let herself out, careful not to make any noise. She remembered passing a Tube station not that far from Leo's house on their journey there the previous night and hurried towards it.

* * *

Nicola's eyes opened and she dared not move. She stared

ahead at the big bay window in David's bedroom, slowly comprehending what had happened during the night. Time passed as she continued to look at the light streaming through the white linen curtains. She felt liberated. She felt alive. She felt better than she had for years.

She slowly turned around to view David, then sat up, quickly realising he wasn't in the bed.

Then the door opened and in he walked, wearing a dressing-gown and carrying a tray with a coffee pot and two cups on it. She pulled up the sheet to cover herself.

"Good morning," he said, placing the tray on the bedside locker.

"Hi," she said, smoothing her hair with her hand.

He poured two cups of coffee and handed one to her.

"What time is it?" she asked.

"Eleven … I guess neither of us will be going in to work today."

"I guess not."

He got on the bed and sat up, resting against the large wooden headboard.

"That was all very … unexpected," he said eventually.

If only you knew the planning that went into it, she thought.

"Your husband will be wondering where you are – if he rings work looking for you."

"He doesn't ring my work." She sipped her coffee.

"He might this morning, to check how the do went last night?"

"My secretary will take his call if he does."

David turned and looked at her. "Look, Nicola, what I'm trying to say is – well, last night we both had a bit too much to drink, things got a bit out of hand. We don't have to let this get in the way of our working relationship. I certainly will never tell anybody what happened and you can go back to your life and just forget about it."

"No!" she spoke urgently. "I don't want to go back to my life. My marriage is over – I'm not going back to it."

His face was shadowed with worry. "But that's nothing to do with last night, is it? Please do not do anything stupid over a one-night stand."

She hated him calling it a one-night stand. But, looking at his worried expression, she knew she had to play it carefully and not frighten him off.

She sighed and, putting the coffee cup on the locker, sat back. "It's nothing to do with last night, David. I didn't lie when I said I've never been unfaithful before but our marriage has been over for a long time. We share the same house but lead separate lives."

"I see," he nodded. "How long have you been married?"

"We've been together for years. I met Oliver when we were very young. I was barely out of college."

He was intrigued. "So when did you fall out of love?"

She shrugged. "I don't know if I ever really loved Oliver. He adored me and offered me all the emotional support I could ever want. He still does. That was enough for me."

"So why are you here then?"

She looked at him. "It's not enough for me any more."

* * *

Stephanie walked up the steps from the underground car-park and came through the wide staff entrance. She stopped at the security office.

"Is my son in yet?" she asked one of the security men on duty.

"He hasn't come through yet, Ms Holden."

"Phone my office when he arrives, please."

She continued over to the elevator and got in. She was livid since the party. She had hardly managed to sleep the previous night she had been so wound up. Leo's blazing row in front of everyone with that girl he was going out with was unforgivable. He had completely shown himself up and undermined her. She remembered him hissing at her to stay out of his life and she saw pure contempt in his face and it had shocked her. She was through with the softly-softly approach with her son.

* * *

The buyer responsible for the book department sat across Stephanie's desk. Stephanie glanced through the lists that had been ordered for the coming season.

"Quite an exciting range coming in," she commented.

"I think so. The publishers of many of them have been on, wanting to do book signings here in Franklyns."

"Excellent, always creates a stir."

"How did Louise Stirling's book do?" Stephanie was curious. She had employed Louise for different marketing campaigns when she had been a model and always found her a laugh.

The book buyer pulled a face. "Not that good, unfortunately. Sales were poor and the reviews even worse. One reviewer used just one word to describe the book in her review."

"Which was?"

The woman paused before saying, "Unnecessary."

The phone rang on Stephanie's desk and she picked up.

"Uh huh ... thanks for letting me know." Stephanie hung up the phone and asked, "Are we finished?"

"Yes, that's about everything."

Having been informed of Leo's arrival, Stephanie marched down the corridors to the office he had been using. She opened the door and walked in. Leo was sitting at his desk, swinging slightly on his swivel-chair, almost looking as if he was daydreaming.

"Glad you decided to turn up," she snapped, closing the door behind her, "albeit it's nearly lunch-time."

He glared at her.

"Do you want to explain to me what that little scene was about last night?" she asked, approaching his desk.

"None of your business," he said, sitting back.

"Yes, it is my business, Leo. It's very much my business. When you come into my workplace and make a bloody show of me, then that's my business. I invited you to come and work here –"

"Nobody asked you to invite me."

"Leo, don't start your usual answer-for-everything routine. I'm really not in the mood! You know I was so nervous about last night, so frightened that it would be screwed up. And then when it was turning into a fantastic night, I was so really proud of you. And then you go and ruin it all, as bloody usual."

"Everybody must have had very little to do to pay attention to me."

"You and that girl were practically screaming your heads off at each other! They couldn't help but look."

Leo threw his feet up on the desk and sat back even further. "So. What do you want me to do?"

"What I *want* is for you to grow up, to stop acting like a surly teenager and take responsibility for your life, and your work here. You act like the world owes you a living. We're not the likes of Nicola Newman and David Stafford – where they come from they have the security of their backgrounds and their families and their wealth to let them get away with acting how they want to. All we have is our brains and our ability to work hard to get us on in life."

"That's all you fucking care about – getting on in life!"

"You forget what it was like, Leo, when you were growing up, having hardly anything."

"I remember it all too well. I never complained, did I? I never wanted the world, did I? Don't try to feed me this bullshit that you worked so hard to become this big hot-shot executive for me."

"I did it for *us* –"

"You did it for *you*!" he shouted.

She was taken aback by his anger.

"You know what, you're pissed off about last night," he went on, "the fact that I showed you up in front of all your fancy friends. You cared more about what they thought than what was happening to me at the time!"

Stephanie kept her voice even. "Leo, whatever was going on between you and that girl, there's a time and a place, and last night was neither."

"Fuck them all."

"Leo!"

"Yes, fuck them all, because I don't care. I met your friend from your band there last night. You know, it's such a pity that I came along and you had to drop out of the music business and put your life on hold for a few years. You could have been Madonna by now if it hadn't been for me. But not to worry, you climbed to the top of the shit heap in the end. Well done, Mum!" His voice dripped sarcasm.

"And what would you have me do? Stay in that council flat? Whether you believe it or not, I wanted to get you away from there, Leo. And I gave you the best chances I could and now you're throwing them away!"

"I didn't want chances when I was growing up. I wanted a mother who cared a little bit more about me than her spreadsheets!"

Stephanie felt her eyes brimming with tears. "Leo, that's not fair! You know, you weren't a bowl of fruit yourself. It was bloody hard work trying to raise you. You always found the very worst company to keep. You were always in trouble and that attitude –"

"And I wanted a father." Leo stood up and stared at her.

Stephanie was stunned to hear him say this. They never discussed Leo's father. When Leo was much younger she had openly discussed his father and how she had known him. He didn't want to know him or many details, and she had been relieved by that.

She stood in silence.

"You know – me and you, we just don't get on, and I don't think we should bother any more." He walked past her and out of the room.

* * *

Stephanie sat on her swivel-chair, facing away from her desk, as she stared across at the Knightsbridge skyline. All the anger and resentment that Leo had hidden for years just erupting like that had knocked her out. She didn't know what he expected of her. Millions of women went out working every day. Millions of mothers. What could she have done differently? She couldn't just live in poverty, raise her son in poverty.

It was hard being on her own and Leo was a difficult teenager. It was such a mess. She buried her face in her hands.

There was a knock on the door.

She turned around. "Come in!"

A security man came in. "This was delivered by hand for you." He handed her a letter.

"Thanks," she said, taking it.

The security man left and she opened the letter.

Dear Stephanie,

It was such a delight to see you again last night. We looked for you later in the night to say our goodbyes but couldn't find you. As we discussed, let's have a proper catch-up. We're having a few friends come down to our Wiltshire estate this weekend. Will you come? Please do.

Love, Hetty & Danny

PS Don't bother with driving, much easier for you to get the train and we'll collect you from the station. Get the seven o'clock from Waterloo to Salisbury xx

* * *

Rachel felt exhausted from the previous night and the last thing she wanted was to be standing behind the Chanel counter. Daniella hadn't shown up for work and she wondered where she was. Her mobile started to ring under the counter and Rachel bent down to answer it, hiding from any passing management.

It was Daniella's number.

"Daniella, where are you?" Rachel demanded.

"At Heathrow, darling, where else would I be?"

"Well, behind the Chanel counter at Franklyns for a start."

"I'm through with Franklyns, darling! I'm going to Rome with Giovanni."

"Please tell me you're joking me, Daniella. You've just met him and you don't know anything about him."

"Actually we clicked like I've rarely clicked with anyone before. And I did a Google search on him and he is a very respected and very successful Italian businessman."

"I can't believe this, Daniella – what about Leo?"

"What about him? I'm through with him as well."

"And have you bothered to tell him?"

"I texted him this morning."

"That's a real lousy thing to do, even for you."

"I think it was lousier for him to invite me to a do and expect me to work there!"

"You're just looking for an excuse for your behaviour now," said Rachel.

"Don't be like that, Rachel. Come out and visit us in Italy! I'd better run, our plane is boarding. I'll phone you from Rome. *Ciao!*"

* * *

Stephanie spotted Rachel serving a customer. She waited until the customer was gone before she went up to her.

"Rachel, isn't it?"

Rachel was surprised to see Stephanie and nervous that she was about to be given out to for her role in Daniella and Leo's scene.

"Eh, yes." She managed a smile.

Stephanie looked awkward. "I just wanted to say thanks. Not only for helping out last night but also for your intervention in the row. You managed to defuse a tricky situation."

"Er . . . no problem, really."

"Anyway, I just wanted to say thanks." Stephanie nodded and turned to walk off.

Taken aback but thinking quickly, Rachel decided this was her chance. It would take barefaced cheek but wasn't that how Leo led his life?

"Eh, Stephanie!" Rachel called.

Surprised, Stephanie turned around.

"I mean, Ms Holden . . . could I have a word with you sometime?"

"A word? About what?"

"Well, just about . . . employment prospects really."

"Oh!" She glanced at her watch. "Come up to my office at four." She turned and walked off.

* * *

It was a day of bliss for Nicola, hanging around David's house dressed in one of his bathrobes. David had disappeared to the upstairs office to do some work, leaving her with her thoughts down in the sitting-room. She knew exactly what she had to do.

She went into the kitchen and cooked them an omelette in the afternoon. She laughed at the thought of herself there, cooking in his dressing-gown. She rarely cooked at home, leaving it all to their housekeeper or Oliver, who was a terrific chef. And she had certainly never worn Oliver's dressing-gown – ever.

"Lunch is ready!" she called up to him.

He came down wearing jeans and a black T-shirt. She had never seen him in anything other than a suit before.

"You shouldn't have bothered," he said, sitting down. "I'd have sent out for something."

"No bother!" she smiled as they sat down at the round glass table in his kitchen area.

"Did you get much done upstairs?" she asked casually.

"A little bit. I should really have gone in to the office today – too much to do."

The mobile rang in his pocket and he took it out and answered it, getting up from the table and walking over to the patio doors.

"Conrad?" said David.

"Just checking how the rest of the night went?"

"Very successful actually. I think everyone was happy and we managed to instil confidence."

"Maybe," said Conrad. "I've had a few emails from concerned shareholders today."

"Concerned about what?" said David, surprised and a little alarmed.

"Well, some of them didn't take to Stephanie at all to be truthful. In fact, they are quite hostile to her."

David glanced quickly over at Nicola who was pretending not to listen as she continued to eat. He quickly unlocked the patio doors and walked out into his long garden.

"What do you mean hostile?" he asked.

"They just think she's wrong for the store and the job."

"Well, if it was up to them they would still have Furstin in charge of the mess!" David pointed out.

"I suppose. In truth – what do you think of her after working with her?"

"I like her a lot. I think she's doing a tremendous job. I

think we should continue to back her," David said decisively. "Most importantly the city respects her, and if we are to have a successful stock-market launch, her name is crucial."

"Okay, we'll continue to roll with the punches then."

* * *

As Nicola looked out the patio window at David pacing up and down the garden talking to Conrad, she was irritated she couldn't hear the conversation. But she had heard enough to guess that her subtle campaign against Stephanie Holden the previous night had paid off. Maybe it would now only be a matter of time until she was kicked out on her glamorous and irritating ass. And then she and David would run the store together.

Chapter 50

After spending thirty minutes asking her about her experience, Stephanie studied Rachel's CV. She put it on the desk and looked up at Rachel.

"You got your hands on a CV quickly. Do you often keep copies in your bag to hand out to passing chief executives?"

Rachel blushed. "I had a spare one in my locker."

"So what are you actually looking for?" Stephanie crossed her legs.

"I'm looking for something in the press office as a publicist – or in the marketing department."

Stephanie studied the girl. She had seemed very charming and capable at the shareholders' party. She had good qualifications. She had good experience but not so much that she would want to do things her way rather than Stephanie's. And having spoken to her for a while she seemed very articulate, pleasant and together.

"Rachel, I am about to recruit a junior publicist to assist me. I'm going to have a little think about this and get your file from Personnel."

Rachel's face suddenly dropped. "I see."

Stephanie saw her reaction. "Is there a problem with that?"

Rachel sighed. "I may as well be honest with you. Nicola Newman doesn't like me and has told me I don't have a future in the store."

"I see!" Stephanie sat back. "Did she give you any reason for this?"

"She said my face doesn't fit."

Stephanie stared for a moment. "Okay . . . but with that knowledge you still approached me to ask for a job."

Rachel nodded, feeling crushed. "I'm sorry for wasting your time."

"You must want a promotion very much?"

Rachel nodded. "I do."

"Leave it with me. I'll have a word with Paul Stewart."

Rachel's expression became concerned.

Noticing this, Stephanie said, "Don't tell me there's a problem with Paul as well?"

Rachel was not confident what Paul would say, but what could she do?

"No – no problem at all." Rachel forced a smile.

"Good. Leave me your mobile number."

* * *

Nicola looked at her watch and seeing it was half five realised she had to go soon. She knew Oliver would be leaving lots of messages on her turned-off mobile phone. She had to go back to The Dorchester and book out. She had to go home. But she never wanted to leave David's place.

David called her a taxi and she knew she looked stupid as she changed into her floaty blue dress again. As the taxi beeped outside, she stood awkwardly in David's hallway.

"Well, eh, see you tomorrow!" he said.

"Yes." She reached forward and kissed him quickly before rushing out to the waiting taxi.

* * *

Stephanie walked into Paul's office.

"Good night last night, everyone seemed happy," said Paul.

"Yes, and thanks for all your help, Paul. You made them all feel at ease and gave a sense of continuity."

"Well, I am part of the team!" he said confidently.

"Yes." Stephanie looked slightly uneasy when he said this as his future was still undecided. "Paul, I just want to ask you about a salesgirl on the ground floor – Rachel Healy – do you know her?"

"Rachel, yes, she was there last night."

"That's right. What's she like?"

He was confused. "Why do you want to know?"

"I'm considering her for a publicist position."

"I see." He was taken aback. He hadn't thought Rachel would be so ambitious as to go over Nicola's head.

"Well?" She was concerned by his hesitancy.

"Rachel has been one of the best salesgirls we've ever had. She consistently breaks targets. A high flyer. I'd be sorry to lose her from the sales team – but I know she's very ambitious to get on so I wouldn't hold her back."

"I think I'll give her a chance then."

"You're after giving me a fucking headache in that case," said Paul.

"Why?"

"Well, Daniella phoned in and quit today as well.

That's two of my best salesgirls gone!"

"Everybody's replaceable, Paul," shrugged Stephanie, taking in the information about Daniella and wondering why she had quit.

Stephanie made her way to the ground floor. She spotted Rachel selling enthusiastically and waited until she had finished with the customer before approaching her.

"Right, you've got the job. You got a glowing reference from Paul. Start first thing on Monday. Stop off at Personnel first to let them know of your change of status so they can make the necessary pay adjustment."

Rachel stared in amazement. "Yes. Thank you. Thank you very much!"

* * *

It was closing time and security men were herding customers out of the store as Rachel made her way to Paul's office.

He looked up from his paperwork at her knock.

"I just wanted to say thanks a million for the reference. Stephanie gave me the job."

He studied her excitement with bemusement. "How do you know I gave you a good reference?"

"Stephanie told me you did."

"Did she? Glad my opinion stills carries some weight then.".

"Of course it does!" She smiled broadly and left.

She took out her mobile to ring Leo to thank him next and check how he was, but his phone was off.

Chapter 51

Nicola prepared herself when she saw Oliver's car as she pulled into their driveway. She had changed out of her gown into a navy dress.

She got out and steadied herself as she let herself in the front door.

"Nicola?" Oliver called urgently from the lounge. She walked in and saw him standing there, his face a cloud of worry.

"Nicola! I've left countless messages on your phone. I tried your office and they said you weren't in. I've been sick with worry!"

"I know, I'm sorry."

"Where have you been?"

"Just at meetings outside the store."

"You could have phoned to let me know you were all right. I've been worried, especially after what happened before."

"Oliver, I need to talk to you," she said, sitting down on the couch. "What about?"

"Please sit down, Oliver. You're making me nervous."

He went and sat in an armchair.

"What's wrong?" he asked.

"Everything and nothing . . . I don't know. I've been doing a lot of thinking, Oliver, and I need a little time for myself."

"I don't understand."

She knew what to say, how to phrase it, how to attract his understanding and let her get away.

"I don't understand myself, Oliver. Ever since the attack . . . well, I haven't been myself."

"I know." He sat forward eagerly. He visualised her on the CCTV footage half-running across the station. He wanted to ask her what she was doing that morning. But he knew that if he asked her anything she would get angry, would feel he was doubting her. He didn't want to upset her more.

"I just haven't felt the same and I'm often scared being here in the house on my own."

"Are you?"

"You're often working late at conferences or something."

He looked at his wife, feeling so sorry for her. She had never been frightened of anything before. "Well, I'll just stop working late then. I'll make sure I'm here before you every evening."

"That won't help me, Oliver. It's running much deeper than that. I could be in the middle of Fort Knox and still not feel safe. That's what being attacked does to you. You of all people should understand the impact of crime on a person."

"I do! I do! But what can we do to help you back to how you were?"

"Well, I just need to rebuild my confidence, slowly. And nobody can do that but me. I need to rely on myself again, not you. I need to build myself up to how I used to be. I think the best way to do that is to – well, as I said, take some time for myself."

"So what are you proposing?"

"I'm going to leave here for a while and rent an apartment in London."

"What?" He was alarmed.

"I need to come out of my cosy environment, get out into the real world and get my confidence going again."

"But you can't just leave, go and live on your own –"

"You want your old wife back, don't you?"

"More than anything!"

"Then, won't you support me with this?" She reached her hand out to him.

He was in utter confusion and shock as he didn't know what to say. He reached out and took her hand.

* * *

Rachel tried ringing Leo again when she got home but his phone was still off. She was worried about him because of Daniella dumping him. She also was unsure how he might react to his mother recruiting her – maybe he wouldn't like it, so she wanted to check it with him first.

She had a shower and then left another message on Leo's phone.

"Leo, hi, it's Rachel here. I know that you and Daniella are through, and I'm worried about you. Call me back to let me know everything's okay."

Then she spent some time ringing family and friends back home to tell them about her promotion. They were all thrilled for her and time flew as she chatted.

When she finally put down the phone it was nearly

nine thirty so she jumped off the couch, changed and headed out.

As she got the lift up to the Oxo Tower Bar, she was hoping Leo would be there.

Walking into the bar she scanned the crowd but couldn't see him. Then she spotted Tom and the other stockbroker friends of Leo's and hurried over to them.

"Hi! Tom, isn't it?" she asked, tapping him on the shoulder.

"Yeah! Hi there, again!"

"Is Leo here?"

"No, not tonight. Can I get you a drink?"

"Is he going to be in later?"

"We're not expecting him. The Brandy Alexanders are fab – you have to try one!"

"Thanks. Another time maybe."

Walking slowly down the South Bank, she sighed. She needed to know he was all right. She needed to know he would be all right about her working for his mother. She flagged down a taxi.

As the taxi pulled up outside Leo's house, she saw there were no lights on.

"Can you hold on a second?" she asked the driver as she jumped out. She knocked on the door a few times and looked up at the house, sighing.

There was another place she could try. She gave the taxi driver directions how to get to The Chambers. It was eleven by the time she walked up to the entrance of the club. She was filled with nerves as she approached the doormen.

They recognised her from the night before and looked at her warily.

"Leo asked me to meet him here," she said confidently,

trying to imitate the assertiveness Leo had shown at Mahiki.

They glanced at each other and moved out of her way. She hoped they hadn't noticed that she was shivering slightly with nerves.

The club was packed with the same type of unsavoury characters as before.

A sleazy guy immediately appeared in front of her. "I like you. You're with me now," he said.

She looked at him incredulously. "I don't think so." She moved to walk past him.

He reached out and grabbed her arm.

She turned to him and looked him squarely in the face. Her eyes furious, she said, "Let go of my fucking arm before I fucking kill you!"

He glared at her and she returned his stare, before he let her go and walked away. She remembered Leo's words that she wouldn't last two minutes without him. She needed to quickly scour the club, find him and get away from this awful place.

A cheaply dressed woman stood in front of her.

"Twenty for the bracelet," she said, nodding at the gold jewellery around Rachel's wrist.

"It's not for sale," Rachel said firmly.

"Then I'll just take it," said the woman, as she reached down to grab the bracelet.

"I said it was not for sale!" Rachel shouted in her face.

Surprised, the woman backed off.

Slightly trembling, Rachel continued through the club.

With relief she spotted Leo at the bar drinking on his own. She quickly went up to him.

"I think I'll take that beer now, if it's still on offer," she said.

He swung around. "Rachel! What the fuck are you doing here?"

"I'm looking for you!"

"You shouldn't even be walking around this area, let alone come in here on your own. You're fucking mad!"

"Did you not get my messages?"

"I've had my phone off. Come on. Let's get out of here." He stood up quickly.

"I really could do with that drink," she said.

"You can have it back at mine. Come on. Let's split." He grabbed her arm and they headed for the door.

* * *

"That was a really stupid thing to do, going in there on your own," snapped Leo, as they got out of the taxi at his house.

"I can look after myself," said Rachel.

"No, you can't, not in a place like that. You don't know the kind of scum that hangs out in there." He was searching his pockets for money for the taxi fare. "You got any cash on you?"

"Oh, sure." Rachel quickly reached into her handbag and paid the taxi driver.

Leo let them into his house and went to the kitchen. Taking out a bottle of vodka he poured two strong drinks. She followed him into the kitchen and he handed her one.

"I needed to speak to you and you weren't at work today."

"I was but I left early. What did you want to talk to me about that was so urgent you trawled your ass across the city at this time of night?"

"I was speaking to Daniella and she told me it's over between the two of you."

"And so?"

"And so … I wanted to know you were all right."

Looking at her, he tried to fathom her. He laughed out loud. "What did you think I was going to do? Something stupid? Throw myself in the Thames?"

"No, I'm not saying that. It's just you were very upset when she left the party with that Italian."

"I was upset for all of ten minutes because I don't like being made to look a fool! Honey, believe me, I would not top myself over an airhead like Daniella."

Studying him, she tried to decide if he was speaking the truth or putting on a brave face. She guessed it was a bit of both.

He opened a kitchen cupboard, and took out some tobacco and started to roll a joint.

"Well … that's good then," she said. "There's no need for me to be worried."

"No, there isn't," he said as he continued to roll the joint.

"There's another thing, Leo . . . I asked your mum for a promotion today and she gave it to me. I'm to be a junior publicist – assisting her."

He looked up, startled.

"I don't know how you feel about that," she went on. "In a way I took advantage of knowing you. She came and thanked me for helping out on the yacht and I took the opportunity to pounce. I've been trying to get a promotion in Franklyns since I arrived there."

He looked down and continued rolling. "Good for you."

"You're not annoyed or upset?"

"No, I'd have done the same myself," he said.

"I know ... and in a way that's what made me ask her. Seeing how you work life. So you won't mind me working close to your mother?"

"It doesn't concern me in the least, because I'm finished with the place."

"What? But why? Is it because Daniella has left?"

He laughed out loud again. "Nothing to do with her. I had a blazing row with my mother. It was over the argument I had with Daniella. She thinks I showed her up."

"But that's no reason to leave your job!"

"I don't actually have a job at Franklyns, Rachel. I'm on the payroll doing nothing. They gave me that party to organise because they couldn't think of anything else for me to do. Mum made a job up for me because we've grown really far apart and she thought it would bring us back together. It was a crap idea and I'm glad it's over."

"And what'll you do now?"

"I'll do what I've always done – survive."

"She didn't just give you a job, Leo. She was giving you an opportunity and you've thrown it back in her face."

"I'm not going to be a charity case, Rach. It's true what Nicola Newman said to me when I started – I had absolutely no experience or anything to offer the store. I should have walked out then."

"Nicola Newman! I really wouldn't mind that bitch – she more or less said the same to me!"

Leo was surprised. "Did she?"

"She told me I had no future in the store – that my face didn't fit! People like Nicola thrive on making other people feel bad about themselves. In a way your mum has given both of us opportunities and I'm not throwing mine back in her face."

Leo didn't respond. Silently he led her out into his back garden where they sat on garden chairs in the warm summer's night. The garden was long and unkempt and beyond the trees at the back were dozens of tower blocks in the not-too-far distance.

"I could pretty much do my own thing as a teenager. Mum was always there for me – she was home every night. But she had a lot of other things on her mind. And there was only her – so I became an expert at deceiving her. When she thought I was out at football practice, I was getting up to all sorts." He took a long drag on the joint.

He offered it to Rachel. She looked at it hesitantly. Then she reached forward and took it.

"I haven't done this since college," she said.

"I'm surprised you even did it then."

"I didn't do it much, I can assure you. But who cares tonight? I'm celebrating my promotion." She put it between her lips and drew in.

"I'll make a rebel out of you yet!" he mocked.

"I sense a lot of anger in you, Leo. Are you angry with your mum?"

He was usually very guarded but that night, sitting there, he felt he could talk about anything to Rachel.

"I'm really not angry with her, you know. She did the best she could under difficult circumstances. Getting pregnant that early, being on her own. I sometimes wonder where she would have got to if I hadn't come along. I took her youth and all the opportunities she could have had."

"God, Leo – that's where your anger comes from! You feel guilty because you feel you took her life away from her. You're not angry at her, you're angry at you!"

He looked straight ahead, feeling exposed, feeling he had said too much.

Sensing this, she put her hand on his arm. "Anything we say won't go any further, Leo. You can trust me."

"You know, we're put on this planet to procreate. Pure and simple. Continue the race. That's why all this shit about careers and waiting till you meet the right person and the right time is bullshit."

You would think along those lines, thought Rachel – it helps you make sense of your own conception.

"So then you still think I was mad to leave my boyfriend in Dublin to pursue a career in London?" she asked.

"Yes, I do . . . but I'm kind of glad you did though." He reached over and took the joint from her. "Here, I want you to try something. You'll get a real buzz from it. Open your mouth when I tell you to." He took a large inhalation of smoke and moved his face in front of her. Then he nodded and said, "Now."

Feeling anxious, she opened her mouth. He brought his mouth close to hers. She edged back slightly, not sure what he was going to do. He then exhaled the smoke into her mouth. Choking slightly she breathed in the smoke, the fumes making her feel intoxicated. She got a rush to her head and closed her eyes.

She breathed the smoke out slowly.

She opened her eyes. Leo was still positioned in front of her, smiling.

"Did you enjoy that?" he asked.

She nodded. "Yes."

Their mouths hovered close to each other and then he stopped smiling as their eyes met. Then they inched closer together and kissed.

Chapter 52

Stephanie had opened a bottle of wine at home and as she topped up her glass she looked down at the invitation from Danny and Hetty on the glass coffee table in front of her. She thought it so arrogant that they hadn't left a number or even an address for her to contact to say she couldn't make it. They just expected her to turn up without question. She didn't know what to do. Did she really want to be in their company after so many years? Although Hetty had seemed perfectly charming at the party, she could detect the same bitchy undercurrents she always used to have. *'But who'd ever have thought you would have done so well in life?'* Hetty was a master at making a compliment sound like an insult.

And then there was Danny. There was no denying that all the memories had been evoked when she saw him again. She was curious to see his and Hetty's life up close. The truth was, when Danny had dumped her and become engaged to Hetty and she had slept with Gary Cosgrave and become pregnant, the course of her whole life had changed forever. This had blown a normal break-up of a relationship into something much more profound and she had carried it over the years. She had spent years imagining Danny and Hetty's lives as perfection while hers was such a struggle. Maybe it was time to see their lives close up and try to deal with her jealousy. But more importantly after Leo's outburst, she now knew that it was an issue for Leo that he never knew his father. She might be quite happy never to hear the name of Gary Cosgrave again but for Leo she needed to address the situation. She didn't know what Leo wanted. Did he want to meet him? The whole thought of bringing up the past made her shudder. The idea of telling Gary Cosgrave that he had a son. How would he react? He probably couldn't even remember her. She was a one-night stand he had had back in the eighties. Anyway, she needed to start by at least finding out what Gary was doing now and where he was.

And the only people who might know were Danny and Hetty. So she needed to go down to Wiltshire and try to find out what she could.

* * *

Leo and Rachel were in his bed in the semi-darkness. After they had made love they had just lain there while Leo talked about his life. She marvelled at how much he could talk without saying too much. He spoke about what he'd got up to growing up but she felt he stopped short of telling her everything. She knew by the way he was that, whatever he might think of his mother, he was loved very much growing up. Finally they drifted off to sleep.

Leo woke with a jolt and sat up quickly, causing Rachel to waken as well.

"Hey – hey," she soothed. "It's all right."

He looked around and lay back down.

"You were having a bad dream?" she asked.

"Can't remember."

She sat up and rested on one arm, looking down at him. "Leo ... I want you to know that I didn't come here last night looking for this. It was the last thing on my mind."

"Why are you saying that?"

"I don't know ... I'm wondering what this looks like. In bed with my best friend in London's boyfriend."

"Ex-boyfriend," he corrected.

"For all of two minutes . . . I don't know what it says about me . . . I don't know what it says about you . . . was this a rebound or something?"

He shrugged. "Shit happens."

She smirked. "Is that your answer to everything?"

"Look, Daniella is probably sailing around the Med as we speak. I don't think she'd be too concerned."

Rachel lay back down. After a while she started chuckling.

"What's so funny?" he asked.

"I'm just thinking – if everyone I know at home could see me now! In a place like that club last night, coming back and being given a good seeing-to in a terrace in the East End by a guy who didn't even have the taxi fare!"

"Nobody forced you." He shrugged defensively.

She leaned over and kissed him. "I wouldn't want to be anywhere else."

"I guess that doctor guy you were seeing back in Dublin always had the taxi fare?"

"Sure he did. In fact he would try to control me by not letting me spend anything. I hated it . . . I have felt more alive with you this past twenty-four hours than I did with him in a year."

She glanced at her watch and saw it was six thirty.

"Shit! I'd better get going." She got out of bed. "I'm going to be late for work. I have to get back to mine and change. Are you going in to work today?"

"I told you, I'm finished with the place."

"It's your choice but why don't you think about it very carefully before you throw it all away?"

Chapter 53

Nicola looked around the large modern apartment in the Docklands.

"It's one of the finest rental properties we have on our books at the moment," assured the agent. The apartment had large floor-to-ceiling windows that looked out across the Docklands. There was luxury cream carpet throughout and beautiful modern furniture. She imagined David would love it when he saw it. The rent was exorbitant but she didn't care. It would be perfect for her to begin her new life.

"I'll take it!" she said to the agent.

She made her way to the plaza in front of the Canary Wharf Tube station. She loved the place, the high-rise buildings, the grandeur of the marble-floored designer-filled shopping malls, the international news from Reuters zipping across the public monitors everywhere, the legions of teeming workers booted and suited, fitting shopping trips in the malls or drinking and eating in the dockside bars and restaurants into their hectic work schedule. This was her new life. This was where she wanted her new life with David to be.

It was four o'clock by the time she got back to Knightsbridge. It was Friday afternoon and David hadn't made contact with her since she had left his place the previous evening. She would go and pack her stuff that night and leave home. She didn't want to waste any time. She needed to leave Oliver straightaway. It would be easier all round.

As she walked in front of Franklyns, she decided she would go straight to David's office and maybe arrange to meet him on the following day, Saturday. Everything was moving so fast and she was so excited. Suddenly she spotted David outside the store with a suitcase, trying to flag down a taxi. She hurried over to him.

"David?" she said, as a cab pulled over to him.

He turned around and looked embarrassed to see her.

"Oh, hi!" he said.

"I was just going to pop up to see you," she said, looking down at his suitcase.

"Right, yeah . . . I'm off to France for the weekend."

"Oh!" She was filled with surprise and disappointment.

"Yeah, it's a friend's stag."

"I see. When are you back?"

"Monday morning."

"Right."

"Look, I'd really better rush or I'll miss the plane. Maybe we'll meet Monday, have a catch-up then?"

"Eh, sure," she nodded.

He jumped into the taxi and it took off leaving her staring after it.

* * *

Nicola went storming out of the lift and made for her office. She spotted Rachel sitting waiting for her. That was all she needed, that fool of a girl hassling her for a promotion again. Did she not take no for an answer?

"Any messages?" she snapped at Yvette.

"No. Just this girl waiting to see you," said Yvette.

Nicola raised her eyes to heaven and turning to Rachel ordered, "Follow me through."

Nervously, Rachel did as she was bid and walked after Nicola into her office.

"What is it this time?" Nicola snapped as she sat at her desk.

"Eh, it's just Stephanie Holden told me to contact HR about my new position."

"What new position?" Nicola demanded.

"Stephanie had appointed me as a publicist."

"She has *what?"* Nicola almost shouted.

Rachel started to tremble slightly. An angry Nicola Newman was not an attractive sight.

"Are you trying to tell me that, after I expressly told you there was no position for you at Franklyns, you went over my head and contacted Stephanie Holden?"

Rachel nodded.

"How bloody dare you! We'll see about this." Nicola picked up the phone and began to dial Stephanie's number.

Rachel felt a headache coming on. She had known it was all too good to be true and Nicola wouldn't allow it.

Then Nicola paused before she continued dialling. She remembered the run-in she had with Stephanie on the yacht, when she had accused Stephanie of wanting to sleep with David. In light of what had happened since then with David, she didn't want to get into any dispute with Stephanie today.

Nicola slammed down the phone.

"Go and see Yvette – she'll sort out some temporary contract for you. And I'm watching you. The first slip-up and I'll have you kicked out of here. Now get out of my sight."

Rachel quickly exited and, sighing, went over to Yvette's desk.

"Did she give you a hard time?" Yvette smiled sympathetically.

"How do you stick her?" Rachel asked with genuine interest.

"I guess I'm a masochist."

"You should go and see a therapist about that," Rachel advised.

Rachel spent the rest of the afternoon behind the Chanel counter like a zombie. She was exhausted from lack of sleep from the last two nights and was dreaming of her bed. That evening after work, she let herself into her apartment and fell straight into bed and into a sound sleep.

Chapter 54

Oliver lifted Nicola's suitcases into the back of her Mercedes and closed the boot. He stood there looking at her. She felt guilty but her excitement about her new life outweighed her guilt. Last night as they lay in bed, she was sure she could hear him quietly crying, something he never did.

"I'm really worried about you, Nicola. Living on your own. What if something happens to you?"

"Don't be silly, Oliver. The apartment I'm renting in Canary Wharf is so safe."

"I think I should go and check it out for you."

"As I explained, I need to do this on my own. That's what I need to do, live on my own and rebuild my confidence." She leaned forward and kissed his cheek. "Don't look so worried . . . everybody has to leave home sometime." She got into the car and drove off.

* * *

Oliver sat in the living-room in his favourite armchair, a large port in his hand. He couldn't believe she was gone.

The house felt so empty, his life felt empty.

They had made a lot of progress since arresting Jason Cody. They had finally managed to crack him and he had given them the name of the man he had sold Nicola's jewellery to, a criminal called Jason Maguire. Maguire was well known to the police as being a cunning and ruthless criminal. They had a warrant out for his arrest. But he had gone underground and they couldn't find him.

Oliver took a swig of port, his frustration growing at the thought of Maguire's still being free.

He took out his mobile and rang the officer in charge of the case.

"Any luck finding Maguire?" Oliver demanded.

"No luck so far. We're using all our contacts to try and locate him."

"Try harder. I want Joseph Maguire found and found quickly."

"Yes, sir."

* * *

Stephanie got on the train at Waterloo and found a comfortable seat. She had a few magazines to keep her entertained on the journey to Salisbury. Half of her was dreading the weekend and the other half was actually excited by it. It really would be good to spend some time with Danny after all these years and see what his life was like now, reminisce a bit, and of course find out what happened to Leo's dad.

Her mobile bleeped and she opened the text. It was from Neil Blackthorn asking if she was around for dinner the next night. She texted him back to say she was away for the weekend and would give him a call on Monday.

She smiled, thinking about him. Maybe when things were settled down a bit at work she'd take a week off for a holiday and ask Neil to go away with her. He'd probably want to go to Dubai or Monaco, but she fancied something simple, like a driving holiday in France. He'd be perfect company driving through the little towns and villages. She was always putting things off but she resolved to have a chat with him about it after the weekend. She settled back into her seat as the train started to move.

* * *

Stephanie woke up with a start and, looking out the window, saw the train was at Salisbury station.

"Ohh!" she cried loudly, jumping up, grabbing her bag and rushing off the train.

She walked down the platform and through to the main station.

She felt a knot in her stomach as she looked around for Danny or Hetty. She walked around the station and there was no sign of them. She realised she didn't even have a mobile phone number to ring. She began to think how flimsy the whole arrangement was when a middle-aged man suddenly appeared beside her wearing a chauffeur's outfit.

"Ms Holden?"

"Emm – yes?"

"If you'd like to follow me, I'll drive you to Barrington Hall." He reached forward and took her bag.

"Eh . . . okay," she said, surprised and then again not surprised that Danny and Hetty hadn't come to meet her themselves.

Outside in the carpark, he opened the back of a black Bentley and put her bag inside.

Then he opened the back door for her.

She nodded at him as she sat in and then he sat into the front and started the engine.

"Is it far to . . . er . . . Barrington Hall?" she enquired.

"About an hour's drive," he said.

"Oh, *that* far? I might as well make myself comfortable then!" she said, settling back into the seat.

* * *

The Bentley turned into the gateway of Barrington Hall and began its journey up the long avenue to the stately house. Even though she'd seen the house in numerous magazine layouts, none of them did any justice to the grandeur of the place. As the car came to a halt, she got out and stared up at the three-storey building.

"This way, Ms Holden," said the driver, taking her bag from the car's boot and walking up the steps to the main entrance.

Any misgivings Stephanie had were now replaced by a burning curiosity. She entered the large hallway and admired the marble floor and wide winding staircase.

"There you are!" came a voice behind her. She turned to view Hetty coming out through the double doors of another room, followed by a smiling Danny.

"We were just about giving up on you! Whatever kept you?"

Stephanie didn't know what to say. She had followed their arrangement, their itinerary – surely they would know what time she would be arriving?

Hetty embraced her and gave her two kisses on the cheek. Then Danny stepped forward, put an arm around her and placed a tender kiss on her right cheek.

Danny was dressed in an Armani suit and Hetty in a glamorous evening dress.

Stephanie was still wearing her business suit and Hetty gave her a quick look up and down.

"You go quickly and change into something more suitable," she said. "The other guests are simply starving! They are in danger of raiding the kitchens if we don't serve dinner soon! Cook will go mad if they do! Do hurry!"

"See you in a couple of minutes," Danny smiled at her.

Confused, Stephanie followed the driver carrying her bag up the stairs. She glanced at her watch and it was approaching ten. It was late, yes, but surely they would have known what time she would be arriving, since they had set her travel plans? The driver showed her down a long corridor and into a beautiful bedroom with a lovely four-poster bed, and an exquisite ensuite bathroom.

"Is that all?" asked the driver.

"Yes, and thank you," said Stephanie.

He left, closing the door after him. She longed for a hot shower after her day's work and the journey, but guessed she wouldn't have time for one. She unpacked her bag and quickly changed into a chic black dress. She touched up her make-up, fixed her hair hastily and made her way downstairs.

"Here she is at last!" said Hetty as Stephanie walked into the large opulent lounge. A fire crackled in the fireplace. Danny stood beside the fireplace, a glass of port in his hand.

There were a further three people in the room: two men aged around forty, dressed in suits, and a younger woman probably in her early thirties sitting on an elaborate gold-embroidered sofa. Stephanie didn't even need the men to speak to know that they were from the same background as Hetty. The woman was striking and Stephanie recognised her as being a former model.

"Stephanie, this is Rupert and this is Jasper," said Hetty.

The two men came smiling to her and she shook their hands.

"And this is Polly," said Hetty.

Polly Carter, remembered Stephanie – she had been a name on the modelling circuit ten years ago and then had just disappeared.

"Hello!" said Polly, very friendly as she stood up and shook Stephanie's hand.

"Stephanie, these people are starving," said Hetty, "so let's get quickly into the dining-room. Come on, everybody! Cook is going to be furious if that dinner is ruined!"

As they all followed Hetty out through the hall to the dining-room, Stephanie was irritated by Hetty giving the impression that she was late. Suddenly she felt an arm around her waist and she turned to see it was Danny.

"Good to see you again," he said smiling.

The dining table was beautifully arranged, with a host of delicious foods laid out. Langoustines were served as a starter. They then moved on to the main course which was a huge roast goose on a central silver dish.

Danny was at the head of the table, facing Stephanie at the other. Hetty and Jasper were to one side of Stephanie, while Rupert and Polly were to the other. Stephanie quickly discovered that Polly and Rupert were not only a couple but a very tactile and loving couple.

"Would you like some roast potatoes with that?" Rupert asked Polly as he gently rubbed her arm.

"That would be lovely," she said in her London accent as she stroked his chin.

Jasper, it was explained, owned a large advertising company and was recounting some tale of a big advertising campaign they had recently had.

"The model we used was an absolute bitch. *Sooo* demanding, *sooo* up her own arse!"

"Was she blonde, was she fair?" asked Polly as she toyed with her own long blonde tresses.

"No – dark," said Jasper.

"Oh," Polly said, sounding disappointed as she stopped messing with her hair.

"I always thought Stephanie would have made a fantastic model," said Hetty, staring at Stephanie.

"Hardly," laughed Stephanie self-consciously.

"Stephanie used to be a backing singer for The Yell," Hetty explained to the others. "She was the cutest little thing you could imagine. She's running Franklyns now. Imagine!"

Stephanie felt Hetty's tone was condescending but managed to smile at her.

"You disappeared the night of the shareholder party without saying goodbye," said Danny.

"You always just disappear," said Hetty. "You did the same years ago – just took off without even a goodbye."

"It was a long and tiring night," explained Stephanie.

"How was your son after it all?" Hetty stared at her pointedly.

"Leo?"

"Yes, that fight he had with that girl. We were a bit shocked – it looked quite vicious."

Stephanie felt herself become irritated. "It was nothing."

"It didn't look like nothing from where we were," Hetty pursued.

"It was nothing," Stephanie said decisively.

"Leo was all right though?" Danny asked. Unlike Hetty there seemed genuine concern in his face.

"He was fine," Stephanie nodded.

"You'd never think it but Stephanie has a grown-up son," Hetty said to the others.

"What age is he again?" asked Danny.

"Twenty-two," Stephanie said decisively.

* * *

They had returned to the lounge for drinks after dinner and as Stephanie sat beside the fire observing them all, she wondered how the Danny she had known and loved all those years ago could be bothered listening to all their vacuous chat. She decided she disliked Hetty as much now as back then.

Danny came and sat beside her. "Really is great seeing you again," he said smiling.

"And you," she nodded.

She decided to see if she could find out anything about Gary Cosgrave. "Do you keep in contact much with the group?"

"Yeah, me and the lads meet up every so often and we play some music."

"That sounds like a lot of fun."

"It is!"

"And what about the rest of the crew? Do you see much of them?"

Polly suddenly yawned loudly. "I think I'll hit the hay!" she said, standing up.

"Good idea," said Rupert.

They said their goodbyes and headed off, arms around each other.

The smaller group made it impossible for Stephanie to extract information from Danny.

"I was very surprised to see you at the party that night," she said. "Have you been shareholders at Franklyns for long?"

"The Barringtons have been shareholders there for generations," explained Hetty. "Who'd ever have thought our investment would end up being in *your* hands!"

* * *

Stephanie made her way down the corridor to her bedroom. It was after one and she was exhausted. The whole night had been emotional, not just because of meeting Danny again but because of all the reminders of the past. She chose to ignore Hetty's constant sniping.

She suddenly heard shouting coming from one of the bedrooms. Alarmed, she went over to listen and recognised Polly and Rupert's voices.

"You should have told me!" screamed Polly. *"You should have told me before I moved in with you!"*

"Yeah, I did try to tell you, didn't I?" Rupert's voice was more relaxed but goading.

"You should have told me! This changes everything. Why didn't you tell me?"

"I did, yeah. But you never listen, do you? You never listen!"

Stephanie quickly walked away from the door to her own room, wondering what on earth they were rowing about. Considering how loved-up they had seemed earlier, whatever had been revealed was obviously terrible to provoke such a row.

Stephanie entered her bedroom and locked the door behind her.

Chapter 55

Stephanie stepped out of the shower and wrapped a huge terry towel around her. She had slept late. Hetty had mentioned something about breakfast being served at nine but Stephanie was so tired after a broken night's sleep that she had slept on until nine thirty.

She went into the bedroom and looked out across the view of the rolling countryside. She wondered again why Hetty and Danny had invited her. Hetty had always wanted her out of the way years ago so she could have a clear run at Danny. Was it because she was now somebody, running Franklyns, that they wanted her to be in their circle? As for Danny, he was as attractive and nice as ever. She had hoped being in his company for a period of time now would kill the feelings she had nursed for him over the years. That was failing to happen.

"Late again!" declared Hetty as Stephanie entered the dining-room. "Breakfast is almost burnt! Cook hates you! Absolutely hates you!"

"Sorry, I had a disturbed night's sleep," said Stephanie, taking the seat left vacant for her.

Everyone was there waiting for her.

"You should have just started without me – I would have in your place!" said Stephanie. She felt quite confused. She had never stayed anywhere before where there was a formal sit-down breakfast at a specific time.

"That's not the etiquette we follow at Barrington Hall," Hetty reprimanded her.

Stephanie raised her eyes and sighed.

Stephanie glanced over to Rupert and Polly and was surprised to see them holding hands affectionately, their screaming match of the previous night obviously forgotten. Polly obviously had seen fit to get over whatever Rupert should have told her before she moved in.

"How are you this morning?" asked Danny.

"Fine," she smiled over at him.

"I have another couple joining us tonight," said Hetty.

"Dinner's at eight so do try and be on time for a change, Stephanie. For Cook's sake, if nothing else."

"I'll try!" Stephanie smiled falsely at her.

"Very trying!" quipped Hetty.

More snobs to endure, thought Stephanie. How could Danny be bothered with them all? Hetty was as pushy as ever. Inventing issues where there were none, just so she could assert her authority.

"Do you ride, Stephanie?" asked Rupert.

"Em, no," said Stephanie.

"Shame! We're all off cross country for the afternoon," said Hetty.

"Tally-ho!" Stephanie didn't try to hide her sarcasm.

"That's all right, Steph. You can keep me company. I don't ride either," Danny winked at her.

* * *

Stephanie and Danny stood in the courtyard as they waved the others off on the horses.

"Why did you never learn to ride?" she asked, her hands in her blazer pockets.

"Never my scene. Don't laugh but I got up on a horse twenty years ago and had a panic attack and they had to get me down. You don't know how fucking high it is up on one of those animals!"

"I can imagine. Hetty seems to have no problem with it."

They watched Hetty gallop to the front of the party.

"Well, she was born to it."

"You'd think you were too. You fit in a treat in these surroundings, with these people." There was a trace of disapproval in her voice.

"Well, I've had enough practice at this stage." He smiled at her. "So, Stephanie, anyone special in your life?"

She shook her head casually. "Nobody special."

"I heard you were seeing one of the Blackthorn brothers."

Stephanie laughed out loud.

"What's so funny?" asked Danny.

"It's just that Neil Blackthorn and I thought we were being so discreet and everybody in London seems to bloody know about us!"

They walked out of the courtyard and started to stroll along a path that led through fields.

"Where are your daughters?" she asked.

"Away for the weekend. Three are off on protests for their different causes and Pru is at some fashion do."

"Pity. I would have liked to meet them."

"Yes, pity."

They continued in silence and then she commented

with a smile, "You still haven't lost your local accent."

"Guess not. Think the kids are embarrassed by it sometimes," he joked.

"I would have thought this lot would have stuffed some plums in your mouth by now."

"You don't like them much, do you?"

"I've no reason to dislike them . . . You know, I've seen you posing for photographs in so many magazines but it's really odd seeing you here."

"Why's that?"

She stopped and looked at him "Because you haven't changed a bit. I can still see you up on a stage singing your heart out or in the recording studio. Don't you miss it?"

"Nah! Not that side of it. I had my day and knew when to leave. I didn't want to end up jumping around a stage like Mick Jagger!"

"You retired early." She started walking again.

"And you retired even earlier. You had a big music career ahead of you and you just walked away."

"What? A big music career as a backing singer?" she said sarcastically.

"No, I think you could have broken through and made it solo. When you left, I made enquiries everywhere to try and track you down but no luck."

She felt herself becoming annoyed. "What did you want to track me down for, Danny? An invitation to your wedding? You were engaged to Hetty so why not just get on with your new life?"

"But we were good friends!"

"You know, that was the problem, Danny. We were more than just friends, in case you can't remember. We were lovers. We were seeing each other. You never bothered even breaking it off with me. You just arrived in with Hetty Barrington and an engagement announcement." The hurt she had nursed all through the years came pouring out.

"I guess I was a bit of a bastard. But I didn't mean to be."

"I know you didn't mean to be. You were a big star and you thought you could behave any way you liked, even if that meant using a silly love-struck girl."

"Now, don't play the victim, Stephanie. You were the one who pursued me, remember?"

She sighed. "I know, more fool me! As if I thought I could compete with all this!" She waved her hand at Barrington Hall in the distance. "I was deluded."

"You know, me and Hetty have had a great marriage. We complement each other. As I told you years ago, you and me were too alike. I often thought about you during the years. Really missed you. And now I know why you ran away – at last." He stopped walking and looked at her.

Stephanie stopped abruptly, her mind suddenly clouded.

"Stephanie, whatever I've done and whatever mistakes I made, I'm now ready to put things right."

"I don't understand you."

"Leo . . . .. I know he's my son. I know you lied about his age. He told me he was twenty-three which means I'm the father. I know you – I was the only guy you were ever with back then."

She stared at him in stunned silence.

"I haven't spoken to Hetty about it yet. But it doesn't matter. I really want to get to know him, play a part in his life, be there for him. He's seems really nice and you've done a terrific job with him. I know it mustn't have been easy. I feel so guilty that I never gave you the opportunity to tell me you were pregnant. And you were selfless enough to run away because you didn't want to jeopardise my marriage with Hetty. You've coped long enough on your own, Stephanie, and I want to step in and help."

Stephanie turned quickly and walked away a few steps, then stood staring out at the countryside.

"You know, I'm a happy man, Steph. I love my life. I've everything I want. But there's always been something missing, and now I know what it is. It's Leo, my son. When I saw Leo that night, I just knew . . . everything made sense . . . why you took off." He walked behind her and put a hand on her shoulder "Let me get to know him, Steph . . . please."

Stephanie turned around. "Danny, I don't know what to say to you. In a way I'd love nothing more than what you're asking for. There have been times over the years that I would have loved Leo to be yours . . . I would have loved for you to have needed something from me, like you've just shown . . . but the truth is, you're not Leo's father. I'm sorry you jumped to the wrong conclusion."

His hand dropped from his shoulder and he looked agitated. "I don't believe you. You lied about his age. You weren't with anybody else!"

"Yes, I lied, I didn't want to complicate the issue – like has just happened . . . so I pretended he was younger so the thought wouldn't even cross your mind that it was yours."

Disappointment spread across Danny's face.

"I guess that's the reason I was invited up here this weekend," Stephanie said, sighing. "It makes sense now . . . and I guess I need to be honest as well. I came up here to find out what happened to Gary Cosgrave."

"Gary Cosgrave . . . our old tour manager?" Danny sounded confused.

"Yeah . . . I was with Gary before I left the band. I did it out of spite to show myself I didn't need you. Gary is Leo's dad. In a way Leo does owe his existence to you – I slept with Gary trying to get some silly revenge on you."

Danny's disappointment gave way to shock at Stephanie's revelation.

"Are you still in contact with him – with Gary?"

"Steph . . . Gary killed himself with drink about ten years ago. You know he always had a drink problem and after the The Yell stopped touring – well, nobody else would hire him because of his drinking. It just got worse and worse. I tried to help him as much as I could. But in the end nobody could help him . . . I'm sorry, Steph."

* * *

Stephanie lay on the four-poster bed trying to stifle her sobs. The tears poured down her face. It was all too much for her, finding out Gary had died. She was consumed with guilt. Guilt that she never told Gary he had a son. Guilt that Leo would never know his father. She had always despised herself for going with Gary that night and been angry with herself and angry with life. She was headstrong and wanted to do everything herself, her way. Now she could see how selfish she had been.

She had been busy nursing a lost love through the years that she now realised had been a waste of time. And being jealous of Hetty Barrington when now it was plain to see that Hetty was just a silly cow with too much time and money on her hands.

She wanted to get away from this place, away from these people and back to her life in London and her son.

* * *

Stephanie glanced at herself in the full-length mirror and looked at her watch. It was seven thirty and Hetty had said dinner would be at eight. She would go and wait in the lounge before the rest arrived so Hetty couldn't make a song and dance about her being late again. She would make some excuse to leave early the following morning and get back to her life. She could just about suffer another night with these people. It was strange that what had looked so glossy and perfect in the magazines was just uninteresting in reality. She wondered if she had ever really loved Danny or if she had been just a teenager infatuated with a star? What a mess she had made of her life! She left her room and walked down the corridor. She could hear screaming coming from Polly and Rupert's room and hurried over to listen.

"I should have listened to what all my friends said about you – they were all right!" came Rupert's voice.

"What do you mean – they were right?" Polly screamed. *"Who are you talking about? I always got on with all your fucking friends!"*

"And my family. I should have listened to my parents – they tried to warn me about you!"

"What are you talking about? I always got on with your fucking parents – in fact I always got on with them better than you ever fucking did!"

Stephanie, feeling baffled, moved quickly on down the corridor.

She was seated on the couch sipping a glass of wine when Hetty and Danny arrived.

"Stephanie! Early for a change!" commented Hetty.

"Well, I thought I'd make an effort . . . for Cook," Stephanie said sarcastically.

"I'm afraid you're beyond redemption as far as Cook is concerned – you've inconvenienced her far too much this weekend with your tardiness."

Danny had a look of gloom about him and avoided eye contact with Stephanie. She was surprised at how excited he had been at the idea of Leo being his.

Then, to her astonishment, in walked Polly and Rupert hand in hand, smiling lovingly at each other as if the blazing row she had heard earlier had never occurred.

"Jasper had to head off, crisis in the office," explained Rupert.

"Oh damn!" said Hetty.

"Whatever will Cook say?" smiled Stephanie just as another couple walked into the room. She smiled over at them, hoping that Hetty's new guests would be more interesting than the others. Her eyes went first to the woman who looked very familiar, dressed exquisitely in a tight cream dress, wearing spectacular jewels, with her vivid blonde hair worn up.

As Stephanie tried to place her, she glanced at her partner and felt a shiver run up and down her spine as Karl Furstin's steely grey-blue eyes penetrated hers. She was immediately transported back to the day of the takeover when he had treated her viciously. She then realised why the woman looked so familiar – she had seen Elka Furstin's photo a million times in the papers. The couple stared at her as if she was the only other person in the room, cold hard stares that made her feel sick.

"Ah, and these are my other guests I was telling you would be coming tonight. Elka and Karl, I think you know

Polly and Rupert and this is an old friend of ours, Stephanie Holden."

"We've had the pleasure of meeting before," said Karl.

Stephanie forced herself to speak. "I can't remember anything being pleasurable about that meeting."

She looked quickly at Polly and Rupert and then at Danny to see if she could see any indication in their faces that they were in on what was going on. But they obviously hadn't heard what she had said and seemed immune to the tension in the air. Only Hetty had a knowing expression.

"Shall we make our way into the dining-room?" suggested Hetty.

Stephanie didn't move while everyone else started walking out. She didn't know what to do. She felt like just going straight to her room. She didn't want to be in Furstin's company. It was plain to see this whole weekend had been orchestrated. She doubted Danny was in cahoots with the Furstins but Hetty certainly was. But to what purpose?

"Stephanie, are you coming?" Hetty was waiting at the door for her.

Stephanie stood up quickly and, still holding her drink, walked quickly up to her saying, "Wouldn't miss it for the world. Are the Furstins staying here at Barrington Hall tonight?"

"Well, of course," said Hetty. "They are based in Vienna at the moment – they are hardly heading back there tonight."

Danny and Hetty sat at either end of the table. Stephanie found herself seated opposite Karl and Elka. She found it strange that as intimidating as Karl Furstin's forbidding presence was, Elka was just as unnerving. She was such a familiar face in the media that you felt you knew her when she was there in front of you. But it was always just photos of her in the press, she never gave interviews. And as she sat there that night she hardly spoke either. Occasionally she would say something in an undertone to Hetty but mostly she just sat there silently in all her stupendous beauty like some Renaissance masterpiece, her cool blue eyes fixed icily on Stephanie.

"So how is everything at Franklyns?" asked Karl as steak was served to all.

Stephanie noted that the Furstins both liked their steak extremely rare. Stephanie herself always liked meat very well done, and as Karl cut into his steak and blood seeped out she felt ill.

"Everything is going very well, sales up, costs down," Stephanie said confidently. "We're turning that place inside out – it needed it."

"Excellent – so all will be well for this big stock-market launch?" said Karl.

"I hope so."

Karl looked at the other guests around the table. "Ms Holden is responsible for taking away my store, my empire, my . . . reason for being."

"I didn't take it. You lost it."

"It's the same thing."

"And you weren't particularly gracious when you lost it, as I recall."

His eyes continued to penetrate her. "And what would you expect me to do – wrap it up with a ribbon for you?"

As hard as it was, Stephanie forced herself to return his stare. She had been intimidated once by this man – she wouldn't let it happen again. She didn't know what games were being played that night but she would stand her ground.

The others were silent, riveted by this exchange.

"I would have expected you to act a little more professionally," Stephanie said.

"When someone takes everything you love from *you* one day – let's see how you act," said Furstin. "A business is like a child – you never stop loving it. And it might stray but it always comes back to you."

"From what I can see of the mess you left the finances in, I think Franklyns is one prodigal who won't be returning to you."

"And how is all the gang? Nicola? She's a very great lady – I believe she hasn't made life easy for you." Stephanie began to worry as to how he was getting information.

"And Paul Stewart? How is he coping with it all? Not so good, I hear. Paul likes to play the big important man but he needs direction. I made Paul what he is, so without me around for him I believe he's running around like a chicken without a head."

"Actually Paul has been nothing but a help to us. He's embraced the whole takeover and continues to manage the store expertly."

"Oh, excellent! Then you'll make his position permanent, will you, and put him out of his misery? I'm sure that will be such a relief for him, particularly as he and his wife are starting IVF."

Stephanie blinked a few times, feeling unnerved at his level of information.

"And then there's that charming young man, David Stafford, your partner in crime. Conrad Richardson really found a gem in him. A man who can give a charming smile as he plunges in the knife – now *that's* a talent. Even you and I could learn a few tricks from him, Stephanie."

Where was all this information coming from?

"And then look who's just joined this happy ship – your son, Leo! I'd keep an eye on that one, Stephanie. I think he could be trouble with a personality like his . . . or end up in a lot of trouble."

Stephanie spoke evenly. "Please don't talk about my son."

Karl waved his hand in the air. "As you wish. You still live at Chelsea Harbour, don't you? I've always admired the security in that place, although I have a friend who lives there who was broken into last year . . . Which floor do you actually live on? The 10th or the 11th?"

"I've lost my appetite," Stephanie said, standing up abruptly and glaring at Karl. "Please excuse me."

"Steph!" Danny called out after her, but she kept walking.

* * *

Stephanie woke up in the middle of the night. There was some sound and she quickly reached over, put on her bedside lamp and sat up. She saw the doorknob was being turned. Somebody was trying to get in. Luckily, she had locked the door.

"Hello!" she called. "There's somebody in here!"

The twisting of the doorknob stopped for a moment and then suddenly it started turning violently again.

"Who is it?" called Stephanie loudly. "Hetty? Danny?"

There was no answer but the doorknob stopped moving again. She was heaving a sigh of relief when it started up again.

Stephanie pulled her legs up and huddled on the bed, her heart thudding.

The twisting of the doorknob continued for some time and she was so unnerved by it that it took ages after that for her to fall asleep.

* * *

Stephanie stirred in her sleep. She was having another bad night, drifting in and out of dreams.

She opened her eyes and Karl Furstin was sitting on the side of her bed staring down at her.

Her heart leapt to her throat and she sat up.

"What the fuck are you doing in here?" she demanded "Get out!"

How had he got in? The door had been locked!

"Maybe I didn't make myself clear when you came into my office that day but I don't want you in my store," he said calmly. "I might have been a bit rude then so I'm asking you nicely now – leave Franklyns. Hand in your notice first thing Monday. Next time I won't ask politely."

He got up slowly from the bed and walked over to the door, opened it and exited. Stephanie, her heart pounding, jumped out of the bed and raced over to the door. The key was not in the lock. Then she saw it lying on the floor. She picked it up and locked the door shut. Realising he had still managed to open the door despite her locking it previously, she grabbed a chair and wedged it under the handle, then went and huddled on the bed.

* * *

Stephanie quickly made her way down the corridor with

her suitcase very early on Sunday morning. As she passed by Polly and Rupert's door they were having another argument.

"Well, that was particularly psychotic behaviour, even for you!" screeched Polly.

She went and waited on the steps of Barrington Hall. Nobody was up in the house yet and the early morning dew sparkled on the grass.

She felt absolute relief when she saw the taxi come up the driveway. She hadn't actually known where Barrington Hall was to give directions to a taxi firm but she finally located one in Salisbury who said they knew how to get there.

She jumped into the back of the taxi.

"Get me out of here – quick!" she said.

Chapter 56

Rachel had spent most of the weekend in her tracksuit. She was somebody who needed her sleep and she spent most of Saturday catching up, only popping down to the shop for the paper and milk. Sunday, she forced herself to get ready and go into the West End. She needed some outfits for the new job she was starting Monday. She bought a couple of nice business suits.

What had happened between her and Leo wasn't far from her thoughts at any time. She was very surprised but didn't regret it. She would never have thought she'd be interested in somebody like Leo and yet he somehow pressed the right buttons for her. As she walked down the street to her home, returning from Selfridges on Sunday afternoon with her shopping bags, she heard somebody shout her name. She squinted and spotted Leo sitting at a table outside the pub on the corner of the street waving at her. She was surprised and delighted as she headed towards him.

She sat down in the free seat opposite him and he leaned forward and greeted her with a kiss.

The barman came out.

She looked down at Leo's pint of Heineken and said, "I'll have the same as him."

"I thought you didn't drink beer," said Leo.

"I'm doing a lot of things recently that I didn't do, beer being the least of them. I wasn't sure I'd see you again."

"Would it have bothered you if you didn't?"

"I don't know. It might have been safer if I didn't."

He laughed. "Why? Are you scared of Big Bad Leo?"

"I'm not scared of you, no. A bit scared of how you live, maybe."

The waiter brought her pint.

They spent the afternoon drinking, talking and having fun.

"You did *what*?" Rachel nearly choked on her drink.

"I wrote in big letters *'Fuck Off, You Dog'* and stuck it over Newman's car," Leo said, proud of himself.

"I can't believe you did that to Nicola Newman!"

"Why not? That'll teach her to be a stuck-up bitch . . . Anyway, I won't have to see that silly cow again."

"So, you definitely are not going back?"

"I don't think there's anything for me there."

"Instead of discussing it with your mother, why don't you go and see somebody else in charge?"

"What – like Nicola Newman? Don't think so."

"Of course, not her. Go see Paul Stewart – he's a nice enough guy."

"He gives me dagger looks every time he sees me."

"Probably because you're quaffing champagne and oysters in the Food Halls – what do you expect? Or even David Stafford – he's supposed to be a straightforward enough fella. He could find you something in finance maybe."

"Mum suggested before that I should see David or Paul."

"So why didn't you do it then?" She looked at his blank face "Because you're a stubborn bastard. Don't waste any more time and get in and do it tomorrow."

They walked up the street in the evening to her apartment.

"I'm feeling a bit pissed. This is ridiculous. I'm starting my new job tomorrow and I should have a clear head. You're a bad influence, Leo."

She let them into her apartment and opened a bottle of wine while he rolled a joint.

* * *

"Thanks for coming over," Stephanie said as she opened the door to Neil Blackthorn.

He saw the look of stress on her face and hugged her.

"What's wrong, luv?" he asked.

Stephanie knew it was a trait in her that she could never show weakness, always had to be in control, regardless of the maelstrom of emotions that could be going on inside her. It would be easy to let go there in front of somebody she trusted as much as Neil but she pulled herself together. She pulled away from him and, pouring them both a drink, sat down and told him everything about the weekend.

"Furstin is the creepiest fuck I've ever had the misfortune to meet," said Stephanie.

"I know. I've met him too . . . But did he threaten you?"

"Yes, he made very ugly threats in his office the day of the takeover. He was less explicit last night but he said he wouldn't 'ask politely' the next time if I didn't resign. And earlier at dinner he had made some veiled threats. He said Leo could get in a lot of trouble and made a point of mentioning that he knew where I lived and that he knew someone in my apartment block who was broken into last year."

"You could go to the police," urged Neil. "It's a clear case of intimidation."

"Oh, no, I couldn't." The thought filled her with dread. "It would be all in the papers – Franklyns boss threatened by the Baron of Knightsbridge. Anyway he'd just deny it – deny he meant anything by what he said at dinner. Besides, he and that walking doll of a wife of his are living in Vienna now."

"There is another solution – why don't you just quit? Do you really need all this hassle? Fuck them and fuck the store! There's your old job waiting for you at Blackthorns at any time, not to mention another hundred retail organisations that would be delighted to get you."

"Thanks, Neil, I appreciate the offer. But if I left Franklyns now, I would be seen to have failed and I doubt too many other companies would want me then. You're as good as your last gig."

"But, okay, so he gets what he wants and you resign – that still doesn't mean that, as if by magic, he gets Franklyns back. It's still owned by Barons Bank."

"He's obviously up to something and from the information he gave me is also keeping close tabs on everything."

* * *

Rachel drew deeply on the marijuana and handed it back to Leo.

"I guess I can kiss goodbye to a clear head at work tomorrow," she said.

He moved his arm around her and pulled her close.

"Leo – I don't know what's going on here between us – but I want you to know I'm not a game-player."

"I know that."

"I'm not like Daniella and the rest of the girls you've been with. It's harder for me. I wear my heart on my sleeve and ... well, I can't be your latest trophy."

"I don't get you."

"I sometimes thought that you and Daniella saw each other as accessories, in the same way you view your designer clothes and sunglasses. I'm not that fickle, Leo."

"Whoever said I was like that?"

"Well, Daniella certainly was."

Leo studied her. "Is that the impression Daniella gave about me?"

"No! Look, Leo, I don't want to get into all that. What happened between you and Daniella is your own business. I'm just saying I'm quite a serious person when it comes to relationships and I have to protect myself. So whatever feelings I'm beginning to feel for you, I do need to protect myself, okay?"

He looked at her for a long time before nodding and then she reached up and kissed him.

* * *

Nicola had classical music playing on the sound system in her new apartment late on Sunday night. She had settled into the apartment and unpacked her clothes. The weekend had been very quiet after that. She had met her mother for lunch in Islington the previous day. She did not mention that she had left Oliver. She didn't want to cause her parents to panic or to get on to Oliver and cause him any more panic. She had just said that they had got an apartment in the Docklands as she was finding the constant commute tiring. Her mother accepted this, even thought it a great idea.

Nicola was surprised when she got back to Canary Wharf late on Saturday afternoon to see how empty the huge mausoleums of the Canary Wharf Tube station and shopping malls seemed without the office workers who were there during the week. It seemed quite lonely. She thought about David all the time, wondering how he was getting on in France. She selected an outfit to wear for work the next morning and then went to bed.

Chapter 57

Nicola got into her office before anybody got into work. She left instructions for security to phone her once David arrived. She waited expectantly.

"Mr Stafford has just come through the staff entrance," informed the security man when he rang up to her at eleven in the morning.

"Did he come up from the carpark?" she asked.

"No, from the street. I saw him get out of a taxi on the CCTV."

"Did he have a suitcase with him?"

"Yes, ma'am."

She hung up the phone. He had come straight from the airport. Her mind started ticking over.

* * *

Rachel was seated in Stephanie's reception. She'd had a cold shower that morning to try and clear her mind. What a stupid thing to do to get drunk and stoned with Leo the night before she started in her new position!

Stephanie came out of the lift and down the corridor.

"Morning, Rachel, follow me through."

Rachel did, blushing slightly at the thought of Stephanie finding out about her and Leo last night.

Stephanie handed her a huge pile of papers.

"These are all enquiries we've had over the past few weeks about publicity opportunities. I've been too busy to look through them and since the old press office was let go during restructuring they've mounted up. Go through them all and pick out the ones you feel we should go ahead and do and the ones that are no-hopers. I don't go by this 'all publicity is good publicity' mantra. I think bad publicity can be very damaging to a store like Franklyns and so be very choosy what you select. Okay?"

"Okay!" Rachel took the huge pile of papers.

"The press office is on the floor below this beside HR. You'll be working from there."

Great, thought Rachel. She would be in close proximity to Nicola Newman and she could do without that added pressure.

"No problem, Stephanie," said Rachel as she hurried away.

Stephanie watched her go. She looked great in her business suit. She would be a good image for the store. Stephanie had of course, gone through all the enquiries and knew exactly which ones would be right for Franklyns and which would be wrong. She would now quickly find out if Rachel would be any good at the job.

Rachel shifted through the enquiries. They ranged from everything from television breakfast shows wanting to do a special from Franklyns, to a film studio that wanted to shoot a scene for some big blockbuster movie in the store, to a children's charity wanting to launch a new fund-raising campaign in the toy department. She was buzzing with excitement dealing with it all and kept

Stephanie's advice to be ruthless in mind.

* * *

Anna was working from home. She had administered the daily injection to herself that morning and decided to work from home that day. She turned on her laptop at the kitchen table and went to check her emails. She always put her email address at the bottom of her column every Sunday and there was usually a ton of emails waiting for her on the Monday, reacting to what she had written. A lot of columnists didn't like to give an email address as some of the responses could be quite abusive. Anna loved sifting through the different reactions to her opinions.

Her mobile rang and she smiled, seeing it was Paul calling her.

"How are you feeling?" His voice was full of concern.

"I'm fine, absolutely fine."

"No adverse reactions so far?"

"A little tired but that's about it."

"If you don't feel well, just call me and I'll be straight home to you."

"Thank you, darling. No, seriously, I feel fine. I'm just here in the kitchen going through my emails from the public."

"Any cranks or weirdos today?" he asked laughing.

"There's always cranks and weirdos but not too many today thankfully."

"Okay, gotta rush. See ya later. Love ya!" Paul hung up

* * *

As the day wore on Nicola realised David was not going to make contact with her that day. She had to see him today.

If she left it any longer, their night together would just become a one-off, an embarrassing encounter that neither of them would know how to handle and so they would end up avoiding each other. She knew what made David tick. She saw how impressed he was by Stephanie Holden. She saw how impressed he was by her father. If she was coming across as just a Home Counties housewife then he wasn't going to be interested in her. The Merc, the sexy clothes, the glamorous hair might not be enough. She might have to go even further to convince him they were soul mates.

She picked up the phone and rang the security at the staff entrance.

"Has David Stafford left work yet?"

"No, ma'am."

"Right, I want you to phone my mobile the moment he leaves the building, do you understand?" She hung up the phone and rushed out of her office.

* * *

"This is the pile I think would make good publicity opportunities for Franklyns and these are the ones I think would either be damaging or just not worth it," said Rachel, putting the two piles of papers on Stephanie's desk.

"I see," said Stephanie, looking at the slim pile that got the thumbs-up. "You were very choosy."

"As you said, I think we need to be in order to protect Franklyns' image."

Stephanie quickly scanned through the papers and was very impressed that Rachel had selected all the opportunities she had earmarked herself.

"Okay, good!" Stephanie handed her back the paperwork. "Start making contact tomorrow with these ones you agree with and start making the arrangements to proceed. I think most enquiries came from PR managers so you shouldn't have any problem getting through. Before you agree to anything, give me a look at all the details, all right?"

"Sure … is there anything else you want me to do now?"

"It's nearly six – home time, I think."

"Right! I'll see you tomorrow then!" Rachel smiled broadly and turned to leave.

Rachel!" Stephanie called.

"Yes?"

"How come you were asked to volunteer to work on the yacht last week? Who asked you to?"

Rachel felt herself go red, not wanting to give away information. "Daniella did. I worked alongside her at Chanel."

"From the familiarity with which you spoke to both Daniella and my son that night when they were rowing, I presume you're good friends with both of them?"

Rachel was obviously uncomfortable. "Yeah."

"I believe Daniella has left Franklyns. Is she still seeing Leo?"

"Rachel felt herself going bright red. "I'm sorry, Stephanie, but you'd really have to ask your son that. It's none of my business."

Stephanie nodded, admiring her stance. "Very well . . . and I shouldn't have asked you that. I put you in an awkward situation, I'm sorry."

Rachel smiled, relieved she was dropping it. "It's not a problem."

"But Rachel, I've been trying to contact Leo all day and his phone is off. If you are speaking to Daniella or even Leo himself, could you pass on a message for him to call me – it's quite important."

Rachel nodded and left quickly.

* * *

Nicola was parked in her car down the sidestreet that the staff entrance was on. She had the roof down and was wearing big sunglasses. Her phone rang.

It was the security man at Franklyns. "Mr Stafford has just left the building, ma'am."

"Good – thanks," Nicola closed over her phone.

She spotted David walking towards busy Brompton Street. She pulled out of her parking space, drove up the street and pulled up beside him.

"Hi there!" she called.

"Nicola!" David said, surprise written across his face. She looked relaxed and happy, one arm stretched over the passenger seat, her hair glossy, sunglasses pushed up on her head.

"How was France?" she asked

"Eh – great – good – you know how it is – lots of drink, then recovering by the pool the next day."

"I don't know how it is actually – I've never been on a stag!"

"Glad to hear it!"

She reached over and opened the passenger door.

"Hop in and I'll give you a lift."

"There's really no need. I'm just going to grab the Tube."

"Rubbish! The last thing you want is to be in a packed boiling-hot Tube when I'm going in your direction anyway."

He hesitated for a second and then shrugged, putting his suitcase into the back seat and climbing into the front. She smiled at him and then roared off down the road.

The wind blew through their hair as Nicola drove them through the city.

"This isn't actually the way to my gaff," David pointed out.

"I know. I've got a surprise for you." Nicola glanced over and smiled at him.

"I'm not really sure I'm in the mood for a surprise," David said with genuine concern.

"Oh, you'll like this surprise."

"I feel as though I'm being kidnapped!"

"Well, you couldn't have been kidnapped by a nicer person, in that case!" said Nicola.

* * *

David stood in the middle of the living-room, looking out at the breathtaking views across Canary Wharf in Nicola's new apartment.

"What do you think?" she asked.

"Pretty impressive gaff," he said. She had changed into tight jeans and a white T-shirt.

"Must cost a bomb!" he remarked.

She shrugged and smiled. "I can afford it! I've been a very successful businesswoman all my life. I work hard and think I should be rewarded with the good things in life, don't you?"

"That's always been my philosophy," he said as he tinkered with the elaborate sound system. "And what are you going to do with your country house?"

"We'll probably just sell it once the divorce comes through."

"You've filed for divorce?" He looked up from the sound system, concerned..

"Months ago," she quickly lied. "Look, there's this gorgeous pub up the road, looks out on the docks – let's go and have a drink and something to eat."

"Actually – I've rugby practice on tonight."

She couldn't hide the disappointment on her face.

He thought for a while. "I'll give the rugby a miss tonight – I'm a bit shattered after France anyway."

"Great! I'll just grab my bag!" She ran off to the bedroom.

Nicola wished she hadn't suggested the pub in question as you had to walk through a series of cobbled streets to get there, and she had to do all she could not to fall in the very high heels she was wearing. Once or twice she had to reach out and hold David to balance herself. But once they got to the pub, she realised it was worth it. They chose a table beside a big open window that looked down on the flowing water of the docks. He drank gin and tonic while she sipped her wine.

"I was very nearly an accountant myself," she lied. "I really wanted to be one. I don't know what stopped me. Actually I do know – success stopped me! When I started off in Harrods after university I was moved around a lot and they gave me the personnel department to organise, and I did such a good job they wouldn't let me leave it."

"You headed personnel at Harrods?"

"Yes, I did," she lied.

"You must have been awfully young then to get such a responsible position."

"I was very ambitious. As soon as I left university I was going to take the business world by storm."

"Your reputation certainly precedes you in Franklyns."

"I haven't stopped yet . . . I might even end up in politics."

"Really?" He was amazed.

"Well, it's in the blood, with my father being who he is."

"Sure . . . sure. It must have been very exciting growing up in your household."

"Yes. Margaret Thatcher was a regular visitor."

"Really?" his eyes widened.

"Yes. I think our house was one of the few places where she could relax. In fact I think she came up with some of her more prudent fiscal policies around our kitchen table."

"Amazing ringside seat to history!"

"Well, between just me and you . . ." She leaned close to him and then shook her head. "No, I really can't say. Official Secrets Act and all that."

Half an hour later she was still lying.

"I'm a huge fan of rugby, you know – my brother played for Oxford."

"Get away!" said David.

"I think there's some plaque up commemorating him in some corridor somewhere there. He's one of the top-earning hedge fund managers on Wall Street – you and he would have so much in common."

"Gosh!"

And now for the *pièce-de-résistance,* she thought. If she could explain away the marriage she was home and dry. She closed her eyes for a second and then opened them. "I knew from the moment I met Oliver that he would go to the top. Maybe I never really loved Oliver, the way a wife should love a husband, but he was doing so much to change the way this city is run, and I needed to be there beside him, helping him direct police policy as best I could. A marriage that maybe didn't have romance at its centre but put a city's wellbeing first."

"Crikey!" said David.

* * *

"Oh, David!" yelled Nicola as David lay on top of her, roughly having sex.

Chapter 58

Leo sat in a chair opposite David on the Tuesday morning, his hands behind his head.

"So what position do you want me to take in your department?" asked Leo.

"Well, I was going to put you into credit control but I've another position that I just think might suit your personality."

"Sock it to me."

"Debt control." David opened a drawer, pulled out a large file and handed it to Leo. Leo began to flick through the pages.

"That is a list of all the people who have accounts in Franklyns. As you can see there is a lot of money outstanding and I need to bring that cash back in."

"But . . . this is fucking ridiculous! Some of these people owe over a hundred grand and it's going back years!"

"I know. Franklyns is known as the posh people's shop but unfortunately a lot of posh people do not like to part with their money. Some of those families have a running tab going back to the sixties."

"Fucking madness! And did the last geezer not try to get them to pay up?"

"Well, you see, these people think that they are doing Franklyns a favour shopping here."

"It's no wonder the place went bust."

"I'd like you to get that money in and I'll leave it up to you how you think best to do it." David then handed him another file. "Another area of your job will be theft control. These are the kind of losses we are also incurring in theft."

"Theft?" Leo looked up.

"Yeah. There's been a big problem with shoplifting and unfortunately also with staff robbing merchandise and money from tills."

Leo whistled as he looked through the list. "Some losses!"

"It all adds up. I want you to see how we can stop this. Work with security to try to bring down these outrageous figures."

* * *

Paul was dropping some files into the finance department when he spotted David coming out of his office with Leo. He watched them shake hands, smile broadly and share a joke while David gave Leo a slap on the back. Not wanting to get caught up talking to David, Paul turned quickly to walk out.

"Paul!"

Paul turned around as David jogged over to him, leaving Leo to head off in the other direction.

"How's it going, Paul?"

"No complaints . . . was that Stephanie's boy I saw with you there?"

"Yeah, Leo – he's coming to work in the finance department here."

"As what exactly?" Paul rolled his eyes to heaven.

"The kid worked in the City for a couple of years, got lots of experience in finance."

"Well, the only thing I've seen him do since he arrived here is chat up pretty young salesgirls. And then he had that huge row at the shareholders' party." Paul was irritated.

"Anyway – are you around for a drink tonight?" David asked.

"No, sorry, I've something on."

David clapped a hand on Paul's shoulder and squeezed hard. "Really, I could do with a bit of advice from a friend."

Well, go and ask one of your hundreds of friends then, thought Paul.

"No, sorry, David, I'd like to, but I genuinely have a lot on at home at the moment," said Paul. For once he wasn't lying.

David managed to squeeze his shoulder even more tightly and winked at him before urging, "Please."

"Oh, all right then – I'll see you across in the Blue Posts at six. And it can't be a late one, and I mean it!"

* * *

Anna hadn't been too pleased that Paul wasn't coming straight home and he couldn't blame her. She needed him at home while she was taking the treatment for the IVF.

He sat on a bar stool waiting for David to arrive. The pub was already packed with workers from Franklyns. He hadn't been in since they started the IVF programme and he had to admit he had missed the place. He spotted Rachel coming in and did a double-take. She looked quite the businesswoman in her elegant suit. He was glad he had been able to do something for her with the reference and that things were okay between them now. He watched her as she made her way through the pub and was surprised to see her join Leo at a table and more surprised when they started laughing and joking together. He was studying them when David arrived on the bar stool beside him.

"Really appreciate you meeting me tonight," said David who then ordered two more drinks for them.

"No problem. What are – friends for?"

David sat there almost in a trance for a short while.

"So what was so urgent?" Paul pressed.

"Can I talk to you in absolute confidence? Like for nobody else to ever find out?"

Paul shrugged his shoulders. "Sure."

"I've kind of got myself into a difficult situation."

"Go on," Paul urged, leaning a little closer, thinking that the perfect David might have fucked up the company finances somehow.

"If I mentioned . . . Nicola Newman to you . . . what would you say?"

"What would I say?" Paul looked perplexed. "I'd say . . . ball-breaker . . . snob . . . hard . . . respectably dull . . . bully. There's any number of adjectives I could use to describe Nicola. Why?" He raised his pint and took a drink.

David drew breath. "I'm shagging her!"

Paul choked on his drink and the beer came spraying out of his mouth across David's face and pin-striped suit.

"For fuck's sake!" said David as he wiped the beer off his face. "Thanks for that!" He grabbed some tissues and started drying his face and suit.

"Did I just hear you right? Did you say you were shagging Nicola Newman?"

"Yes, and keep your voice down," David said and flung the tissues across the bar into a bin.

Paul started laughing. "I actually don't believe you!"

"It's true." David looked a great deal less than happy about it.

"But Nicola never puts a foot wrong. She's married to the Police Commissioner. She would never screw around."

"She *was* married to him – they're separated now."

"You're joking!"

"Look, you've been here years and so has she. Is that true, what you just said, that she doesn't screw around?"

"There has never been a whiff of scandal about that woman in all her years here. How did it happen?"

"She came on to me after the party last week and we spent the night together."

"This is priceless!"

"I didn't take her seriously at first. I thought it was just a drunken one-night stand, but she's been making it clear ever since she wants more than that."

Paul was trying his best to picture David and Nicola together but was finding it impossible. "And what do *you* want?"

"Well, I don't know at this stage. She's just so not the type I've ever gone for. I usually go for them a bit younger."

"Nicola isn't actually that much older than us at all. She just comes across as a lot older."

"I know, that's what I mean. And I hate baggage! And they don't come more baggaged than being married to the Police Commissioner."

Paul could see where he was coming from. "Look, David, I haven't seen you for a long while but you seem the same as you were back in school. I mean – can I be honest?"

"Please do."

"From what I can see you've never put a step wrong in your life. Everything is perfect from your career to your hair. I imagine the girls you see are the same type you saw back then. Uncomplicated girls with equally perfect lives and hair, with no mistakes in their past. Certainly no mistakes like a sixteen-year marriage to the Police Commissioner."

David looked pensively into his pint. "But she's so fucking impressive, Paul. All the stuff she's achieved and done. She's so independent. I'm intrigued by her."

"Is she?" laughed Paul, wondering what he was talking about. All Nicola had done was bully a store all her life. "Only you could be intrigued by a battleaxe."

David looked up, his face puzzled.

"I'm sorry," Paul held out his hands. "It's just – it's just it's taking me a while to get my head around this." He paused, then suddenly said out loud, "For fuck's sake!"

"What's wrong?"

"Well, look who's just walked in!"

David followed Paul's stare. Nicola had walked into the pub wearing very high heels and a chic cream minidress, her blonde hair gleaming.

She spotted them and cut through the crowd.

"Nicola!" said Paul, his mouth open. "It's very unusual to see you in here."

"Hi, boys! Mine's a white wine," she said, sitting up on the spare stool in front of them.

"I – eh – I think I need to go out and have a cigarette!" David said, standing up and walking out.

"Nicola – you look – different!" Paul said, his mouth still open. Her hair was blonder, the make-up heavier and the clothes very sexy.

She leaned forward. "Shut your fucking mouth and get me a drink."

* * *

Paul finished brushing his teeth and came out of the en-suite.

"Paul, when you come home with gossip like that, you have my permission to go to the pub every night of the week!" said Anna, who was lying out on the bed, glancing through a magazine.

"I'm still in shock. I don't know who I'm more shocked by – him or her."

"Well, put it in perspective. David has only known Nicola since she metamorphosed into this sassy sports-car-driving sex bomb. He never really knew the tweed-and-pearl-wearing Nicola of old."

Remembering David's icon of old, Margaret Thatcher, Paul wondered whether tweed and pearls mightn't be more of a turn-on for him!

"I tell you one thing," he said. "He was swearing me to secrecy but when she arrived in they were making it very obvious something was happening between them. Although, to be fair, she was making it more obvious than him." He lay out on the bed beside her. "Are you okay?"

She cuddled into him. "The doctor from the clinic was on to me today just confirming everything was fine for us to go to the clinic Friday week. You have booked that day off work?"

"Of course, I have."

"Well, it'll be all over by the end of the weekend. And then it's just a waiting game to see if it was successful."

"It will be," he insisted. "Don't worry about it."

* * *

The Blue Posts had emptied out at this stage and as Leo and Rachel left they looked over at David and Nicola. Her legs crossed, she was leaning towards him and laughing her head off at something he was saying.

"What the fuck is going on there?" asked Leo as they stepped out into the street.

"Very odd!" agreed Rachel. "I thought that woman was incapable of laughing."

"Hmmm, so did I. Speaking of David, thanks again for the great suggestion to contact him to get a position in finance."

"Your mum did tell you to contact David long before I suggested it."

"Hmmm."

"So I suggest it and it's a great idea but anything your mum says is just disregarded?"

"Let's not go there."

"Did you ring your mum today?"

"No."

"Leo! She asked me to pass on a message to make contact."

"So now you've passed on the message and it's up to me what I do, okay?"

"You're a stubborn bastard!" She hit his arm

"One of my many qualities! Your place or mine?"

"Mine, it's nearer."

* * *

Leo was looking through photos from home that Rachel was showing him. He stared at her family's beautiful large house.

"I didn't realise you were that rich," he said.

"We're not rich," she objected.

"That's rich in my book." He held up the photo of the house.

"Well, the Beckhams are rich in my book! So is Richard Branson! And Mr Michael O'Leary!"

"No – I'm not just talking about money," he continued, looking through the photos. "I'm talking about – I don't know, class maybe. I'm looking through these photos and I'm seeing a way of life that's very alien to me. You've never wanted for anything, you know where you're from, you have a place in society that was just given to you. In fact, what the fuck are you doing over here struggling on the shop floor in Franklyns when you could be home enjoying all this?"

"I'm not on the shop floor any more, in case you haven't noticed."

"I know. But you're like a lot of the birds there – you're just there for the glamour. Unlike the likes of me and Daniella who were there because we needed the bread."

"Everyone needs to pay their own way in the world, Leo."

"Yeah, but you had options. Lots of them." He looked at photos of her smiling with her parents and with friends. "And a lot of support."

Chapter 59

Leo was shown his new office which was down the corridor from David in Finance. He looked through the list that David had given him of people who owed money to Franklyns and decided to start with the biggest. A certain Lady Felladale owed £130,000 on her account. She sent in a couple of thousand every couple of months but her shopping expenses for that period were usually about the same. Leo got on to the internet and did a Google search on her. He dialled her number at her Belgravia home.

"Yes?" said the woman who answered the phone.

"May I speak to Lady Felladale, please?" said Leo.

"This is she."

"Ah, Lady Felladale, it's Leo Holden from Franklyns. I'm just phoning you about your account."

"What about it?"

"Well – it's in considerable arrears."

"Really? Oh, I'll get the accountant to send in some money. I have guests, so you'll have to excuse me."

"Hold on – just how much are you thinking of sending in?"

"Well, I don't know. The usual payment I presume – two thousand. Now if you'll excuse me –"

"Well, actually, you owe £130,000 and it's time to pay up."

"How dare you speak to me in that manner! I'll report you to Paul Stewart."

"I think you'll find Paul Stewart doesn't hold much sway here any more."

"I have been going into Franklyns for forty years. I have always maintained my account a certain way and I see no reason to change it now just because the store has been taken over by a rabble. Now if you persist, I will take my custom elsewhere."

"Off you go but you're settling that £130,000 first."

"You'll be paid when I deem fit."

"You are the same Lady Felladale who was listed in the *Sunday Times* Rich List this year?"

"What of it?"

"Now, listen, Grandma. If you don't get your accountant to send in that money pronto and I mean by the end of the week, I'm going to get on to *The Sunday Times* and give them a copy of your bill here and say you won't pay it."

"This is outrageous!"

"No, what is outrageous is that you think you never have to pay this bill by just running it as a continuous tab. You've got till Friday or I'll be on to *The Times*."

* * *

Oliver sat in an undercover police car across the road from a house they were surveying in Brixton. He couldn't remember the last time he was out on an actual job.

But this job was different. This was for Nicola and he wanted to make sure he was there so that nothing would go wrong. It had taken a long time to track down the man Jason Cody had sold the jewellery to, but an informant finally came through to them and told them that Joseph Maguire was operating from a house in Brixton. Joseph Maguire was a particularly nasty criminal, with his activities stretching to many areas. He was running a very profitable business getting low life like Cody to rob, and then he acted as a middleman selling the goods on. He had been in and out of prison for years and he didn't care what he handled as long as there was money in it for him.

"Maguire was definitely seen going in?" checked Oliver.

"Yes. And he's still there."

"Okay – give them the go-ahead!" authorised Oliver.

The officer spoke into his phone. "Are you stationed at the back? We're going in now."

Oliver went across the street with the two officers from the car and rang the doorbell.

"There's a television on inside," he said as he rang the bell again.

The door opened and a tired-looking Eastern European woman in a dressing-gown stood leaning against the doorway.

"What?" she asked.

Oliver took out the warrant. "I have a search warrant to search these premises."

"Why?" demanded the woman. "There is nothing here!"

Oliver pushed the door open and they entered the house. The inside of the house was dingy, with wallpaper peeling off the wall and a smell of mould throughout. In the living room a television was blaring and another four younger Eastern European women were lounging around, all in dressing-gowns.

Oliver and the two officers went up the stairs, while other officers came in the back. The bedrooms were unoccupied but the bathroom door was locked.

"Maguire! Open the door!" shouted Oliver.

There was no response. Oliver stepped back from the door and then kicked it, sending it flying. Joseph Maguire was emptying the last of a sachet of heroin down the toilet. He turned around to them, smiled, and then flushed the toilet.

* * *

Leo was down in the large security department at the back of the store. He was with Paul and the Head of Store Security, Steve Elliott. There had been an issue of a sales girl in the fashion department suspected of stealing from the till for a number of months. The amount being stolen was getting larger and larger and was enough for David to now be very concerned. Paul stood there with his arms folded, eyeing Leo up suspiciously. Paul thought Leo had been arrogant enough when he wasn't doing much. Now he had become David Stafford's blue-eyed boy it was like he owned the store. They were looking at CCTV footage of the girl in question as she cashed up her till.

"She's just too clever," said Steve. "I don't know how she's doing it – we can't catch her on CCTV."

"How do we know it's her then?" asked Leo.

"Because she's on every till that's short," said Paul.

"We've randomly checked her handbag when she's leaving and even her locker but can't ever catch her with any of the large sums of money she has stolen."

"Leave it with me and I'll see what I can come up with," said Leo.

"If Steve and the guys can't catch her, I can't see what luck you'll have," said Paul, annoyed with his arrogance.

"Leave it to me!" Leo said and winked.

* * *

Leo spent two days staring at the camera trained on the girl and indeed security was right, she didn't put a foot wrong. He was just about to give up on the second day when he spotted her serving a woman that he recognised from the day before. He sat up and scrutinised the monitor. The woman bought something small and paid in cash.

* * *

"What exactly are we waiting for?" demanded Paul on the Friday afternoon.

He, Leo and Steve Elliott were in Paul's office. All the monitors on the wall were trained on the girl in the fashion department as she went about her business serving customers.

"There she is!" said Leo. "The same woman again! Get your store detective over there! She's giving out too much change. That's how she's getting the money out of the store. Handing it over to her partner in crime."

Steve spoke into his walkie-talkie. As the woman was handed back her change, the store detective pounced.

As they watched on the monitors, two security guards arrived at the counter. There was a disturbance and then the salesgirl and the woman were escorted away.

"Caught red-handed!" shouted Leo.

"The clever little thieving bitch!" said Steve.

Paul managed to smile at the ecstatic Leo and said, "Well done."

* * *

Stephanie was on the third floor with a group of merchandisers.

"I want this electrical department reduced in size by a third. I want to free up all this area here for an expansion of designer clothes." She waved her arms to show the areas she meant.

"Stephanie!" said David, approaching her.

"Hi, David."

"Look at this." He handed her over a cheque.

"What's this? My bonus?" She smiled wryly.

"No, it's a cheque from a certain Lady Felladale who's been using this place as a personal expense account for years. Leo got on to her and had her paying up in two days."

"He's working with you?"

"Yeah. Your lad is priceless. Threatened the old bat that he'd go to the press. He's not afraid of anything. Took it on himself the other day to just ring up one of our major suppliers and demand credit terms be extended by thirty days. He's a gift – thank you!"

* * *

Stephanie was relieved that Leo had returned to work but was frustrated that he was ignoring her calls. It was as if everything had gone back to the way it had been before he had started at Franklyns.

She spotted him striding across the third floor and hurried after him.

"Leo! I've been looking for you. I really think we need to sit down and have a chat."

He kept walking and she was forced to keep pace with him. "Sorry, Mum, I'm far too busy at the moment to stop. Security want me down to see this buyer. I noticed there was an irregularity between the stock he was ordering and what was in store. I told security and they checked his locker. Fucking packed full with mobile phones. He's been on the take for months."

"That's excellent, Leo. Well done . . . but when are you free for that chat?"

"You know, I'm just so busy. I'll drop by to you when I'm free."

As he raced off, her heart sank as she realised he had no intention of doing so.

I'm such a bloody fool, she thought. I pushed him away by moaning about work to him.

Chapter 60

"Aren't you clever!" said Rachel as they got out of the Tube near his home after he had recounted the story of how he snared the buyer. After work that evening they had been out for something to eat in Covent Garden.

"I just need to pop in here to get a couple of things," he said as they passed a petrol station.

She followed him through into the small supermarket and glanced through magazines as he got some milk, bacon and chocolate.

"Are you all right?" he asked as he walked past her with the plastic bag of shopping. She replaced the magazine and followed him.

Outside the shop in the forecourt of the petrol station there was a row of small drums of motor oil for sale. Leo looked around quickly and, as he walked past, bent down, picked one up and kept walking.

Confused, Rachel asked, "What are you doing?"

"Nothing. Just keep on walking."

"Leo, I didn't hear you asking for that up at the till or paying for it."

"That's because I didn't."

"So you just stole that drum of oil?" She stopped walking.

"Will you come on and stop attracting attention," he snapped at her.

She continued walking alongside him. "Leo, go back into that shop and pay for that."

"No, why should I?"

"Because you don't just take something because you fancy it. Do you even need that oil?"

"Not really," he shrugged as they turned into his street.

"So why the fuck did you take it then?"

He put the key in his door, opened it and said, "Because I could!"

"I don't believe you!" She shook her head as she followed him in. "What a pointless thing to do."

He smirked at her. "It wasn't pointless. It's worth a few quid, that."

"Yes, a few quid to the garage!"

"They shouldn't have left them out in the forecourt then, should they?" he laughed.

"All over dinner you've been boasting about catching those thieves who worked at Franklyns," said Rachel, "and then you just rob something yourself!"

"But that's different! They deserved to be caught – because they were caught!"

"So, let me get this right. In the wonderful commonsense world of Leo Holden, it's only wrong if you get caught?"

"That's about the size of it. Say, want to buy a drum of oil? I'll give it to you for a knockdown price!" He winked at her.

Rachel shook her head, sighing, and put her hands on her hips. "What am I doing here? Have I lost leave of my senses? We're from different worlds."

"Opposites attract! Look, what's your problem? You just don't understand the basic rules of commerce. That's your problem."

"And would you care to explain them to me?"

"Something's only worth what somebody is prepared to pay for it. I wasn't prepared to pay anything for that drum of oil – so it's worthless – so I took it!"

"But you'd be happy to take £100 from somebody else for it?"

"If someone saw fit to pay that, then yeah. It's done all the time. People buy and sell stocks and shares. People are being ripped off all the time. Those designer gowns we flog at Franklyns, there's no fucking way they're worth a few grand each. But if somebody is stupid enough to pay for it, isn't that still robbing them? I mean, how can you justify selling a piece of fabric for £10,000?"

"You're missing the point, Leo. In all these other transactions there's a case of request and permission. That petrol shop owner did not give you permission to take that oil."

He shrugged. "A mere technicality!"

Rachel stood thinking and then turned to go. She picked up her jacket and bag and headed for the door.

"Where are you going?"

"Home."

"You're being stupid."

She turned and looked at him."No, Leo . . . I need some time to think. This has all gone very quickly for me, too quickly. I don't move this fast normally. Daniella was hardly gone and we ended up in bed together. I feel bad about that and I'm feeling like I'm just a replacement. And although I love your very unique way of thinking, it's driving me bonkers. There's a lot been going on recently with the new job and you. I've been carried away by the excitement of it all . . . I need a bit of time to think. I'll talk to you later." She turned again to leave.

"I don't know what you're being so high and mighty about. Given the situation, anybody has it in them to commit a crime."

She turned again and looked at him. "That's just taking cynicism a little bit too far for me, Leo."

"One day you'll compromise yourself," he said.

"I don't think so," she said and walked out.

* * *

Leo sat on his couch at home. Radiohead's 'Creep' was playing on his sound system. He had the necklace he bought off Joseph Maguire in his hand and he toyed with it as he thought about Rachel. He had planned to have such a great weekend with her and now he had been left on his own. Looking at the necklace he knew what he would do on Monday at work.

* * *

Nicola had a wonderful weekend. She really felt she was an independent girl about town. David stayed with her on the Friday night. Then she packed an overnight bag and stayed with him on the Saturday. He had something on Sunday evening so she happily went back to her own apartment and planned her wardrobe for the coming week. She felt so confident in herself and her allure.

Chapter 61

On Monday morning the lift door opened on the fifth floor and Rachel walked out and went through the main reception area towards the press office. Walking past the HR department, she saw Nicola emerging. Rachel did a double-take. Nicola was dressed in a mini-dress and high heels and was literally strutting.

"Hi, Nicola," said Rachel as she passed her.

Nicola ignored her and continued towards the lifts.

Rachel went down the corridor into the press office and went to her desk.

She hadn't heard anything from Leo. Not that she expected to. She knew just how stubborn he was. She wasn't sure if she wanted to hear from him or not. Everything about him was warning her to stay away and yet she couldn't understand it but she loved being around him. He excited her. The danger that was in him that warned her also excited her. He had occupied her thoughts for the whole weekend. The phone on her desk rang.

"Rachel, it's Stephanie. Seemingly Arielle Moore is in the store. She's down with Paul Stewart in the jeweller's. Seemingly there's a big swarm of media waiting for her outside the store. I'm tied up in meetings. Can you go down and help Paul out?"

"Of course!" said Rachel.

Rachel excitedly made her way to the third floor. Arielle Moore was a huge Hollywood movie star, an A-lister that the paparazzi followed everywhere.

She couldn't wait to see her in reality.

Arielle Moore was surrounded by her bodyguards who in turn were surrounded by Franklyns' security. Often when stars came into the store, customers approached them looking for autographs. There would be no such access to a star of Arielle Moore's stature. Paul was beside her as she selected items of jewellery.

The bodyguards blocked Rachel as she tried to make her way to the star.

"It's all right. Let her through!" called Paul.

They made a gap for her to enter.

"Arielle, this is our store publicist, Rachel Healy," said Paul.

She got a huge buzz from the introduction. It wasn't true either. She was a junior publicist assisting Stephanie. But she still liked the description. *This* was what she had come to London for!

Arielle smiled and nodded at her. She was smaller than Rachel expected, a woman in her forties who thanks to cosmetic surgery and various exhaustive exercise routines could pass for twenty years younger. She was dressed in a man's tight black waistcoat with nothing underneath it and tight jeans and was wearing oversized sunglasses. Not many people could get away with the look but Arielle could. Rachel tried not to stare at her as she selected various items and bought them. Paul acted with the ease of somebody who was used to dealing with such big names in the store.

"Not interrupting your coffee break, are we?" Paul whispered to Rachel with a smirk, reminding her of the time he asked her to assist in the sale of watches to an Arab.

"I've been intrigued by Arielle Moore for years. I'd sacrifice every coffee break in my life for this chance to see her up close!"

"Is she what you expected?" Paul was curious. He was immune to celebrity but the reaction of people to the stars when they came to the store never ceased to amaze him.

"She's looks a bit like a plastic doll," Rachel whispered.

"Okay, I think I'm through!" said Arielle.

Paul did a quick mental arithmetic sum of the items she had placed on the counter.

"On behalf of Franklyns, we would like to offer you these items compliments of the store," said Paul.

"Thank you!" said Areille, almost as if she expected it.

"Pass me some bags," said Paul to the sales girl behind the counter. The girl passed some small bags out that matched the items' size.

"No, the big bags!" Paul hissed at her.

The sales girl quickly did what she was told. Paul placed each item into a big bag.

Arielle's assistants took the bags while Paul held onto one bag himself.

"Okay, how are we going to do this?" asked her chief bodyguard. "Can we leave by a back exit?"

"I'm afraid not," said Paul. "The press are expecting that and are camped out at every door. The best thing is to leave by the front. It's the clearest way to make a getaway. If she leaves by the other exits, her car might get blocked on the sideroads."

The bodyguard started talking into his radio.

They moved quickly through the store, surrounded by security, Paul and Rachel either side of Arielle.

When they reached the main entrance Paul handed Rachel the bag and whispered to her, "When the press start snapping, I want you to hold up this bag as close as possible to Arielle so it's in as many of the photos as possible. Okay?"

Rachel nodded. "Okay."

As they left the store and walked towards the limousine Rachel was taken aback by the number of photographers there were shouting Arielle's name and snapping cameras. Paul put an arm protectively around Arielle as the security pushed their way through the crowd. Arielle kept her head down all the time.

Paul opened the back door of the car and Arielle went to step in. It was the clearest shot the press had of her.

"Don't forget this bag!" said Rachel loudly, lifting the Franklyns' bag to the level of Arielle's shoulder. Arielle paused for a second, then took the bag before getting into the car.

The car then sped off followed by her bodyguards' cars and the paparazzi, until it was just Paul and Rachel standing on the pavement.

"Well done! If they print that shot you've had your first press coup!" Paul said to Rachel.

"Well, it was you who masterminded it," said Rachel. "I didn't know what you were doing insisting on the big bags! You wanted the bag clearly seen in the photos."

"If she is photographed with a Franklyns' bag, you can't buy press like that!"

"And do we often give freebies out like that?" She was surprised to hear her use the word 'we' when referring to Franklyns.

"When they are as big a star as Arielle, then yes we do. We often give visiting celebrities something. It's good for business. Although David Stafford might put a stop to all that."

As Rachel watched the circus that was Arielle's entourage disappear down the road she asked, "How can she live like that? With that level of fame and attention with her wherever she goes."

"She's just driven by ambition. We all are to a certain extent. How far would you go to get success, Rachel?" He looked at her curiously.

* * *

Paul swung open the door of the press office. Rachel looked up from her paperwork as he beamed a smile and sat on her desk. He threw a copy of the *Evening Standard* in front of her.

"Congratulations, you're famous!"

Rachel took up the paper. On the front page was a large photo of Rachel handing Arielle Moore the shopping bag as she got into her limousine. Over the photo was the heading: *'Arielle Shops at Franklyns.'*

Rachel suddenly felt exposed in having her photo on the front page.

"I didn't realise they'd put me in the shot!" She sounded horrified.

"The main thing is that the Franklyns shopping bag is hugely visible. You can't buy that kind of brand placement." He smiled at her and walked out.

Rachel made her way to Stephanie's office. On reaching it, she knocked and entered. Rachel had waited for Stephanie to give her permission to enter her office the previous day and Stephanie had told her that in future she should come straight in. Rachel loved her relaxed attitude which was so different from the rest of the Franklyns' stuffy protocol.

"I just wanted to leave these itinerary plans for those press events for your approval before I give the go-ahead," said Rachel, putting the papers on Stephanie's desk.

"That's fine, Rachel," said Stephanie. "I'll look through them tonight and let you know in the morning."

"Okay, thanks," Rachel said. "See you tomorrow."

"Oh, and Rachel. I saw *The Standard* – great press, well done!"

"It was really Paul Stewart who organised it all. I just did what he told me."

Stephanie smiled and nodded as Rachel left. Then she sat down at her desk and started going through the large amount of paperwork which Rachel had just added to.

* * *

Later Stephanie joined Rachel in the press office to look through photos that had been commissioned by the store.

"I like these ones," said Stephanie eventually, handing a selection to Rachel. "I think we'll go with these for the feature."

David walked into the office. "Oh, sorry, Stephanie, for disturbing you. I'm looking for Rachel Healy."

"Eh, that's me," said Rachel.

"Rachel, could I have a quick word?"

"Sure," said Rachel and walked over to him at the door.

He smiled at her. "I believe we had Arielle in the store yesterday?"

"Yes, that's right," smiled Rachel.

"She was given quite a substantial amount of gifts free gratis."

"Eh, yes." Rachel's smile hovered.

"Rachel, I know it was customary to give visiting stars freebies in the past but that's all stopping now. You really shouldn't have given those gifts without written permission from somebody superior. Because you didn't know this change in policy that'll be the end of it, but it's not to happen again, understand?"

Rachel's smile dropped as she struggled for something to say.

Stephanie looked up from her photos. "Sorry for interrupting you, David, but Rachel was only assisting with Arielle. The freebies were given by Paul Stewart."

"Oh!" said David. "I'll have a word with Paul in that case." He smiled at Rachel and walked out.

Rachel turned around and walked slowly back to the desk, her face full of concern.

Noticing her downbeat expression, Stephanie said,

"You have to speak up for yourself, Rachel. You can't take the blame for somebody else's actions."

"Oh, I know," said Rachel. "I just don't want to get Paul into any trouble."

"I wouldn't worry about it."

* * *

Paul was reading through the letter sent to him and Anna from the IVF clinic, confirming times and dates for Friday.

David strode into Paul's office. Paul quickly put the letter to one side.

"Paul, wanted to have a quick work with you about the freebies you gave Arielle Moore yesterday."

"Yeah? What about it?" Here we go, he thought.

"Did you see what the final bill came to for that?"

"Yeah."

"In case you didn't realise, there's a credit crunch on, you know, Paul. We just can't continue with that old policy of giving people stuff just because they're famous. All right?"

"Come on, David. We got the front page of the *Standard*! You can't buy publicity like that – it was worth whatever we gave Arielle."

"Well, actually, I checked how much it would cost to buy the same amount of advertising space in the paper and it would have worked out much cheaper to just book the advertising space."

You would, thought Paul.

"Yeah, but it wouldn't carry the same weight," objected Paul. "This was a huge photo on the front page with Arielle carrying a Franklyns' shopping bag. There's no amount of advertising can get that wow factor."

David looked bored. "Yeah, I know all that but does it really materialise in any increase of sales? I doubt it. You just can't quantify this kind of stuff, so I'm going to put an immediate ban on it, all right?"

Paul was angry but tried to control it. "Not all right, David. I feel very strongly about this. When a star the size of Arielle comes in and we can get that kind of publicity, then it's worth a few freebies. If you don't object, I think I'll bring it up at the next Board meeting to get everyone else's opinion on it."

David blinked a couple of times. "Sure, if you want to bring it up, then do. See you later." And with a smile he walked out.

* * *

Leo went up to the gift wrap department and spotted a girl called Valerie working on the counter, busy wrapping customers' purchasers in Franklyns' embossed wrapping paper. He had chatted to her a few times and gone for coffee with her in the staff restaurant.

"Valerie, how's it going?" He beamed her a smile and winked at her.

"Hi, Leo! What's up?"

He leaned forward in a conspiratorial manner and lowered his voice. "Could you do me a big favour?"

"Name it."

He glanced around and took out the necklace he bought from Joseph Maguire and handed it over to her.

"Could you wrap that up in a Franklyns' box for me?"

Valerie looked concerned. "Did you buy this in the store?"

"No. It's a gift for someone and it would just look better if it came in a Franklyns' box, get my meaning?"

"I get your meaning, Leo. But that's against all the rules. I can only wrap purchases bought in the store."

His eyes widened at her in a pleading fashion. "But nobody would ever know but us, I promise."

She sighed and gave him a warning look. "They'd better not, Leo, or else I'm in big trouble." She reached behind the counter for a suitably sized gift box and wrapping paper.

"Don't forget to put a big bow on it!" He winked at her.

* * *

Oliver sat across from Joseph Maguire in the interrogation room. Maguire had refused to speak since his arrest. He had built a wall around himself and stared straight ahead. A search of Maguire's house had not shown up any of

Nicola's jewellery. However it had shown up lots of other stolen jewellery which they managed to trace to other women victims of vicious muggings. Oliver could piece together the whole situation. Maguire ran a tight little operation. He sent out drug addicts like Jason Cody to attack well-heeled businesswomen like Nicola who were easy prey. Maguire then took the jewellery and sold it on to a group of trusted buyers. Oliver needed now to know the buyer Maguire had sold Nicola's jewellery to. He had tried everything with Maguire but he refused to talk.

"All right," Oliver said, sitting forward. "You know you're going to prison. We have enough on you. So it's a case of negotiating a lesser charge if you co-operate with me. You help me – and I'll help you."

Maguire suddenly had a flicker of movement in his eyes and he turned and faced Oliver.

"What are you looking for? And what do I get out of it?" Maguire demanded.

Chapter 62

Paul left work and was walking down the street to the Tube station. His mind was preoccupied with going to the clinic that weekend. He was nervous. Anna kept wanting to talk about what would happen if it wasn't successful and she didn't become pregnant. He knew she was just trying to prepare both of them for failure if it didn't work. But he wanted to think positive and for Anna to be positive as well. Suddenly a limousine pulled up beside him. The front passenger door opened up and a suited man stepped out and blocked Paul's continued passage.

Before Paul could say anything, the man opened the car's back door and said, "Get in, please."

"What is this?" demanded Paul.

Suddenly a voice he recognised from the back of the car said, "Get in, Paul, we haven't got all day."

Paul looked into the back seat to see Karl Furstin sitting there.

He hesitated for a few moments, then stepped into the back of the car and sat down next to Karl. The chauffeur closed the back door, then got into the front and drove them away.

If Paul had forgotten what it was like being in the presence of Karl Furstin, he was quickly reminded as he sat beside him in silence as the limousine made its way through Knightsbridge. The car pulled up outside the apartment block where the Furstins lived. The chauffeur got out and opened Karl's door while Paul let himself out the other side. The concierge opened the glass doors of the building and Paul followed Karl through the huge marble lobby to the private elevator. The two men stood in silence in the lift as it brought them to the top floor.

Paul mind was racing, wondering what Furstin wanted, getting that old claustrophobic feeling he used to get around Karl.

Karl stepped into the huge lounge of his penthouse, Paul nervously following him. To his surprise Elka was there as well, standing with her back to them as she looked out the windows. Hearing their arrival, she turned around. She was immaculately dressed in a long cream satin gown, her hair and make-up as ever done to perfection. Her glacial face managed to thaw slightly on seeing Paul.

"Good to see you again, Paul," she said and nodded.

"And you, Mrs Furstin," Paul said. Nothing could be further from the truth, he thought, as he shivered slightly to be back in their company.

"Drink, Paul?" said Karl.

"Maybe just a glass of water."

Within a few moments a woman appeared beside him with a glass of water on a tray. He took it and drank a gulp. The woman stood waiting.

"Leave us!" commanded Karl.

The woman turned and left.

"Sit down, Paul," said Karl.

Paul made his way over to one of the huge white sofas and sat down. He hoped they wouldn't spot the beads of sweat that had broken out on his brow.

"And so! How is everything at Franklyns?" asked Karl.

"It's . . . er . . . different," Paul said.

"In what way?"

Paul managed to smile. "In every way! The layout is all changed. Cutbacks all over the place. Massive changes in personnel."

"But they haven't got rid of you?" said Karl.

"Yet," Elka added.

Paul glanced over at Elka. "No, I'm still there."

"And how do you find Stephanie Holden? I believe you have a difficult relationship with her?" said Karl.

"We had a bumpy start but I think we've managed to build a professional relationship."

"You find the changes she's made have been good?" Paul felt the whole conversation invasive and yet he stayed. "I don't like all of them but profits are up. Her work must be good."

"The only place she should be is walking the streets in Kings Cross," said Karl. "But maybe some of the changes were long overdue. They might have done us a favour in the long run."

"In the long run?" asked Paul.

Elka fixed him with ice-cold blue eyes. "We want our store back."

"And we want you to help us get it back," said Karl.

Paul looked from one to the other. "I don't understand."

"We are working on getting the store back at the moment but we need your assistance," said Karl. "Work with us from the inside."

Paul's face creased with worry. "I really don't like the sound of that. If it got out, I'd be sacked immediately. In fact I'd be ruined. "

"You'll be sacked at soon as they've extracted all the use they can from you anyway," said Elka.

"Work with us and when we have the store back you'll have all your former power again," said Karl. "No Stephanie Holden or David Stafford interfering. All your old perks back – expense accounts, company car. You were always an ambitious man, Paul. I'm offering you back what is rightfully yours."

Paul's eyes began to widen.

"And we can do so much more for you," said Elka.

"Forget about that clinic that you and your wife are attending for IVF," said Karl. "We can arrange for you to meet the world's best specialists in a clinic we know in Switzerland."

Paul's mouth dropped as he went cold.

"Can we rely on you?" asked Elka.

"I . . . eh . . . I need some time to think about all of this," he said.

There was a silence.

"Take all the time you need," said Karl eventually.

"But just don't take too long," advised Elka.

"You may go," said Karl. "The car is waiting downstairs and it will take you home."

* * *

As the Furstins' chauffeur drove through the London traffic, Paul's head was spinning with all that had just happened. How did they know about the IVF? He felt worried by their level of knowledge. They were offering him so much. He felt nauseous at the lingering smell of Karl's aftershave in the car. He spotted a Tube station.

"Pull over and let me out," he said to the driver.

"My orders are to deliver you to your home," said the chauffeur.

"Just let me the fuck out!" Paul demanded.

* * *

Paul came into his home and walked right past Anna who was lying out on the couch reading a newspaper. He walked over to the drinks cabinet without saying a word, opened a bottle of Ballintine's whiskey and poured himself a big tumbler.

"Hard day at the office, darling?" Anna smirked over at him as he downed the glass.

"Something like that."

"David Stafford giving you trouble again?"

He poured another glass and turned to face her, resting against the giant marble fireplace. He so wanted to tell her about what had just happened with Furstin, so wanted her opinion. But with her being in the middle of IVF, the last thing he wanted to do was burden her or upset her. And she would be very upset if she knew the Furstins knew about the IVF. *He* was very upset they knew.

He smiled at her. "Yeah, Stafford just getting on my nerves again."

"I guess this weekend at the clinic isn't making things any more relaxed for you?"

He shook his head. "I'm looking forward to just getting on with it now, Anna." He came and sat beside her. "Looking forward to starting our new lives with a kid."

* * *

Rachel popped into Tesco's after work and got some stuff for her dinner that night. As she sat upstairs on the double-decker bus, she looked out at the rain lashing down on Kings Road. She was so engrossed in thinking about Leo and her new job that she nearly missed her stop. She quickly pressed the bell and got off.

Putting up her umbrella, she walked through the streets home. She turned into her street and walked on, her head bent. Starting up the steps of her building she glanced down the street and did a double-take as she spotted Leo sitting outside the pub on the corner in the pouring rain. He waved at her. She shook her head in disbelief and walked down the street to him.

"Hi!" he said when she reached him. He was dressed in a raincoat, a pint of Heineken on the table in front of him with the rain spilling down on him, his hair and face drenched.

"Leo! What the fuck are you doing sitting here in the rain?" she demanded.

"I was waiting for you."

"Wouldn't it have been more sensible to wait inside the pub out of the wet?" She looked down at the raindrops splashing into the top of his pint.

"I would have missed you coming home then."

"You're a nut, do you know that? Come on back to my place. You're going to get pneumonia."

He stood up and walked along with her.

Inside, she put the heating on as he took off the soaking raincoat.

"Leo, go into the bathroom and have a hot shower – I'll get you some dry towels."

"I want to talk to you first," he insisted.

"It would have been simpler if you had just come to my office today."

"I did. You were always with somebody."

"It was a busy day," she conceded. "You could have just phoned me then."

"I didn't think you'd take my call."

She sighed. "I don't play games, Leo – of course I would have. Anyway, what's so important that you want to see me about it?"

"You know what's so important. What happened the other night. I want to give you something." He reached into his pocket, took out a Franklyns bag and handed it to her.

"What's this?" she asked, confused, as she took it.

"Just open it."

She undid the bow and wrapping paper and opened the box. She stared down at the necklace.

"Leo, what's this?"

"I bought it for you."

Amazed, she took out the necklace and studied it.

"Leo, I can't accept this. It's too expensive."

"I want you to have it . . . besides, I got my staff discount with it," he smirked at her.

"I appreciate the gesture, Leo, but I can't take it." She handed it back to him.

His face was overcome with hurt. "I got you this to show you that you aren't just a replacement for Daniella for me. You mean a lot to me, and maybe I piss you off and maybe we are from two different worlds but you're the best thing that's happened to me for a long time, and I just want you to know that."

"Leo . . ." She stared down at the necklace. "You didn't need to buy the necklace – all I really needed was to hear those words. You know, I didn't think somebody like you would ever wear their heart on their sleeve like that."

"I don't as a rule – this is a once-off and don't expect me going around saying soppy things to you all the time, all right?" He winked at her and laughed.

"Well, what are you saying to me then?"

"I'm saying . . . I like having you around." He took the necklace, walked behind her and put it on her. "It was made for you," he whispered into her ear and snuggled his head into her neck.

"I don't know what to say. Maybe I'm not a replacement for Daniella then . . . but I still don't like what you did taking that drum of oil."

"I returned the drum of oil to the forecourt this morning."

"Did you really?" Her face brightened up.

"Scout's honour! See, I need you around to save me from myself! Point out wrong from right."

"I'm not in the mood to save anybody, Leo." She turned around and studied his smiling face. She reached forward and kissed him. "You really had better go and have a hot shower and get out of those wet clothes. I'll go and cook us something to eat."

* * *

That night Paul lay in bed staring at the ceiling. As ever the light was on in the hall, shining dimly through the gap at the side of the bedroom door. Anna lay sleeping soundly beside him.

The conversation with the Furstins kept going through his mind. All his old power and perks back. Goodbye to Stephanie Holden and, more importantly, David Stafford. Back to how he wanted to run things. And safe in his position from the constant threat of being let go. But just what would they want him to do?

Chapter 63

The next morning Paul was walking down the street to work when he spotted Rachel and Leo getting off a bus together. He observed them for a while as they walked down the street hand-in-hand, laughing and chatting. As they got nearer the store, they separated and walked further apart and as they reached the staff entrance they waved goodbye to each other. He had been suspicious that there was something going on between them when he had seen them together before and now it was confirmed. He was surprised. He would have never put the two of them together. And ridiculously, he found himself irritated.

He sat in his office, toying with a pen, deep in thought about the Furstins' offer. They were offering him everything. It was very tempting. But there was just one problem with the offer – the Furstins. He had almost forgotten how unpleasant it was to be in their company. No amount of perks could compensate for being around people who made you feel so uncomfortable. And there were also Karl's other activities. Paul had always turned a blind eye to them, preferring not to know. But now they were asking him to be directly involved in something sinister and, knowing them, seedy. What were they planning to do to Stephanie? He wanted no part of it. In a funny kind of way, even though he was in a very vulnerable position since the takeover, he was at least only answerable to himself. He didn't have to jump around to Furstin's demands any more. Like when he fought back against David the other day about the freebies to Arielle. He wouldn't dream of putting up such a fight with the Furstins. He felt free without Karl in his life and that's what he wanted. And the fact that he knew all about their IVF showed just how underhand and sinister they were. He didn't even want to know how they found out. His mobile rang and he saw Karl's number coming up.

"So much for take all the time you need," he said out loud before answering it. "Karl?"

"Paul . . . have you given much thought to what we discussed?"

" I haven't thought about anything else."

"And?"

"I thank you for your offer but I'm going to have to say no, I'm afraid."

Silence on the other end.

"Karl?" said Paul.

"I'm disappointed in you," said Karl and then the phone went dead.

Paul sighed and sat back in his chair, rubbing his face.

A knock sounded on the open door. "Sorry, Paul, can I have a quick word?" said Rachel.

Paul looked up. "Sure, come in."

"I just wanted to say I hope you didn't think I purposely landed you in any trouble about the free gifts for Arielle. It actually wasn't me who told David Stafford."

"Oh, who was it then?"

Rachel felt herself go red. "Look, I'd rather not say."

He sat back. "No, I'd be surprised if you did say. Don't worry about it. It's not that important."

He saw her face visibly relax and realised she had been very worried about it.

Paul's mobile rang. He picked it up and answered it.

"Yeah . . . Well, you have to have that stock in on Monday, no option." He stood up as he continued to speak and turned and looked out the window behind his desk. "I really couldn't give a fuck," he said down the phone. "A deadline is a deadline and I want that stock in on Monday."

As Rachel waited for him to finish his phone call, her eyes glanced down at the paperwork on his desk. She saw a letter addressed to Paul and Anna Stewart and from the logo saw that it was from a fertility clinic. In the body of the letter she noticed the letters IVF mentioned several times. She quickly looked away and felt herself go bright red. Paul turned around as he continued to speak on the phone and she looked at his monitors, pretending to be concentrating on what was happening in the store.

She looked at Paul and mouthed, "I have to go!"

He nodded and waved at her as he continued to argue on his mobile.

* * *

Yvette stared at Nicola as she walked past her desk.

"Any messages, Yvette?" asked Nicola.

"Just your husband phoned for you again."

"Oh, any others?"

"And David Stafford called for you."

"Get Mr Stafford on the phone for me, will you?"

"Sure. I'm just heading off to lunch – do you want me to get you anything?" Yvette's eyes stared at Nicola's legs through the long slit in her skirt.

"No, it's fine. I'm going out to lunch."

* * *

Yvette was holding court in the staff restaurant with a group of friends from the store around her.

"It's like a fashion show with her every day!" she was saying. "The skirts are getting shorter and shorter! I don't know where it's all going to end!" She rolled her eyes and paused to take a large mouthful of her panini as they all tittered at her unintentional joke. Then her captive audience watched every chew as they hovered on the edges of their seats waiting for her to continue. Yvette had always regaled everybody with stories about Nicola. Most of the stories concerned how much of a bigger bitch Nicola could be. But now they were getting first-hand stories which were much more exciting and shocking.

"The husband rings for her all the time," Yvette continued, "and she rarely takes his calls, telling me to say she's in a meeting."

"Never mind that, get to the point! Her and David Stafford – are they screwing?"

"I've no direct evidence," said Yvette adopting a serious look. "But they have long lunches together, laughing and joking across in the pub every night, ringing for each other all the time and when they are in her office for meetings, they are in there forever!"

"The dirty cow!" they all cried together.

* * *

Nicola sat in the Furstins' penthouse opposite Karl and Elka.

"Well, it's an unfortunate case of the animals taking over the zoo in my opinion," said Nicola. "I've tried to keep standards up in the place but it's hard when there's a juggernaut trying to railroad over you. Do you know what's she's just gone and done now?"

"Holden?" asked Karl.

"Yes. She has opened a Moet bar in the men's designer section. Did you ever hear such nonsense? Some rubbish about the wives and girlfriends can have a glass of champagne while the men try on the clothes. She'll be opening an ice-cream parlour in the women's section next. The mind boggles!"

"Well, Nicola, the reason why we sent for you is because we are in a position to buy back our store," said Karl.

Nicola smiled broadly. "But that's excellent!"

"The trouble is Barons Bank are insistent about putting the store on the stock market."

"So they won't sell it back to you?"

"They think they can get much more on a stock-market float than what we are prepared to pay," said Karl. "We need to derail this stock-market idea."

Nicola's mind drifted to David and what repercussions this could have.

"And what are you suggesting?" she asked.

"The bottom line is we need Stephanie Holden out," said Elka. "The whole stock-market float depends on her being at the helm. She's very much respected in the city."

"I can't imagine why!" said Nicola.

"Just because of the amount of successful stock-market floats she has presided over. If she left, I think Barons Bank would be much more flexible in their dealings with us."

"That woman isn't going anywhere by the look of her," warned Nicola.

"We know. That's why we need you. We need to get something watertight against her, something that will disgrace her so she can't stay . . . it won't be easy. She's as clean as a whistle. Nicola, you were always so – good – at sorting out our problems. Can we rely on you to work on the inside this time?"

"Of course, you can!" said Nicola.

Both Karl and Elka smiled.

"I just have one stipulation," said Nicola. "The new Financial Controller David Stafford. He's simply brilliant. I think we should poach him from Barons Bank and keep him on at Franklyns, whatever it costs."

Karl shrugged. "Whatever you think. We always left personnel decisions to you, Nicola."

"Great!" Nicola smiled.

"It's so good to see you again, Nicola," said Elka. "And you look so well!"

"Thank you."

"And how is your husband? The Commissioner?" asked Karl.

"Oh, good, you know . . . keeping busy."

* * *

That night Nicola stared at David's face as they lay in bed. He was recounting some tale from the day's work. She was only half listening as she couldn't take her eyes off him. She was hardly daring to believe she was there with him.

"So next thing, I get Leo on the job, and he has it sorted out in two minutes flat," David giggled.

"Leo? You mean Leo Holden?" Nicola suddenly became alert.

"Yes."

"And what's he doing working on accounts?"

"He's joined my team in the finance department," explained David.

"He's *what*?" Nicola quickly sat up. "And who said that little grease monkey could go and work in Finance?"

"Well, I did actually."

"David, you can't just hire somebody without going through the proper procedures," said Nicola, looking angry.

"What proper procedures? He's already an employee. What's the big deal?"

"The big deal is I have to give the say-so."

"No. I hire who I want, when I want and I don't answer to anybody, Nicola."

"But there are things in everybody's file that need to be checked to make sure they are suitable for a position. As it happens, Leo Holden is completely unsuitable to be working with the store's finance."

"What makes you say that?"

"A conversation I had with the HR in that City firm he worked in. He was a disaster, lost them a fortune."

"Well, it just goes to show why you shouldn't believe in references, because I've found him brilliant since he started."

"Well, so did they – at the beginning."

"He's in a role where he can't do any damage. He's not in charge of any funds. Nicola, I think this is about that stupid rift you have with Stephanie Holden."

She blinked a few times, wondering how he knew about that. From Stephanie obviously, she thought.

"You both should just get over your dislike for the other and work together to put the store first."

"I always put the store first, David. I know what's right for the store and what's not. And she's *not*! What has she actually achieved since she started at Franklyns?"

"Well, a huge amount actually. She's rearranged everything, cutting departments that weren't making money and maximising money-making departments. She's signed up a load of brilliant money-making designers and dropped loss-makers. She's refurbished areas that need it and hired in brilliant personal shoppers. Profits are up, Nicola. There's no denying it."

"Well, bully for her!"

David stared at her for a few moments. "Do you know, I don't want to have this conversation. I don't want to talk about this any more." He got out of bed and walked out of the room.

Chapter 64

David and Nicola were finishing off their salmon salad in the fifth floor restaurant at Harvey Nichols that Thursday lunch-time.

Since they had had their tiff about Stephanie Holden Nicola had made sure to put on a happy face and pretend nothing had happened. David seemed quite content to do the same. Nicola made a mental note to herself not to challenge him like that again – he obviously reacted badly to it.

Nicola reached over and poured the remains of the bottle of white wine into their glasses as she finished telling a story: "So I told him that we didn't need a liability like him around the store and it was best for all concerned that he leave immediately!"

David roared with laughter. "And he didn't say anything else?"

"He was too afraid to, I can assure you!" Nicola took her glass of wine and took a sip. There was a pause, then she reached over and lightly stroked his hand. "David? Would you ever consider leaving Barons Bank?"

"I haven't given it much thought, why?"

"Just curious. I mean if the right offer came along, would you accept it?"

"Right offer?"

"As in a huge pay increase?"

"Of course, I would. I'd be stupid not to, wouldn't I?"

"Hmmm, that's what I would have thought," said Nicola.

Her mobile started to ring again in her handbag. She had ignored it many times already, not wishing to take it out and turn it off in front of David. She knew it was Oliver.

"Who is that ringing you all through lunch?" demanded David.

Nicola took out her mobile and saw ten missed calls from Oliver. "Oh, just work. I should have just turned it off." She switched it off and put it back in her handbag.

"It's time we were getting back anyway," said David.

"Oh, let's order another drink before we go back," urged Nicola with a mischievous smile, finishing off her glass.

"Nicola! We've already been over two hours here!"

"So what? That place would have fallen apart if it wasn't for me and you – let them survive without us for a while."

He put his hand up to beckon the waitress.

"Yes?"

"Two more glasses of this wine," ordered David, pointing to the label on the empty bottle.

"Oh, just bring another bottle," said Nicola.

"Nicola!" objected David.

"Another bottle," Nicola insisted to the waitress.

The waitress smiled and walked away.

"You're a bad influence on me," said David with a smile.

"And I can assure you, you're a very bad influence on me!"

* * *

The night before Anna and Paul were due to go into the clinic for the IVF procedure, they had a quiet evening in.

"I won't get a wink of sleep tonight," said Anna as they slowly ate their meal at the kitchen table.

"You'll have to try," Paul encouraged. "The next couple of days are going to be exhausting for you."

"Paul . . . will we go again . . . if it's not successful?"

"Let's just cross every bridge as it comes, huh?"

"I guess," she sighed and continued to play with the food on her plate with her fork.

* * *

The following morning felt so weird because of its normality. Paul felt it was such an important day and yet the sun shone as normal. The news came on as normal. They got ready as normal. They didn't even speak about it, both lost in their own thoughts. Anna drove in silence to the clinic.

They sat in the car for a minute before going in and then gave each other a quick supportive smile and got out. They held hands tightly as they walked into the clinic.

* * *

Nicola sat in her office wondering excitedly what the weekend would bring with David. She picked up her phone and dialled his office.

"Just me, just checking what you're up to for the weekend?" she quizzed.

"I'm off on a skiing trip to Switzerland after work this evening. Did I not mention?"

"No – no, you didn't." She didn't try to hide the disappointment in her voice.

"Well, you might have assumed I was off when you saw me packing a suitcase and bringing it to work this morning."

She had hoped he was coming to stay at her apartment for the weekend.

She forced herself to sound cheery. "Well, have a lovely weekend!"

He obviously felt a little guilty because then he said, "Listen, why not come and watch me play rugby on Monday evening?"

"I'd love that!"

"Cool. Talk later." He hung up the phone.

She swivelled lightly in her chair. He had such a busy fulfilled life. He was always off doing something exciting. After a long marriage, there were a lot of gaps in her life without a husband. As if on cue her mobile rang and she knew it was Oliver before looking at the ID. She raised her eyes to heaven and decided to answer.

"What is it, Oliver?" she sounded sharp.

"Nicola, I've been trying to get through to you for three days now. The message minder is gone from your mobile and I don't think that secretary of yours is passing on my messages."

"I must have switched the message minder off by accident. What do you want?"

"I need to talk to you."

"Well, you're talking to me now. Go on."

"What I have to say is too important to say over the phone. I need to meet you. There's been a dramatic development in the search for your stolen jewellery."

That fucking jewellery, she wanted to shout.

"What dramatic development? For goodness sake, Oliver, it's hardly the Great Train Robbery!"

"I need to see you."

She sighed. She wouldn't be doing anything else over the weekend by the looks of it.

"I'll drive up to the house tomorrow. See you then," she said and switched off the phone before he could continue the conversation.

* * *

Rachel had been run off her feet all week but had enjoyed every minute of it. Now she was looking forward to the weekend. She had met Leo nearly every night and he intrigued her more and more the closer she got to him.

As Rachel came down the escalator around mid-morning, thinking about Leo, there was suddenly a huge commotion at the bottom of the lift. She stared as a youth was wrestled to the ground by security men. He was screaming loudly, causing shocked shoppers to stare. As she got to the bottom of the escalator she saw him being reefed up and a teddy bear being taken out of a holdall bag he had and he was carted off by the security men. The Security Manager was looking on and Rachel went up to him.

"What's going on?" she asked.

"That little fucker was just caught stealing red-handed."

"But he looks so young!"

"That's when you have to get them, before they cause any real damage."

"What did he steal?"

"A teddy bear."

"For goodness sake, Steve, was there any reason for such a dramatic arrest for somebody so young for something so minor?"

He looked at her, disgusted. "What's minor about it? Look, love, you do your job and leave me to do mine, all right?"

Rachel felt unnerved for the rest of the day. She didn't like to see violence and she felt the security staff had used excessive force with the youth. Leo had wanted to go out to dinner that night but she rang him up and asked if they could have a quiet night in instead.

It was six o'clock as she made her way up to Stephanie's office. She knocked and entered. Stephanie was standing behind her desk, looking out the window.

"Stephanie, I'll just leave these for you to sign on your desk, all right?"

Stephanie didn't move and said nothing.

"Stephanie?" Rachel pushed.

Stephanie turned around quickly. "Sorry! I was a million miles away. Eh – yes, leave those there and I'll go through them all later."

Stephanie kept her face down but Rachel spotted immediately that she had been crying.

"Okay, if there's nothing else?" Rachel said.

"That's all. Have a nice weekend."

* * *

Rachel had changed into casual clothes and was resting on

the couch in her flat listening to Kate Nash singing 'Foundations', when she heard the buzzer ring. She got up, pressed the buzzer and unhitched the lock on the door.

She turned Kate Nash down slightly and went back to the couch.

"Hiya!" said Leo as he bounced in, closing the door behind him. He went to her and gave her a hug.

She managed to smile back. "I'll just go put the dinner on." She got up and went into the kitchen.

* * *

Leo observed Rachel sitting on the sofa across from him after dinner as they both drank wine.

"Okay, what have I done?" he asked.

"Sorry?" She looked up from her glass.

"What have I done this time? You've hardly said two words all evening. What have I done to piss you off?"

She smiled and shook her head. "Nothing, Leo."

"So what's wrong?"

"I'm just being stupid. This kid in the store was arrested today for stealing some teddy bear."

"I heard something about it. So what?"

"I saw them arrest him, Leo. It was horrible to watch. They wrestled him to the floor and he was screaming. There were three security men on top of him. It disturbed me to see it. And of course he shouldn't have taken the blasted teddy and of course he needs to be taught a lesson, but it didn't need such force. And do you know what really pissed me off?"

"Go on."

She took a gulp of her drink. "That a little while back Arielle Moore was in the store and they threw a huge amount of goods at her for free. Watches, bracelets, you name it – all she had to do was point at something and she was getting it free. What kind of a crazy fucked-up world do we live in that we can shower a face-lifted Barbie Doll with thousands of pounds' worth of free gifts and yet throw a kid into a prison cell over taking a teddy bear?"

He got up and went over to her. Putting an arm around her, he pulled her tight.

"That's just the way things are. You can't change the world, baby. All you can do is make sure you know how it works so you're on the winning team."

"The more I think about things the more I realise that your philosophy on life isn't so crazy."

"Are you trying to tell me that you've realised that I'm always right?" he smirked at her.

She shrugged and smiled. "You've opened my eyes to a lot of things. And maybe it's my turn to wear my heart on my sleeve . . . I think I'm falling for you. And I'm not going to run away from it. I'm going to grab hold of it."

He studied her intently and kissed her hair and held her tightly.

Chapter 65

"Feeling a bit better?" asked Leo on Saturday morning as he and Rachel got ready to walk up to Kings Road to go shopping.

"Yeah. Thanks for being supportive and listening to me."

"Hey – what am I here for?"

She stopped putting on her make-up in the mirror and turned to face him. "There is something you could do to make me feel happier."

"Name it."

"Phone your mum and meet her."

His face soured as he turned and continued to button up his shirt while he looked out the window.

"Leo?"

"I wonder what Tom's party is going to be like tonight? He's usually throws a good bash."

"Leo – your mother?"

He ignored her which provoked her into saying, "I know when I see somebody in pain and, Leo, your mother is in pain."

"What are you talking about?"

"Last night when I went to her office with some papers, she had been crying, Leo."

He turned around, looked at himself in the mirror and started fixing his hair.

"Leo!" Rachel got up and walked over to him. "You know there's a problem between you and your mother. You knows she's desperate to talk to you!"

"What do you know about anything? Coming from your Bambi upbringing!"

"Probably not a lot. But how do you think I feel knowing that I'm spending the weekend with you happily going to parties, while you won't give your mother an hour? It's not fair on her. I can't face her on Monday."

"Really – what do you care?"

"I know your mother is a very decent, fair and hardworking mother and she doesn't deserve this rejection from you, just because you won't allow yourself to discuss things that have been pent up for years," she said angrily. "Now you told me that you needed me to point out what's right and wrong to you – well, I'm now screaming at you that not talking to your mother is very wrong."

"So what would you have me do?" he asked eventually.

She walked over to the phone and threw it at him.

"Ring her and arrange to meet her!" she said as he caught it.

"I can't meet her today. We're going shopping and we have Tom's party tonight."

"You have all tomorrow."

He looked at the phone for a long while and then dialled Stephanie's number.

"Leo?" Stephanie asked excitedly.

"Are you around tomorrow to talk?"

* * *

As she drove into the driveway of their house, Nicola felt nostalgic. It felt safe and warm to her, but not enough for her to want to stay there. She let herself in and Oliver was waiting for her in the lounge. He looked delighted to see her, came up and gave her a big hug and kiss on the cheek. It all felt very secure. She wanted to leave.

"You look great! How are you feeling?" he asked, still hugging her.

"All right." She removed herself from his arms. "A little better, if the truth be known. But it's going to take a long time for me to be myself again."

He nodded understandingly. "Maybe you should sit down before I say what I'm about to say."

She sat down on the couch.

"We've found the guy who bought the jewellery off the scum who attacked you. A real low life called Joseph Maguire. He's the brains behind it all. Doesn't get his own hands dirty but employs the likes of the guy who mugged you to steal and supply back to him."

"Well, at least he's off the streets," said Nicola.

"Now I want you to be brave about this, Nicola . . . he's admitted that he had your wedding ring and engagement ring melted down and refashioned into something else and sold off. They no longer exist."

Nicola wanted to kick her shoes off and do a dance.

"It might take me a little longer to get over all this," she said, managing to sound sad.

"I know. I know. However, he did admit to us who he sold your necklace to." He stopped and said nothing for a while.

Oh good, I would like the necklace back, thought Nicola.

"So what's the problem? Just arrest the bastard and get on with it," she urged.

"He sold the necklace to a fellow called Leo Holden."

"Leo Holden?" Nicola tried to register the news.

"We did a quick investigation. He's known to the local police and has quite a reputation for dealing stuff. More of a wide boy than a true criminal. We tracked him down to his address in the East End and discovered he's working at Franklyns. He's Stephanie Holden's son."

Nicola was speechless.

"We were about to arrest him but I thought, because of the circumstances, I'd better talk to you beforehand."

"Yes . . . Oliver, you did right . . . what would he be charged with exactly?"

"Receiving stolen goods."

"Could he not just say that he didn't know they were stolen?"

"Not with all the evidence Maguire gave us. Besides, we've built quite a portfolio against Holden. Once we started digging we discovered he has received quite a lot of knocked-off goods over the years. He's sunk this time."

"Oliver . . . this will have repercussions for Franklyns. Can you just sit on this for a short while, until I decide how to handle this in the store?"

"Of course – anything you want. I was about to cook lunch. Will you stay for something to eat?"

She stood up. "No, I'd better get back to London. Thanks, Oliver."

As she pulled out of the driveway, with Oliver waving her off, she was already dialling Karl Furstin's number.

"Karl, it's Nicola . . . I think we've got her."

* * *

Rachel felt happy as she and Leo, arms around each other's waist, walked down the street to Tom's house. Tom lived on a street full of large semi-detached houses in south London. It was now Leo's turn to be on edge. He was dreading going to his mother's apartment the next day. After their last confrontation there had been too many wounds opened that would now have to go under analysis and he would just prefer not to go through it. He was even more surprised that he had phoned Stephanie. And as he and Rachel walked up to Tom's front door and rang the doorbell, he was amazed at the lengths he obviously would go to for Rachel.

The front door of the house door swung open and there was Tom, a bottle of whiskey in one hand and a bottle of bourbon in the other.

"Here's the man!" declared Tom as he slapped his arm around Leo's back and they headed in to the party.

"Tom, you remember Rachel, don't you?"

"How could I forget? Leo, you trade girlfriends quicker than I trade British Airways shares!"

Rachel's smile dropped at Tom's words and she turned and walked into the sitting-room.

Leo handed Tom a bottle of vodka and snapped, "Maybe I should ram this down that gob of yours! Less of the wisecracks!" He quickly went into the sitting-room to find Rachel.

"Has everyone lost their sense of humour all of a sudden?" called Tom.

The party wasn't very packed but Rachel found the people friendly. Most of them worked with Tom and used to work with Leo when he had been at their City firm.

She guessed most of them were barrow boys – working-class people who had gone to work on the trading floor at the Stock Exchange and worked their way up by sheer sweat, toil and aggression. She imagined money came and went quickly with them as did everything else in their life. There was a barbecue going on out in the garden and she and Leo went outside to eat some food while reggae music played.

Noticing she was being a little quiet, Leo said, "Tom was only joking. He only meant that he was used to seeing me with Daniella and now I'm here with her friend."

"I know what he meant!" she snapped. "He's only pointing out what I'm trying not to think about myself!"

He put her arm around the waist. "You can't help the circumstances in which you meet the person you fall in love with."

She turned to him quickly. "Those are strong words you're using."

"I know. I can't explain how I feel about you. From the first time I met you."

She snuggled closer to him.

Rachel began to relax and the party started to swing. The reggae music was pumped up higher and people started to dance and laugh a lot. Here she was at a brilliant party in London, with her dream job, and the man she felt she had waited all her life to meet. She had been so scared about her move to London and yet everything had eventually worked out fine.

* * *

They had been at the party for a couple of hours. Rachel

was out in the garden talking to some of people who used to work with Leo. Leo had been missing for a while and she wondered where he had got to. She went into the house and looked for him.

She spotted a pretty girl called Katie who seemed to be Tom's girlfriend – for the night if nothing else – and went over to her.

"You didn't see Leo anywhere, did you?" Rachel asked with a smile.

"Oh, I saw him disappear with Tom. I would say they won't be long," said Katie.

"Can I get you anything?"

Katie was obviously playing the hostess, thought Rachel. She looked down at her empty glass "Yeah, another glass of wine would be lovely, thanks." Rachel handed her glass over.

Katie looked at the glass, confused "Not quite what I meant, love. I mean do you want me to get you *anything?*"

"I don't quite get you?"

"Cocaine, speed, ecstasy? It's all going a-begging if you want some?"

"Oh!" Rachel looked surprised "No, I'm fine, thanks all the same."

Katie shrugged and studied Rachel "How long have you been going out with Leo anyway?"

"Really not that long – why?"

"You just don't seem his normal type. That's all."

"And what's his normal type?"

"Well, a little more relaxed and laid back than you seem to be for a start, love."

"I'm very relaxed and enjoying myself, thank you very much."

"Not what I'd call relaxed." Katie shrugged again and

smiled at her. "I'll just go get you a top-up."

Katie headed off to fill Rachel's glass, then Leo arrived back at her side with Tom.

"Where were you?" asked Rachel.

"Just talking a bit of business," said Leo, put his arm around her waist. "Enjoying yourself?"

"Yeah, it's fun," Rachel nodded.

Katie arrived back with the glass "Now, Rachel, this will help you relax, love."

* * *

Leo opened Rachel's door while at the same time holding onto her in case she slid down onto the floor. He had one of her arms around his neck and his own arm around her waist supporting her. He kicked the door shut behind them and half-carried her into her bedroom.

"Such a brilliant party! I enjoyed every minute of it!" she said, her speech slurred.

"Sure. Come on now. Take it easy," he said as he lay her down on the bed.

"I feel fantastic!" she declared.

"You won't in the morning!" He went into the kitchen, poured a pint glass of water and got himself a can of beer from the fridge. Returning to her room, he sat on the bed and she managed to sit up with encouragement.

"Drink this," he insisted, raising the glass to her mouth and forcing her to drink.

After drinking as much as she could, she lay back on the bed and smiled inanely at Leo.

"I've never met anybody like you."

"I don't know if that's a good thing for you."

He studied her intently. He'd never seen her like this

before. She hadn't had that many drinks so he was mystified how she could be *that* drunk.

"Just try and get some sleep. You're going to have a thumping headache tomorrow, I can assure you."

He thought about the party. She had been fine and then had gone completely out of it in a matter of minutes. He remembered Katie bringing Rachel a drink.

He went into the living-room and dialled Tom on his mobile. When Tom answered he could hear the party still going on in the background.

"Tom, Rachel is in a bad way. What's the fucking story? She didn't drink that much."

"Eh, sorry, but I think Katie gave her a little pick-me-up."

"She spiked her drink?"

"Yeah. Katie said she was all uptight and needed something to relax her. Katie said you'd get bored with her pretty quickly otherwise and she was doing her a favour."

"She's some dozy cow, that Katie. Rachel's not like that, Tom. She doesn't touch drugs or anything like that."

"Ah, relax, she wasn't given anything too strong."

"I'm really pissed off about this," said Leo and he turned his mobile off.

Back in the bedroom he lay out beside Rachel, leaning on his elbow looking down at her as she dozed off to sleep. He took a gulp from his can as he remembered the party. How she had suddenly been as high as a kite and she yapped to everyone there. How she had knocked back the drink and insisted that he roll her a joint, which she had proceeded to hungrily smoke. How she had wanted to do a line of coke when she saw some of his friends snorting it. He stroked her hair protectively as he remembered her trying to climb up on a table to dance, before he finally convinced her the party was over and they needed to go home.

Chapter 66

Rachel tried to sit up but the whole room was swimming around her.

"Leo!" she called.

"In here!" he called from the sitting-room.

She swung her legs off the bed and immediately felt a retching in her stomach. She hung her head down while she tried to remember the night. She was wasted. She struggled up and carefully made her way into the sitting room where Leo was showered and dressed and looking full of health and life as he drank a cup of coffee.

"I have never felt so bad in my life." Her voice was barely audible as she clutched her stomach and closed her eyes.

"Do you want something to eat or drink?" he asked.

She suddenly raced into the bathroom and slammed the door. He winced as he heard grotesque vomiting sounds coming from the bathroom. She didn't emerge for fifteen minutes. She was as white as a sheet when she came out, her hand over her face.

"I need to get back to bed. I feel like shit," she said, heading back to the bedroom.

"Okay. I'm going over to meet my mum, remember?"

He could see her manage to nod before she climbed into bed again.

* * *

Leo paced up and down outside Chelsea Harbour while he finished off a cigarette. He glanced at his watch. He was already thirty minutes late. He threw the cigarette on the ground and stamped on it.

* * *

Her arms folded, Stephanie walked up and down by the glass windows of her apartment. The view of the river below her looked lovely in the Sunday sunshine.

Just when she decided that Leo wasn't coming, there was a knock on her door. She steadied herself and went over and answered it.

Leo stood there looking uneasy.

"Come in!" she said. "Do you want anything to eat or drink? Have you had lunch?"

"No, I'm fine . . . thanks." He strolled over to the windows.

There was an awkward silence and she realised he was leaving it to her to do the talking. Didn't he always? She decided to break the ice. "Leo . . . I've been hearing great things about you. David Stafford is singing your praises, saying you're amazing."

He shrugged. "I wouldn't want to embarrass you."

"I've been so upset since we had that argument at work . . . I've been under such huge pressure and I'm sorry if I came across as too strong."

"Well, I'm doing nothing to jeopardise your position now, am I?"

"No, as I said, David can't say enough good things about you."

"Good. I wouldn't want to fuck up your career the way I fucked up your life."

She felt his words were like a slap. "Whoever said you fucked up my life? Whatever gave you that impression?" He continued to stare at her.

She went over to the couch and sat down. Rubbing her temples she said, "I did . . . obviously."

He studied her and saw how upset she really was.

"You know, somebody said something to me recently and it got me thinking," he said slowly. "She told me that I felt guilty because I took a great future from you when you got pregnant so soon and you had to give up your singing career and the great life you were having back then. You swapped it all for a dingy council flat and me. I never looked at it like that before. I resented you for being so pre-occupied with your career when in fact I was angry with myself for causing you to have a bad life."

Stephanie looked up at him. "I was expecting you to tell me I was a bad mother, and I could take that, but I think it's worse to hear you blaming yourself, Leo. Whatever has happened in my life and whatever has gone wrong or right, I'm responsible, not you and it's just stupid to blame yourself . . . I got us into that dingy council flat, not you . . . and I was the one who had to get us out, which I managed to do as well . . . But I couldn't do everything on my own, something had to give and I should have given you more direction in life."

"I've never said you were a bad mother."

"But I know you think it. Why else do you ignore my calls, never meet me, pretend I don't exist?"

"Because we're awkward together . . . we've grown apart . . . and I don't want to cause you any more hassle."

"Hassle? I'm your mother. That's what I'm here for – to deal with your hassle."

He laughed hollowly. "You don't know just how much hassle I could cause you . . . you're better off keeping a distance from me, for your own sake . . . unless you want that brilliant career you've worked at so hard to come tumbling down."

She got up and raised her voice. "What are you talking about, Leo? My career has always come second to you. I only worked so hard so I could give you things. If you're ever in trouble, I want to be there with you."

"I can take care of myself. I've been doing it for a long time and nobody can get the better of me."

"Leo, youth is very arrogant. You don't know what's around the corner to bring us crashing down. I know. I've been there."

He threw his hands in the air. "And we're back to the point where your life came crashing down because of me!"

"Look, I thought at the time it was crashing down . . . but it wasn't . . . it was just changing direction and for the better. I admit over the years I've nursed dreams of what might have been. But recently I had an opportunity to see what my life might have been like. And I didn't want it. I'm so glad for the life I've had. I really am. I wouldn't want it any other way. Except that I want things to be better between us . . . that's more important than anything else to me now."

Leo looked steadily at her. "You really mean that?"

"I mean it."

He nodded. "I'll be around – if you want to meet up any time."

She smiled. "I would love that."

He looked at his watch and thought about Rachel. She was in such a state when he left her flat. He wanted to get back to her to see if she was all right.

"Listen, I'm not being funny but I have to be somewhere. I'm going to have to run."

"Okay," she nodded.

"Maybe we'll meet up for dinner during the week?" he suggested.

"I would love that," she said.

She walked him to the door and opened it. They stood eyeing each other for a few seconds.

"Is this where I fall into your arms and declare 'Mama?'" he said with a grin.

"You're such a cynical person!" she said, but she was half laughing.

"See you tomorrow at work." He gave her a kiss on the cheek and headed quickly off to the elevator.

* * *

Rachel had given Leo a key to her apartment and he let himself in.

He found her curled up on the couch in her dressing-gown, clutching her stomach, but she had some more colour in her cheeks.

"How are you feeling?" he said sitting beside her and hugging her.

"Oh, Leo, I feel like shit!"

"I shouldn't have left you. Did you manage to eat something?"

"I tried, but I just barfed it up again."

"You'll be fine . . . you just need to rest and drink lots of water." He hugged her tightly.

* * *

It was Sunday night and Nicola was alone in her apartment. She had been watching television, her legs up on the couch. She hadn't heard from David all weekend. She turned off the television with the remote, got up off the couch and closed the curtains, blocking off the fantastic view of Canary Wharf. She turned on the sound system and put on some classical music, then went and sat back on the couch. She felt very alone and poured herself another glass of wine.

Chapter 67

Nicola was walking through the store on Monday morning when she saw two salesgirls behind a counter staring at her. One whispered something to the other and they both started giggling. Hardly believing the audacity of them, she marched over to them.

"What exactly do you think you're laughing at?" she demanded.

"Nothing, Mrs Newman," said one as their faces went poker-straight but their eyes still seemed to be laughing.

"Get on with your work!" she snapped and walked away. As she turned a corner she heard them erupt into giggles. She was going to turn and reprimand them again, but something stopped her.

* * *

Rachel had felt better that morning. She had a long hot shower and got ready to go to work.

"I've never had a headache like that before," she said as she and Leo got off the bus outside Franklyns.

"You were in a bad way all right," said Leo. "Are you

okay to work today?"

"I have to be. I've too much on and it would look very bad pulling a sickie so soon into the job. I'm just going over to Starbucks to get a coffee. Are you still on for tonight?"

"Yeah. Come round to my place," said Leo.

"BBC are filming something in the store, so I might be late."

"I'll see you when I see you then." He bent forward and kissed her, then bounced down the street.

Paul was walking down the street and saw them kiss. He caught up with Rachel.

"Good weekend?" he asked.

"Eh, yeah, busy."

"That's good. Can I ask you a personal question?"

"Sure," she shrugged.

"Are you seeing that Holden guy?"

She felt herself go bright red. "Yes, what of it?"

"I wouldn't have put the two of you together, that's all."

"Why not?"

"Well, I know his type. He's full of himself and full of trouble."

"I think I'll be the judge of that."

They reached the staff entrance and he stopped and turned to face her. "I know he might be Stephanie Holden's son but you're barking up the wrong tree if you think you'll sleep your way to the top with him. It's David Stafford whose door you should be knocking on."

She stared at him and her eyes became teary with anger. "You're a fucking asshole," she said before pushing past him and walking into the store.

* * *

Stephanie was in her office looking through sketches. She reached over to answer her ringing phone.

"There's a Danny McKay on the phone for you, Ms Holden," said Reception.

Stephanie paused, not knowing what to do.

"Ms Holden?"

"Yes, put him through." She kept her voice steady. "Hi, Danny."

"Stephanie, how are you?"

"I'm all right."

"Listen, I'm actually in London today. Can I meet up with you?"

"Do you know, I don't think that's such a good idea, Danny. I'm very busy and –"

"For old times' sake?"

She sighed. "What time and where?"

She arranged to meet him at three, surprised that he picked a little café in a back street in Kensington.

He smiled at her brightly as she entered the café. He was seated in a far corner and she made her way over to him.

He got up and kissed her on the cheek.

"Just a coffee," she said over to the waitress.

He stirred his own coffee. "You left Barrington Hall without saying goodbye."

"Do you blame me?"

"I don't understand."

"I don't take kindly to waking up in the middle of the night and having a stranger sitting on my bed!"

"What?"

"Karl Furstin. I don't know what the fuck was going on but I do know the whole weekend was some kind of a plan to get me to meet Karl Furstin."

Danny's face was full of concern. "I had no part in that, Stephanie."

She watched him for a while. "I believe you hadn't. But that stupid bitch you're married to was in on it, I can assure you."

"You mustn't be unkind about Hetty, Stephanie."

"Why bloody not?" Stephanie demanded, her face angry. "She's a twit who hasn't done a day's work all her life. She takes everything as if it's her birthright and she's friends with horrendous people like Karl Furstin. You know, I spent years being consumed with envy for that woman. I mean, look at it from my point of view. I was in love with you but you were seduced by all her wealth and connections. I was living on social handouts with a young child looking at you two in glossy magazines with this unbelievable lifestyle."

Danny's eyes widened more with every word she spoke.

"And you know what," she continued, leaning forward, her face animated. "I was envious of a silly dream. Because when I went and saw your life close up, I didn't want it. In fact, I ran away from it. And so I've spent years thinking I loved somebody that I really didn't and being envious of a life that I really despised."

"Well, that's not my fault or Hetty's."

"I know. It's mine. And I'm angry with myself for missing opportunities with people that could have made me happy. I've spent the last twenty-odd years being bitter and not allowing myself to take happiness where I could find it. With my son, with other men who were actually real and who actually might have cared for me if I had given them the chance and taken down my walls. Instead of some fading pop star in a glossy magazine who I once had a thing with!"

Danny laid a hand on her arm as if to halt her.

"Stephanie. You're right. That's all in the past now. But today I've come here as a friend, an old friend. A friend who has something important to say." He paused. "I've known the Furstins a long time and they are not nice people. Don't take them on."

* * *

Conrad Richardson sat in disbelief in his office at Barons Bank as Nicola told the story about Leo Holden. David Stafford sat to his right, equally shocked.

"I can't believe it . . . it's very, very disturbing," Conrad said eventually.

"I know. I'm in shock myself," said Nicola. "But unfortunately it's the truth. Leo Holden is nothing but a common thief, presently employed at Franklyns on his mother's insistence. I managed to use my contacts to hold off Leo being arrested so the store can act quickly to limit the damage that has been done. The type of crime that he is associated with is nasty and horrible. Violent physical attacks and robbery on defenceless women. I should know – I was a victim of it myself."

"He wasn't directly involved in the attacks though, was he?" asked David.

"Does it matter? He received the goods and mud sticks. Once Leo is arrested, it will be only a matter of time before it becomes common knowledge and Franklyns will be seriously damaged. I can see the headlines now: *Franklyns' Boss in Violent Theft Scandal.*"

"We must act to distance ourselves and the store from Stephanie Holden immediately," said Conrad. "We'll summon her tomorrow and fire her."

"My very thoughts," agreed Nicola.

"This is going to have major repercussions for the stock-market float," warned David. "It will significantly delay it. In fact we're in a crisis. Once Stephanie leaves and the facts of her son's arrest emerge, it will just scare the city. The store won't be ready in time for the float. Who's going to replace her? The investors won't touch us."

Nicola nodded in agreement. But *our* future is very bright, she thought looking at David.

* * *

That evening David charged through the rugby field with the ball, avoiding tackles as the onlookers cheered.

"Come on, David! Come on, David!" Nicola screamed from the sidelines.

When victory came for David's side Nicola shouted for joy, jumping up and down.

His team-mates looked curiously at her as they made their way to the changing rooms. He jogged over to her and she threw her arms around him and hugged him tightly.

"You were brilliant! Absolutely brilliant!" she screamed.

"Steady!" David said half-laughing and half-serious, conscious of some of his friends looking on bemused.

"I never saw anybody play as well as you!" Nicola said, too loud by far.

"You obviously don't watch much rugby then! Listen, give me a chance to clean up and then we usually go across to that pub for a few drinks, okay?" He nodded over to a bar across the road.

"Okay!" She swelled with happiness.

* * *

The pub was packed after the game as Nicola fought her way through to the bar and ordered drinks.

"There you go!" She put a bottle of Miller in David's hand and chinked her own bottle against his.

Nicola was dressed in a designer dress and David felt he should he have pointed out to her beforehand that everyone would be casually dressed at the match. Having said that, he was slightly baffled that he would have to point such a thing out. Even more baffled that Nicola didn't seem to notice that she was the only one dressed up to the nines.

"I so enjoyed the game. It was magnificent!"

A couple of David's friends heard her and laughed quietly.

"Hardly magnificent, Nicola. It was an average game."

"So modest!"

She looked at him dreamily for a while, and spotted his face clouding with concern.

"What's wrong?" she asked.

"I'm just thinking of this whole Leo Holden thing. It's shocking."

Nicola tried to avoid a 'told you so' expression. She failed.

"I mean, he seemed like a spirited kid. But I didn't think he'd be involved in this kind of thing."

"I did warn you!"

"I know you did." His tone was irritated. "This has really fucked up the store. I don't know what we're going to do. Just when everything was going so well. I was really confident about the float with all the changes Stephanie was making. Now I have to recommend that we suspend the stock-market float indefinitely. And how is Barons Bank going to recoup our losses now?"

"I wouldn't worry too much. Life has a habit of delivering nice surprises!" said Nicola.

She handed him her bottle of Miller. "Just hold that, will you, while I pop to the loo."

As she walked away, one of his friends came up to him and put a hand on his shoulder

"Is that your new squeeze, David?"

"Umm, yeah, I guess," said David.

"She's certainly different!"

* * *

Rachel let herself into Leo's house with the key he had given her.

"Hi, it's just me!" she said as she walked down the small hall into the living-room.

She stopped in her tracks as she saw Daniella seated on the couch, her legs crossed, both her arms stretched out along the back of the couch, smiling and looking as glamorous as ever.

"Hello, darling!" said Daniella smiling. "Long time no see!"

"Daniella!" Rachel looked around. "Where's Leo?"

Leo came out of the kitchen drying his hands.

"Hiya. See who's back?" he said casually.

"Yes, I see! But . . . why aren't you in Italy?"

"Oh, don't mention the war, sweetie! Giovanni turned out to be a big disappointment in every way. It started with a drink . . . and it ended in tears!"

Rachel looked at Leo, searching for some indication of

what was going on, some reassurance from him.

"I would have brought you back a prezzie but I kind of needed to get out of Rome in a hurry – you know what it's like!"

"Not really, but –"

"Back to my Leo! I've behaved like a right bitch, I admit it. But you forgive me, don't you, darling?" Daniella got up and went to Leo and put her arms around him.

Rachel stared in disbelief as Leo looked back at her, expressionless.

"Leo?" Rachel asked, a pleading look on her face.

"You know how it is, Rachel," was all Leo said with a shrug.

"Thanks for keeping an eye on this one for me, for keeping the seat warm, as it were," said Daniella. "Leo said you've been an absolute star!"

"I –" Rachel began.

"But I'm back now, so you're a little surplus to requirement," Daniella smiled.

Rachel felt herself overcome by humiliation and anger as she threw Leo's door key down on the table and turned to leave.

"Oh, and Rachel – the necklace?" Leo called after her.

She snapped off the necklace in disbelief, threw it at him and ran out of the house.

He caught the necklace as it came through the air at him and listened as the front door banged.

Chapter 68

On Tuesday, Nicola was sitting in her office, on the phone to Karl Furstin.

"Everyone's shocked, of course. Stephanie Holden has been called to Barons Bank for a meeting at two where she will be fired. From what I hear, the stock-market float is being shelved. The road is wide open for you, Karl."

"What can I say, Nicola? You have surpassed yourself."

* * *

Rachel didn't venture out of her office all day as she buried herself in work. She was terrified of bumping into Leo and at the same time half hoping he would come into her office, to give her some explanation, to say that what had happened last night with Daniella was a silly joke. But she knew he wouldn't come.

* * *

Conrad, David and Nicola were sitting in Conrad's office at Barons's Bank waiting for Stephanie's arrival. It was almost two. Nicola tried not to look too pleased as the two men looked so unhappy but she was so looking forward to Stephanie's dismissal and humiliation. There was a knock on the door and the three gave each other a look of expectation. The door opened and Conrad's secretary came in.

"You can show Ms Holden straight in," said Conrad to the secretary.

"She's actually not here yet. I'm just delivering this letter that arrived by courier." She approached his desk and handed over the white envelope with Conrad's name on it. He looked at the envelope, then opened it, unfolded the letter inside and read.

Dear Conrad,

I resign my position as Brand Director at Franklyns from today,

Yours sincerely,

Stephanie Holden

Conrad looked up at the others, stunned.

* * *

Leo walked down the Embankment looking out at the Thames as it drifted slowly by in the night air. He stopped and looked out across the water. He reached into his pocket and took out the necklace. Looking at it, he gently rubbed the precious stones. Then he fired it into the air and watched it drop into the river.

Chapter 69

Nicola was on her mobile to Oliver outside Conrad's office.

"There's something up, Oliver. She didn't turn up to the meeting to fire her and instead sent in a resignation letter. I've just checked with the store and Leo Holden didn't show up for work today."

"They must have got wind of what was going on, somehow," said Oliver.

"Well, don't waste any more time then. Get over to his house and arrest the bastard!"

She closed over her phone and re-entered Conrad's office.

"This is all a bit of a coincidence. Leo didn't show up for work today either. I've just been on to the police and they're going over to his house to arrest him now," Nicola explained.

"Thank goodness for your police contacts, Nicola. We would be completely in the dark otherwise."

"Hmmm," said David pensively.

Nicola sat down in her chair. "They'll ring back as soon as they've arrested him."

Half an hour later and Nicola's mobile rang again. She picked it up and answered it, seeing it was Oliver's number.

"Yes?" She looked at Conrad and David's worried faces as she spoke.

"Nicola, he's gone!" said Oliver. "We've just been over to his house and there's no sign of him. The house is cleared out. He's done a runner."

"I cannot believe it! How did they find out what was going to happen? There must be some leak in your office!"

"There isn't, Nicola," Oliver spoke sternly.

"Well, what can we do now?"

"I'd say he's long gone. I'll go to his mother to see if we can find out anything from her."

"Well, get over to her before she does a runner too!"

Nicola snapped her mobile shut. "Did you hear that? He's done a runner!"

Conrad and David looked visibly relaxed.

"That's quite a relief," said Conrad.

"What do you mean? He's escaped!" said Nicola.

"I know but it's for the best," said Conrad. "If Leo can't be arrested then this won't come out. Stephanie has resigned and so the crisis is over. Nobody need find out about this grubby little business but ourselves."

"I don't know if I can believe your attitude!" said Nicola, outraged.

"Oh, come Nicola, live in the real world," said Conrad. "We can just say Stephanie left due to personal reasons. There will be no court appearance for the son. Everything's fine."

Nicola tried to contain her anger.

"Except for the stock-market float," David said looking at Conrad. "Without Stephanie, we really have to shelve that."

* * *

Stephanie stood in the middle of Waterloo Station with Danny.

"Oh, where is he?" said Stephanie looking at her watch. "He's going to miss the train!" She looked down at the Eurostar ticket she was holding for him.

"Here he is now!" Danny pointed in the other direction.

Leo was racing through the station, a bag over his shoulder.

"Leo! I thought they'd got you or something!" said Stephanie as she hugged him.

"You know me, always late!" said Leo, grinning.

"Here's your ticket and here's something to keep you going," She handed him the ticket and a wallet. He opened the wallet and it was stacked with Euros.

"No, I don't want this." He pushed the wallet forcibly back at her.

She shook her head. "I'll never understand you, Leo. You'd take from strangers but you wouldn't take from me?"

"You work too hard for it."

"I have plenty." She put the wallet in his jacket pocket. "And what's the good of it all if I can't share it with you. Will you be all right?"

"Yes, I've got some good friends in Paris."

"Promise me you'll stay out of trouble?" she pleaded.

"I promise."

"Seriously, if Danny hadn't tipped us off you'd be in a prison cell now."

"As I told you, I didn't steal that necklace. I bought it

but I admit I did know it was knocked off."

"Oh, Leo, just please be careful! And promise me you'll keep in regular contact with me?"

"I will . . . I'll never forgive myself for ruining things for you at Franklyns, ruining your career after you've worked so hard to get to where you are."

"I'll recover. As I said to you on Sunday, my career was never my priority – you are."

"I know that now," said Leo.

"You'd really better go or you'll miss that train," urged Danny.

Leo shook Danny's hand. "Thanks for tipping us off. I'd like meet you again and have a proper talk."

"You will – now just go!" urged Danny.

Leo gave Stephanie a hug and then ran off to the train. Stephanie and Danny watched as he got on and waved at him.

Danny put an arm around her. "You all right?"

"Yes. I think at last Leo and I are all right, regardless of the circumstances. Nothing else matters after that."

The train pulled out of the station.

They turned and walked away.

"I'll never be able to thank you enough for letting us know what Furstin had planned, Danny. If it wasn't for you, I'd be sacked now and disgraced and Leo would be arrested. I owe you so much."

Stephanie thought back to the previous day in the café in Kensington when he told her that the police had arrested a criminal called Joseph Maguire who had sold a stolen necklace on to Leo. They were now about to arrest Leo. Also Barons Bank had found out through Nicola's husband and were about to fire her and destroy her because of the robbery. Hetty knew through her close friendship with the Furstins, who were preparing to move in for the kill once Stephanie was fired. She remembered racing back to Franklyns from the café and storming into Leo's office and telling him what was happening.

"Hetty won't find out, will she?" she asked Danny now. "You won't get into trouble at home over this?"

"Hetty wouldn't think in a million years that I would tip you off. Anyway I'm going to make a few changes when I get back to Barrington Hall. I do not like that friendship she has with Elka Furstin."

They came to the entrance of the station. They stopped walking and faced each other.

"Well, anyway, I'll always be grateful," said Stephanie

"And I didn't do it just for you," said Danny. "When I found out that Leo was Gary Cosgrave's son ... well, I couldn't stand back and see him go down. I was friends with Gary right up to the end and he was always in trouble – and I was always stepping in and rescuing him. He had that way about him, kept drawing you back no matter what he did. He'd expect me to look out for Leo."

"He sounds a bit like Leo . . . I never really knew him, I guess, and it's too late now."

Chapter 70

Paul was driving home from work that evening when he spotted Rachel standing at a bus stop. He quickly pulled over and wound down the passenger window.

"Hi there, want a lift?"

She looked at him, surprised to see him. "There will be a bus coming along in a couple of minutes," she said.

"Don't be daft. I'll drive you right to the door."

She hesitated for a moment, then opened the door and sat in.

She gave him the directions to her flat in a cold voice.

"That's on my way. I live in Wimbledon. I mostly get the Tube. But I'm not ending up in the pub after work as much these days and so I'm driving."

"Really." She stared right ahead.

"Listen, Rachel. I want to apologise. You were right. I was a complete asshole with what I said yesterday. I didn't mean it. I'd just had a stressful weekend and I think I was trying to be funny."

She glanced at him. "Ha ha! Really hilarious, accusing somebody of wanting to sleep their way to the top."

"It was a daft thing to say. Really sorry. Why are we

always having some falling out over something or other?"

"Maybe we're destined to just not get on and should avoid each other in the future."

He looked quickly over at her and then concentrated on the traffic. "That would be daft. I like you, Rachel. I really do."

She turned to face him and her eyes burned with tears.

"Well, if you like me, why did you say such an upsetting thing?"

"Because I'm a fucking asshole, as you said."

He drove in silence for a while. He pulled into her street.

"Just here on the right," she said.

He parked the car and turned to her. "Rachel – I want to –"

"You know," she interrupted angrily, "I spent all day yesterday thinking about what you said. Wondering if other people would think the same thing. That I was seeing Leo just because of who his mother is! I didn't want to start seeing Leo . . . I did everything I could to avoid going out with him! It just happened!"

"Hey-hey-hey!" He was taken aback by her anger. "What's all this about?"

She dabbed her eyes with a handkerchief.

He put a hand on her shoulder. "It was just a dumb remark. It's really not worth getting this upset about. I am really sorry."

She got out of the car, slammed the door shut and walked across the pavement and up the steps to her door.

Paul jumped out of the car and followed her.

"Rachel – I can't let you go like this – are you all right?" he asked, full of concern.

"Forget about it, Paul. I'm overreacting. It doesn't matter any more anyway."

"Come on – let's go up and have a chat," he urged, seeing how distressed she was.

"You don't need to listen to my problems," she said.

"I don't, but I'd like to."

She thought for a moment. "Come on up," she said, opening the door.

They went inside.

"Nice flat," admired Paul, looking around the living-room.

"Isn't it? Leo found it for me," she said, not disguising the bitterness in her voice.

He followed her into the kitchen and spotted two empty bottles of wine on the table. She went to a cupboard and took out another bottle of red and, opening it, poured herself a hefty glass.

"Drink?" she asked.

"Just a small one. I'm driving."

She poured him a glass and handed him it to him, then walked out into the living-room and sat on the couch.

"So what's all this about?" he asked. "You're not this upset over an ignorant throwaway remark by me, are you?"

"No – I'm this upset because I'm a fucking fool."

He sat down opposite her on the other sofa.

"Why?"

"Leo's dumped me. He didn't have the courtesy to tell me he'd dumped me. He just started up again with the glamorous Daniella. Remember her?"

"Yeah . . . I'm sorry."

She took a big gulp. "So am I."

"But you looked very together yesterday when I saw you."

"That's what I thought too. I can't believe how stupid

I've been. Every sense I had was screaming at me to stay away from him. He was so obviously bad news. So obviously self-serving and selfish. He didn't even try to hide it! In fact he boasted about it! And I just wander blindly into falling in love with him."

"Sometimes we can't help ourselves," Paul offered.

"Or we choose not to help ourselves." She stood up and went to look out the window, holding her glass.

"Is that your excuse?"

"Huh?"

"For sleeping with Christine and whoever else you've had affairs with?" She turned around to face him.

"Maybe."

"That's a fucking lame excuse. I never particularly liked Christine but you treated her in the same way that Leo has treated me. Using somebody and then just discarding them!"

"I have no excuse for past behaviour, Rachel, only to say I regret it."

"I've met your wife and she's lovely. She doesn't deserve how you've treated her."

He shrugged. "I know."

She poured herself another large glass of wine. "So why don't you just do yourself and her a favour and end your sham of a marriage?"

He was taken aback by the bitter tone in her voice. "I actually love Anna very much."

"Well, it doesn't look like it from where I'm standing," said Rachel.

Paul was surprised by her cynicism, her simplified way of looking at things. And yet that was how his marriage might look to her.

"You've so much going for you, Rachel. Don't let this

experience with Leo Holden make you bitter and cynical."

"Leo used to say cynical is good – you never get disappointed when you're cynical. He was right. He has taught me so much."

* * *

Oliver and a police officer arrived at Chelsea Harbour and got the concierge to call up to Stephanie to say they wanted to speak to her. The concierge directed them up to her apartment.

To Oliver's surprise, he was greeted by a man in his fifties wearing glasses at Stephanie's door.

"We're here to interview Stephanie Holden," said Oliver to the man.

"Yes, come on in. She's here."

They walked into the apartment and found Stephanie seated on the couch, in front of the windows with the darkening skyline of London behind her.

"I am Commissioner Oliver Newman and this is DI James Parter. We wish to speak to Stephanie Holden."

"This is Ms Holden," said the man. "And I am Alex Amhurst of Amhurst & Co, Solicitors."

Oliver looked at the solicitor in surprise. "I see. Ms Holden, we have a few questions about your son. We're investigating him over an allegation of receiving stolen goods as a result of a violent robbery."

"My client is happy to answer any questions you have," said Alex.

Oliver looked at Alex in irritation. He studied Stephanie who was sitting confidently and relaxed, her legs crossed.

"When did you last see your son, Ms Holden?" asked Oliver.

"My client last saw her son at work yesterday," said Alex.

Oliver looked at Alex with more irritation, then back at Stephanie. "Have you spoken to your son today?"

"My client last spoke to her son yesterday at work. There has been no communication between them today."

"Are you aware that your son is not at his home and his house is cleared of all personal possessions?"

"My client is not aware of that, no."

"Do you know where your son is now, Ms Holden?"

"My client is not aware of her son's whereabouts."

"Do you have a new contact number for your son, Ms Holden? As his old one seems to be disconnected. "

"My client does not have any new contact number for her son."

"Ms Holden, I believe you resigned from your position at Franklyns today. Why?"

"My client resigned due to a personality clash with another member of management, a Mrs Nicola Newman. She's considering taking a tribunal case against Mrs Newman for bullying."

Oliver shot a look of shock from Alex to Stephanie. "Your resignation was nothing to do then with your son's impending arrest?"

"How could it be, when she knew nothing of it?" said Alex.

"And how come her solicitor just happened to be here when we called tonight then?" asked Oliver, a grim smile on his face.

"I often take late tea with Ms Holden. We share a mutual hobby – botany."

Oliver looked at his DI with a knowing but helpless look. He studied Stephanie, sitting there in her cool confidence and realised they had been beaten.

"Any further questions?" asked Alex.

"Just one," said Oliver. "Does Ms Holden ever speak for herself."

"Why should she?" said Stephanie. "When she can afford one of London's top lawyers to do the talking for her?"

* * *

Rachel had finished the bottle of wine and opened another. She filled Paul's glass again.

"I'm driving, Rachel, I can't drink another one," he said, looking at his watch.

"Just leave your car here and get a taxi," she said. "You know, we've worked together quite a while now and we've never socialised together properly."

He took out his mobile phone and texted Anna to say he would be late home. He was genuinely worried about Rachel. But, also, after the intensity of the past few days it was good to have a break.

"I know about you and Anna having IVF," Rachel said, sitting down.

"What?"

"I saw the letter on your desk from a clinic," she explained.

"I should be more careful." He was annoyed with himself.

"When are you due to go through it?"

"We did . . . at the weekend. We're waiting to find out if we're successful."

"Right." She was surprised. "Best of luck with it."

"Thank you." He took a large gulp of wine.

"I'm sorry but . . . do you really think that your marriage to Anna is strong enough to bring a child into it? Considering your affairs?"

Paul got annoyed and stood up "You don't know the first thing about my marriage to Anna. She's my life. They weren't affairs! They were drunken one-night stands. I didn't cheat on her in long deliberate affairs."

"You can excuse yourself for anything! I'm sure Leo is excusing how he treated me at this moment. On second thoughts, he probably doesn't give a damn. At least you are trying to excuse yourself. Leo would just say that's the way the world is."

* * *

Nicola paced up and down her apartment that night as she spoke on the phone to Oliver.

"I just simply can't believe it! They get away with it! Is there nothing else you can do?"

"Stephanie Holden sat there and wouldn't even speak. She had that hot-shot lawyer there – you know, the one who got that pop star off that fraud case last year, and he left us nowhere to go with questioning. There was nothing we could do. Even made some threat about taking you to a tribunal for bullying."

"The bloody bitch! You know something, I wouldn't put it past her if she did and she would probably win! I'm absolutely furious!"

"Well, if you had answered your phone when I was trying to get through to you last week we could have acted sooner and he'd be under lock and key now and she would be exposed!"

"Yes, all right, Oliver, don't go on."

* * *

Paul looked at the empty wine bottles on Rachel's kitchen table as she went to open another.

"How much have you been drinking lately?" he asked.

"What do you care?" She filled both their glasses again.

"Rachel, I know you're very hurt about Leo but you mustn't let it get you down."

"You're right." She walked out into the living-room. "You know, I've been too soft all my life. I'm not like you or Leo who can just have flings and not care about them or who gets hurt . . . or at least I was like that . . . but I'm going to change. Leo has shown me how to change. I would have never got the promotion I did if I didn't take the step and be brave enough as Leo showed me how. In future I'm going to take what I want, when I want. I'm going to step over people to get what I want and nobody is going to get in my way. Leo thinks he's ruthless but I'm going to show him I'm going to be much more." She stared at Paul. Then she walked over to him and kissed his lips tenderly.

She pulled back.

"Did you enjoy that?" she asked.

"Yes," he said.

She went to kiss him again.

He turned his head quickly and walked away.

"What are you doing, Rachel?" he snapped.

"What do you think I'm doing?" she demanded.

"But this isn't you!"

"It's the new me. Come on, be honest, Paul. Tell me you didn't find me attractive from the moment we met . . . I'll be honest with you, I found you attractive, very attractive."

"You are very attractive," he said, shaking his head.

"So what's the big deal then? It's not as if you've never been unfaithful before, is it?"

"Rachel . . . you've drunk too much.

"So what if I have? You used it as an excuse for your one-night stands. We can use it as an excuse for what's going to happen between us now."

"You're emotional and exhausted. You're angry with the world and you're looking to take revenge on Leo by sleeping with the first person who comes your way."

"Maybe . . . but tell me that we didn't have something between us from the moment we met."

"Yes, there has been something there. And if I wasn't married; I would love to see what could happen between us. But I am married."

"I'm going to take just what I want. Why shouldn't I? I'm going to be just like Leo."

She walked over to him and started to kiss him again. He responded and started kissing back as the two of them fell on to the sofa.

He suddenly stopped and looked down at her.

"I can't do this, Rachel. I'm sorry." He got up. "I've risked everything with Anna in the past. I'm not going to risk anything in the future."

She sat up and put her head in her hands.

"This isn't you, Rachel. This is just a rebound thing. You're hurt and you're lonely but you're not this tough bitch who takes what she wants. And if you pretend to be, you'll be the one who gets hurt the most in the future."

She took her hands away from her face and looked up at him.

"I'm sorry, Paul. And I'm sorry I tried to do that to Anna. Go home to your wife and realise how lucky you are

– and how lucky both of you are."

"Will you be all right?" he asked.

"Yeah, just go on home."

"I'll see you at work tomorrow."

He walked to the door and left the flat.

Chapter 71

Rachel sat in her office staring down at the paperwork on her desk. She felt mortified, thinking about the previous night. To blatantly come on to Paul Stewart – had she lost leave of her senses? All she could do was be grateful he had stopped it. She was dreading meeting him.

There was a knock on her door and Paul walked in. She went bright red. He spotted her blush and how uncomfortable she looked but pretended nothing had happened the previous night. He acted as if it was business as normal.

"Rachel, there have been some big changes. Stephanie Holden has resigned."

"What?"

"I just came from a meeting with David Stafford. I'm not really sure what's going on. Stephanie gave in her notice yesterday. But the press are going to be on so you're going to have to deal with it, being our only publicist at the moment. You tell everyone who phones that Franklyns has no comment to make on her resignation but we will be making a statement in the next week, all right?"

"Okay," she nodded, nervous about being on her own

without Stephanie for guidance.

"Don't worry. If anything is too much for you then just come to me."

"All right."

"I'll probably need you to sit in on some meetings, so you can keep abreast of what's going on."

"Sure."

He turned to leave. "Oh, and Rachel. Just so you know, Leo Holden has left too."

* * *

Nicola was in David's house the following night, Thursday. "So where to for Franklyns now?" she asked.

"We've arranged to meet Karl Furstin next week. Looks like we'll accept the offer he's made to buy the store back. I mean, with the way the stock markets are so volatile right now, it's just not worth continuing with that now Stephanie's gone. It's not giving the investors confidence. And then with the banking crisis, you know, we just need to get our money back. So even though we're not happy with Furstin's offer, we'll cut our losses. How will you feel to have your old boss back?"

"Karl?" She gave a small laugh. "Karl does what I say. I'll be quite glad to have him back actually."

"I'm sure Paul Stewart will be as well. His job's secure now."

"Yes, I'd say he's delighted. What are we doing for the weekend?"

"Eh, I'm out with mates from Barons Bank on Friday. We're going up the city. Saturday, out with my college crew. Sunday, I'm at home with the parents – we're having a big family dinner."

"Right." She tried to hide her disappointment.

He noticed her downbeat face and thought for a while. "Say – why don't you come too?"

She perked up. "To which one?"

He thought quickly. "On Saturday. Meet my college friends. They're kind of my best friends."

She nodded. He had so many groups of friends she wasn't sure who his best friends were.

"Yes, I'd love to. What's going on exactly?"

"One Saturday every month we pick a pub and just go boozing for the afternoon. It's great fun and we all get to catch up."

"Right. Can't wait!"

* * *

Paul had been right. They were inundated with enquiries from the press demanding to know what was going on after word got out about Stephanie's resignation. Rachel was glad as it kept her mind off everything that had happened. Her hurt over Leo was only matched by her shame at trying to seduce Paul. He had been absolutely right: she had been drunk and hurt and looking to get back at Leo. She was so grateful that nothing had happened.

Because she was snowed under with enquiries, with no assistance, Paul came into the press office to help her out a lot. After the third day she managed to stop blushing bright red all the time. He made no reference to that night and she adored him for that. As ever she could only stand back and admire the deft way he handled himself and the press who were demanding answers.

After work she would just go home and sit and think about Leo, wondering where he was. She imagined him and Daniella living it up somewhere, quaffing champagne and driving around in his sports car, probably having a good laugh about Rachel Healy, the square girl who Leo showed London to. She wasn't sure what effect Leo had had on her. She needed to get back to being herself.

Chapter 72

On the Friday night, Nicola had arranged to meet some acquaintances from the business group she was in and went out for dinner. It was civilised and interactive and slightly boring. All her real friends were really mutual friends she shared with Oliver and she just couldn't go there at the moment. Considering how busy a life David had, she would have to make a proactive effort to build a social life. What would David think of her if he was out with his friends from Barons Bank having a whopping time and she was stuck in, watching television?

She got up early the next morning. She couldn't wait to meet David and his friends from college for an afternoon of drinking. What a lovely idea, just to go to a pub and drink the day away! Something that would have been alien to her life with Oliver. She selected a sexy white designer dress and started to do her make-up.

* * *

Nicola walked through Battersea Square to The Woodman pub on the Saturday afternoon. It was sunny and people were sitting out and eating at the different restaurants and bars on the square. She found The Woodman. She looked at her watch and saw it was a quarter past two and she was slightly late. She walked into the pub and spotted David immediately. He and his friends were seated at a very large wooden table in the beer garden at the back of the pub. There were twelve there in total.

He waved to her and smiled. She made her way over.

She was relieved he had kept a space for her beside him.

"Everyone, this is Nicola," said David who then proceeded to name everyone around the table. The guys all had names like Harry and Zac, the girls were all Jessicas and Francescas. They were all accountants or hedge fund managers. The girls were all very good looking in a natural wholesome way, dressed casually with little make-up and yet managing to look very groomed at the same time. She felt out of place. Even though they all greeted her in a friendly manner, she felt they looked at her as a curiosity. As the conversation developed she discovered they were all quite incestuous as well. It was revealed as the afternoon wore on that Harry had gone out with Sarah who in turn had gone out with Zac who in turn had gone out with Melanie. Nicola was sure that David was tied up in this intertwined history of past relationships and wondered who he had gone out with as she jealously inspected the girls.

The rounds of drinks kept coming as they amused each other with their tales. Nicola tried to participate as best she could.

"Did you hear about that row at Jake's party recently?" Harry asked David.

"I heard something. What happened?"

"Jacqui arrives in quite late to the party – you know, that French bird. And she actually doesn't really know anybody there. So me being the gentleman that I am, I take her under my wing and start taking her around and introducing her to everybody . . . and then she causes this huge scene as if I'm trying to get into her knickers or something!"

"As if!" said Zac.

"I know! As if!" said Harry.

Zac's mobile suddenly rang and he answered it. "Hi? Yeah? No, dump that stock, just dump it now. Sell it! It's not going to go any higher." Zac finished the call and then said simply "Hong Kong," by way of explanation.

"What Uni did you go to, Nicola?" asked Jessica.

"University? I went to St Joan's."

There was a blank look on everyone's face.

"St Joan's? Where's that?" asked Zac.

"Em . . . it's in Islington."

"St Joan's, the *art* school?" said Jessica.

"That's the one," said Nicola.

"*Art*?" David said it as if it was a dirty word. "What were you doing in an art college?"

"That's what I did at college. I studied History of Art."

"But – but I assumed you had a business degree," said David.

"No," Nicola managed to smile. "I did History of Art."

"Well, why aren't you teaching art or something like that then, instead of what you're doing?" demanded David. "How did you end up in HR?"

"A friend of my family sorted me out with a job in Harrods when I left college."

David stared at her while the others looked slightly bemused.

As the afternoon wore on she did enjoy their company, especially as she drank more. But there was such a chasm between her life experience and theirs. She was a married woman of sixteen years. About six at the table were married, to each other of course, but that was only in the past couple of years. Although they were all at least in their mid-thirties they lived life as if they were free as birds. They spoke about bands she had never heard of and parties that all sorts went on at.

Nicola put her arm around David's waist and he smiled at her.

He bent forward and whispered to her, "Everything all right?"

"Yes, they're all lovely." She smiled at him.

"Good. Listen . . . just a word of advice. Take a look at the way the other girls are dressed here. You don't have to make such an effort every time you come out, you know."

"I don't understand?" She shook her head in confusion.

"Well, everyone else is dressed casually, appropriately . . . and there's you sitting there looking like . . . Zsa Zsa Gabor!"

Nicola turned and stared ahead, her eyes wide.

* * *

It was Nicola's turn to go to the bar and she tried to remember all their drinks as the barman placed them on a tray for her.

"You'd better come back for the rest," he advised as the tray was full.

She turned and began to walk back to the beer garden. She felt self-conscious after David's comment and wished she had worn a longer dress and lower heels.

As she entered the beer garden, Zac shouted, "Here she is!"

She smiled and suddenly felt her ankle go under her as her heel got caught in one of the pavement cracks. As she tried to dislodge her heel, the tray of drinks suddenly went flying and crashed to the ground.

She looked up to see David who was now standing, arms folded, and looking unimpressed.

"Oh, Nicola!" said Zac.

* * *

The taxi cab pulled up outside David's house and he and Nicola got out. He paid the taxi driver and they made their way up to his front door. It was ten at night and they had been drinking with his friends all day.

"I really enjoyed the day!" said Nicola as he opened the door with his key.

"Hmmm, it was good all right . . . apart from you dropping all the drinks."

"I couldn't help it."

"Maybe if you wore heels that you could actually walk in, you might stand a better chance of remaining vertical," he said, closing the door after them.

* * *

Across the road from behind one of the leafy trees lining it, Oliver stepped out and stared over at the house. Watching as David went around closing all the curtains.

* * *

They were in David's living-room. He opened a bottle of wine and put some music on the sound system. She was in the mood for some soothing Burt Bacharach music, but instead the Arctic Monkeys came blasting out of his sound system.

"And what's all this about you studying art?" he suddenly said. "You always made out you had a business background."

"I do have a business background. I've been heading HR for years. I practically ran Franklyns."

"Yeah, I know all that, but suddenly a lot of things are becoming clearer. It's quite obvious really that you don't have a business degree because I traced some of the most ludicrous business decisions during Furstin's time back to your door." He handed her a glass of red wine.

"What do you mean?" she asked, irritated.

"I mean, Nicola, there's no rhyme or reason to a lot of the stuff you've done. Let's face it, the personnel of that store was in a heap before I arrived. You had too many staff in some areas and not enough in others."

"Well, that wasn't my sole decision," said Nicola, flushing. "There was Furstin and Paul Stewart and the department managers. It wasn't all down to me!"

"Well, no, it was, actually. I really researched this when I waded through the mess that is Franklyns and all those decisions were yours. And then there's the weird promotion structure you employ. Like, are you aware that the head of security actually had little or no security background before he started his job?"

"Steve is an excellent security manager."

"He might be now but he learned on the job. I shudder to think the amount of stealing that was going on before he learned his trade. Whatever possessed you to give him such a high position with no experience?"

Nicola became very angry, the drink accentuating her fury.

"I don't need an MBA from the London School of Economics to know what's right or wrong, David. With all your bloody education and so-called experience you still couldn't spot a common thief like Leo Holden, could you? Not to mention his conniving mother who ran rings around you and Conrad Richardson! And I mightn't be an accountant like Jessica and Francesca, but at least I know how to put on a bit of glamour!"

David stared at her calmly. He then put down his glass.

"You know, I think we'd better stop having this conversation right now. I want to stop talking about this."

Chapter 73

Karl Furstin sat opposite Conrad Richardson and David in Conrad's office at Barons Bank on Tuesday afternoon.

"And so! We can do business," said Karl.

"Yes," said Conrad. "We would like to accept your offer to buy back Franklyns at the agreed amount."

"Excellent!" smiled Karl. "A pleasure doing business with you, gentlemen."

"Congratulations, you have your store back, Karl," said Conrad.

"Yes. Franklyns was just an investment for you; it's everything to me. Owning it will put us back where we belong!"

"Could I just ask, out of curiosity," said Conrad. "Where did you get the funds to buy back the store?"

"We've been in Vienna a lot. Vienna is the head of OPEC. There is suddenly a lot of petro dollars floating around with the huge oil prices in recent years. The Arabs and the Russians. If you know the right people they are anxious to invest their money in long-term projects. They are buying up massive swathes of the West with their petro dollars. And like they did in the seventies, the last time there was an oil boom. They are looking to invest in prime real estate in London. They don't come more prime than Franklyns."

"So you're a front man for a consortium?" asked David.

"Maybe . . . but I'm the one in control. And now, if there's nothing else?" Karl stood up and shook Conrad's hand and then David's. He held David's hand too long and his eyes bored into him.

"Mr Stafford, may I have a private word with you?" he asked.

* * *

Nicola looked at the young security man sitting across her desk and spoke to him sharply. "Your lateness record is abominable. Your manager has asked me to speak to you. Consider this a verbal warning. You're on your last chance."

The young man had a smirk across his face.

"Do you hear me?" she snapped.

He nodded as though not too concerned and continued to smirk.

She looked at him in disbelief. Staff usually quivered when she was giving out to them. It was as if he was not taking her seriously.

"What are you smirking at?" she demanded.

"Nothing much," he shrugged but the smirk remained.

She was about to start shouting at him when the phone rang on her desk.

"What, Yvette?"

"Your Bank Manager, Mr Woodbridge, is on the line for you," said Yvette.

"Put him through." She covered the mouthpiece and said to the young man, "Get out and don't let me see you back here again."

The young man slouched off the chair and left, his smirk still in place.

Perplexed, Nicola turned her attention to Adam Woodbridge.

"Hello, Nicola, how are you?" said Adam's sing-song friendly voice.

"I'm well, Adam, thanks. What's up?"

"Just thought I'd better have a quick word with you to check everything is all right?"

"Why shouldn't it be?"

"Well, it's just your and Oliver's account – there's been a lot of irregularity recently. Basically huge sums of money going out all the time. Massive spending. I'm just looking at your statement now. There's huge money going out to some property company every month."

"Yes, we're renting a place in Canary Wharf. It's easier for the commute."

"Gosh, what are you renting – the actual Canary Wharf building itself or something?"

"Yes, I know it's a bit pricey."

"Those Mercs are pretty expensive too, aren't they?"

"Yes, they are," Nicola became impatient.

"And then who's Karen Millen? And why are you paying her exorbitant amounts of money every month? Is she blackmailing you or something?" He allowed himself a little laugh.

She coughed slightly. "It's clothes, actually, Adam. Karen Millen is nothing more sinister than a fashion house."

"Gosh, and Gucci shoes and Gina shoes and Prada . . .

it's all adds up, doesn't it? And then there's the jewellery. Look, if everything's all right, then that's fine. I just thought I'd better check in because your funds are literally flying out the door. If you need to have a chat with me about money issues, my door's always open, Nicola."

"Thanks, Adam."

She hung up the phone, mortified. How much money had she actually gone through? She would have to look at the balances later. So, she had gone a little mad recently. Wasn't she allowed to live a little? She quickly got up. She was meeting David and was late. She was dying to find out all about the offer Furstin made him. After their little argument on Saturday night, they didn't refer to it the next morning. David was in a rush to get to his family dinner so in a way it was lucky they didn't have time to discuss it. Not that she would have anyway. Note to mental self, she thought, don't provoke him or criticise his friends. She hadn't seen him all day Monday because he was under pressure at work and then he had rushed off for his rugby practice that evening, no invitation extended to her. They were due to meet at Canary Wharf that evening. She knew he was meeting Furstin at Barons Bank and she couldn't wait to see his reaction to the offer Karl was making to him.

* * *

Nicola made the journey to Canary Wharf by Tube. It was half five by the time she made her way up the gigantically long escalators at the Tube station. The baritone opera-singer busker's voice boomed around the station. She loved the way David just brought a suitcase into work on a Friday and flew out somewhere for the weekend after.

She might suggest they go somewhere this weekend. Maybe Amsterdam. Now Stephanie was gone and all the hassle associated with her, they deserved a little break. She came out of the station and into the central plaza. She walked to Smollenskys on the plaza and saw David sitting at one of the tables outside, his legs crossed, his sunglasses on, enjoying the sun, a gin and tonic in front of him.

"Hello, sorry I'm late." She bent down and kissed him quickly. David wasn't one for big displays of affection and so she didn't linger.

She sat down opposite him and ordered wine, which came immediately. He removed his sunglasses.

"You came straight from Barons?" she asked.

"Yep."

"And how did it go with Furstin?"

"Smooth. He is now the owner of Franklyns again. And that place is no longer my problem."

"Well, it's no longer Barons' problem but it's still yours," she corrected him.

"Hmmm?"

"Well, the offer Furstin made you means you're still working there."

He looked confused. "You knew about that offer?"

"Yes, Furstin rang me and told me about it. I thought I'd let him surprise you with it. So what did he offer you exactly?" she asked excitedly.

"Oh, he made me an offer all right but I didn't accept it."

"*What?*" she cried, astounded. "But I know Furstin – you could have named your price!"

"No amount of money would induce me to work for that man," David said decisively. "First of all, his reputation is pretty shit. And secondly, the things I've uncovered about him and that bonkers wife of his would definitely make me run a mile. Everything from paying for Latvians' hair to something very weird going on with his personal staff which I never got to the bottom of. I'm kind of glad I didn't get to the bottom of it – he gives me the creeps enough as it is."

"But you'll never get an offer like that again!" She flung her hands into the air in agitation. She was astonished by his rejection of the offer she had so carefully set up for him, and unable to comprehend the way he both casually rejected the offer and Franklyns.

"I don't really care. Look, I'm not Paul Stewart relying on the likes of Furstin to get me ahead. I'm a highly sought-after accountant who can name my terms."

"I see," Nicola said, full of disappointment that all her planning had been for nothing. "Well, where is Barons Bank sending you next then?"

"Wall Street."

"*What*?" Nicola shouted, causing people to stare.

"A bank in Wall Street we've taken over is in trouble and I'm going out there to sort it out. It'll only be for six months or so."

"But you can't go!"

"Of course, I'm going. I always wanted to do a stint on Wall Street."

"But what about me?"

"Well, I'll be flying back some weekends. I can see you then. And it's not for ever."

"No, David, you don't understand. There's no way our relationship will survive if you go there. It just won't! How could it?"

He became disturbed at her intensity. "Look, I would love us to remain friends –"

"Friends! The last thing you need is more friends,

David! You've got more friends than anybody I've ever met! We have something special here. And we just can't let it go!"

"We've had a lot of fun –"

"I love you!" she nearly shouted. "I've thrown everything away for you! And I'd do it all again tomorrow."

He looked very uncomfortable and spoke in measured tones. "What are you talking about, Nicola? This was a bit of fun. We've both had a good time. Now work is taking me away, so we're going to have to cool it, okay? It's no big deal."

She sat back, staring at him in disbelief. "That was really all this ever was to you, wasn't it? One person's fling is another person's relationship."

"We have never discussed any plans, any future together," he said coolly. "No promises were made. I have been completely honest with you from the beginning and I hoped you had been with me."

"There was never any room for me in your life, was there? In fact, is there room for anybody?"

"Look, maybe we should just give it a miss tonight. I think I'd better go home."

"But what's going to happen to you, David? Are you just going to keep on going the way you are? Never settle down? Going from sorting out company to company? Going from skiing trips to stags? Rugby matches to friends' parties? Will you eventually marry one of those accountant girls just because all your friends are doing it? Or will you just keep going the way you are? What will become of you?"

David stood up and put on his sunglasses. "My life's pretty cool, Nicola. Why don't you concentrate on thinking about yours."

He walked off towards the Tube station.

* * *

Nicola managed to get back to her apartment from Smollensky's. She sat on the couch in absolute silence, unable to express any emotion.

Chapter 74

David walked into Paul's office with his briefcase the next day, Wednesday.

"Right. There've been quite a few more changes, Paul," he said. "In fact, there's been a fucking huge amount of shit going on. But all you need to know is Karl Furstin has bought back the store."

Paul sat back, his eyes widening in surprise.

"I know – it's all come as a bit of a shock to me as well. I'm literally finishing up now. Just cleared out my office. Furstin is taking over today."

"I don't know what to say . . ."

"Well, you should be delighted. No more Stephanie, no more me interfering in the way you do things. Your job is safe back with Furstin. And no doubt he'll hand you back your Beamer and all the other perks you enjoyed with him. And the store can go back to its old inefficient ways."

If only you knew how I didn't co-operate with Furstin to help him get the store back, thought Paul. His position was more at risk than ever.

"And what about you?" he asked.

"I'm off to Wall Street. For six months anyway. Barons

have just taken over a bank that's in trouble because of the sub-prime crisis over there. I've being sent in to sort it out."

"I see. And what about you and Nicola?"

"We're through. It really wasn't ever going anywhere long-term, I don't think."

"Right. Well, best of luck, David."

"Same to you. No doubt I'll see you sometime . . . in twenty years' time again maybe!"

"David, can I ask you something?" Paul sat forward.

"Fire ahead."

"Why did you try to help me so much when the store was taken over here? Why did you bother to keep giving me advice? It wasn't like we were ever good friends or anything and yet you seemed to genuinely care what happened to me."

David paused. "You never really liked me, did you, Paul? Not back then when we were at school and not now either."

"If I have to be honest . . . then no."

"Why?"

"To be honest again, I've thought about this and I just don't know why."

David seemed lost in thought. "Hmmm . . . maybe that's it. I've never not been liked by anybody before. I didn't know how to deal with it. I wanted you to like me."

"You can't control things like that."

"Hmmm . . .anyway, Paul, I'd better go. If you're ever in Wall Street over the next few months . . ."

Paul shook David's offered hand.

"Goodbye, Paul," said David and he walked out.

Paul barely had time to digest the information when his phone rang.

"Paul Stewart speaking."

"Stewart, I'm back in my office on the sixth floor. Come up immediately," said Karl's voice and the phone went dead.

* * *

Paul made his way to the sixth floor and was surprised to see it a hive of activity. He recognised a lot of Karl's old staff busily moving back into their offices and some new staff as well. It was weird seeing the floor so busy, as it had been occupied only by Stephanie for so long, apart from meetings. He made his way down to Karl's office.

He steadied himself before he entered. He knew how Karl operated. His revenge for not helping him would be swift and ruthless. Paul expected to be fired immediately.

There was Karl, standing in the middle of his office, with a large group of cleaners at work.

"I want every inch scrubbed and scrubbed again!" he ordered.

Removal men were taking out the old furniture and bringing in new. Paul got the old feeling of claustrophobia that he got around Karl. Anyway, his business would be brief.

"Congratulations, Karl, on getting your store back," he said.

"You know, I'll never be able to get this office clean again," said Karl surveying the work. "The smell of her cheap perfume when I entered the place. It'll reek for months!"

Paul just ignored him. Stephanie Holden always wore the most beautiful light fragrance and could teach Karl and his wife a lesson about their overpowering style.

Paul waited, preparing himself for what was coming next.

"I want to do a tour of the store at three, so make yourself available. See what damage she's inflicted on the place."

Paul blinked a few times and then nodded. "See you at three."

Chapter 75

Nicola had called in sick the day after David had delivered his bombshell. That night she could hardly sleep. On the Thursday morning she made her way to work as usual, almost in a trance. She had a meeting with Karl Furstin at eleven. She instructed Yvette to cancel all other meetings during the day and told her she would not take any calls. She managed to force herself to try and act normally as she made her way up to see Karl. He was waiting for her, seated behind his big desk, a smile on his face.

"Back where I belong, Nicola."

"Yes," she smiled as she sat down opposite him.

"And a big thanks to you!"

"Glad to be of help."

"I spoke to your boyfriend about offering him a position here but he didn't seem interested," said Karl.

She blinked a few times, feeling horribly exposed that Karl knew she had been seeing David.

"Rare to get a man who can't be bought. I quite liked him. I see what you saw in him."

She felt very awkward. She didn't want Karl knowing about what had been happening in her life. She wanted him to see her the way he always did.

Karl fixed her with his penetrating gaze. "I've got some bad news for you, Nicola," he said. He leaned forward and paused.

Nicola felt uneasy, wondering what could possibly be wrong.

"I'm afraid your position is no longer tenable."

"What?"

"I'm going to have to let you go."

"But why?" she demanded, her voice shrill.

"Quite simply, I can't have a slut working in senior management."

She sat in stunned silence.

"It's common knowledge that you've been fucking David Stafford, left your husband, carrying on . . . you've lost all respect with the staff in the store. They laugh about you behind your back. They don't take you seriously any more and so you can't continue in HR."

Nicola felt anger rising within her. As his steely cold eyes bored into her, she knew what he was like, what he was capable of. How he frightened everybody. But he never frightened her. Nobody frightened her.

"I can't believe you are saying this to me so blatantly! So it's all right for Paul Stewart to go around screwing everyone he wants, and it doesn't affect his position, but because I'm a woman I'm being fired!"

"Paul was never indiscreet about his dalliances. In fact he always went to great effort to conceal them, as far as I know. Embarrassed by them almost."

"That is not the issue. The plain truth is you are firing me because of my personal life. That is illegal. I know employment law inside out and you're picking on the wrong person. If you fire me, Karl, I will immediately bring legal action against you and I will win." She sat forward aggressively, pointing her finger at him.

"Oh, Nicola, Nicola . . . you've lost your memory as well as your morals. Correct me if I'm wrong but when Franklyns was taken over by Barons Bank, you terminated your contract with Franklyns and signed a new contract with Barons Bank directly, didn't you?"

Nicola sat back. Realisation dawning on her of the implications of this. She said quietly, "Yes."

"Then your contract was with Barons Bank and not with Franklyns. And since Barons Bank no longer owns Franklyns, then that contract is null and void. You can't bring legal action against us because officially you don't work here any more."

Nicola sat in silence as she realised that what he was saying was true.

"I'm sorry, Nicola, but your face just doesn't fit here any more."

* * *

When Paul found out about Nicola Newman being sacked he was shocked. But in a strange kind of way he knew Furstin wouldn't tolerate the new Nicola. He had lost all respect for her. Word had got out quickly about Nicola's dismissal that morning and the store was buzzing with rumours.

He sat in Furstin's office that afternoon, having given Karl a full appraisal of the many changes that had taken place in the store.

"I suppose we don't have to undo some of the changes made," concluded Karl. "Maybe some of them were overdue. I'll take a look around and make up my own mind."

As if you would do anything else, thought Paul.

"There have been so many changes in personnel," said Karl, irritated. "I need to get a whole new finance department since they fired everyone. Make some calls and see if we can get some of them back."

"Will do," Paul nodded. He doubted many of them would come back if they had found new positions. Why would they come back to listen to Furstin hollering at them all the time? Unless the money was right.

"And I need to find a new HR Manager on top of everything else," Karl said crossly. "Preferably one who doesn't drop her drawers the first time a bit of hot stuff comes along."

Paul coughed slightly.

"And what's the story with the PR department?" Karl demanded.

"Wipe-out there as well, I'm afraid. They let Gordon and everyone go. Stephanie Holden was herself handling the press office enquiries but the work stacked up. She recently appointed a press officer to assist her. And since Stephanie went, the same girl is handling everything brilliantly, despite being thrown in at the deep end."

"What's her name?"

"Rachel Healy.

"Never heard of her. Who was she with before?"

"She was in the press office in Brown Thomas and worked in a couple of departments here before being promoted."

"What age?"

"Mid-twenties."

Karl scoffed. "She's much too junior to become the principal press officer, if that's what you're suggesting."

"I'm not suggesting anything," said Paul. "Just

reminding you that most people thought I was too junior to become General Manager when you appointed me from Sales Manager. She's very ambitious, Karl. She was determined to get into the press office from the moment she arrived here."

"Set up an appointment for me to see her tomorrow."

* * *

Rachel tried to concentrate on the press release she was working on but couldn't. The fourth-floor restaurant had just hired a well-known TV chef to oversee the menu and she was letting all the appropriate papers know. Actually, it had been Stephanie who had hired the famous chef and it was quite a coup. She had been so immersed in coping with what had happened with Leo that she was only coming to think about her career now. With Stephanie gone, did she still have a position any more? Without Stephanie's patronage, she was sure Nicola Newman would have her back behind the Chanel counter by close of business, which she couldn't cope with. But now there was a rumour wildly circulating that Nicola had been fired. Her nerves were so stretched that when the press office door opened she jumped out of her seat.

It was Paul, and seeing her look so worried, he said, "It's all right. It's just me!"

"Oh Paul! What's been going on? The whole shop is shaking with rumours. Is Nicola Newman gone?"

"As gone as last Christmas."

"I can't believe it."

"Bit of a shock all right. Furstin has taken back the store."

"Oh!" She slumped back into her chair. "That's me for the chop then."

"Why?" he shrugged.

"Don't you remember when he wanted me to join his personal staff and I said no. I might as well pack now."

"He won't even remember that. Sorry to tell you but you're just not important enough for him to remember."

"But he's a creep, isn't he?" she shuddered.

"Maybe. But he's a powerful man and he's in a position to give you what you want."

"I don't get you."

"I've just given him a low-down on the position of all the departments and I gave you a glowing reference, saying you were manning the ship here in the press office. He wants to meet you."

"So, you mean he might keep me on here in my position?"

"Yes, and it might be an opportunity for you. If you impress him, there's a clear run for you remaining a publicist and maybe even heading the press office team some day. If Furstin likes you he can accelerate your career at an amazing pace. He did it for me."

"That's all very well, Paul. But I don't think I have the experience to head the press office here."

"I didn't have the experience to be General Manager either. You sink or swim, and believe me, Rachel, you'll swim."

"But I don't know if I want to work for a man like that, from what I hear."

"You're being stupid."

"No, Paul. There are rumours going around about him."

"Rachel, I know about those rumours. And I'm not pretending he's an easy person to work for. In fact he's a complete bastard. But you'll never get a chance like this again. Even see it as a short term thing, get your experience and move on."

"Like you did?" she asked cynically.

"Well, then, I'm living proof that the benefits can outweigh the cons of working for Furstin. I'm still here, aren't I?"

"Yeah, but did you sell your soul?" She looked at him curiously.

"Rachel! Just meet him, and see what he has to offer. Okay?"

Rachel nodded "Okay."

"Try to impress him," urged Paul.

"But how could I possibly impress Karl Furstin?"

"Think Nicola Newman before she decided to become Marilyn Monroe. I checked with his PA and she's set up an appointment for you to meet him tomorrow morning at eleven."

"For fuck's sake!" Rachel nearly shouted. "This is all a nightmare. I wish I'd never left Dublin. Nothing is working out for me. I wish I'd stayed at home!"

"Rachel, pull yourself together. This is an opportunity for you. Grab it."

The door suddenly opened and they both looked up to see Anna race in, looking flushed.

"Anna!" Paul stood up from where he had been sitting on Rachel's desk.

"Paul, Reception said I'd find you here. I need to speak to you!" She glanced down at Rachel "Oh, hi! Rachel, isn't it? I'm going to have to borrow him for a minute." Rachel smiled, though feeling on edge at seeing Paul's wife after she had made a pass at him.

Paul went to Anna and casually put his arm around her as the two of them walked out of the press office. He didn't close the door and Rachel watched them as they walked a little way down the corridor. She saw them stop and face each other as Anna spoke excitedly. Then Paul put his arms out and Anna jumped into them happily and they laughed and hugged each other.

Chapter 76

It was Friday and Rachel couldn't wait for the weekend to take a breather from all that was happening. She was sitting outside Karl Furstin's office, three snooty PAs looking at her suspiciously. She had gone out shopping the night before. She was fully aware of how much she was spending but she justified it as an investment in her future. Mindful of Paul's advice, she had selected a black Gucci trouser suit with a slim jacket buttoned at the waist. Her hair was caught back loosely at the nape of the neck. The look was finished off with elegant black court shoes. She had limited her jewellery to a watch. A slim briefcase was placed by her side. She sat upright and tried to ooze confidence. It was an act – she was shaking on the inside. She remembered how informal everything was when Stephanie worked from this office. No PAs, no security at the lifts as you came on to the floor. Everyone could just go straight up to her door and walk in. She loved Stephanie's management style.

The phone rang on one of the PA's desks. She answered it and then put the receiver back down.

"You may go in to Mr Furstin now," she said.

Rachel nodded and stood up. She braced herself and walked across to the big double doors. She gave a knock, then opened the door and walked in. She closed the door behind her and absorbed the atmosphere.

Even though the office looked the same, it felt so different from when Stephanie was there. Karl sat behind the giant desk scrutinising her. She immediately felt overcome by the same nauseous feeling she had got when she had seen him before. She wanted to turn and run from the place. She quickly reminded herself how important this was to her.

She smiled and walked confidently across the floor, stretching her hand out as she approached his desk.

"Good afternoon, Mr Furstin, and thank you for meeting me," she said, casually smiling.

He surveyed her hand for a moment without taking it but she didn't falter and then he reached forward and gave it a quick shake.

She looked down at the vacant chair, glanced over at him and smiled.

"You may sit," he said.

"Thank you." She sat down and crossed her legs.

"You look familiar. Have we met before?" he queried.

"No, I don't think so."

"And so – Paul Stewart tells me you've been keeping things together in the press office."

"I've certainly been busy trying to keep everything under control."

"Just trying?"

"Keeping everything under control," she nodded. She realised that to show any weakness in front of this man would mean he immediately lost respect for you.

"I haven't much time to talk to you. The woman that

was in charge here fired my very good and competent press office staff and I'm left with just you."

"Maybe if I talked about what I've been doing recently. Last week we had a competition live on GMTV which was a big success –"

"Enough!" He held up his hand.

Immediately her confidence evaporated. His penetrating eyes stared at her face, examining every inch of it. And then his stare trailed down as he sized her up. She sat in silence.

"Paul Stewart suggested you as a candidate to actually run the press office in the future . . . My last principal press officer was a chief political correspondent for the BBC. Do you really think you can compare to that?"

"No, I'm not trying to. I think Paul might have oversung my praises."

"So what are you offering me?"

"Just to give my work one hundred and fifty per cent."

He looked down at her fingers "Married?"

"No."

"Boyfriend."

"Em . . . no."

"Good . . . I need complete dedication from my management. If I need you to work until midnight, you work until midnight. If I phone you at three in the morning, then you answer that phone. If I need you to attend a function with me in the evenings, then you attend. The job comes first. Understood?"

She nodded her head nervously. "Yes, I understand."

"Then continue in the press office with what you are doing. We'll be working closely over the coming weeks. I'll be monitoring you to see if you're up to the job. Understood?"

She nodded. She sat in silence for a while as he continued to look at her.

"Well . . . go!" he suddenly snapped, giving her a start.

"Yes, and thank you," she said getting up quickly and making her way to the door, realising her heart was thumping in her chest.

Rachel went straight back to her office and sat at her desk. The work was piled up in front of her but she couldn't concentrate as she thought of her meeting with Furstin.

She should be delighted – he was telling her she was staying in the press office and was even going to consider her for running the office. But the whole experience had unnerved her. He was offering her everything she wanted. The dream job. What she had come to London for. She would have exceeded her expectations. But it would mean working closely with the man. And the thought of that frightened her.

She looked at her watch and seeing it was nearly one, she realised she needed to get out and get some fresh air and some lunch.

Lost in thought, Rachel made her way out of the staff entrance and headed towards a coffee shop she liked in Knightsbridge. As she walked along the street, a gleaming black limo pulled up ahead of her. The chauffeur got out of the car and opened the back door. Out stepped a middle-aged smartly dressed man and a glamorous young woman. Rachel did a double take as she realised the young woman was Daniella. She watched in amazement as the two walked towards an exclusive restaurant. They had their arms around each other's waists and as they drew level with the restaurant they kissed.

Burning with anger, Rachel ran and stood in front of them.

"What do you think you're doing?" she demanded.

"Eh, Rachel!" Daniella looked surprised and uncomfortable but smiled broadly. "Darling, let me introduce you to Ricky. He's a television producer. He produces reality shows, and, guess what? He's going to put me in his next one."

"And does Leo know about Ricky?" demanded Rachel.

"Eh, darling, you're being a bit loud."

"I don't give a fuck! What do you think you're playing at? You swan back and break me and Leo up and then as ever you dump him as soon as the first rich old guy comes along, you vacuous cow!"

"Hey!" shouted Ricky.

"He's hardly old,darling, he's only fifty! Isn't that the new forty?"

"*Daniella!*" Rachel nearly shouted.

Daniella sighed and slowly removed herself from Ricky's grip.

"Okay," she said and turned to Ricky. "Listen Ricky-tick-a-tick-tick you go on in and order the starter and I'll join you in as quick a time as you can say low-fat mayonnaise."

Ricky gave Rachel a dirty look and proceeded into the restaurant. Daniella turned to Rachel.

"All right, let's get into the car and have a chat," suggested Daniella.

"Let's."

They walked back to the limo. The chauffeur opened the back door for them and they sat into the back.

"Once round the block," Daniella instructed the chauffeur.

"I've never met anybody like you, Daniella!" Rachel burst out as they drove off. "You're the most greedy, self-centred, horrible person I've ever met!"

"Steady with the compliments, darling!"

"Why are you treating Leo like this? You're not interested in him obviously when you're off with that television producer, so why bother coming back into his life?"

Daniella sighed loudly "Okay, darling, I guess the game is up . . . I'm not back with Leo, I never was."

"I don't understand!"

"Leo ran into trouble with the police. I think it was over that necklace he had given you. I think it was hot property. He needed to get it back off you."

"So why didn't he just ask for the fucking thing back?"

"He didn't want to tell you – you know how moralising you can be. So he rang me up and asked me to pretend we were back together. I thought I put on a good Oscar-winning performance."

"That's a fucking cowardly way to get a stupid necklace back!"

"Yeah, well, it wasn't just about the necklace. He really did want to finish with you and he thought this would be the quickest, easiest way out."

"Oh, I see." Rachel sighed and looked ahead.

Daniella turned around to her. "No, you don't. He wanted to finish with you because he thought he was no good for you. He had to go on the run from the police the next day and he didn't want to drag you down with him."

"Drag me down?"

"Yes, he said you'd just landed the job of your dreams and he didn't want to fuck things up for you."

Rachel shook her head in amazement. "The bloody fool! Why didn't he just explain things to me properly? And why didn't you tell me?"

"Because I thought what he was saying was true! On top of all that, there was what happened at the party. You both went to a party at Tom's on the Saturday night, yeah?"

"Yes."

"He said some girl spiked your drink and you were sick after it."

"What?" Rachel was astounded. "Oh, now it makes sense why I was so ill."

"He felt terrible about it. He said you were worlds apart and he was no good for you and, you know, I kind of agree with him."

"And where's he now?" asked Rachel.

Daniella shrugged.

"*Daniella!*" Rachel demanded.

"He's in Paris, darling."

* * *

Rachel sat at her desk after work, thinking about what Daniella had told her. She couldn't concentrate as she tried to take it all in. Suddenly the phone rang on her desk, giving her a jolt.

"Press office," she said answering the phone.

"Rachel, this is Mr. Furstin's PA. He would like you to work late tonight. Please come to his office at seven this evening."

Rachel sat speechless.

"Rachel?" snapped the PA.

"Yes?"

"Seven this evening, Mr Furstin's office. Do you understand?"

"This evening? But that's very short notice," said Rachel.

There was a pause before the PA spoke "Cancel any plans you have. When Mr Furstin tells you to be somewhere, be there. Even if he gives you two minutes' notice. Get used to it. And don't be late."

Chapter 77

"What do you think of Susan if it's a girl?" asked Anna.

It was six thirty that evening and they were walking to a local Italian restaurant near where they lived.

"Hmm, that's nice. And if we have a boy?"

"I'm not sure . . . oh, I know – how about Karl?" She savoured the look of horror on his face.

"Eh, no thanks. I would prefer my son not to be named after that man."

"I don't know, you've always said you would never have got to where you are without him. You must be delighted he's back in charge at Franklyns. No more Stephanie Holden or David Stafford. Your job safe again."

"Oh, my job is certainly safe again. I've even been told I can collect my new company BMW next week whenever I want. Or *Beamer*, as David Stafford would call it." Paul did an impression of David's voice.

"Wonderful! You must be delighted!" said Anna, looking for a reaction.

"I am . . . He's keeping Rachel on in the press office, remember her?"

"Yes, an all-round good result for everybody then, isn't

it? Except for poor Nicola, of course."

* * *

The lift door opened and Rachel stepped out into the sixth floor, clutching a pen and a pad of A4 lined paper, her handbag slung over her shoulder. She hadn't known what she should bring with her as she had no idea what Furstin wanted her to do. She looked around and realised all the office staff had gone home. In fact the whole store was empty by now. She knew this was ridiculous – asking her to work late at such short notice. But she guessed she would have to get used to it. She was being considered for a very high-powered position and this was what you had to sacrifice to get on in the world.

She made her way down the corridor to Karl's reception. The place seemed eerie. And even more so when she realised that his PAs had gone home too.

She nervously looked at his door and saw that it was ajar. She walked towards it and knocked. No answer. She peeped through the slit on the door and couldn't see anybody. She knocked again, more loudly.

A voice called, "Come in!"

She pushed the door open and walked in. She looked around but there was no sign of anybody.

"Mr Furstin?" she called.

There was no response. The whole situation felt wrong to her and she began to feel frightened. Her eyes searched around the office but there was no sign of anybody. Suddenly slow classical music began to play.

"Hello?" she called again.

"Come here!" The voice sounded muffled and now almost drowned out by the music which was increasing in volume all the time.

"Mr Furstin?"

"In here . . ."

She realised the voice was coming from a large ornate door which was standing half-open. She approached the door cautiously, her heart thudding, alarm bells ringing in her head.

The music was becoming louder and louder.

She stepped into the doorway and pushed the door back.

It was a bathroom, huge and marble and opulent. Classical music blared.

In the middle of the floor was a large sunken bath, clouds of steam rising from it. In it lay Karl Furstin, his penetrating eyes staring right into hers.

Rachel turned and raced through the office and down the corridor. Dropping the pad and pen, she frantically pushed the button of the lift and the door slid open. She could hear footsteps behind her but dared not look around. Jumping in, she pushed the button for the ground floor. She breathed heavily, hearing her heart beat at the same time. On the fourth floor the lift stalled. Terrified, she hit the button to open the door and when it did she leapt out. She raced for the stairs and tore down them from one floor to the next, her heart beating faster and faster. On the ground floor she raced through the empty cosmetics department to the staff entrance.

She didn't relax until she got back to her flat and locked the door after her.

Chapter 78

On the Saturday morning Paul and Anna lay in bed. Paul lay awake staring at the ceiling, thinking of all the events that had happened recently. Suddenly his work mobile started ringing on the bedside table.

"It didn't take that shit long to start phoning at all times. Tell Furstin to piss off," Anna mumbled, her eyes still closed.

"Hello?" said Paul into the phone as he jumped out of bed, put on his dressing-gown and walked out of the room.

"Paul, hi, it's Rachel. I'm so sorry for ringing you at the weekend."

"Rachel!" Paul was surprised. He had given her his mobile number when she had been left to run the press office in case of emergencies. He padded down the stairs into the sitting-room. "What's up?" he asked.

"Paul, I'm handing in my notice. With Nicola and Stephanie gone, there's nobody left to hand in my notice to, except you."

"Handing in your notice! But why? This is the opportunity you've been dying for. And what's the urgency?"

"I know. But I just can't work for that man, Paul. I'm sorry. I don't want to be anywhere near him."

Paul was silent, shocking thoughts racing through his head. Another casualty of the sixth floor. What had Furstin done to her? He didn't want to ask but felt he owed it to her. It was difficult to give voice to his unspoken fears – he was so accustomed to repressing them.

"What happened, Rachel?" he said, dreading the answer. "What did he do to you?"

"Nothing, Paul. Don't worry. I got myself out of there in the nick of time."

"I'm sorry, Rachel. I feel responsible."

"Don't. I'm all grown up. I'm responsible for myself. And I want to thank you for putting me forward for the job and recommending me for it. And I want to thank you for everything since I began at Franklyns. You've been great, in more ways than one."

Paul searched for words to express his feelings. "I was wrong to encourage you to stay. You're doing the right thing, Rachel. You have too much integrity to work for Furstin. I wish I had your strength of mind."

"I'm sure you have, Paul."

"That remains to be seen."

"Well, good luck, Paul.And thanks again."

"Good luck, Rachel."

He closed over his mobile and thought about her. He wondered where she was going, why she had left, what made her tick. He'd got used to having her around and he would miss her. He turned around and headed back upstairs and into the bedroom.

"What did Furstin want?" Anna asked.

"It wasn't him. It was Rachel – you know, from the press office."

"Oh! And what did she want?"

"She just wanted to hand in her notice. She's leaving Franklyns. She doesn't want to work for Furstin."

"Clever girl!" said Anna. "Now there's somebody who knows there's more to life than Franklyns." Anna yawned and turned on her side and drifted back to sleep.

Chapter 79

Christine Mountcharles had not had a good time of it since she had left Franklyns. Sales Management jobs were hard to come by and, even though she had gone for interviews, nothing had materialised. She became more bitter by the day with the way she was treated by Franklyns. By the way she was treated by Paul Stewart. Because of their affair she should have been last on the list of people let go. But instead she had been put top of the list. And then Paul had just sailed on with his perfect job and his perfect marriage. It was only perfect because his wife didn't know what a bastard she was married to. She picked up the Sunday newspaper and read through Anna Stewart's column. More drivel from Wimbledon. She studied Anna's smiling photo atop the column and felt so angry she could hardly stand it. At the bottom of the column she spotted Anna's email address as per usual. Put there no doubt so Anna could receive feedback from the readers telling her how wonderful her opinions were. As the anger continued inside Christine, she got up and went to her computer. She would send Anna an email. But not one telling her how much she had enjoyed her column, but one telling her how much she had enjoyed her husband. She would smash Anna and Paul's happy little life in Wimbledon to pieces by telling Anna all about her affair with Paul. That would give her something to write about in her next column. Christine began to compose the email.

* * *

On Sunday night Nicola sat in her apartment looking out at the view, classical music playing. She had spent the time between breaking up with David and being fired by Furstin almost in a trance. She had thought a lot, and drunk a lot, and slept a lot. On Saturday she went for lunch with her mother and sister. They weren't even aware she had broken up with Oliver so she didn't let on anything was wrong. On Sunday she had walked around Covent Garden for a few hours. And now here she sat, feeling very alone, the remainder of half a bottle of wine on the table in front of her, the balances of her and her husband's bank accounts, heavily hit by her spending, scattered on the floor.

Chapter 80

On Monday Paul sat outside Karl's office, waiting to be summoned into his presence.

"You can go in," the PA said to Paul.

Paul nodded and getting up walked over to the doors and let himself into Karl's office. Karl sat there behind his desk glaring at Paul.

"You wanted to see me?" said Paul, approaching the desk.

"This bitch that you recommended to take over the press office. She was supposed to come to my office on Friday evening for a meeting and she didn't show up. My staff have been trying to contact the press office and there's no answer."

"Ah, yes, Rachel. I'm afraid she's handed in her notice," explained Paul.

"She's done what?" Karl shouted.

"I don't know why. She just decided to leave." Karl slammed his hand on the table "Nobody leaves unless I tell them to. Get her back, I don't care what it costs."

"You're wasting your time, Karl. She's not interested in

the job. Anyway I don't even know where she's gone to."

"You told me she wanted this job. You said she was ambitious."

"Obviously not as ambitious as I thought."

"I do not enjoy being made a fool of!" Karl's face was reddening with anger.

Paul stared at him. With everything that had been going on, he had nearly forgotten how demanding Karl was, how unreasonable, how horrible. Paul had been so used to him over the years that he had become slightly immune to him. But now he could see why Rachel, looking at him with fresh eyes, would have run out of the place.

"Look, what's the big deal, Karl? There's loads of publicists out there."

"I wanted *her*!"

Paul sighed and rubbed the centre of his forehead with his index finger while looking down at the floor. Then he looked up quickly and spoke firmly. "Well, you can't have her."

"I can have what I want."

Paul felt exasperated. "Well, what do you want me to do? Seriously, what the fuck can I do? She's left, end of story."

"Don't you talk to me like that!" shouted Karl, standing up and slamming his desk with both his hands. Paul watched the man grow angrier and saw his future. He didn't like it and he didn't want it.

Paul stood up too. "And I'm leaving too. Goodbye, Karl."

"What do you mean you're leaving?"

"You can add the position of general manager to the list of all the other department head positions you need to fill." Paul turned and started walking out of the office.

"Get back here, Paul. You get back here!" Karl screamed after him. "I'm warning you. Don't leave here! Don't leave me!"

Paul opened the door and walked out, Karl's threats echoing behind him. He made his way to his office, grabbed his personal possessions and then quickly left the building. As he walked out into the busy street he found himself smiling. And the further he got away from Franklyns, the more quickly he walked until he realised he was nearly running.

* * *

Paul opened the front door and came into the house.

"Anna?"

"In the kitchen!" she answered.

He walked in and found her at her laptop at the kitchen table.

He enveloped her in a hug from behind and kissed her. "How are you feeling?" He touched her stomach.

"Fine – we're doing just fine," she smiled at him.

He sat down on a chair beside her.

"Anna, I've got some news for you. I want you to brace yourself."

"What is it?" she asked in alarm, seeing his concerned face.

"I've . . . eh . . . quit the job.".

"Really?" she said and she began to smile.

"You don't seem too worried."

"Paul, I'm delighted! I've been at you for years to leave that place."

"You know, if the store hadn't gone into receivership, I don't know if I'd ever have had the confidence to leave

Furstin. But having all that change forced on me makes me realise I can do it. And I want to do it. And with the baby coming, this is like a new beginning for us. And I don't want the baggage of Franklyns any more. You know what Furstin is like. I just don't want to be associated with him any more, I don't want our child having an association with somebody like that."

"Good." She nodded. "If you feel the time is right, then do it."

"I've already spoken to a couple of recruitment agencies today and they sounded really optimistic, in spite of the downturn, and said to email on my CV straight away."

"You've made your mind up. I'm proud of you. How did Furstin take it?"

"Not very well. I left him roaring down the corridor after me."

"All the more reason why it's wonderful you've left."

"Actually, there's no time like the present. The recruitment agency was anxious to get my CV today. Can I use the laptop to email it to them?"

"Of course, fire ahead. I'm just going through all my fans' emails," she joked.

"Oh, it's crank Monday, isn't it?" He laughed. "How many of the public want to hang you this week?"

She stood up and smiled. "I'll just go give my mum a quick call while you're sending it."

He sat in her chair while she went out into the hall and went upstairs. He looked at the emails still on the computer screen and smiled. What possessed all these people to bother writing in and commenting on a column? He'd read some of the emails in the past and they got so worked up about ridiculous issues. Cranks.

He was about to log out of Anna's email account when he spotted the email. From christinemountcharles@yahoo.com. The subject was marked *Private.* He stared at the email and then quickly opened it.

Dear Anna,

I haven't met you but I'm sure you've heard my name mentioned by Paul. I was going to visit your office at the newspaper but I spotted your email address at the bottom of your column and thought this might be the easier way for us all. As you are probably aware I used to work in Franklyns with Paul. What you are probably not aware of is that I had an affair with Paul. Our affair started at the Christmas party last year – corny, I know. I've wrestled with my conscience and I felt I had to let you know about his behaviour. Unfortunately I was not a one-off affair for Paul but the last in a list of women. Maybe not even the last – it has been a while since I left Franklyns. I can only imagine what he has got up to since. Before me, there was the buyer, there was the personal shopper – it is common knowledge throughout the store who he has slept with.

I'm sorry to break the news to you like this, and I know how this must make you feel. But if it was me, I'd want to know. If you need further details you have my email address.

Goodbye, Anna,

Christine Mountcharles

Paul sat still staring at the screen. Hearing Anna come down the hallway to the kitchen quickly spurred him into action and he rapidly eliminated the email.

"Mum sends her love," said Anna, coming into the kitchen.

Paul quickly logged out of Anna's account.

"Are you finished?" she asked, coming over behind him and putting her hands on his shoulders.

"Eh, no! I haven't sent it yet. I couldn't find my CV on the laptop." He held her hands tightly. "Did I do the right thing, Anna, leaving Franklyns?"

"Oh, I think you're right to go, Paul." Anna leaned down and wrapped her arms around him and put her face next to his. "With the baby, I think we need a new start, don't you?"

"Yes, I definitely do," he agreed.

* * *

That Monday evening Nicola drove through the countryside, her suitcases packed in the back of the car. She pulled into the driveway and saw Oliver's Range Rover parked there. She steadied herself and then got out of the car and let herself into the house.

She looked into the lounge and couldn't see him there. Feeling a breeze, she realised he must be out the back. She walked to the open French windows and saw him at the garden table working on his laptop. She stepped through the doors and stood there. He looked up, surprised to see her.

She nervously and gently rubbed her hands together. Then she slowly stretched her arms out, palms up in an open gesture and said, "I'm back."

He watched her for a while and then he nodded and stood up.

"I'll go make us a cup of tea," he said.

Chapter 81

Stephanie came out of the Tube station at Oxford Circus and walked down Argyll Street and into The Argyll pub. She went up the stairs to the restaurant part and spotted Neil sitting there in their normal window seat. She waved over to him.

As soon as she had kissed him and sat down he said, "There's a strong rumour circulating that you have left Franklyns. Can you confirm or deny?"

"Confirmed!"

"I'm shocked. Why?"

"It's a long story."

"I've got all afternoon."

"It would probably take longer than that."

"Are you all right? Has it anything to do with Furstin?"

"I'm fine, Neil. In fact I'm finer than I've been in ages. I feel free and liberated."

"Well, that's good."

"Yes, it is. Thanks for meeting me today. I wanted to talk to you a bit about my future and it kind of involves you, if you want it to."

"I'm listening." He sat forward.

"Is the job offer at Blackthorns still open?"

"Eh, yes! Of course, it is. We'd love to have you back."

"Well, then I would love to come back. You know, I've worked in a lot of places and I've never been happier than when I was at Blackthorns. It's like family to me."

"Great. It will be just like old times."

"The only thing is, Neil. I don't want to be in the office until ten every night any more. I don't want to work Saturdays and Sundays."

"I'm glad to hear it! I was always nagging at you to slow down."

"And I want to take lunch breaks, proper lunch breaks."

"Good! We can come up here every day!" he laughed.

"And take holidays. I suppose what I'm trying to say is that I want to have more to life than just work. I want to have a life outside work."

"You're preaching to the converted here," he insisted.

She allowed herself a laugh. "I know. Which brings me on to what else I want to discuss with you . . . I *do* want a life outside work and I want that to include you. You always said that I didn't give what we had a chance."

"Well, you didn't."

"Well, I'd like to now."

"But you always said I was too much of a playboy."

"I wouldn't mind taking a bit of that playtime with you now," she said.

"So what exactly are you suggesting?" He was leaning closer to her all the time.

"Us in a proper relationship."

"I don't think you could do it! Between mobiles ringing, faxes faxing, emails emailing. I don't think you could switch off from work long enough for a proper relationship."

"Try me!" Her eyes twinkled at him.

He thought for a second, then poured two glasses of wine from the bottle on the table and raised his glass.

"Okay – I'm game!"

She took her glass up and chinked it against his. "I can't wait."

Chapter 82

Nicola and Oliver were at an art auction in Chelsea Town Hall. All the paintings were on exhibition in the hall and the crowd went around anxiously inspecting what was on offer before the auction began.

"What do you think of this one?" asked Oliver, stopping at a landscape painting.

"It's a little dull," Nicola mused. "I just haven't seen anything that takes my fancy yet."

"You continue looking here and I'll go and start looking at the other end and see what we can come up with, all right?"

"All right. Meet you back here in fifteen minutes."

She continued walking down the hall, inspecting some portraits.

"Nicola?" said a voice behind her. She turned around and saw it was their friend, Liz.

"Where have you been?" demanded Liz and she kissed both Nicola's cheeks. "Myself and Edward had literally given up on the two of you. We've left that many messages with you!"

"I know. I'm sorry, Liz. Things have been a bit mad. I

was genuinely going to phone you this week."

"I can't stop now. I'm trying to find Edward – we're illegally parked down the road. What are you and Oliver doing on Friday? Will you come to us for dinner and we can have a proper catch-up?"

"That would be lovely, Liz," Nicola smiled.

"Okay. We'll save it all till then. See you around eight." She kissed her again and went off into the crowd.

Nicola looked after her and then started to inspect a painting in front of her.

She stood still for quite a while looking at the painting and then she realised she wasn't looking at the painting at all but was staring off into space. Her eyes started to fill with tears. There was nothing she could do as the tears started falling down her face. And suddenly she was sobbing aloud. People started to look at her.

"Nicola? Nicola!" said Oliver as he rushed over to her. He stood in front of her, looking at her crying face.

He put an arm around her and gently turned her and started to lead her to the exit. People stared as she continued crying loudly.

Liz came running up to them and demanded, "Nicola, what's wrong?"

Oliver shook his head at Liz and she backed away as he continued to gently direct Nicola to the door.

"I'm sorry, Oliver. I'm sorry," Nicola said between sobs.

"It's all right. Let's just get you home," he said gently.

Chapter 83

Leo walked up the street he had moved to in Paris. He was coming from work and stopped off in a couple of the small shops that lined the street to get some groceries.

His French was atrocious, he had to admit, as he managed to communicate with the people working in the shops with a mixture of sign language, broken English and pidgin French. Still he managed to get what he wanted. It was a pleasant evening.

He had been lucky since arriving in Paris. The friend he used to buy knock-down champagne from all the time and sell it on had an office in Paris. He had given him a job there, mainly taking orders from English-speaking customers. Hardly taxing on the brain-power but it was a start. When he thought of what the alternative would have been if he had stayed in London, he was very grateful for his new life in Paris. His mobile bleeped as he approached the building his apartment was in. It was from his mother asking how he was. He smiled to himself and texted her back: **'Everything fine, love Leo'.**

The building he lived in was a typical Parisian building that had been divided up into small flats. He got out his key as he approached the front door and, laden with shopping, awkwardly managed to open it.

"Do you want a hand with that?" said a voice behind him.

He turned around to see Rachel standing there.

"Rach!" he said, nearly dropped the shopping.

"Here, let me help you!" She reached forward and took one of the bags of shopping.

He stood staring at her.

"Aren't you going to invite me in?" she asked.

"Eh, yeah, come on up," he said and they entered the building.

They got into the little lift and went up to the fourth floor where he let them into a tiny flat.

She glanced around. "Very artistic!" she said.

"How did you find me?" Leo asked.

"I ran into Daniella and bullied her into giving me the address. She sends her love incidentally. She's about to become a reality television star seemingly."

He put the shopping bags down on the table and opened the double windows, letting in the sounds of the street below.

Rachel put the bag she was holding next to his.

"Rach – what are you doing here?"

"What do you think I'm doing here, you big idiot. I'm here for you!"

"But we're finished!"

"Leo, I also bullied Daniella into telling me everything. I know you're not really back with Daniella."

Leo sighed loudly. "I didn't want to hurt you. I thought it better to be cruel to be kind."

"I know why you did what you did."

A police siren wailed somewhere in the distance.

"Listen, head back to London on the next plane, sweetheart, because there is nothing for you here in Paris."

"Well, there's nothing for me in London either. I quit my job."

"For fuck's sake, Rachel, why did you do that?" He was angry.

"Many reasons. But the main reason is what you told me once about not putting a career first if you find something better. And I've found something better, Leo. I've found you."

"Doll, you don't know me. That necklace – I didn't buy it in Franklyns – it was stolen!"

"I know that."

"I've dealt in more knock-off goods than you've had hot dinners."

"I know that." She smiled and nodded.

He was becoming exasperated. "The reason you were sick after Tom's party is because your drink was spiked with a drug. Even my respectable friends are dodgy !"

"I know that."

"I'm trouble!"

"I know that too!"

"Those companies I ran, they were all scams. I was fired from my job in the City. The sports car I had was on hire purchase and I was behind on repayments. I was behind on the rent for the house as well and yet I was still wasting money I didn't have quaffing champagne and living the high life."

"I don't care about any of it. Do you really think I was impressed by sports cars and champagne lifestyles?"

"Yes . . . no! I don't know!"

She came over and hugged him tightly.

"You've tried to get rid of me and failed. I guess you're

stuck with me now."

"You're ruining everything you've worked for. I don't want to drag you down."

"Do you really think I was enjoying that job? The reality was far different from the dream. Now stop being so negative. You're not going to drag me down because you're not going down. We're going up in the world together."

"But I am negative, remember? And cynical."

She smiled at him and kissed him "And cynical is good, because you never get disappointed when you're cynical, yeah?"

He kissed her back. "Exactly!"

"Well, I'm very cynical about sports cars and champagne lifestyles. I don't want that. I just want you to be you. How does that sound?"

"Good," he smiled at her.

"Then you want me to stay?" she asked the question, confident of the answer. Confident she really knew Leo.

"Of course, I do. I thought I'd lost you forever." He hugged her tightly. "How's your French?" he asked smiling.

"Not bad. Just about good enough to get me a job behind a sales counter in a store somewhere."

"Well . . . it's a start," he said. "Everyone has to start somewhere."

THE END

Also published by Poolbeg Press

Property

A.O' Connor

The boom has been good to the Cunninghams. Property baron Cormac has taken the family business to new heights, building luxury homes for Ireland's élite. And always by his side, and on the cover of the property supplements, is his beautiful wife Denise.

Lisa, Cormac's sister, enjoys the good life as one of Dublin's high-flying estate agents – working for the dynamic and handsome Michael Farrell. And Michael is enjoying himself too, working on bigger and more outrageous stunts to promote the Cunninghams' developments.

But when award-winning journalist Ali O'Mara storms into this glitzy world she raises awkward questions. What lies at the heart of Denise and Cormac's unconventional marriage? What lengths will Lisa go to, to get the man she craves? And when Ali and Michael's romance threatens the Cunningham empire, can they survive the backlash together?

ISBN 978-1-84223-277-4

Also published by Poolbeg Press

Exclusive

A. O' Connor

Celebrity – glamorous, addictive, destructive

As manager of an exclusive nightclub, Kathryn Foy knows what celebrities want and makes sure they get it. Now it is her turn to take centre stage – but she is desperate to keep her personal life in the dark.

Party-animal Lana Curtis suddenly finds herself in the limelight when her tycoon father runs for election – not a good thing when you have an addictive personality and a dangerous lifestyle.

Rock-star Cathal Fitzgerald is well used to the glare of publicity. When he meets Lana, they become the latest golden couple. But he lives in fear of a shady past resurfacing.

Nicole Donnelly, psychotherapist, is delighted when her partner Tony O'Brien lands a job in celebrity magazine Hi Life – until he is seduced by the glitzy lifestyle. How far will she go to hold on to him? And how far will he go to succeed?

THEIR LIVES ARE RULED BY CELEBRITY – BUT THEN, ISN'T THAT TRUE OF US ALL?

ISBN 978-1-84223-239-2

Also published by Poolbeg Press

This Model Life

A.O' Connor

Top Irish model Audrey Driver is a well-known face around Dublin's social circles. And her connected solicitor boyfriend Aran Murphy is the perfect catch. Set to land a big American contract, Audrey wonders can life get any better than this?

PR guru Peter Murphy is at the peak of his game and the Childwatch Fashion Show will cement his reputation. His prestige-obsessed wife Lynn is pushing him to succeed and there is no room for mistakes.

Takeover Queen Chloe Gallagher has climbed to the top of Macken PR, thanks to an appetite for destruction and underhand tactics. She will stop at nothing to get what she wants and hates it when someone else is in the limelight.

As their paths cross, sparks fly, mettles are tested and they are forced to face up to their real strengths and weaknesses.

ISBN 978-1-84223-197-5